About the a

Vivien Brown lives in Uxbridge, on the outskirts of London, with her husband and two cats. After a career in banking and accountancy and the birth of her twin daughters, she gave up working with numbers and moved into working with words and has never looked back.

In recent years, as a pre-school reading specialist and library storyteller, she has helped hundreds of young children to explore and enjoy books, has written extensively for pre-school and nursery magazines, and has had numerous short stories and children's poems published. Vivien loves reading romance novels and psychological thrillers (or better still, stories that combine the two), watching and taking part in TV quiz shows, and tackling really tricky cryptic crosswords, ideally in a sunny garden and with a bar of chocolate and an ice-cold Diet Pepsi close at hand.

Lily Alone

Vivien Brown

harper
impulse

HarperImpulse an imprint of
HarperCollins*Publishers*
1 London Bridge Street
London SE1 9GF

www.harpercollins.co.uk

This paperback edition published by Harper*Impulse* 2017

First published in Great Britain in ebook format by Harper*Impulse* 2017

A catalogue record for this book
is available from the British Library

ISBN: 9780008252113

This novel is entirely a work of fiction.
The names, characters and incidents portrayed in it are
the work of the author's imagination. Any resemblance to
actual persons, living or dead, events or localities is
entirely coincidental.

Set in Birka by Type-it AS, Norway

Printed and bound in Great Britain by
CPI Group (UK) Ltd, Croydon CR0 4YY

MIX
Paper from
responsible sources
FSC® C007454

FSC is a non-profit international organisation established
to promote the responsible management of the world's forests.
Products carrying the FSC label are independently certified
to assure consumers that they come from forests that are managed
to meet the social, economic and ecological needs
of present and future generations.

Find out more about HarperCollins and the environment at
www.harpercollins.co.uk/green

To Penny, who is almost the same age as Lily,
but will never be alone.

PROLOGUE

Ruby

There's a face looking down at me. Big and blurry, not quite in focus. I close my eyes and open them again, slowly, but it's still there. Go away. I don't know who you are. Let me sleep. I need to sleep.

Other faces now, working their way into shot, waving about around the edges like the petals of a daisy, opening and closing, opening and closing. My back feels cold, and I'm lying on something hard. And wet. I don't know how I got here. Or where here is.

'It's okay, sweetheart. Don't try to move.'

Mike. Mike always calls me sweetheart. Calls everybody sweetheart. Is he here?

'You've been in an accident. Just hold on there. The ambulance is on its way.'

It's a woman now, bending down next to me. What does she mean, hold on? What am I supposed to hold on to? I try to reach for her hand, but mine won't move. It just lies there, like a piece of dead meat. Disconnected.

The woman's knees are bony, pressed against my side, and

7

there's water running off her mac and dripping onto my hand. I'm lying in the road. And it's raining. How did I end up in the road? She touches my shoulder. Her face is white, really white, as if she's had a shock; seen a ghost or something.

Why do I feel so cold? Did I forget to put the heating on? Where's my duvet? I just want everyone to go away and leave me alone, so I can close my eyes and go back to sleep. But there's so much noise. People talking, whispering, crying. Why is someone crying? Sirens now. Getting louder, closer.

And a minute later – or is it five? ten? – the thumping of a door. Two people in bright yellow jackets are squatting in front of me, touching me, talking to me, asking me my name. I stare at the yellow. It's the same yellow as Lily's new pyjamas, but without the rabbits. Lily likes rabbits. My stomach lurches. Lily. Where's Lily?

'Your name, sweetheart,' one of them says again. 'Can you tell us your name?'

I try to lift my head, to look for her. She should be here, with me, but she isn't. My head falls back down, hard, as if I can't hold its weight. Someone is clamping something around my neck now, and I can't move any more. The sky is everywhere. It's all I can see, like a thick grey blanket falling over me. I can feel the wetness at the back of my head, running down my neck, creeping inside my hood. It's warm, sticky. Not like rain at all. Something – everything – hurts. Really hurts.

'Lily . . .' I say. 'Lily . . .'

And then I'm gone.

PART ONE

CHAPTER ONE

Archie was hungry. Lily let his wet ear slip out of her mouth. She rubbed a sweaty hand over her eyelids and yawned, cuddled Archie up tight to her chest, then threw the covers back and held him up at arm's length, tugging his little knitted trousers off over his feet.

Archie should have pyjamas for when he went to bed. Or to wear in the daytime sometimes, when there was nothing special to get dressed for. Lily had been wearing hers all morning, and so had Mummy.

Lily's pyjamas were yellow, with bunnies on, and yellow was her new favourite colour. When they got a garden of their own she would grow yellow daffodils, and have a real live bunny of her own too. Mummy had promised.

The curtains were half closed, but little shadows of light darted about like jumping frogs on the ceiling. There was a lot of noise outside. Loud noise. Lily didn't like loud noise. When people shouted, or fireworks banged, or balloons popped. She hated those things. You had to close your eyes and put your hands over your ears when they happened. She didn't want fireworks or balloons at her birthday party. Just presents. Mummy said she was going to be three. She'd held up her fingers to show Lily what three looked like. Baa baa black sheep. Three bags full. She'd like a bouncy castle too, at her party, but castles were very big and cost lots of money so she didn't think Mummy would really get one. But maybe she'd get her a bunny, if they had a garden by then.

Out in the street, there was a wailing, screeching sound, like she imagined the big bad wolf would sound if he was very angry and coming after the pigs. Mummy had left one of the little windows open right up at the top, and the wind was blowing in, making the bottom of the curtain move. *I'll huff and I'll puff and I'll blow your house down . . .*

Lily remembered the story of the wolf and the pigs. One of the ladies at the nursery had read it to them, when they all sat in a circle before they went home, but Lily didn't like it. She didn't like the story, and she didn't like the noise. She tried to cover her ears and pull the quilt up over her head all at the same time, making sure she hung on tightly to Archie to keep him safe, and to stop him from being scared.

The noise went away. She peeped cautiously over the top of the covers and, when she was sure there was no wolf, she settled Archie on the pillow beside her and sat up in bed. She'd only had a nap, not an all-night sleep, but her nappy felt heavy, and she was thirsty. She wanted some juice. Bena juice. That was her favourite, except maybe Coke, but she wasn't allowed that very often. Only on special days. Lily didn't think this was a special day.

Maybe Archie could have some juice too, as he'd been good. She yawned, and called out for Mummy, fiddling with a black thread that had come loose from Archie's eye and was hanging down over his nose. Mummy would mend that, with something from her big red sewing tin that used to have biscuits in it, or with the glue that Lily wasn't allowed to touch. Mummy was good at mending things. It saved buying new, she always said.

Lily waited but Mummy didn't come, so she called again, louder this time.

Lily climbed out of bed, her foot springing onto the book she'd left open on the rug, flipping the pages over and making the spine snap shut. The baby in the flat upstairs was crying. It did that sometimes. Today it was doing it lots. It sounded sad, like Archie. Maybe it wanted some juice too. She walked over to the door, peered out into the empty hall, and called out again.

'Mummy . . .'

But Mummy didn't come. Nobody came.

*

Agnes Munro looked up from her crossword. There were sirens going off in the street again, the honking of horns, a motorcycle revving its engine and screeching off into the distance, probably bumping up and over the pavement in the process. That's what they usually did when there was a jam.

That was the trouble with living in London. Even here, on the outskirts, it was too busy, too noisy. There was no real sense of community. Nobody seemed to care about anything much, let alone the state of the roads or trying to preserve a bit of peace and quiet. Always something going on, even at the weekend, and not always something good. What now? A broken-down bus, some impatient driver carelessly thumping his bonnet into somebody else's boot, or yet another robbery on the high street?

She tried to push the sudden thought of her old home out of her mind and concentrate on the two final clues she'd been puzzling over for the last five minutes. Oh, how she hated leaving a crossword unfinished. In fact, she wouldn't, couldn't. If it took all day, she'd make sure she finished it somehow, but crosswords, like just about everything else, seemed to be taking her so much longer these days. Her body certainly wasn't as fast or efficient as it used to be. The creaking in her knees as she moved told her that. Perhaps her mind was starting to go the same way. And those little empty white squares looked so forlorn, and so untidy.

She wondered if the dictionary might help, but it was in the bookcase under the window, out of reach. Smudge was dozing on her lap, twitching in his sleep, and she didn't want to disturb him. She leant across, very carefully, to the small lace-covered table beside her, picked up her tea and took a warming sip, tapping her pen idly against the side of the china mug as she struggled with the letters of an anagram in her head.

Life had always been so peaceful before, when she'd lived in the old cottage. The home that they'd told her was too rundown, too big, too isolated now she was getting older. Much better here in town, they said, where they could keep an eye on her, where the shops were just a short walk away, where the buses ran right past the door. And a ground floor flat too. No stairs and so much easier for her to manage, especially with arthritis setting in with a vengeance, giving her painful, knobbly fingers and stiffening knees.

Downsizing. That's what they had called it when the idea had first been mooted eighteen months ago. Her son William, and his ever-efficient wife. They had made it sound quite exciting back then, like a big adventure, something wonderful to be embraced and thankful for. Downsizing, indeed! Agnes could think of a better word, but she dared not say it out loud. They didn't like it when she swore. Not that there was a 'they' any more. Now her daughter-in-law had gone – good riddance – and there was just William. She chuckled to herself. Just William. Wasn't that the name of a naughty boy in some old children's book?

Agnes gave up on the anagram. Her mind was too busy jumping about elsewhere. That was one of the hazards of living alone. Too much time to think, and nothing of any real importance to think about. Well, nothing she could do much about, anyway.

She finished her tea and tried to replace her empty mug on the table without moving Smudge, but the big grey cat woke up, stretched and jumped down, ambled over to his cat flap and let himself out into the communal hall with a clatter of rebounding plastic. He would sit for a while on the coir doormat outside her flat, preening, then wait at the front door of the block, as he always did, until one of the other residents, either coming in or going out, eventually let him through. Sometimes he would walk steadily up the three flights of stairs to the top of the building where he could sit and gaze out from the grimy windowsill on the landing at the birds twittering away, up high in the one and only tree. Agnes had followed him up all those stairs once, just to see where he went, but she'd had to stop and rest after each flight, and had needed some strong tea and a couple of paracetamol as soon as her aching joints had made it safely back down again.

She took off her reading glasses and tried to switch to the other pair she kept for distance, the two pairs dangling side by side from adjacent chains around her neck. The chains were tangled together today and it took her a few moments to unwind them. She muttered to herself and winced as she stood. Her knees were playing up again, as usual.

Going to the window, she lifted the edge of her newly washed nets, popped on the right specs and peered out into the street. Dull, grey, October drizzle, with another winter not far off. Traffic bumper to bumper, wipers swishing across grimy screens, the male drivers drumming their hands on their steering wheels, the women taking the opportunity to peer into mirrors and redo their make-up or neaten their hair. An ambulance was trying to make its way through. Was there really any need for the siren? Sometimes she thought the drivers just did it to make themselves feel important. It's not as if it couldn't be seen, what with the blue light and all the cars doing their best to mount the kerb and get out of its way. More cracks in the pavement! It's a wonder more folk didn't trip and sue the council for compensation.

From two floors above, she could hear that baby screaming again, probably woken up by the racket going on outside. She thought of going up there to complain, but she couldn't face the stairs, and what good would it do, anyway? How could she tell a baby to be quiet, or expect its mother to make it? Babies couldn't help it, could they? Crying came naturally to them. Their way of saying something was wrong. Perhaps she should try a bit of weeping and wailing and see if it helped. See if anyone came running to pander to her every whim, to make things right again. She smiled to herself. She was just being grouchy, that was all. Blame it on the knees. Silly old woman!

Ah, well. She might as well watch some telly now she was up and about. Her favourite antiques programme would be starting soon. The one where they found hidden treasures in people's lofts. As if! All they'd found in hers when she moved was Donald's old army pay book, some dressing-up clothes from William's am-dram days, and a pile of dusty photos, mostly of people she didn't even recognise, let alone remember.

Still, they might have some teapots on the programme today, if she was lucky. Agnes liked teapots. They were a passion of hers. Old ones, obviously, and some of the more unusual, novelty ones too. Not to use, of course. Oh, no, she had to admit that, being by herself so much of the time, a teabag dunked straight into a cup of hot water did the trick quite nicely these days. But there was something undeniably beautiful about teapots. To look at, and to touch. Such smooth shapes, such elegant spouts and handles. In fact, she'd built up quite a nice collection over the years, even if they were all boxed up in William's garage now because she didn't have the room.

She sighed. What was the use of thinking about all that stuff? Her life had changed, and she knew full well it was never going to change back again. At least having the telly on, perhaps a bit louder than necessary, might just help to drown out all the incessant noise.

*

The plane lurched as it hit yet another air pocket, knocking a passing stewardess, hip first, into the side of Patsy's seat.

'Sorry, Madam.' The girl carried on up the aisle, totally unfazed, small uniformed hips wiggling easily from side to side. All in a day's work, probably. Patsy closed her eyes, took a deep breath, and thanked God she didn't have to do a job like that.

'It's just a bit of turbulence, sweetheart.' Michael picked up Patsy's hand and stroked it reassuringly, fingering the new diamond ring that sparkled under the overhead lights. The ring he had laughingly told her he still couldn't quite get used to, even though he'd put it there himself, only two days before. 'Nothing to worry about. We'll be landing soon.'

Patsy smiled at him, trying really hard not to be sick. She was not a good air traveller, and if there was one thing guaranteed to put a man off for life, it was watching a girl being sick. She'd done it once, after a party. Vomited all over the front seat of some boy's shiny new car. She could still remember the acid taste and the pervasive smell of it, clogging her nostrils, caked onto her dress and mixed into her hair, as it spewed out between her trembling fingers when she tried to hold it back. The huge dollops of it running down the upholstery and onto the rubber mat at her feet. And the look of utter horror on the boy's face as he pulled over and stopped the engine and watched her lean out over the kerb, spilling the remaining contents of her alcohol-fuelled stomach all over the road. She could no longer remember his name, but she would never ever forget that face. Or that feeling.

Oh, no, if she was going to be sick, it had to be somewhere else, out of sight, away from Michael. She stood up, unsteadily. 'Won't be long,' she said, slipping her hand out of his and edging into the aisle.

'Seatbelt signs are on, Pats. Maybe you should stay here for now . . .'

But the loo was only a few feet away, and she needed privacy, some time alone before they landed. She shook her head, tried to smile, and stumbled into the cubicle, sliding the bolt across, and landing with a thump on top of the loo seat.

You're going to have to get used to sick if you're going to be a stepmum, she thought. And temper tantrums, and potties, and God knows what else. She bit down hard on her lip. She wanted to do this. Of course she did. For Michael. He'd already missed too big a chunk of Lily's life. And that was mostly down to that vengeful ex of his. Since they'd been away, Ruby hadn't even let him speak to his daughter on the phone, and they both felt sure that the little presents they'd so carefully chosen and posted to her had probably never been opened. Most women left alone with a child would be banging on the door of the Child Support Agency demanding what they felt they were due, but oh no, not Ruby. She wanted nothing from Michael. She'd made that abundantly clear. Not even if that meant Lily went without. Well, it couldn't go on. As Michael had said, thumping his fist on the table in anger when yet another bank statement showed she had failed to cash any of his cheques, something definitely had to change.

Patsy closed her eyes and tried to picture the Ruby she'd met a couple of times, a while back, before Michael had made the decision to leave, but all she had seen then was a mouse of a girl utterly lacking in confidence, thrown unexpectedly into motherhood far too young and trying way too hard to be a grown-up. She had felt almost sorry for her back then. There was a flicker of guilt too, for her own part in what had happened. If she and Michael hadn't met, hadn't fallen in love, then maybe he would still be there now, with Ruby and his daughter. They may have been far from the perfect family, but they had been a family nonetheless. But then, nothing is ever quite as straightforward, or as one-sided, as it appears, is it? Michael may have been the one to cheat, the one to walk away, but . . .

Patsy had insisted from the start that he talk to her about it, about what his life with Ruby was like, so she could make up her own mind and understand just what she was getting herself involved in, what harm they might be causing if he was to walk away. She still found Michael's reluctance tricky to deal with sometimes. It was as if he just wanted to bury his head in the sand and pretend Ruby didn't exist, so she still didn't know it all, and probably never would, but it seemed there was another side to Ruby. Since Michael had gradually filled in some of the blanks, the meek and mild person Patsy thought she had seen had morphed into someone far more fiery and unpredictable, and feeling sorry for her had become a whole lot harder.

Still, it was Lily who mattered now, much more than Ruby. Lily needed her daddy back in her life, and it was Lily they were coming home for.

She held her finger up and looked again at the sparkling new ring that still felt heavy and unfamiliar. It was beautiful, but it had to mean more than just a decoration, an extra glitzy jewel to add to her collection. It came with responsibilities, conditions that had so far been left largely unspoken but were nevertheless very real. No, it was up to her to support him, to help him fight to find a way back into Lily's life, to show him she was up to the task. Motherhood, even just part time, was going to be a big thing, a major commitment, especially trying to mother someone else's child, a constant reminder of the woman – no, the girl – who came before. She shivered, hugging her arms around herself, and tried to breathe slowly and calmly as the plane lurched menacingly beneath her.

Maybe they'd even have a baby of their own one day. Not for a year or two yet, obviously. Or more like five or six. She was still only twenty-seven, and she had her career to think of, after all. She certainly hadn't reached the point where a career break, even of just a few months, could possibly work. It was a small company, still growing, and she wanted to grow with it. The board were counting on her to get this European project up and running. It was her big chance to prove herself. But one day, when she was ready, when the biological clock that people talked about started to tick – if it ever did – then maybe.

Getting to know Lily would be a start though, wouldn't it? Like a practice run, to see if things worked out. But things had to work out, didn't they? There was no other option. Not if she wanted to keep the ring on her finger, become Mrs Payne, keep Michael happy . . .

The plane tipped and jolted, suddenly bouncing her bottom up off the seat and depositing her back down again, hard. She only just had time to swivel round in the tiny space between the toilet and the basin and the door, press her hands hard against the wall and line her head up with the pan before she was violently sick. She looked down at the spatter of pale gloopy drops that had somehow bypassed the edge and splashed out onto the floor around her. She'd missed her new Jimmy Choos by a whisker.

Somehow, even that small piece of luck didn't make her feel any better.

CHAPTER TWO

Geraldine Payne stood among the crowds in the arrivals hall at Gatwick, watching the passengers as they trundled through the doors, sporting new suntans, pushing over-laden trolleys, carrying white plastic bags stuffed with cigarettes and booze, their clothes all crumpled from their flights.

Michael had called her before he boarded, told her that he and Patsy had something important to tell her just as soon as they got home, and would she mind coming to Gatwick to pick them up? Well, it could only be one of two things, couldn't it? Either an engagement, or the girl was pregnant. Given the choice, and remembering what had happened the last time, she wasn't at all sure which she should hope for. But Michael was a grown man and he wouldn't thank her for voicing her opinions. She couldn't tell him what to do any more. She'd tried that before, and look where it had got her.

She checked her watch again and compared it with the time on the arrivals board. This was the right flight, wasn't it? Lisbon. Two forty-five. It had to be. Where were they? Too busy canoodling to get themselves out here on time, she shouldn't wonder. Unless they'd been stopped by Customs, of course. The amount of bling that girl carted about on her wrists, and even round her ankles on occasion, they'd probably mistaken her for a jewel smuggler. Not the sort of girl he might have met had he stayed at the bank. A good, steady job he'd had there. None of this big contract, sweeping-himself-off-to-far-flung-corners-of-Europe stuff he'd got himself mixed up with these days. Too much risk, too much change, too much she didn't understand. It wasn't what Geraldine was used to at all. She knew she was a creature of habit, the sort of woman who liked to stick with what she knew. There was safety, and an element of comfort, in the familiar, wasn't there? The everyday normality of life ticking along the way it always had. Ironing his work shirts, choosing the chops for his tea, the sound of his key turning in the lock at half past five . . .

But all of that was gone. Long gone. Things were different now, and likely to stay that way.

Where on earth were they? At these exorbitant airport prices, she had been hoping to get away with just an hour's car parking, and more than half of that had gone already. She was a busy woman, with things to do. She had a shop to run, and it was Saturday, the busiest shopping day of the week. She never liked to leave Kerry in charge for any longer than necessary, and a whole afternoon felt like way too long. The girl meant well, and she was as honest as the day was long, but she didn't have a lot going on between the ears. It would only take one wrong delivery or a dispute over change and she'd go to pieces.

Geraldine opened her bag and took out two of her migraine pills, the pink ones. The last two in the packet. She could feel one of her heads coming on, and there was still the drive back home to have to cope with. She didn't have the time to be ill. At sixty-two, if her life had turned out differently and she didn't have to constantly battle on with everything alone, she'd have been seriously thinking about retiring by now. But there was the house to manage, and a garden just a little too big for her to tackle with any real success, and the business to keep afloat. And now Michael was coming back after four months away and with heaven knows what bombshell about to be dropped at her feet. Sometimes all she wanted to do was bury herself under a duvet and sleep for a week. The trouble was, she knew it would all still be there waiting for her when she woke up again.

She thought about seeking out a cup of tea. There was nothing quite like a spot of tea and sympathy, even if all the sympathy she could muster was for herself, but they'd be here any minute now and she didn't want to miss them. Airport tea would probably be horribly expensive anyhow, or just plain horrible. She tipped the pills to the back of her throat without the benefit of any liquid to help them on their way, and swallowed, still feeling the little dry lump in her throat after they'd fought their way down. Bloody Ken. Why did he have to go and die, just when life was finally looking like it might turn out okay after all? And why did she still feel so angry with him? It's not as if he'd done it on purpose.

She shook the thoughts away and rummaged about for her phone. Better check that Kerry was all right. She dialled the familiar number and heard it ring and ring, but the girl didn't answer. Eventually the answer phone kicked in, sending her own voice hurtling back at her, telling her the shop was closed for now, and inviting her to leave a message. It wasn't closed, of course. Well, she bloody well hoped not! No, either the shop was so busy that Kerry couldn't get to the phone in time or – God forbid – something dreadful had happened. Geraldine bit down on her lower lip and wondered when she had become such a worrier.

With jumbled images flooding into her brain – of armed robbery, heart attacks, fire engines or worse – she finally saw her son walking across the terminal towards her, and felt the tears welling up quite unexpectedly from somewhere deep inside her as she rushed forward and threw herself into his open arms.

*

William Munro took off his glasses and rubbed his tired eyes. He was worried about his mother. Since his divorce had come through – a quickie, his wife had called it, not unlike their rare forays into a sex life – and Susan, with hardly a backward glance, had driven away to pastures new, he'd suddenly found he had more time on his hands, and a lot more space in his head.

Susan had been the main breadwinner and had borne the brunt of the costs, but not without a lot of spitting and hissing along the way. If this was a quickie, he hated to think what a long and protracted divorce would have been like. But it was over now. After all the bitter rows and sleepless nights, the letters bargaining and counter-bargaining, and a pile of solicitors' bills that added up to more than the cost of his latest car, at last the house was his again. Originally quite rundown and shabby, it had been William's long before Susan's arrival, but it had become their marital home, added to and preened over the last few years to within an inch of its life, until it met her exacting executive requirements. And now she'd gone, and both he and the house seemed to be on the decline again.

Quite apart from the salary she brought home from the publishing house where she worked, a staggering figure which seemed to rise by leaps and bounds as she clawed her way by her long shiny fingernails towards the top of the corporate tree, she'd been sitting on a sizeable nest egg since the death of her parents and had been persuaded to use a small percentage of it to reluctantly pay off what was left of the mortgage, so at least he wasn't weighed down by a debt he had no way of repaying. She had even been ordered, by a surprisingly understanding judge, to settle a small additional lump sum in William's favour at the time of the divorce, which she had done grudgingly and with predictably bad grace. He hadn't felt too sure about that. It wasn't quite right, was it? A husband being seen as dependent on his wife, not able to provide for himself. But now the money nestled expectantly in his bank account until he made up his mind what to do with it, and finally he had the time to stop and take stock of his life. And what a mess he had made of it.

Agnes, his mother, had never particularly liked Susan. She had never actually said it aloud, but he had always known it, and had decided, probably wisely, to ignore it. Susan had been his choice and his mother had respected that, although the thin pursing of her lips and the uncharacteristic silence that surrounded her during their irregular visits had rather given the game away.

Susan had three major faults. In Agnes's eyes, at least.

Number one. She worked, not just from nine to five, or more

likely to seven or eight, but often at the weekends too. She brought paperwork home and shut herself away in the study for hours at a time, leaving William to fend for himself. William hadn't minded too much. At least she was there with him at night, even if she often didn't come to bed until the early hours and usually turned her back towards him as she slept.

William had been proud of his wife's achievements, the successful authors she had discovered and nurtured, and her occasional appearances on TV book programmes and at awards ceremonies, to which he was rarely invited. He had always enjoyed having a go at various DIY projects, but more recently he had become a dab hand at shopping and dusting and cooking too. Well, if he didn't do it, then nobody would. He didn't like the term 'house husband', but perhaps, particularly in the two years or so since he had been made redundant, and with very little prospect of finding another job at his age, that was what he had gradually and unwittingly become. Looking back, that was probably when it had all started to go so horribly wrong, with a vengeance. Susan wasn't the type of woman who wanted to be shackled to a failure, a man in an apron with no real reason even to leave the house every day. As her star rose, his had dropped like a stone, and his self-esteem along with it.

His mother was incensed on his behalf and no longer made any attempt to disguise her feelings. Yes, he was at home all day, and his spaghetti carbonara may have been so good it could win prizes, but it was the principle of the thing. Leaving the domestic side of life to the man of the house was not the way a wife should behave, and certainly not something Agnes, who had devoted her entire adult life to the needs and comfort of her own dear husband Donald until his untimely death, could ever understand.

Fault number two. Susan had never wanted children. An only child herself, and determined to stick to her belief that there were other more rewarding, and less messy and demanding things to be enjoyed in life, she had made William's promise not to cajole, trick or persuade her an absolute condition of their marriage. And, short of signing in his own blood, William, who had met and married her a little late in life and had already resigned himself to the probability of a childless future, had felt there was no option but to agree, thus depriving Agnes of the grandchildren she could now only dream of.

And then there was number three. Susan didn't like cats. This, in his mother's eyes, was beyond all reason, and utterly unforgivable. Whenever they had visited Agnes in her old cottage, poor Smudge had been banished to the garden or the bedroom, his pathetic cries and the claw marks he scratched into the panelling of the old oak door frames failing to touch even the tiniest part of Susan's cold, unfeeling soul.

Now that Susan was gone, William had found he had both the time and licence to consider his mother's opinions, and had realised, to his dismay, that, on all three counts, she just might have been right all along. Susan wasn't the woman he had hoped she was and, looking back, it was hard to figure out just why she had married him in the first place. He had certainly believed, at the time, that it had been for love, but Susan's idea of love had turned out not to be quite the same as his.

With his own parents' marriage the only model he could base his expectations on, he knew he would have liked a wife who, if not necessarily putting her husband first in all things in that old-fashioned way his mother had done, would at least have sat with him on the sofa in the evenings and rubbed his feet, or massaged his neck as they watched the news; brought him a nice mug of tea every now and then, and a couple of digestives to go with it. Perhaps, in the early years, before her career had exploded into the all-consuming passion that seemed to overshadow all else, that just might have been a possibility, but it had never happened. It was just the way she was.

In truth, she had probably accepted his proposal in the same way a drowning woman accepts a lifebelt. She was getting older, she was embarrassingly single, and he was there. He was presentable enough, and solid, and convenient. They had met during the rehearsals for an amateur production of *The Sound of Music*, she having just moved to the area and keen to find something to do, and someone to do it with, and him doing battle with producing lights and sounds from an ancient backstage control panel, understudying for just about all the walk-on parts, including the nuns, and wishing he'd had the nerve to try out for the part of Captain Von Trapp.

As it turned out, she had quickly realised that treading the boards was not for her and had moved on to joining, and then running, the book club at the library, and he had discovered that messing about with spotlights was far less stressful than standing beneath them. Still, some sort of spark had been lit and they had found that they enjoyed being in each other's company and later, as things progressed, in each other's beds. He may not have been her Mister Darcy but he just might have been her last chance. Nowadays, he thought, she probably wished she had simply carried on bobbing along without him.

He would have liked a child, of course – maybe two – to bounce on his knee, someone to inherit his house, and his money (what little of it there was), and the flecked brown of the Munro eyes, but barring that one time when her period had been late and, just for a few frantic days, he'd felt a tiny flicker of rapidly extinguished hope, that had never really been on the cards either. And, as for poor Smudge, well . . .

William knew he had made mistakes. He had almost forced his mother and her beloved cat into that London flat. Susan's idea, of course. Selling the old cottage, she had insisted, before it needed some serious maintenance, before Agnes's impending and inevitable frailty forced their hand, surely made sense. Good financial sense. But money in the bank didn't bring happiness. After sixteen years of half-hearted marriage, and with very little to show for it, he knew that only too well.

William was fifty seven years old. He was too chubby around the middle, and his hair was not only thinning on top but what was left of it was going decidedly grey at the sides. When he looked in the mirror he hardly recognised the face that looked back at him through his thick rimmed spectacles. Where had his life gone? How could everything had gone so horribly wrong? He wasn't happy. He probably hadn't been happy for years, but he'd never stopped to think about it before. And, worst of all, he was ashamed to realise that he didn't know if his mother was happy either.

He'd call her. Yes, that's what he would do. Or, better still, go round there. Unexpected, uninvited, like he used to in his bachelor days, turning up on her doorstep, out of the blue, with flowers and a hug, and sometimes a bag of laundry, and knowing there'd be tea in the pot – whichever of the many pots was his mother's favourite at the time – and cake in the tin. But that, of course, had been before Susan. Susan had changed things, prised open a little gap between his mother and himself that had slowly, as the years passed, widened and deepened into an almost unbridgeable gulf.

It was time to do something about it, before it was too late. His mother wasn't getting any younger. Neither was he, come to think of it. And, now that Susan had gone, there was nothing to stop him from being a part of her life again, and letting her be a part of his. They were both alone now. Lonely, even. Well, he knew he was. He had no idea if she felt the same. She did have old Smudge for company, of course, so there was always somebody for her to talk to, even if that somebody never talked back. Which was more than he had. William rubbed the tips of his fingers over his eyelids and yawned. He had to snap out of this self-pitying phase before he started to go all maudlin.

Only one thing for it. He'd go tomorrow, surprise her and take her out for lunch somewhere. A nice roast, with all the trimmings. She'd like that. He'd stop off on the way and buy freesias. Lots of freesias, in lovely bright colours. They were always her favourites. And cat food for Smudge. Tuna, or chicken. The expensive chunky stuff in the little foil cartons. Or maybe something tasty from the butchers, if he could find one open on a Sunday.

He hadn't realised it before, but he'd missed that old cat.

Almost as much as he'd missed his old mum. He had to admit it. Susan certainly had a lot to answer for.

*

Laura had been on shift for five hours already and her feet ached. Saturdays were notoriously busy in A & E, even in the mornings, what with the hangovers and drunken falls from the night before, and then came all the football and rugby injuries, half-dressed men trailing the mud from their boots and the drips from hastily applied bloody bandages across the newly mopped floor. And the mums who hadn't wanted to take their sick children out of school or risk having their pay docked for taking a day off work, and preferred instead to queue up for hours at the weekend to get their five minutes with a doctor, fretting about meningitis or appendicitis, only to be told that the symptoms they were so concerned about pointed to nothing more serious than a bad cold or a touch of tummy ache. No wonder the NHS was in trouble. But at least she didn't have to deal with those, even though she got to hear all about them from her flatmate Gina who had trained as a paediatric nurse and had been working here in Children's A & E ever since she'd qualified. No, Laura only dealt with adult patients, not the kids or, thank God, their parents. Good job really, or she'd probably be tempted to say something she shouldn't.

After six months in the job, she was getting used to it all now. When she'd first transferred down from the men's surgical ward, she'd found A & E quite terrifying. Everything she'd had to do before just flew right out of the window. There was never any order. No chance to plan or prepare, so little time to stop and think. You never knew what was going to come through the door next. One minute a dad-to-be dashing in with a wife already in labour and just missing giving birth in the car on the way here, the next an old lady with a twisted ankle or some idiot with his penis stuck up a hoover tube and trying to hide it underneath his coat. From the trivial to the life-and-death to the 'you wouldn't believe it!', it all just threw itself at her from the moment she arrived until she found herself exhausted, shell-shocked and waiting outside for the bus home.

The road accidents were the worst. No matter how many seatbelts and speed cameras and anti-drinking campaigns there were in the world, the accidents just kept on happening. She stood now, gazing down at the latest victim as the doctor bent over her, shining a light into her eyes, assessing the extent of the damage. The poor girl didn't look much older than Laura herself, perhaps even younger, and she was in a bad way, the victim of a hit and run. Her clothes and hair were soaking wet, at least one leg was obviously broken, there was a nasty gash on the back of her head, and although she'd apparently been briefly conscious and trying to talk at the scene, there had been no response beyond a few incoherent mumblings since she'd been brought in, and she still hadn't opened her eyes.

'Can we try to get an ID? Did she have a bag with her?'

Laura turned to Bob and Sarah, the paramedics. They both looked tired, and Sarah was stretching and rubbing her back with both hands, through the folds of her fluorescent yellow jacket. Having slid her across from trolley to bed and rattled off a list of readings and what they'd already done to help her, they were getting ready to leave.

'Sorry, no.' Sarah shook her head. 'She hardly spoke before she blacked out. Just muttered her name. Lily. But that's all we have. No bag found with her at the scene. Or phone. Unless some friendly passer-by had already nicked them, of course. It wouldn't be the first time. Couldn't find anything in her pockets either, except a couple of keys. House, not car. There wasn't even anything on the key ring to give us any clues. No company logo to tell us who she works for. Not even one of those Tesco clubcard fob things. Bit of a mystery girl, I'm afraid.'

'A pretty unlucky one, too.' The doctor stood up and wiped a hand over his forehead, a stethoscope strung idly around his thin neck and more than a hint of stubbly shadow on his chin. 'I don't like it when patients can't tell me who they are or where it hurts. We're getting a few sounds out of her, which is good, and she is responding to pain, but I don't like head injuries, and I especially don't like the look of this one. Her airway's clear now, but she is struggling a bit. Can we get an urgent head CT please, nurse? Her blood pressure is pretty low too, so let's cross match some blood. Four units. If she's bleeding into that brain of hers, we'll need to replace that blood ASAP. I think we'll need the neurosurgeons to take a look at her.'

He stood back and wiped a bead of sweat from his brow, then carried on assessing his patient's less worrying injuries. 'Fractured left tib and fib as well as a couple of ribs, I'd say, and some fairly deep lacerations on the arms and hands, but nothing too terrible. We can deal with those. Abdomen feels okay. No distension. No obvious sign of any internal damage, apart from the head. Shame there's no way of knowing who she is.'

And no one there waiting for her when she wakes up, Laura thought, as she returned to the nurses' station and busied herself sorting out the paperwork and making the right calls while her colleagues carried on monitoring and did all they could to keep the girl stable.

Her stomach rumbled ominously, reminding her that she still hadn't found time to eat. Even in the midst of others' suffering, life and lunch had to go on. There was a broken custard cream in her uniform pocket. Emergency supplies. She took a sneaky nibble, dropping a scattering of crumbs on the desk, and glanced at her watch. Quarter to one, and she'd been up since 6.00 a.m. The cereal and toast she'd bolted down before leaving for work were nothing but distant memories.

Laura yawned as discreetly as she could and looked across at the mystery girl, surrounded by staff on all sides, unconscious and totally unaware of what was happening to her. And, with no ID, there was no way of knowing who they should call. Not even anyone to sign the consent forms. She'd want her mum at her side if it was her lying there. And her dad, obviously. But mostly her mum. There's nothing so scary as facing stuff alone. And nothing like a mum to make it right. God, imagine having all that going on inside your own body and not knowing a thing about it. Laura shuddered and pushed the thoughts away. It's a job, she reminded herself. Just a job. Don't let yourself get too involved. But, how awful if the girl should die, anonymous and alone.

Death. In the middle of a normal Saturday, with the traffic

going about its business outside the window, someone coughing into a bowl behind a curtain, the radio in the nurses' kitchen spilling out sports news and tinny pop music and the weather, a vase of droopy flowers and a clutch of Thank You cards propped up along the windowsill. Death, coming out of nowhere, when it's least expected. That was the part of her job she most dreaded, especially when the patient was so young. She knew the next few hours would be critical. Tests, monitors, ventilators, maybe an operation to relieve the pressure on her brain, everyone waiting to see whether the girl woke up or slipped away. Life and death. Such a thin line between the two, and so frighteningly easy to cross.

Quarter of an hour now since she'd been brought in, and they'd come to wheel her away already. One of the other nurses went with her. Her expression remained grim. She looked across at Laura as they entered the lift, and shook her head. There was still no change.

CHAPTER THREE

Ruby

The rain has stopped, but I can't go out to play. I'm not feeling very well. Mrs Castle has put me to bed with a hot water bottle and my favourite doll. She's called Betsy, and I think she's wearing her best yellow dress, but someone has closed the curtains and the room is so dark that I can't tell for sure. Her small plastic hand feels cold against mine. The room is quiet, but I can hear some of the others talking outside. They sound so far away, almost as if they're whispering, but I know they're not. Nobody here ever whispers.

My head hurts and I feel really hot, but I'm shivering with cold. That doesn't make any sense at all, but I do as I'm told and stay tucked up under the blankets, only reaching my arm out when I want to take a sip from the big beaker of water by my bed. My legs ache as if I've been running for miles, but I don't think I have. Mrs Castle says what I have might be catching, so the others can't come and see me. I feel very alone in here, but I know Mrs Castle doesn't mean to be unkind. She's trying to help me get better, and she usually knows what's best. She's not as nice as a real mum, but she's the next best thing, and I do trust her. I hope I don't spill the water in the dark and make her cross.

I must have gone to sleep for a while. One of those deep dark sleeps, with no dreams in it. I don't know how long I was asleep, but when I wake up, something feels different. No, everything feels different.

I can't move my legs. I try hard but nothing happens. I can tell that Betsy has gone. I can't feel her hand any more. In the darkness, I try to find her, but I can't move my arms either. Or my eyes. I can't open my eyes. Why can't I open my eyes?

I try to think, try to remember, try to recapture the colour of the yellow in my head. Betsy's yellow, the brightest happiest yellow ever, but everything's just black. Black and dark and empty. And I know she's not here. Betsy.

Is it Betsy I'm searching for? No, not Betsy. Not Betsy at all. Betsy was a long time ago. It's Lily. Lily was this morning. Where is Lily? I try to call for her, try to speak, but nothing happens. My mouth doesn't open. My voice doesn't come.

Where's Lily? And where am I?

CHAPTER FOUR

Geraldine opened the front door and dropped her bag on the hall table. It was a warm afternoon, despite the drizzle, and she was glad to shrug off her coat and slip out of her damp shoes. The feel of the soft wool carpet between her toes always cheered her up and made her feel instantly glad to be home.

'Anyone for tea?' she said as Michael and Patricia slammed the car boot shut and lugged their cases up the drive behind her. 'Only, I can't stop long. I'll have to go back to the shop, if only to help Kerry cash up the takings and lock up properly. Heaven knows what she will have got up to while I've been gone.' She glanced over her shoulder as they reached the step. 'Shoes, please . . .'

She saw Michael raise his eyes to the sky and shake his head. Once inside the old familiar house, their shoes left at the door, he guided Patricia into the living room and plonked her down in a chair, then followed his mother along the narrow hallway to the kitchen.

'You still haven't asked me,' he said, lowering his voice to a whisper and opening the fridge door to grab the milk.

Geraldine busied herself at the sink, filling the kettle and pulling cups out of the cupboard. 'Asked you what, love?'

'Mum, you know what! Oh, you can be infuriating sometimes.'

She turned to look at him. It hadn't been that long since she'd last seen him but she could have sworn he'd grown. Older, taller, wider, more like his father than ever. And so suntanned, she hardly recognised him any more. Not for the first time she felt a pang of something she couldn't quite put a name to. A feeling that she was losing him, as his life headed off in new directions, slowly but surely, bit by inevitable bit. 'Michael, you know I don't like to pry. Yes, you said on the phone that you had something to tell me, but I was waiting for you to do just that.' Oh, she really shouldn't snap at him quite so abruptly. No wonder he came back home so rarely. Not that he probably saw this house, or Brighton, as his home any more. He'd long since put it all behind him. 'I was waiting for you to tell me, when you were ready, that's all. I didn't realise I was expected to ask . . .'

'Well, come into the front room then, and Patsy and I can tell you together. Leave the tea for a minute. No one's going to die of thirst for having to wait a bit longer.'

Geraldine sighed. She'd have to be blind or stupid not to have spotted the ring on Patricia's finger the moment she'd set eyes on her at the airport, but it wasn't her place to comment, was it? And now she'd have to pretend to be surprised. And pleased.

Michael had that look in his eyes. The same one he would come home from school with when he'd come top in maths or scored a goal at football. He was almost bouncing with the urge to tell her, and she knew she must play her part.

So, with the sound of the kettle starting to bubble and let off steam behind her, she let her son lead her along the hall, hand in hand, glad of those last few precious seconds to part her lips and practise her best 'welcome to the family' smile behind his back.

*

Agnes was worried about Smudge. She looked at the clock on her kitchen wall and gazed out at the small back yard, the rain still bouncing hard against the window. Five o'clock, and it was already starting to get dusky, the shadows fading to big shapeless chunks of grey on the concrete below. Poor old cat. He was quite a big chunk of shapeless grey himself these days. She smiled to herself. He was fifteen years old now, getting stiffer, lazier, just like her, and he didn't usually stay out this long when the weather was bad, although he still liked a prowl around, and still came back with a cut ear or a new battle scar from time to time.

She leaned out over the sink and struggled with the rickety window catch, pushing the window open just enough to feel the rush of chilly air and the splash of rain on her arm.

'Smudge. Smudgey Boy, come on. Dinner time!'

She reached for a can of his favourite cat food from the little cupboard under the sink, feeling the pull in her knees as she slowly bent and straightened again. She would keep the cans somewhere else, if only there was space, but every cupboard and shelf in this tiny kitchen was already jam-packed with stuff. Soup and beans, lined up in military order, labels outwards, and umpteen packets of porridge, all bought in as emergency supplies, for the days she either couldn't or didn't want to trudge to the shops. Mugs and glasses and cups. Far too many cups. As if an army of visitors was likely to appear, demanding tea. And the teapot itself, of course. The best one. Her favourite, blue and white Wedgwood, far too good to use, but such a joy to look at. She remembered the day she'd rescued it from the storage boxes, just before they were consigned to William's dusty garage.

She slotted the can into the opener on the wall and pressed the button, watching the thing turn and the lid disengage easily, smoothly, like magic. Whatever next? Self-filling kettles? Bin bags that took themselves out to the dustbin? Sheets that fitted themselves onto the bed? How technology was moving on, changing, sweeping everything along with it! And here she was, trying so hard just to stand still.

'Here, Smudge. Smudgey, Smudge. It's tuna time . . .' She was aware of how silly she sounded, her voice high and shrill as it penetrated the near-silence of the small yard outside the window, but she didn't really care. Not any more. You reach an age when what other people think of you no longer matters, when you can finally say and feel and do as you please, and for Agnes that age had come a while back, soon after the big house move, and the loss of her garden, and the rather symbolic removal of the teapots, when she'd felt, as she still did, that she'd allowed others to take control of her life for long enough and there was nothing much else left to lose.

And then there had been Susan's departure, of course, and her son left shell-shocked and alone. That was when Agnes had finally let it all out. Let rip, as they say in the American films on the telly, and told her son what she really thought. She may even have used a few swear words. In fact, she was sure she had.

The look on William's face! The frustration, the anger, the sense of loss, out it had all tumbled. If only it had raised its head a little sooner, she might have told that bloody wife of his what she'd really thought of her. To her face, instead of shouting it at William, who just stood there, like an empty shell, and said nothing at all.

Vigorously she scraped out half the contents of the cat food can into a bowl and rattled the fork against the side as a 'come-home' signal, her eyes scanning the fence line and the roofs of the sheds beyond. It was surprising just how quiet it was back here, compared to the bustle of the street at the front. High buildings, all close together, high fences and walls. It was how she imagined it must feel peering out from a prison cell at the boundaries built with no other purpose but to keep you in. And there was that crying again, breaking the peace and quiet, like a knife slicing through butter. And it was in bloody stereo now! Two kids bawling their heads off, from two different flats up above. And she'd been worried the other residents might object to her having a pet!

She was about to shout something through the window, suggesting they keep the noise down, but that was when she saw a movement in the corner of the yard. Two front paws appeared like little Punch and Judy finger puppets on the top of the fence and Smudge hauled himself up and over, then scrabbled clumsily down the wooden panel in a flurry of damp fur and scraping claws. She knew what he would do now. A leap up and through the small kitchen window was a bit too tricky for the poor old cat, so he would stroll around the edge of the yard, squeeze through the gap under the side gate that led out to the pavement, climb the concrete steps and wait to be let in at the front door.

Agnes pulled the window shut with a satisfying slam, sending little splashes of rainwater dancing all over the draining board, and lowered the blind, then went out of her flat into the shared hallway to open the front door and await the return of the warrior.

*

Lily woke up on the carpet, curled into a tight little ball, pressed against the side of the sofa. She had fallen asleep crying, in great noisy gulps, and now her cheeks were sore, and she was cold. The curtains were open, and the tree out on the pavement was swaying in the wind and rain, its leaves making scary shadowy patterns on the wall. Lily felt around for Archie and found him under a cushion.

She remembered that she had been playing tea parties with her dolls, talking to them so the room didn't feel so quiet and empty. She'd put the TV on. She knew how to do that, pressing the buttons on the mote. There were no kiddie programmes on, just grown-up things, but she'd left it on to stop the quiet, and gone over to the sofa and climbed up, but then she'd leant over too far to grab for Archie and they'd both fallen off it, and she'd banged her head a little bit and that had made her cry.

The TV was still on now as she woke up, turned up a bit too loud. The dolls were lying down on their sides. Maybe they had needed a nap too. All the plastic cups and plates were still spread over the floor, and the little cardboard packets too, the ones she used when she pretended the flat was a shop and Mummy came and bought things with money from her purse. But none of it was real food, and she was hungry. Archie was hungry too.

When they went into the kitchen, Lily's bare feet slapping on the hard lino floor, there was nothing cooking. Everything was still and quiet. The big ironing board was up, a pile of clothes on top of it, the wire from the iron hanging down to the floor but not plugged in. Lily reached up and touched the iron, very carefully with one finger, in case it was still hot. It wasn't. It was cold. Mummy must have finished the ironing but forgotten to put the iron away. Mummy always put the iron away. But Mummy still wasn't here.

She opened the door of the fridge, looking for food, and the light came on, showing her what was inside. She would have liked to eat a biscuit best, but the biscuits were always kept in a tin high up in a cupboard she couldn't reach, and Mummy never let her have one before her dinner. But the fridge was where Mummy kept the things she was allowed to eat. The fruit and carrots, and things dinner was made of. She felt in the see-through drawer at the bottom and found a baby tomato. It was icy cold, and the juicy pips spurted out as she bit, dribbling in a sticky line down the front of her pyjamas. She offered one to Archie, holding it to his furry lips, but he wasn't very hungry after all, and he whispered that Lily could eat it for him if she wanted to. When she shut the fridge, the light went out and the kitchen felt all horrible and spooky. Quickly, she reopened the door, pulling it all the way back until it stayed there and dragging a chair over to wedge against it, and the bright light shone out like a shiny white square in the corner of the cold grey gloom.

She needed to do a wee. The nappy she was wearing was only meant to be for nap times now that she was nearly three. Not for when she was awake. She didn't know if she should just wee in the nappy. It felt really heavy already, and Mummy might be annoyed with her if she didn't try to hold on until she could climb up onto the toilet or use the potty.

Maybe she should just wait. Hold on. Jiggle up and down. That sometimes helped, like when they were in the supermarket and they had to leave the trolley with all the shopping in it and run off to the Ladies, the one with the pink door. She had to jiggle then, and squash her legs together, which made running much harder to do, but they always got there just in time, and Mummy would laugh as they walked back afterwards, and wondered if they would remember which aisle they'd left the shopping in.

Maybe Mummy had gone to the shops now. But she'd never gone by herself before. Never left Lily behind. The wee feeling was getting stronger. She didn't know what to do. Maybe she could ring Mummy. She walked to the phone. It was on the table by the front door, its long green wire hanging down, all curly like a snake. She picked it up and listened. There was just a buzzing noise and she wasn't sure what to do next. What buttons to press.

'Mummy?'

Nobody spoke. There was just the buzzing noise.

'Mummy?'

But the phone just kept on buzzing in her hand.

The wee was trying really hard to come out now, and she was trying really hard to stop it. She dropped the phone, still buzzing, onto the table, and tugged at the sticky strips sticking up over the waistband of her pyjama bottoms, the strips that held the nappy on. She had never had to take her own nappy off before. She managed to tear off one of the strips and that side of the nappy slipped crookedly and soggily down inside her pyjamas towards her knees. But it was too hard to get it right off. It was taking too long. The pyjamas were in the way. Her fingers wouldn't work.

And then it was too late to find the potty. She couldn't hold it in any longer, no matter how hard she jiggled, and the warm liquid flowed down her legs, leaving a long damp trail down her pyjama bottoms and making a big slippery puddle that she could hardly see on the floor around her cold bare feet.

CHAPTER FIVE

Ruby

I'm sitting on the grass in the park. The others are all chasing a ball around, glad to be outside for a while, shouting to each other and squealing with excitement, but I'm happier here under the tree with my book.

Every now and then I lay it down on my lap and watch the people going by. Mums pushing prams, toddlers stopping to pick daisies in the grass, the occasional man out from his office, lighting up a cigarette, tugging his collar open and loosening his tie as he sweats in his business suit.

There's an old lady today, with a little grey dog. She's walking very slowly, her big coat open and flapping in the breeze, and it's obvious the dog just wants to run on ahead, but she doesn't let him. She grips on to his lead as if she's holding back a great raging lion, but he's just a little dog. A poodle, I think. Anyone can see he's dying to chase leaves and bring back sticks and do what dogs are supposed to do, but the old lady finds a bench and lowers herself onto it, tying the end of the lead round the slats at the back and closing her eyes against the sun.

After a while she opens a pack of sandwiches, little square

ones she's made at home and wrapped up in a greaseproof paper bundle. I watch as her jaw grinds up and down rhythmically, and she pushes a chunk of something – maybe cheese – into the dog's mouth and throws a few crusts for the birds, and then the dog gives up trying to escape, rolls onto his side and goes to sleep on the path.

I like it when we come out like this. Get a look at the real world, a world populated by families and grannies and dogs. I don't have any of those things. I have never had any of those things. Not properly. Not to keep.

Someone nearly took me once. Did all the papers and took me out on trips and stuff. They seemed nice enough. Him with his shiny shoes, and her with her shiny eyes. But it didn't happen in the end. It's a big decision, I suppose, taking on a kid who isn't yours. A bit like choosing a dog. You have to be in it for the long haul, prepared to get on with it, take what comes, ups and downs, good and bad, no matter what. Not just for Christmas. Maybe they just couldn't go through with it, face the enormity of it. I like to think that maybe they found out they were having a baby of their own, or decided to get a cat instead, or realised they could be happy just in each other's company after all. I hope they didn't choose some other child to adopt, that it wasn't just me they rejected.

Mrs Castle is rounding us all up now. It's time to go back to the children's home, nearly time for tea. She's herding us back to the mini-bus like wayward, weary sheep. I get up and flick stalks of dried grass from my clothes, pop the bookmark inside my book ready to pick up the story later, exactly where I left off, and climb up the steep step, heading for my favourite seat by the window, in the middle row, on the left.

I must have gone to sleep. The rhythm of the wheels on the road, the gentle chatter of the other children's voices all around me, the heat of the dying sun working its way into the skin of my forehead through the glass, layer by layer, making me feel all muzzy and only halfway here.

And now someone is touching my arm, whispering so quietly I can hardly hear, as if they are a long, long way away. 'Lily . . .' a voice is saying, cool steady fingers pressing against my wrist. A female voice I don't recognise. Not Mrs Castle. Not my mother. But then I realise I don't quite remember what my mother's voice sounds like. It's so long since I've seen her. Or heard her say my name.

And, through my dreams I'm thinking: Yes, Lily. I like Lily. It's a nice name. When I'm a mother, I'm going to call my baby Lily. Or Betsy, like my doll. And love her properly, never leave her, never let her go. But the voice fades away, and I can't conjure up a face that fits it, and the wheels keep turning, and my left leg has gone to sleep pressed against the throbbing side of the bus.

And I'm not ready to wake up yet.

CHAPTER SIX

Laura checked her watch. Ten to eight. She had managed to run and catch the bus just as it was about to pull away from the stop, puffing heavily and with the beginnings of a stitch in her side – she really must lose a few pounds, she was so unfit – but glad to have made it, as the next wasn't due for twenty minutes.

The traffic had not been as heavy as usual and the bus had sailed through several sets of lights just as they were about to turn red, so now she was here with time to spare. That made a change. She stood in the lobby, early-morning empty, a pale imitation of the bustling hive of activity it would soon become, once the coffee shop opened and the visitors started to arrive, armed with cards and grapes and Lucozade and flowers.

There was a pile of thick Sunday newspapers, colour supplements in plastic casing spilling out of the sides, tied up with string in the still-closed doorway of the hospital shop, and Laura waved through the glass at her friend Fiona, overall on, getting ready to open on the dot of eight, tipping coins into the till from a small plastic bag with one hand as she waved back, sleepily, with the other.

Vivien Brown

For some reason she could not fully explain, despite one of Gina's casseroles, an early night and not the smallest trace of alcohol, Laura had slept fitfully. Images of the girl from yesterday, the one hit by the car, had kept flashing up on her dream screen. It was never easy, seeing people hurt, unconscious, sometimes not being able to help them. As a nurse, she knew she had to switch off, try not to take it home with her, keep it all out of her head. But some times were harder than others. Some patients had more impact, tugging harder at the heart strings.

This girl, the one from yesterday, had got to her, crept in under the radar. Perhaps it was the fact that she was unconscious and unidentified. Just Lily, if that was even her name. Poor sick deep-sleeping Lily. No bag, no address, no medical records, no family sobbing at her bedside. Or perhaps it was because she was so near to Laura's own age, or seemed to be. No wedding ring, but somewhere there would be parents, brothers, sisters, a boyfriend maybe, all blissfully unaware . . . Surely someone would have reported her missing by now?

Laura pushed the button for the sixth floor and waited for the lift to arrive. She had ten minutes – okay, only eight now – before she was due to start work. Just long enough to pop up to the intensive care unit and see if anyone had come to claim Lily, or if she had woken up yet.

*

William put the key in the ignition and turned. There was a splutter, an ominous sort of chug, and then nothing but a whine. He tried again and got just the whine this time. The sodding battery was flat. Just when he'd finally psyched himself up to go and see his mother too. Best shirt, shoes polished, and a handful of loose change clanking in his pocket, ready to pick up some flowers on the way. Could you buy freesias in October? He had no idea. Still, they'd be bound to have something nice at the Asian 24-hour place on the corner, or at the petrol station, something bright and cheerful that would sit in a vase on his mother's windowsill and help him break the proverbial ice.

Cars! More trouble than they were worth. He would have liked to get out and give the damn thing a good kicking, vent his frustrations on the already rusting bodywork, but then it would have a sodding great dent in the side as well as a dead battery, so what was the point, other than to make himself feel better? Instead, he rooted about in the glove compartment, looking for the breakdown cover documents. William knew very little about cars, beyond how much they cost to run, and that was frightening enough these days. Even if he could track down the breakdown policy, would someone come out, to his own driveway, just to give him some kind of a bump start, and on a Sunday too? He didn't know if they – he – had the full cover or just the basic roadside deal. He'd always left that kind of stuff to Susan and, now she'd gone, he had no idea where she would have put the papers, or even if she'd bothered to renew the thing at all. Her own car, considerably newer than his, was a company one and no doubt came with all manner of guarantees that his old banger had long since outlived.

He found it right at the back. A small plastic folder marked 'RAC' in Susan's flowery handwriting, a bit bent and tucked in behind an old spare pair of glasses, an open packet of Polos and one of those things you use to check the pressure of the tyres. He hadn't done that for a while either. But when he pulled out the papers inside, the thing had run out. Expired, just three weeks ago. Why on earth hadn't they written to him, reminded him it was due? But then he remembered the pile of letters propped up by the clock, the bills and junk mail and suspiciously official looking brown envelopes that he hadn't quite got around to tackling yet, and knew that they probably had.

What would have taken ten minutes by car was a forty minute bus ride, on a good day. They'd done it once, both ways, he and Susan, noting down the right bus number to catch, and the times it departed and arrived, then stop-watching themselves from door to door, just to show Agnes how easy it would be for her to come and visit, but she never had. Getting on and off buses was a struggle, she said, with their high steps and her bad knees, although he knew she could do it if she tried. But William was starting to feel that way himself these days. It was all a bit too much of a bother, and there'd probably be a much longer wait anyway, it being a Sunday. Buses never ran as frequently on a Sunday.

He opened up the bonnet and managed to disconnect the battery, getting great blobs of oil and muck all over his sleeves in the process, and then lugged it through into the garage. He knew he had a charger somewhere amongst all the cluttered detritus of his life. It must have been years since he'd had a good clear-out and even longer since he'd been able to actually park a car in there.

Eventually, he went back into the house and threw his oily jacket down on a chair already littered with discarded jumpers, crumpled sweatshirts and screwed-up socks. He'd put the kettle on and have some tea while he decided what to do. After all, it wasn't as if his mother was expecting him, so not turning up wasn't about to break any hearts. He flipped the TV on as he waited for the kettle to boil. There was an old film on. Something black and white, from the 1930s or 40s by the look of it. The kind of film his father used to watch on a Sunday, all dapper-looking men in evening suits and elegant women swishing their long satin skirts, cigarettes in long slim holders poised at their lips and a big band playing in the background.

He still missed his father. Donald Munro had been a force to be reckoned with. Upright, honest, an all-round good egg. An organiser too. Even at his funeral, it had been as if he was still there, taking charge, making sure everything ran like clockwork. He'd left strict instructions. Music, coffin, memorial, even where the after-party should be held and who should be invited. Left a special account too, with just the right amount of cash in it to see himself safely out of this world and into the next.

Now that Susan's gone, perhaps I should make plans, William thought, pouring the hot water onto his teabag and flopping back down in front of the film. A new will. Decisions about what happens next. Who to leave it all to. But, of course, there was no one. Only his mother, who by the law of averages would go first. No brothers or sisters, the only cousin being a girl he'd not met since he was three and who now lived in Australia. He should have had children. He wished he'd had children. But it wasn't going to happen now, was it? Maybe he should start investigating charities, leave it all to the NSPCC or a dogs' home somewhere. Cats, even. His mother would approve of that.

On the screen, a man in a top hat was sweeping a woman off her feet, whirling her around in mid-air, his tap shoes tap-tapping away on an impossibly shiny over-polished floor. William looked down at his own feet. He'd kicked his shoes off at the door. Old habits. Susan never allowed shoes on inside the house. There was a hole in one of his socks, half a big toe peeping through, and a line of crumbs on the carpet around his armchair from too many late-night digestives. His toenails needed a trim too, by the look of the one escaping from his sock.

It was no good denying it. He missed having a woman around. Even a cold-hearted bitch like Susan. At least she was someone he could have left it all to. All his worldly goods. Clichéd though it sounded, there was a sodding great hole in his life these days, not just in his sock. And they both needed mending, but he had no idea how. Or even where the mending kit was kept.

*

The whiney noise kept coming from the phone near the front door. She didn't know what it was, and she didn't like it. It wasn't the buzzy noise she'd heard before, when she'd tried to talk to Mummy. This was different. Scarier. Like the nee-naw noises the fire engines made. Loud, then quiet, then loud again. It kept coming out of the phone she'd put down on the table. Maybe the long curly wire really was a snake and it was trying to get her. Chase her. Eat her. She wasn't going to go near it. Not until it stopped. Only, it didn't.

Lily was naked from the waist down. Her yellow pyjamas were too wet to wear. They were in the laundry basket, where she'd put them last night, where Mummy always put the dirty things. But she couldn't find any clean ones. Her other pairs were in there too, right at the bottom. She had seen them, one pair stripey, and one with little pink teddies, through a gap in the plastic, so there was nothing to wear. Only her jeans and tops and pretty dresses, but you weren't supposed to wear proper clothes to go to sleep in.

She'd stood on the bed and pulled at the light cord, so the Winnie the Pooh light on the ceiling had been on all night. It was what Mummy called a night light, not too bright, and it made a soft pink circle on the ceiling that was supposed to stop her being scared when she was by herself, but it hadn't worked. Now the daylight was streaming in too, through the still-open curtains, and the traffic was getting loud outside just like every morning. But this morning was different to other mornings.

She had tried to find some pull-ups last night but there weren't any left in the packet. Mummy said they cost a lot of money and big girls could manage to use the proper toilet in the daytime now, couldn't they? But she couldn't go to bed without a nappy on. She always wore a nappy to go to bed. So she'd tried to put a proper one on, one with the sticky sides, but it hadn't stuck properly and the knickers she had worn to try to make it stay there were now even wetter than the pyjamas. So was her bed. It smelled of stale warmth and wee, and so did she.

The smell didn't go away. It seemed to follow her as she padded through the flat, room by room. There was no Mummy. Still no Mummy. She was thirsty. She wanted to cry again, but she was a big girl now. Mummy had said so. And big girls know how to get their own drink. She walked into the kitchen, her feet sticky as they reached the place where she'd made the puddle. It was nearly all dried up now, and the floor felt warm where the sun was coming in. She was glad. She didn't want Mummy to see the puddle when she came back. Big girls didn't make puddles on the floor. Big girls used the potty, or sat on the big toilet on the special seat Mummy had bought at the charity shop. The day they got the yellow pyjamas, and Mummy's new shoes.

Lily went to the sink. She pulled the plastic step over – the one Mummy called the kiddie step – and climbed up so she could reach the taps, the way she did when they'd been baking cakes and Mummy said she had to wash her hands to get the last of the mixture off, even though she'd already licked them clean. Then she picked up the plug on the end of its metal chain and pushed it firmly into the plug hole, the way Mummy had shown her, so she could make the water stay and go all soapy without it running away down the drain.

The cold tap was the one nearest to the kitchen door. She was only allowed to touch the cold tap. Not the hot. Mummy had taught her about which tap was which. Left and right, but that was too hard to remember, even when they'd practised holding up both hands or picking out which shoe to put on which foot. It was much easier to just know that the cold tap was the one nearest to the door.

Her favourite cup was upside down on the draining board. It had a row of baby ducks on it, going right round in a circle, all following their mummy. She turned it over. The tap was stiff. She needed both hands to make it turn, and then the water came out in a big gush that made her jump and splashed all over her top. Lily caught some water in the cup and took a big swig before dropping the cup back into the water in the sink and washing it with the little bar of soap they kept in a dish at the side, playing with the creamy bubbles and rubbing them right up to her elbows, soaking the ends of her sleeves, as slowly the sink began to fill.

Then, suddenly, there was a bang at the front door. Someone was there. Lily froze. What if it was the Big Bad Wolf, come to get her? Or a nasty stranger? She wasn't allowed to open the door, especially to strangers. Or to talk to them in the street, or in the park. Strangers were dangerous, like dogs. The door was right next to the curly snake that was still making the scary noise, so she couldn't go there, even if she wanted to.

'Hello?'

It was a man's voice, coming from behind the door. From the hall outside.

'Hello? Ruby? You in there?' He was shouting louder now.

Lily stood very still.

'Ruby? Your neighbours from upstairs were just coming out and they let me into the hall. Don't know if you're at home, but I'll leave the stuff out here, love. Should be safe enough. Be back tomorrow to collect it, along with the last lot, okay?'

Then it went quiet again.

Lily didn't know if he had gone away. She hoped he had. But she still wanted to see. She edged towards the door, her hands over her ears to stop the whiney noise, keeping her eyes on the wiry green snake in case it tried to move and bite her. But she had to look and see who was out there. She had to be brave. She *was* brave. Mummy had said so when she let the dentist man look inside her mouth. She had got a sticker for that. A sticker that said she was a brave girl.

She lay down on the floor, pressed tight onto the mat. There was an old cat flap low down in the door, left by the people who had lived here before them. The big cat from downstairs had tried to come in once, prodding it with his paw, but Mummy had opened the door and shooed him away before he got right through, and he had run away scared and had never come back again. Mummy said she didn't want it to come inside. She had never had an animal before, and she wasn't used to them, didn't know how to look after them properly. But they were going to get a rabbit. She knew they were. Mummy had said so.

Mummy always said she was going to find something to block the flap up with, but then she forgot again. Lily didn't want it blocked up. She liked looking through it, flapping the square of scratchy plastic in and out so it rattled, watching what was happening, at ankle level, out in the hall. Spiders, leaves, dust. She saw a mouse once, but it had soon disappeared. Maybe the cat ate it. Sometimes she liked to pretend she was an animal in the zoo, like a lion or a tiger, and that the cat flap was her own little door and she could climb through it and escape when nobody was looking and scare all the visitors, but she had tried it once and it was much too small. She could get her arm through but that was all.

Very carefully now, she pushed it open just a little bit so she could peer out. She could only see his boots, big muddy black boots, moving away from her, making big loud thuds as he walked, and the corner of the big box he'd left in the hall. But then, as he went further away and started to go down the stairs, she could see more of him, and she knew who it was. His big blue jacket, his dirty jeans, his shiny bald head. It was the iron man. Not really a stranger. So maybe she was allowed to talk to him. She could ask him where Mummy was, see if he could help find her, but it was too late now. He disappeared from view, clunking away from her, and the big front door downstairs slammed shut and he was gone.

Lily's tummy growled just like the lion she was pretending to be. She stood up and ran quickly away from the phone, roaring at it and holding out her claws as she passed, to see if it would make it stop. It didn't.

She was very hungry now. She had eaten up the rest of the tomatoes last night, and a piece of cheese and a big carrot, even though she didn't like carrots all that much. She'd unwrapped a bit of paper with two sausages in it and taken a bite off the end of one, but it was all cold and pink because Mummy hadn't cooked it yet, and it tasted horrible, so she'd spat it out. She had struggled to get the lid off the big blue tub that had the ice cream in it, but when she had, the ice cream was all runny and she'd spilled most of it when she'd tried to drink it on a spoon. Then she'd finished off the last of the milk straight from the bottle but it had tasted horrible. All warm and smelly, and a lump of something yellow had caught in her throat and nearly made her sick.

With big tears running down her face, she had pushed the chair away and the fridge door had swung shut, but the dark had still been too dark, too scary, and she'd quickly opened it again, which didn't matter because all the food that was in there had gone and now there was some water dripping down the inside and trickling out onto the floor.

Now it was the next day, because she had been to sleep, and she had a tummy ache, and so did Archie. She thought she might need to do a poo but it wasn't quite ready to come out yet. Mummy sometimes gave her Cowpol when she had a tummy ache, or a cold, or when her head hurt, which it did sometimes when she was tired. A big sugary-sweet pink spoonful that tasted nice and always made her feel better. She didn't know why it was called Cowpol. Maybe they used it at the farm when the cows were sick. They would need a huge spoon though. Cows had big mouths and great big, long, licky tongues.

She could hear the water running in the sink and remembered she'd left the tap on when she'd heard someone banging at the door. She climbed back up and tried to turn it off, but it was so stiff. It went most of the way but wouldn't go any more. She could hear it going drip-drip-drip, splashing into the water already there in the sink, bouncing off her ducky cup, as she climbed down from the step and went to look for the medicine.

*

Agnes was in her dressing gown with the tea stain down the front she still hadn't got around to scrubbing. Her slippers were looking tatty too, but it didn't seem to matter all that much. Nobody was going to see them but her.

Sundays had been special once, when Donald was still alive. When she would wake early and make bacon and eggs and thinly sliced toast soldiers, and a proper pot of tea, and they'd put on their good clothes and walk together, arm in arm, to church or go for a spin in the car before coming home to a real fire and roast lamb and something nice on the telly. Not any more. Now Sundays merged into all the other days, indistinguishable, ordinary, disappointing.

She poured porridge oats from one of the many packets lined up like giant cardboard dominoes in the cupboard and stood gazing out at nothing in particular through the window as the milk warmed in the pan. It was a bit late to call it breakfast but porridge for lunch was okay, wasn't it? Why not? She had no one else to please.

There was a boil-in-the-bag cod in butter sauce in the freezer for later and a few peas, plenty for one, with perhaps a corner of the fish left over for Smudge. No need for potatoes at her age. They just filled up space, in the already over-stuffed cupboards, and in her own stomach. You didn't need the same amount of stodge when you went nowhere, did nothing to burn it off. The paper would be on the mat in the hall by now, so there'd be a bit of scandal to read and a crossword to work on later. She'd maybe sort out her smalls and put a wash load on, pop her dressing gown in too, to see if it would get the stain out. Flip a duster round the place. Other than that, nothing. No grand plan for the day.

The kettle wheezed its way to boiling point and she made herself some strong tea, avoiding the one good pot as usual and just plopping a teabag into the cup. Then she carried it through to her armchair, using both hands, the cup shaking between them and slopping a little tea onto her dressing gown where it slowly sank in unnoticed to join and expand the existing stain like some shapeless wishy-washy brown amoeba. Yes, she'd definitely have to tackle the washing today.

The rain had stopped and there was a watery sun trying to peep between the slow-moving clouds. Agnes arranged herself in her chair, closed her eyes and turned her face towards the light coming in through the window.

From somewhere above her head, she could hear the sound of something being scraped along the floor. It grated, put her teeth on edge, like chalk squealing across a blackboard. Reluctantly, she leaned over and switched on the telly. That was the trouble with flats. In her old cottage, every room, every floor, every inch was hers. No noisy neighbours, no crying babies. She could summon silence at will. Now it was cooking programmes or politics or the God slot, or some old Sunday film. It was the only way she knew to drown out the world.

*

Laura and Fiona were taking a break. They sat, as they often did, on the wall outside the hospital, watching the world go by, assorted pre-packed sandwiches in plastic triangles open beside them. Fiona was allowed to reduce prices as sell-by dates were reached, and then there was her usual staff discount on top, so it made sense to take advantage. Whatever flavour wasn't selling so well . . . that's what they'd eat. They weren't too fussy. Variety is the spice of life, after all.

At least they were out in the fresh air. There were a few wilting pansies, the last of the season, in a basket by the main doors, a narrow patch of well-trodden grass at their feet, and they could just about hear the fountain above the noise from the car park, and the occasional wail of incoming ambulances. All in all, better than the canteen. And, anyway, they both agreed that it was so much easier to buy ready-made food than to be messing about with slicing cheese and cutting up salad at seven in the morning, when heating up the hair straighteners and finding a clean pair of knickers were much more important priorities. Not that either of them were likely to find a lot of salad just lying about in their fridges, if they were absolutely honest about it.

As nurses go, Laura was only too aware that she was not among the fittest and healthiest of specimens. Her changing shift patterns, early morning starts and late finishes, and day-off trips home to see her parents left little enough opportunity to have any kind of meaningful social life, let alone find the time for proper cooking or to go to the gym. Her uniform was starting to strain a bit around the hips and bum, and she already needed the fingers of a whole hand to count the number of times she'd eaten chips this week.

'He was all right, I suppose,' Fiona was saying. 'If you like that sort of thing . . .'

'What sort of thing?' Laura took a bite out of the soggy white bread, now slightly pink from being saturated in over-ripe tomato. 'I thought when you went on these dating sites, you could ask for exactly what you wanted. You know, list all his attributes, try before you buy!'

'Well, yes, I'd seen his photo, obviously. And we'd chatted online, but it's not the same, is it? There are things you're never going to be able to tell until you meet in the flesh.'

Laura's mind boggled. 'Like?'

'Well, like his breath for one thing. Onions, garlic, tobacco. You name it, he must have eaten it – and the big lips didn't help. Yuk! Like rubber. I know now why he had his mouth shut so tightly in the picture.'

Laura laughed, almost choking on a chunk of cucumber. 'Never again, then?'

'Oh, I wouldn't say that. You have to kiss a lot of frogs before your prince comes along, as they say. So, it's onwards and upwards. Plenty more fish in the murky waters of the sea. And tonight it's Harry.'

'Harry?'

'Yep. Same agency, 'cos I do have to try to get my moneys' worth before I knock it on the head. But this one looks all right. Bit weedy, maybe. More sprat than shark, if you know what I mean. But he works in some city insurance place, so he's bound to be minted. We're meeting for cocktails, then dinner. No cut-price sarnies for me tonight. Well, if I play my cards right, anyhow. Little black dress, and condoms at the ready!'

'Fiona, you are terrible. You will be careful though, won't you?'

'I told you. Condoms packed and ready to go. How much more careful do you want me to be?'

'Oh, I don't know. Life's shit sometimes. He's a stranger. Things happen. Just look after yourself, that's all I'm saying. But you go and have fun. And eat yourself silly. Why not, if he's paying? Don't take any notice of me. I'm probably just jealous, that's all.'

They screwed up their wrappers and walked them over to the

overflowing bin where a couple of drowsy wasps were diving in and out among the leftovers.

'See you tomorrow? You can tell me all about it.'

'Yeah, sure. I might even persuade you to have a go yourself. Wish me luck, anyway.' And Fiona was off, her high heels clacking noisily across the concrete, hastily checking her phone one last time before the sliding glass doors pulled her back inside and quickly swallowed her up.

Laura stood for a moment. Luck. That's what it all comes down to in the end. Who you meet, what you look like, what happens to you. Did she choose this job, this friend, these hips? Or did they just happen? Fate. Destiny. Luck. Who knows what's waiting around the corner?

She glanced at her watch, its overlarge face hanging upside down from a silver chain above her breast. Was there time before she was due back? Yes, there was.

There was a queue for the lifts. Sunday visiting, straight after lunch. Always a busy time. When the first one came, she squeezed inside, along with at least a dozen others. There was a smell of pungent flowers, lukewarm burgers, lots of sweat. A small boy eased his way to the front, his hand outstretched, eager to be the one to push the buttons. 'Six, please,' Laura said, when it was her turn to tell him where she wanted to go, and the lift rumbled its way upwards, stopping at just about every floor to let people out and a few replacement people in, several of them grumbling that it was going up when they really wanted it to go down and sending the boy into a frenzy of excited button-pushing, until the woman with him grabbed him by the sleeve and hauled him out at level five.

Intensive Care was always quiet. There was a rather sad air, a mixture of fear and expectation that hit her as soon as the doors opened to Laura's push of the intercom. She went inside, closing the doors as silently as she could behind her.

'You back again?' the sister called across to her. It was the same one from earlier, the jolly black one with curly grey hair pulled back into a straggly bun. Cora Jenkins, according to her badge. Laura couldn't remember ever seeing a black person with such grey hair before. It was very distinctive. Striking. Cora pushed the file she was writing in aside and beckoned her over. 'Anyone would think you were family!'

'No, but until one appears, I'll have to do.' Laura dunked her hands under the anti-bac dispenser on the wall and rubbed them hastily together before moving to the nurses' station. 'Still nothing?'

'Not a thing. We're no nearer to knowing who she is. There were just the keys in her pocket and a cross around her neck. Ordinary high street clothes, no bag, no tattoos or anything like that. Nothing to help ID her at all. The police are on to it, but nobody's been. Seems like, wherever she's come from, our mystery girl hasn't even been missed. Sad, isn't it?'

'And how is she? Has she opened her eyes? Tried to talk? Anything?'

'Not yet, I'm afraid. The leg's been sorted, as you know. They've done what they can in theatre to relieve the pressure on her brain and her blood pressure is more or less back on track. Look, lovey, she's as stable as she can be under the cir-cumstances.' She shook her head. 'They want to keep her under a while longer, give her a chance to recover before they try to wake her up, so she won't be back with us and talking just yet. It's still early days . . .'

'Can I go in?'

'Course you can, my love. You know where I am if you need me.' And she turned her attention back to her paperwork as Laura made her way along the corridor of little side rooms, each patient encased in their own private bubble, until she reached the right door.

She eased it open quietly, nodding to a nurse who was just replacing the clipboard at the end of the bed and was about to leave. 'No change,' she whispered, touching Laura's arm. 'We're still doing the breathing for her, just for now anyway. To help her along while she rests, make things easier for her. She did take a very nasty bang to the head. The surgeons have done what they can, but there's no knowing if there's any lasting damage. Not until she . . . well, as it's you, I'll be honest and say . . .'

'*If* she wakes up?'

The girl nodded and opened the door 'Let's hope someone comes to claim her soon, eh?'

Before it's too late, Laura thought, but quickly shook the idea away.

'Oh, and there's one more thing. I don't know if I should tell you, but as you're staff . . .'

'Yes?'

'She has a caesarean scar. At some time, not too long ago, she's had a baby.' And then the nurse was gone, her shoes clicking away into the distance along the corridor, and Laura and the girl were alone.

'So, Lily . . .' Laura moved towards the bed, surrounded by machinery, and looked down into the still, bruised face. There was a tube fitted into the girl's mouth, a bandage wrapped around her head, wires attached to her chest, the incessant beeping of monitors, providing the background noise like crickets on a summer's night in some Spanish holiday resort. 'What are we going to do with you?' she muttered, picturing this girl with a baby in her arms. And where was that baby now? 'How are we going to find your family?'

She pulled a chair nearer to the bed and slid her hand over Lily's, spotting the nibbled nails and noting again the absence of a ring.

'Hello. Can you hear me?'

There was no response, which was no surprise, but that wasn't going to stop her from talking.

'They say coma patients can hear sometimes, you know. People wake up and say they've heard every word spoken while they've been asleep, family chatting, music, all sorts, but they just didn't have the power to answer back. Maybe that's happening with you? Maybe you're hearing me now. Lying there scared and trapped, not understanding where you are, or what's going on?'

Still nothing.

'I want to help you, Lily. I don't even know if that's really your name, but I'll call you Lily anyway. I'm Laura. I'm a nurse. I know you have nobody else here to talk to you, to tell you where or how you are; what the weather's like outside. Would you like me to be that person, Lily? For now, anyway, just until someone comes?'

The girl just lay there. Not a flicker. Laura squeezed her hand and half hoped she might feel it move, that it might try to squeeze her back, but no. Just the beeps, marking out the seconds, one by one, and the sound of the ventilator breathing in and out, in and out, in and out.

'You're in the hospital. We don't know what happened to you. Hit by a car that didn't stop, so they say. Your leg's broken, so that might hurt a bit. And your ribs. And your head's going to feel sore. You're being kept asleep, just until your brain decides to get better and start working properly again by itself. Don't worry about that. Or the noise, or the tubes. It's all here to help you. All perfectly normal. Don't be afraid. All you have to do is lie there and sleep, and let yourself heal.'

Laura looked at the watch on her chest. It was time to get back to work already.

'It's a nice day, Lily. It's rained a lot the last day or two, but the sun's out now, and there are trees outside the window. Lovely, tall, green trees. I think I can even see a little nest. You'll be able to see it for yourself when you wake up. And hear the birds. If you can't already . . .'

She withdrew her hand, and resisted a sudden compulsion to lean over and kiss Lily on the cheek. No, that would be wrong. Crossing professional boundaries. But maybe she was doing that already, just by being here?

The lift was empty this time, depositing her back on the ground floor with a bump. She hurried back into A & E and checked the screen for new patients, any developments since she'd been gone. Nothing of any significance. Things were remarkably quiet. Until the Sunday afternoon football and rugby players started to roll in, the amateur ones with proper jobs who played just for the exercise, and the beer afterwards, and the fun – some fun! – with their split lips and bloodied noses and broken ankles. Three o'clock loomed. Kick-off time. It wouldn't be long now.

CHAPTER SEVEN

Ruby

Michael is nice. More than nice. Michael is handsome, gorgeous, wonderful. Michael is the best thing ever to happen to me. Only he hasn't happened to me. Not really. Not yet.

He did speak to me today. Only to say thank you. But he said it in such a lovely way. With his eyes, not just his voice. Like he really meant it.

Mrs Castle lets me run errands now. She says that a children's home is for children and I'm not a child any more, that she is going to give me more responsibility, prepare me for the outside world. When she's in her office she lets me help her sometimes. A bit of filing, answering the phone. All good practice for when I get a job, that's what she says. I'm sixteen now, and I have always known I can't stay here forever.

Today she sent me down to the bank. Not with tons of money. That would be too dangerous. I could get mugged or something. But she'd been collecting up coins in jars for weeks and she let me bag them up and walk them down to the bank to pay them in. Nobody robs you for ten pence pieces, do they? Not worth the effort.

Michael's long fingers reached across the desk and hooked the bags in, under the see-through dip that separates him from the queue, lifting them one at a time, dropping them onto the scales, ticking them off on the slip with his pen. I know his name is Michael because he wears a badge. Michael Payne. He's so much younger than the rest of the staff, who all have grey hair and bored faces and look like they've been there forever. He's older than me though. Maybe twenty or twenty-one. So, not by all that much. Not enough to matter. And he has the most brilliant blue eyes. The eyes that said thank you, all by themselves.

In my mind, I can still feel his hand, touching the top of mine, ever so lightly, as he takes the coin bags, making the tiny hairs stand to attention all along my arm. And then, later, touching my cheek, touching my body under my clothes, touching with soft gentle strokes where nobody has ever touched me before. And then it's gone again. The hand. And suddenly all I can hear is the sound of my own breathing struggling in my throat as the very thought of him stops me in my tracks, sends the blood rushing to my head, to my heart, and almost takes my breath away.

He could charm the birds out of the trees, that one. It's one of Mrs Castle's sayings, and it's as if I can hear her still saying it now. Birds. Trees. My mind's all over the place, whirling around like I'm in a spin dryer, but I know what I felt. In that one delicious moment at the bank, I felt it. The beginnings of love.

I am in love. Head over heels, birds in the trees love. With a man I don't even know. And his name is Michael Payne.

CHAPTER EIGHT

Patsy reached across the lumpy bed for Michael. He wasn't there.

It was ridiculous to feel so tired after such a short flight, but perhaps the months of intense work had finally caught up with her. Now she'd sealed the latest contract she could take a couple of weeks off and relax a bit before Phase Two. The hefty bonus coming her way would help too. She could feel a spot of retail therapy coming on, just as soon as they could get up to London and hit the shops.

They'd had a meal at the local pub with Michael's mother last night, but it had proved to be a rather strained affair. They'd both been putting on smiles for his benefit, but underneath the surface they'd been squaring up, marking their corners. Womens' stuff, that Michael wouldn't have noticed. But she knew. Geraldine did not like her, did not really want her here.

Michael had clearly felt a bit awkward about sharing the bed. It was his mother's house. The last time he'd properly lived here was a long time ago and he'd been a single man for most of that time. She'd still done his washing, hoovered his room, made his meals. Even when Ruby had arrived, he'd told her, it hadn't felt like this. Ruby had been like family to start with, like a younger sister, just there living alongside him in the house, until things had suddenly and stupidly changed between them. Things had moved so quickly then, into an intimacy he had never felt ready for. A shared room, a shared bed, a baby on the way, but always something lacking. Now he was finding it hard to make this new transition, to bring his own fiancée, a woman his mother hardly knew, into the house, take her into his old room and do the kind of things he would have done if they'd been back in Portugal, where walls did not have ears. His mother's ears, anyway. And things he had never done with Ruby.

And so, after the pub outing last night they'd drunk cocoa and made small talk until Geraldine had gone up to bed, and then they'd tiptoed up the stairs like naughty teenagers and gone to sleep curled against each other, with far too many clothes on, the light off, and not so much as a snog, let alone anything that might have made the bedsprings creak.

Patsy had not slept well.

Geraldine had made them breakfast, which they'd all eaten together, squashed around the kitchen table, then she'd made some calls before deciding to get off back to the shop. She didn't usually open on a Sunday, or at least not out of season, but she'd missed a good bit of yesterday and there were things to be done, she'd told them. Paperwork, stock taking, financial stuff. It had sounded like an excuse to get away from the house, and probably from them, but Patsy wasn't complaining.

'At last,' Patsy had said when the front door closed and they'd heard Geraldine's car move off down the road. 'Bed!'

'But we've only just got up,' Michael had pleaded, as she led him back up the stairs, still clutching a slice of cold toast in his hand.

'Oh, no, my lad. You haven't got up at all yet. That's the problem!'

And now, what must be three or four hours later, she was awake again, her clothes scattered in heaps on the carpet, her hair tangled up in post-coital knots, and the other side of the bed empty.

'Michael?' she called, raising her head from the damp sweatiness of the pillowcase, which was made of some sort of shiny nylon. In a sickly pale peach colour, too. Certainly not to her taste, but they wouldn't have to stay here long. Not if she had anything to do with it.

There was no answer, so she swung her legs over the side and sat up. Her head ached. Alcohol from the night before? Unlikely. She was sure she hadn't drunk all that much. No, it must just be the air in here. It was too warm, muggy, like the onset of a storm. And daytime sex didn't help, with no window open, and the curtains closed. Oh, she could do with a coffee. A good strong one. But Geraldine didn't go in for proper coffee. There was no percolator, no filter machine, no fancy coffee pods in her kitchen. Patsy had established that last night. So, instant it would have to be.

'Michael?' she called again, louder this time. 'Can you put the kettle on?'

He was in the back garden when she finally ventured down to find him. The shed door was open, and he had a pile of old tennis rackets, some kind of net thing, and a rusty bike laid out on the grass.

'Just looking out a few bits for when Lily comes down,' he said. 'I didn't want to wake you.'

'Well, I'm awake now, and my head's banging.' She pulled her flimsy gown tightly around her and picked her way barefoot over the grass. 'How about we go out, find a coffee shop, take a walk by the sea? It might blow away the cobwebs a bit. This stuff can wait, can't it? It all looks pretty ancient. Wouldn't she rather have new? And it's not as if you've heard anything yet from Ruby, so we have no idea when Lily's likely to need any of it . . .'

Michael shook his head. 'Leave it an hour or so, eh? You go back in and help yourself to whatever you fancy in the kitchen, have a shower – the water's hot – and then we'll go out for a late lunch. How does that sound?' He slipped his arms around her waist and pulled her in for a kiss. 'Just give me time to get this lot sorted at least, and then I'll be in, okay?'

The kitchen felt cold as she flipped the switch on the kettle and hauled herself onto a high stool to get her feet up off the tiled floor. There was a blob of mud on her big toe and she leant down to wipe it away with a scrap of kitchen roll. Back in Portugal now it would be warm, the sun sending long streaks of pale light through the shutters, and she would have real strong coffee. Lots of it. She had almost forgotten what England was like at this time of year. All brown trees and chilly winds, and the awful driving rain. No wonder they hadn't been brave enough to open the bedroom window. Maybe it was being here near the sea that made it worse. Not the clear blue sea and golden sands she had grown used to, but this harsh grey pounding sea that struck at the endless piles of pebbles Geraldine had laughingly called a beach.

The instant coffee, heaped with more sugar than was good for her, didn't quite hit the spot, but it helped. She gazed out of the window, watched Michael busying himself in his mother's garden, and breathed. Just breathed. She had to tell herself that she was here for a reason. And that reason was Michael. And Lily, of course. She felt her stomach lurch involuntarily as she thought about Lily. They would meet properly soon. This tiny child who still meant so much to Michael, whose absence had left a hole in his life he was so anxious to refill. My new stepdaughter, she thought, trying out the word for the first time. Oh, hell. What do I know about children?

*

Geraldine had tried. Well, not very hard admittedly, but it wasn't easy to like Patricia. Or Patsy, as Michael insisted on calling her. They had met before, of course. Once or twice, in London, before her son had made the big announcement that he was going to go off and work abroad. Something to do with land, and holiday homes by the sea. Project management, he'd called it. Whatever that was.

Moving from Brighton to take up a better position in the bank's head office in London had been bad enough, but she hadn't tried to stop him. Much as she had missed them all, she had to admit it had made sense. A fresh, exciting new start for him and Ruby, and for little Lily, a chance to build a better life together as a family. There were opportunities in London that would never have come his way at home. But then he'd heard about this new company, been offered a job, left the bank behind, grabbed his chance. 'Now, I'm really going places,' he'd said, proudly, as if that was what mattered in life. And within months he was. Moving on from the company's London base and all the way to Portugal. A place too far.

Back then, when she'd first come across her, Patricia hadn't seemed particularly important. Just some girl from work. Michael had not long left the bank and was still settling in at the new place, full of ambition and eager to please. The girl was visiting from their office in Lisbon where she had been making a name for herself. She knew the right people, the right contacts. They spent time together, working on some project or other. There were working lunches and late night meetings. She'd even been to the flat, met Ruby, drunk her tea, shaken her hand.

Geraldine still remembered sitting with Ruby one night, waiting for Michael to come home. With Lily in her pyjamas, clutching that bear of hers, trying to keep her eyes open for a goodnight cuddle from Daddy, and not managing it. And Michael coming back smelling of too much wine and crashing out on the sofa, Ruby pulling a blanket around him and making excuses. He works hard, he's busy, he's doing it all for us . . .

Geraldine had driven back to Brighton in the dark that night, much later than planned. Something didn't feel right, but he was her son. It was her place to worry, but never her place to say. He was an adult now, in charge of his own life, and the last thing she wanted was to be seen as an interfering nag of a mother, trying to tell him what to do. Besides, it was probably all something and nothing. One of those rocky patches all marriages go through when there was a baby involved. Both of them coping with too much change, not enough time for each other, and nowhere near enough sleep. She had no idea then that Patricia had been head-hunting, looking for a suitable candidate for a new post in Portugal, or that it was Michael's head she had set her sights on. And the rest of his body too, so it seemed, and no idea that her little family was about to fracture beyond repair.

Patricia! There was something about the girl that made her hackles rise. The six-inch high heels, the tarty ankle chain, the hair held so immaculately, unnaturally in place. Not that there was anything wrong with making an effort, trying to look your best, but this girl was . . .

Geraldine shuddered. She knew she was being unfair. Michael was his own man. Whatever had happened was as much his fault as Patricia's. Nobody had made him fall for her, leave his life behind, abandon his family. If he had been someone else's son she would have seen things differently, looked down her nose at him and branded him a typical bloody man, following the contents of his trousers instead of his head. But if the girl had dressed more plainly, done up a few more buttons on her bulging blouse, shown some respect for the fact that Michael was a father, then maybe, just maybe . . .

Ruby may not initially have been her ideal choice of daughter-in-law. She was young. Far too young and definitely troubled, but there were reasons for that. And Michael had seemed happy enough and settled with her, and with little Lily. While it lasted, anyway. Until the banns had been read and the flowers had been ordered and the novelty had worn off.

Geraldine sat inside the empty shop, her laptop open and a pile of receipts spread out on the counter. She hadn't looked properly at the accounts in weeks, and today was no different. It was a job she hated, something Ken had always taken care of. Perhaps it was time to pay for some help. Someone good with figures, for just a few hours a week, to take away the burden. It was the sort of thing Ruby and Michael could have helped with, if they'd still been together. They could have made it a family business again, something to build on, for Lily's future.

She stared out of the cluttered window, watching a young family walk by. Mum, Dad, toddler skipping along at their side with a huge balloon in her hand, and a baby snuggled down in a padded buggy, fast asleep. That's what weekends should be about. Family. Not the shop. Not sitting here by herself, stewing over things she couldn't change.

It had been so long since she had seen Lily, but her little face was imprinted on her brain. Such a pretty little thing. Blonde, bouncy, always giggling, just starting to talk in real sentences, develop a mind of her own, and a stubborn streak like her mother's, already learning to answer back . . .

Her only grandchild. Well, as far as she knew. No, she wasn't going to follow that train of thought. She would not go there. She'd promised Ken long ago that she would never talk about that period of her life, that she would put her teenaged mistake behind her, forget about it, never try to find out . . .

Considering the way Ruby had spoken to her the last time she'd called, she knew she was no longer welcome. But Ruby was angry. Hurt. She was just lashing out, not only at Michael but at anyone or anything that reminded her of his betrayal. Geraldine knew that, but it didn't make it any easier to help her. Or to know what to do.

She had tried so hard not to take sides but, for months now, she had been a grandmother in name only. It was all Patricia's fault. How could Michael even think of marrying the girl? She was the reason Ruby had cut off those all-important links between them, kept her at arm's length for so long. The reason there had been no christening, even after she'd dug out the old family robe and bought the most beautiful little silver bangle, engraved with Lily's name. No wedding either. The hat she'd spent hours choosing was still there, at the top of the wardrobe, in a big pink box. All fancy feathers and net. She'd so looked forward to wearing it, but she'd be buggered if she'd get it out for this latest bride-to-be, that was for sure.

Patricia was the reason her granddaughter was lost to her. Stealing her son away from his family, bringing out all the hate and blame and anger in Ruby, feelings that had erupted and spilled out towards Michael, and had somehow marked her, Geraldine, as the enemy too, tearing her dreams for the future and her innocent little granddaughter away from her in one fell swoop. And now she had let the bloody woman into her home. Put the naffest sheets she could find on the bed, hidden the coffee maker, plastered on a smile so false it was almost a match for Patricia's fingernails, or her ridiculously pointy boobs. Small gestures, a silent rebellion that her son, in his Patricia-blindness, would never see.

No, she didn't like her. And if Michael insisted on going ahead with this wedding, then she wasn't overly keen on him either. She loved him, of course, in the way mothers tend to do – no matter what – but right now she didn't like him an awful lot. The sooner he and Patricia sorted things out with

Ruby about access to Lily, and buggered off back where they'd come from the better.

*

Lily had found the medicine easily. It had been left out on the table in the kitchen, next to the empty tomato sauce that Mummy had turned upside down to catch the last drips, and a big pile of letters. She held the small medicine bottle in her even smaller hands and pulled at the lid but she couldn't undo it. She tried twisting and twisting until her wrists hurt but it wouldn't come off. She had seen Mummy open things with a knife before. Slitting into envelopes, opening packets, and forcing lids off things.

Lily knew where the knives were kept, even though she wasn't allowed to use them, except for eating her dinner and that was just a small kiddie knife without the really sharp bit. She stood up on her tippy-toes and pulled the drawer open, blindly dipping her hand inside. Wrapping her fingers around the wooden handle of one of the big knives, she pulled it towards her and lifted it out. It was heavy and it wobbled in her grasp, the blade part all long and flat and shiny. Like the sword you use to kill dragons with. Lily hoped there weren't any dragons in real life. She could still hear the noise from the phone by the door. She was getting used to it now, and she still wasn't sure what it was, but she didn't think it was a dragon.

Lily sat on the floor and held the medicine bottle in one hand and the big knife in the other. She pushed the tip of the knife into the side of the lid, jabbing it hard and then moving it about, like Mummy did, but nothing happened. She pushed harder and harder, but still it didn't come off. And then the knife slipped away from her and the edge of the blade sliced into the flesh at the base of her thumb as it fell. A thin trickle of blood appeared instantly and spread in spidery patterns across her palm. She cried out, more in shock than pain, and clutched her hand closed. Lily didn't like blood. Mummy would have got her a plaster, one with cartoon pictures on it, but Mummy wasn't here. She put her hand down flat, leaving a sticky red handprint on the floor, and levered herself back up onto her feet, but the knife drawer was still open and her head hit the corner of it, hard, bouncing her back.

Lily's hand flew to her head as she fell, the warm wet blood from her thumb oozing out again and mixing with a fresh trickle that was already running from somewhere beneath her hair. She didn't know what to do. It hurt. Everything hurt, but there was nobody to help her. All she could do was scream, cry, curl up on the floor in a tight ball, the sobs racking through her tiny body, until the throbbing, stinging feeling slowly ebbed away and the blood on her head and hands dried into a dark red crust, and she fell asleep.

When she woke up she was hungry again, hungrier than she had ever been. Her head felt better, but she needed something to make her tummy feel better too. And her poorly hand. She wasn't sure if it was her left hand or her right hand. Was it the one nearest to the door? All she knew was that it felt sore again as soon as she tried to open her fingers out.

She had already eaten the last apple from the bowl earlier, right down to the pips, and a very hard slice of half-eaten toast she'd found on a plate on the table. But now her tummy was empty and growling out loud and all she wanted was a biscuit. Mummy always let her have a treat if she'd been brave. And she had. She had real blood now to prove it.

The cupboard with the biscuits in it was very high up. Nearly at the ceiling. Lily stood up slowly and closed the knife drawer, dropping the big bad knife back inside. She looked around for something to help her reach the cupboard, and the biscuit tin. The kiddie step was still there by the sink, standing in a little puddle of water. She dragged it carefully across the kitchen floor, leaving a slippery wet trail behind it, like a snail. Kiddie steps were made for standing on, so she stood on it, but it wasn't tall enough. *She* wasn't tall enough. She still couldn't reach up high enough to get to the biscuit cupboard.

She lifted one leg up high, as high as she could stretch. The right leg. Or maybe the left. She put her foot halfway up the cupboard where the plates were kept, rested it on the long white handle and hauled herself up, the way she always climbed up the frame in the park, wriggling until she was sitting on the worktop, with her bottom next to the kettle and her legs dangling over the edge. It was like being on the side of the swimming pool and looking down into the water. Mummy had taken her once but she didn't like it. The noise, the cold, the not wanting Mummy to let go. The kitchen floor seemed a long way down, and it was wet, just like at the pool, when their bare feet had gone slip-slap on the floor and Mummy had laughed and said they sounded like fish.

But she could get to the top cupboard now, if she just stood up next to the kettle and reached above her head. The floor looked even further away as she pulled herself up. She wobbled as she leaned backwards just enough to pull on the handle of the door where the biscuits lived. She felt the cut in her thumb sting and open up again as she squeezed her fingers tightly around the handle, and then the cupboard swung open towards her, too smoothly, too quickly, and almost knocked her flying, but she had it now, between her hands. The big tin, with the picture of a monkey on it. Cheeky monkey, Mummy always said when Lily asked for another chocolate finger.

Lily bent down and lowered the tin very carefully onto the worktop next to her feet, before starting to shuffle herself back down to a sitting position beside it. Her hip banged against the kettle and she stumbled, one foot tangling itself into the lead, tipping the whole thing over as she bumped herself down. A little stream of cold water poured out and sent her slipping, grabbing for something to hold on to, and knocking the tin, with a very loud crash, to the floor.

By the time Lily had clambered down, the lid was off and the contents were scattered all over the lino. But there were no chocolate fingers today. Just one broken rich tea, which she stuffed hungrily into her mouth in two big bites. And then there were just crumbs. Nothing left but crumbs, a trickle of water, and a trail of sticky red fingerprints all over the cupboard doors.

*

William couldn't settle. The afternoon was slipping by, like so many others. What he needed was a job, a purpose, a life. A woman? No, probably not. He looked around at the mess that had once been their tidy, well-ordered house. His and Susan's. How had he let this happen? The unwashed clothes, the takeaway boxes, the unopened mail . . .

He should do something about it, but it was Sunday. Wasn't Sunday meant to be a day of rest? So, he'd do something about it tomorrow. He'd start cleaning up, start trying to sort himself out. Tomorrow.

There was no Susan any more. Well, there was, obviously. Somewhere. But not here. And that was a good thing. Despite the mess and the loneliness, he knew it was a good thing. And now it was time to be just William again. Just William! He remembered the book with that name that his mother used to read to him, about the naughty schoolboy. Wasn't he a pretty hopeless character too? Covered in mud, with his socks hanging down? Full of half-hearted, dimwit schemes that were usually doomed to fail? The likeness wasn't lost on him.

He went into the kitchen looking for food. When had he last gone shopping for food? Proper shopping, with a trolley and a list? There was a tin of beans at the back of the cupboard, and the final two slices of last week's loaf sat curling in their plastic wrapper on the bread board. They'd have to do for now. Just a little bit of green around the crust, but that didn't matter, did it? He sliced the mouldy edges away with a knife, the blade slipping, slicing a thin slit into the tip of his little finger. It was surprisingly deep, and painful. A spot of bright red blood ran out and dripped onto the bread. He grabbed for a piece of kitchen paper to wrap around it, but the cardboard roll stood empty on its holder. He needed to buy some more. And he needed a plaster. Did he have any? Where were they kept? He had no idea.

He sat down at the table and stuck his finger in his mouth, sucking hard at it, like a baby seeking comfort, until the bleeding eased. He was sick of being on his own, with nobody to talk to, nobody to notice, let alone care, if he were to sit here and slowly bleed to death. Tomorrow he would definitely go and see his mother, if the car battery was charged and working by then. Something told him that fixing the car would probably be a lot easier than the fixing he needed to do on himself.

*

Lily was playing with her bricks in the bedroom, building a house with a chimney like the one where Granny lived, when the poo came out. She didn't get any warning. It just happened, ever so quickly. She'd forgotten she wasn't wearing any knickers, and it slithered out onto the carpet, all runny.

It was too late to get the potty. She'd done it now. But maybe she should try to clean it up, so Mummy wouldn't shout at her when she came back and saw it there. There was a special lock on the cupboard under the sink. Mummy said the lock was to stop her touching the cleaning things because they were dangerous and she mustn't swallow them. So she couldn't get to the big bottle of stuff that Mummy used that smelled like lemons.

Lily stood up. The last bit of runny poo streaked down her leg and onto one of the plastic bricks she was using to make the chimney. She picked the brick up – a red one –.before it made any more of the bricks dirty. The ones for making the walls, and the windows. She didn't want to build a dirty house. Granny's house was clean. She remembered the nice smell of flowers, and that you had to take your shoes off when you went inside before you were allowed to stand on the carpet. Mummy always laughed about that. She said lots of posh ladies did that, but they didn't.

Maybe she could get some paper from the roll hanging in the bathroom to clean herself up with. And a flannel, or a towel, to wash the blob off the carpet. Then she could put it in the washing basket with the pyjamas. Be a good girl.

The smell that followed her was worse than it was before. Not like lemons or flowers. Her bottom felt all squidgy and messy, and a bit sore. Lily tried to reach round and rub it clean with the paper, forgetting she had the brick in her hand, but it just made her hand all nasty, and the brick even nastier. And the kiddie step wasn't here to reach the bathroom sink and wash it off. The step was still in the kitchen, but it was too dark in there and she couldn't reach the light.

But at least her tummy ache had gone now. That was good. She didn't need the Cowpol any more, from the bottle that wouldn't open. Maybe that had a special lock on it too. But it wouldn't be to stop her swallowing it, because she knew she was allowed to swallow Cowpol. It tasted nice and made everything feel better.

Lily wished everything would feel better now, but it didn't. She had never been on her own before, and she didn't like it. It was getting dark outside again, and the tree outside was blowing around, and the wind was rattling the window. She was hungry again, and she wanted something nice to eat, but whatever was left was in the kitchen, and she wanted a plaster for her hand that kept hurting all the time but the plasters were in the cupboard she couldn't open, in the box with a red cross on it under the sink. She wanted to get into her bed with Archie and have Mummy tuck her in, but it was all wet and nasty. And she wanted to cry but when she did it didn't make any difference because nobody came. And she wanted to see Daddy, and Granny, who she hadn't seen for such a long time . . .

But most of all she wanted Mummy. She just wanted Mummy.

*

Dinner was a fraught affair. Patsy had offered to help but had been turned away from the kitchen with a look that could have curdled milk. Now they all sat together around the table in the dining room, very formally, eating some sort of indeterminate pie with waxy potatoes and thin tasteless gravy, and trying to make polite conversation.

It was only half past six. Much too early to be eating, but it wasn't Patsy's house and therefore, according to Michael who was doing his best to keep the peace, not her decision. The meat was chewy, the pastry as hard and tasteless as cardboard, and the gravy was lukewarm, but Michael didn't seem to notice or, if he did, he'd chosen to ignore it.

'Lovely, Mum. Thank you,' he said, clattering his cutlery down and wiping his mouth on a paper serviette with Christmas robins around the edge.

Patsy moved her knife and fork to the side of her plate and left them pressed together at an angle, to signal she had finished, in case the pile of pushed-about uneaten food still on her plate should indicate otherwise.

'Anything wrong, Patricia?' Geraldine smiled at her, her teeth bared like a protective mother tiger. 'Don't you like pastry? Can I get you anything else?'

'No, everything's fine, thank you, Mrs Payne. We ate a late lunch, and I'm not very hungry, that's all.'

'Tart?'

Patsy wasn't sure for a moment whether she was being offered more food or if Geraldine was taking a sly opportunity to tell her just how she felt about her. She looked across at Michael, hoping to see some reaction, but his attention seemed taken up elsewhere, as he gazed out at a tree branch that overhung the fence and watched a bird balancing on it like a mini ballerina, bobbing up and down on its thin little legs.

'It's apple,' Geraldine continued, straight-faced, not batting an eyelid. 'Oh, no, of course, you don't like pastry. Ice cream, then? Or a piece of fruit? We do like to finish with some sort of dessert, don't we, Michael? Even if we think we're full!'

We! We? Why did she think she could speak for Michael? Act like some kind of expert on what he liked to eat. As if he was still five years old. The woman was infuriating. Michael went on watching the bird, oblivious as always.

'No. No, really. Nothing else. But let me help with the clearing up at least.'

Patsy would not rise to it. She would remain on her best behaviour, breathe deeply and say nothing. She started to pile up the plates, turning her back towards the others to hide her frustration, and dropping a greasy fork onto the carpet in the process. It was lying right next to Geraldine Payne's fluffy-slippered foot, and, as she bent to retrieve it, she couldn't help but notice the big thick blue vein that ran haphazardly up the side of her calf like a length of coiled string. Ugh!

There was a gravy mark on the carpet now too, but best not to point it out and risk all the fuss, so she supposed it was up to her to clean it up. She had no idea where to look for the right cloths or cleaning stuff, and no inclination to ask. It would have to be a blob of Fairy on a j-cloth. Or on one of those hideous robin serviettes. Oh, God, how she wanted to get out of here and back to her own cooking and her cold tiled floors.

'Oh, and I do think you should start to call me Geraldine, don't you? We're as good as family now. Mrs Payne sounds so formal, and you'll be calling yourself by that name soon enough, won't you? If everything goes to plan . . .'

Goes to plan? Why shouldn't it go to plan? They were getting married, weren't they?

'So, Michael, when are you going up to see Ruby?' Geraldine's voice had dropped to a whisper but not enough to prevent it reaching Patsy's ears as she stumbled through into the kitchen, catching the heel of her shoe on the door jamb.

'It's okay, Mum. No need to whisper. I don't keep secrets from Pats. But in answer to your question, I don't know. I had hoped Ruby would be reasonable for once and that she'd have been in touch by now. She knows we're here. I'll call her in the morning . . .'

Patsy tried to keep her balance, but hopping on one foot was not easy when she was carrying a pile of plates. Chucking them ahead of her onto the draining board quickly, before they could slip out of her hands, she winced as they landed loudly. Too loudly. But at least they hadn't smashed. 'Oh, sorry,' she said, half-heartedly, over her shoulder, knowing they probably couldn't hear her anyway. 'No harm done.'

But Michael and his mother were already moving off into the front room, the subject changed, and were now deep in conversation about the overhanging tree and whether to talk to the next-door neighbour about cutting it back, leaving her to do the washing-up and try to make something that at least half-resembled a decent cup of coffee.

CHAPTER NINE

Ruby

Click. Click. Click. Something's making that noise, like a clock. Or shoes. Shoes with clattery bottoms, picking their way, carefully, across the floor. It sounds like someone is tiptoeing. Or trying to, but the noise won't quite let them. Click. Click. Click.

Slap. Slap. Slap. Like a fish. Coming closer. Slower. Being extra quiet now, thinking I can't hear. When the noise stops, I wait in the dark, in the silence, for it to start again, but it doesn't.

Mike must be late home again. He's creeping about, trying to make sure he doesn't wake me, or Lily. I feel someone nearby, the sheets move, just a little, and a hand pushing my hair back from my face, gently. So gently. And then the hand is gone.

But, no, it can't be Mike. Mike's gone. Not just the hand. All of him. And it's the night before the wedding. I didn't think I'd be able to sleep at all, but I have. I must have. I feel like I've been asleep for ever. Fuzzy, drowsy. Trying to forget. But I can never forget. So much planning. All shattered. A wedding was meant to be the best day of your life. That's what they say. But not mine. Because there is no wedding. Tomorrow is just a red ring on the calendar, crossed through, as if it never was.

I'm wondering what they're all thinking, crossing it off their calendars too, changing their plans, returning their gifts to whichever shops they'd come from, their dry-cleaned suits hanging in wardrobes behind closed doors, with the tags still on. Geraldine said she'd bought a hat.

What happened to Geraldine's hat?

Geraldine with that disappointed look she has. Sighing. Chest rising. Breath going in and out. In and out. Too loudly. Like something from a horror film. Something evil in a darkened room, in a mask, behind a door. Not Geraldine at all.

It's breaking the silence. The only thing breaking the silence. It's close to my face, whatever it is. Too close. Over my mouth. Held there. Pushing into me, its rhythm whooshing, puffing, hissing, sighing.

Breathing. Against me. With me. For me?

Then I hear it again. Echoing in the empty room. Click. Click. Click. The clock. Time. Shoes. Moving away. A final click, like a door closing and I'm alone again, and still breathing.

CHAPTER TEN

Agnes stretched out for the remote control and clicked the telly off. Why was there never anything decent to watch any more? She could remember the days when all the best programmes were on at the weekends. Variety shows, comedy, a good murder mystery. She used to love *Sunday Night at the London Palladium*, and *Morecambe and Wise*. And there were only three channels to choose from back then, too. Or was it only two? Now there was a list of channels as long as your arm and nothing worth watching at all.

She glanced at the clock, its steady ticking so familiar it was almost imperceptible unless she stopped and listened out especially for it. Not even nine-thirty yet. Too early for bed, and she'd read her newspaper from cover to cover. Another crossword maybe? She'd have a go at some knitting if she thought her old knuckles were up to it, but she'd hate to start something she couldn't finish. And who was there to knit for, anyway?

Even Smudge seemed restless, ambling over to his cat flap and letting himself out for one final prowl before he settled down for the night. Agnes moved slowly to the door and opened it, peered out and then followed the old cat into the shared hallway.

As she stepped across it to reach the main door and let him out onto the street, the automatic light came on, highlighting the buggies pushed up against the far wall and a pile of unclaimed post strewn across the mat. Most of it had been there for days. Probably junk. More menus for pizza, estate agents looking for places to sell, and ads for double glazing. She bent down slowly and scooped it up, so she could take it back with her to sort through, and then probably chuck most of it in the bin.

The house seemed especially lifeless this evening. The two young men on the top floor were rarely in, or if they were, their comings and goings were conducted quietly and at times of day or night when Agnes never got to see them. They'd introduced themselves on the day they'd moved in, but that had been a good while back now and she'd had nothing more than the occasional nod since. Jason and Rob, she thought they were called. Or was it Rick? Something like that. She had wondered briefly if they might be gay, but of course it was none of her business.

Then there was the mousey little grey-haired woman below them, on the second floor. There was often a baby there too, but not always, and the two of them would wander out sometimes, her carrying the baby down the stairs on her shoulder and popping it into the buggy for their walk. Boy or girl? Agnes had taken a peep once, through the window, when the weather was warmer and the baby wasn't buried in a pile of blankets, but it was impossible to tell. Must be the grandchild, Agnes thought, as the woman herself looked too old to have a baby of her own. But you never knew these days, what with test tubes and donors and what have you. But the baby was quiet now. Either that or it wasn't there.

Which was more than you could say for the family on the first floor. That little girl must be about three. All rosy cheeks and bouncing blonde curls, like a doll. Full of beans too, that one! There had been more than the usual amount of banging and scraping and yelling today, the noise coming through Agnes's ceiling like there was a herd of elephants up there, moving the furniture back and having a dance. The father was never about. She hadn't seen him for weeks. No, months, more like. Probably working. But the mother, a thin little person, hardly more than a child herself, came and went. She knocked at Agnes's flat once, said hello, came in and sat down, had a cup of tea, asked if she could help with anything. Ironing, shopping, cleaning. Agnes had thought the girl was just being neighbourly, showing a bit of kindness to an old lady on her own, but no. It turned out she wanted paying. She'd said something about doing the ironing for people while the child went to some nursery for a few hours a week. Free hours, apparently. What was that all about? Another government handout, no doubt. Always after something for nothing, the young ones of today. And, besides, Agnes was still perfectly capable of doing her own ironing.

Still, at least the girl – what was her name again? She wished she could remember – was trying to earn some money by honest means, she'd give her that. Not just having children she couldn't afford to keep, and grabbing every benefit going, like so many of them did these days, if the papers were to be believed.

She and her Donald had waited for seven years after they got married, making sure they had enough saved, before young William came along. There was never any question of a nursery.

No, Agnes believed a child's place was at home, and a mother's place – a good mother's place – was to be right there with it.

Agnes had had very little to do with the girl since then, just said hello in the hall a few times, or watched her through the curtains, lifting the buggy down the steps, chattering away to the child all the time. Proper conversations, as if she had nobody more adult to talk to. Maybe she should make more effort, get to know the girl, invite her and the little one in for a glass of squash and a biscuit or something. But what would a young girl want to spend time with an old lady for? They'd have nothing in common. If she accepted her invitation, it would probably only be because it felt awkward to have to say no. Best leave it, for now. Agnes sighed.

There was crying coming from their flat again now, wafting towards her down the stairs. Not the loud tantrum screams there sometimes were, more just a niggling whine. A child not yet asleep, but who probably should be. No toddler should still be up and about at this time of night. Her William was always bathed and in bed straight after his tea, so she and Donald could get some time to themselves.

Agnes raised her eyes to the ceiling and tried not to be annoyed. It was nothing to do with her. She hardly knew these people, and they wouldn't thank her for interfering. Perhaps the little one was teething anyway, or had a bug of some kind. She still remembered when her William had the measles, as if it was yesterday. How hot and red and upset he had been. How frazzled and frightened she had felt herself, and tired and helpless, and him barely a year old . . . She knew only too well how worrying it could be for the parents when a child was sick or in pain, and how distressing for the child. She glanced up the stairs again. Poor little mite.

Maybe tomorrow, when it was light, she would go up there and see if there was anything she could do. Just what, she wasn't at all sure. But sometimes just knowing someone cared was enough . . .

She retreated back into her own flat, with the bundle of junk mail that would at least give her something productive to do for a few minutes, and closed the door behind her.

*

Laura and Fiona sat in the Red Lion, two halves of lager in front of them on the sticky wooden table. They were sitting too near the door, which kept opening and closing as customers came and went, letting streams of cold air in, so neither had yet removed their coats. It was the only table they'd been able to get at this time of the evening, and they didn't want to brave the weather looking for somewhere else and then finding it just as busy.

It was raining again, that cold, driving rain that soaked into your bones and defeated all but the sturdiest of boots and umbrellas. They watched the raindrops run frantically down the outside of the window in haphazard diagonal lines, as the high heel of one of Fiona's shoes tapped rhythmically against the leg of her chair and her painted nails drummed on the side of her glass.

'So?' Laura had waited long enough. 'You've dragged me here straight from work, still in my tatty going-home-on-the-bus clothes, and in this awful weather too. You do realise I haven't even had the chance to eat yet? And we both know you're supposed to be out on your big date tonight. Look at you in all your bling and your fantastically expensive new shoes. Tell me! What happened? With Harry?'

'*Without* Harry, you mean!' Fiona stopped drumming and started sighing instead. 'It was so humiliating! He just didn't turn up. No sign of him, the rat. I waited at the bar, found a stool, bought myself a drink. The cheapest I could think of, but it was still two pounds sixty. Can you believe it? For a half! And it was flat.'

'Then what?'

'Then nothing. Seven o'clock, he'd said, and seven came and went. Half past. Quarter to eight. I kept watching the door, and the barman kept watching me. Do you know, Laura, I think he felt sorry for me. Sad, single no-hoper, all dressed up with nowhere to go, sipping on a lemonade shandy with a straw in it. How embarrassing is that?'

'Did you try phoning him? Or texting?'

'I don't have his number. It was all done through the website. It's safer that way. That's where we chatted, made the arrangements . . . all online. It's like a kind of chat room. Or chat-up room, I suppose.'

'No mobile numbers. No addresses. Yes, I can see the need for that. But, hey, it's not the end of the world if you can't track him down, is it? You might have hated him anyway, if he'd turned up. Or been disappointed. I bet he used someone else's photo, that's why he bottled out. Didn't want you to see the real Harry, buck teeth and all! At least you haven't had to sit through a whole evening of him. And now you've got me instead.' Laura pulled a funny face, sticking her teeth out, buck-like, over her bottom lip, but Fiona didn't laugh. 'Oh, come on, drink up and I'll get us another and a bag of crisps, as I've had no dinner.'

'Thanks, Laura. You're a mate. I just didn't want to sit on my own any longer tonight. Or go home either. I knew you'd stay and keep me company. It's not as if you had anything better to do, did you? Not having a boyfriend either, I mean. Do you know what? I'm going to buy us a curry later, to say thank you. And because I'm starving. That rat was meant to feed me! Tomorrow you can look at the dating site with me and help me choose my next date as I'm obviously absolutely no good at picking them for myself.'

*

She was on the TV. Only sodding Susan, sitting on a plush pink sofa, squeezed between a stand-up comedian and some newspaper editor he'd never heard of, all spouting on about books. William didn't often watch the arty programmes, but there'd been no film to take his fancy tonight and he'd just flicked about looking for something to tide him over until bedtime.

Susan! It came as a shock, that was all, to find her there in his own living room, and in high def too. He'd not set eyes on her since the divorce. Not in the flesh. And there was a lot of flesh on display tonight, that was for sure. His eyes were drawn to her legs. She had high-heeled shoes on. Black and super-shiny with thin pointed toes, the sort that looked excruciatingly painful, but they made her legs look long and toned and – there was no other word for it – sensational. Hooker shoes. She'd never worn shoes like that for him. Or done her hair that way either. All high and blown back, with blonde streaks running through it. No frizz. No roots. It suited her.

Even as she was waffling on about the latest deadly dull literary discovery, she seemed to have a way of flirting with the other guests, or maybe it was just with the camera. William couldn't help but watch her flicking her hair, licking her glossed-up lips, rubbing one high-heeled foot slowly up the back of the opposite leg. This was Susan. *His* Susan, as was, but she was like some alien creature, not the Susan he knew at all. If he didn't already know what a prize bitch she could be, if he hadn't seen her in curlers and a face pack, if he didn't know that she farted in bed just like everybody else, he would almost have fancied her. Yes, damn it, he *did* fancy her! She looked amazing. Classy. Slimmer than she had been, younger-looking and, it was pretty plain to see, a darn sight happier. Was that what divorcing him had done for her? Let her become someone different? Set her free?

William looked down at himself. Egg-stained shirt, tartan slippers, stubbly chin, the remains of several meals rotting on unwashed plates scattered around him. Divorce had not set him free. It had simply allowed him to stop bothering, to give up, to revert to what he really was. And, if this was what he really was, then no wonder she had gone.

It was too much. He couldn't stand it, couldn't look at Susan a minute longer. She was like a stranger now. Taunting him, laughing at him, flaunting herself, and those endless legs, to the world. Did she know he would be watching? Was it all for his benefit? Showing him her newly reinvented self so he would see what he was missing? Well, it wasn't going to work. He didn't have to look at her. He reached for the remote and switched to another channel, some shopping auction thing with fake jewellery being flogged by what looked like an equally fake woman with an orange tan. But that last image of Susan, dark eyes turned directly towards him, burning into him, stayed there in his head for the rest of the night and refused to go away.

*

Geraldine couldn't sleep. She knew the shop was in trouble. *Bits & Bobs.* A silly name for a shop really, but it had always been called that. Since back in the pre-decimal days when it had been Ken's parents' place and nothing in it had cost much more than a shilling. A bob. God, that dated her. But it had been a long time. She'd started working there as a teenager looking to earn a couple of pounds on a Saturday, started dating Ken, stayed on when she left school and had eventually married into it. And look at it now. *Bits & Bobs* indeed! Falling to bits, and only worth a few bob, what with all the cheap stuff coming in from abroad. But that's what people wanted. A cheap holiday souvenir with Brighton stamped on it. Never mind that it was made in China or Taiwan. Tat, all of it, and hardly any profit to be made.

Not quite at the point of going bust, not just yet, but not going all that well either. She'd looked long and hard at the books today and knew it needed something to drag it up from its knees. Of course, she could sack Kerry and save a few quid that way. Give the girl her cards and a small bonus, and an apology, for what it was worth. Harsh, but it's a harsh world, with no room for sentiment. Where had sentiment ever got her?

Everyone knew that staff costs were one of the biggest outgoings for any business, but without Kerry where would she be? Behind that counter herself, all day, every day, wearing herself into the ground, with no time off to do anything else. No proper lunch break, having to lock the door every time she needed the loo, no daytime trips to the wholesalers, nothing but work, work, work. And now that Michael was back, he was going to try sorting things out with Ruby, and that meant she might be able to see Lily again. Have her down to stay sometimes, maybe. How could she do that if she was stuck in the shop all the time?

Geraldine turned onto her back and leant out to switch on the bedside light. It was no use. She was never going to get to sleep. Maybe she should get up and make a cup of tea, or try to read or something. When had she last even tried to read a book? There was just never any time. But she just lay there, undecided as always, and gazed up at the ceiling, straight at a crack she hadn't spotted before. Where had that come from? Who was going to fix it? For that kind of job, she needed cash, or a man who was handy with a packet of filler and a paintbrush, but since Ken had died she'd been pretty short on both scores, damn him!

She didn't like the thought of selling the family business, not after all these years, but it was starting to look like the only way out. The shop needed more than just an injection of money. It needed energy, ideas, time. All the things that, at sixty-two, she knew she no longer had.

From the next room, she could hear the muffled sounds of

Michael and his girlfriend talking. No, not girlfriend. Fiancée. She'd have to try to get used to calling her that. Sounds of them moving about, getting up to who knows what, on those awful slippery peach-coloured sheets. She couldn't help smiling to herself about the sheets. When the rhythmic banging started, the head of the bed knocking like a hungry woodpecker against the dividing wall, she couldn't stand it any more. Any of it. She just wanted to block it all out. Life, worry, grief, the thought of that woman latched on to her son like a leech, everything. She clicked at the light switch again and tried to push all the intrusions away, tugging the duvet up high over her head to muffle herself away deep inside its enveloping blackness.

Finally, the noise of her son having sex stopped, as suddenly as it had begun. There was a soft giggle, and then even softer footsteps on the landing, and the flushing of the loo. Then another pair of feet tiptoeing about and a failed attempt at a second flush. Michael's bedroom door closed, and everything fell silent. But, even as she drifted into a fitful sleep, all she could see behind her eyes was that damned crack, creeping across the ceiling and laughing at her, somewhere in the darkness above her head.

*

Lily was cold. She was in Mummy's bed, because her own was still wet and smelly. She'd put on her favourite dress, the Disney princess one, even though it was much too small for her now and didn't do up properly, and some pants, to go to sleep in. But the pants had felt all funny and uncomfortable, and they kept getting stuck up between her bottom cheeks, so she had to keep pulling them back out again. She didn't think real princesses ever had to do that.

When she'd climbed into the bed and slid her hand under the pillows she'd found a picture. She thought it was a picture of Daddy, but he looked different, with longer hair than Daddy had. She hadn't seen him for a long time. Mummy didn't like Daddy very much any more. She said bad things about him sometimes that made her cry, but it was a nice picture, and Lily had gone to sleep holding it. But now she was awake again and it was all crumpled and Mummy might be angry, even though she didn't like Daddy and probably didn't even know she'd left the picture under the pillow at all.

The covers had slipped over, and most of them had gone on the floor where she had been kicking at them. She wanted a wee again. She didn't know if it was morning or still night time. Through the open curtains everything was dark and black, and the light was on and, although she could see the clock, she didn't know how to understand the numbers on it yet. She knew that she had to get up and go to the toilet now, so she didn't spoil the pretty pink princess pants or make this bed wet like the other one. Mummy wouldn't like it if her bed got wet. Mummy's bed was nice. It smelled nice, like Mummy, and it had big bouncy pillows. With a picture of her daddy under them.

Archie wanted to come with her to the bathroom, so she held on tightly to him and climbed out of the bed. Lily sat on the toilet and did her wee and wiped her bottom the best she could. She knew she was meant to wash her hands afterwards but she couldn't reach properly without going to find the step.

The step was still in the kitchen. When she went in there the sink was full right up with water and dribbling over the side, so she didn't need to try turning the taps again. She dipped her hands in the water and rubbed some soap into them, then filled up her cup from the bowl and had a drink. The water tasted warm and a bit funny, like the soap. The sleeves of her princess dress were getting all soggy at the ends and her feet slipped as she stepped back down onto the wet floor.

Lily found a box of cereal in the bottom cupboard and dipped her soapy hand in. She knew there wasn't any milk left, so she just scooped the cereal into her mouth with her fingers. It was dry but nice and sugary, each little piece in the shape of an O. She did a big yawn and a mouthful of Os almost spilled back out again.

Mummy's handbag was lying on the table, next to all the letters, where she'd found the toast. Lily wasn't supposed to go through Mummy's bag. She had been told off for doing it lots of times, but Mummy's bag always had interesting things in it. She remembered the eye make-up thing she'd found and used to draw on all her dollies' faces once. Mummy had got angry about that. She liked looking at the money and touching it and putting the coins in piles. There was a lollipop in there once too, one that the lady in the hairdressers had given to Lily for sitting still, but Mummy had hidden it away because it was nearly dinner time and lollies spoil your dinner. Maybe there might be a lolly in there now?

She picked up the upside-down tomato sauce to see if any drips had run down inside so she could lick them up, but it still looked empty. Lily liked sauce. She'd poured some on her rice pudding once and stirred it in until it all went pink. Mummy had tried to throw it away but she liked it. She liked sauce with everything. Especially chips.

The TV was still on in the living room as she went in there, the bag draped over her small arms by its long handles, the weight causing her to almost drag it along the carpet. She hadn't wanted to turn the TV off when she'd gone to bed and hear all that nasty quiet again. Quiet was too scary. So she'd left it on. She wondered if there might be any kiddie programmes on now. She wasn't feeling tired any more, just a bit lonely. Mummy hadn't come home. She could tell. The mote was on the carpet where she'd left it. Everything was where she'd left it. Nothing had been tidied away or cleaned up.

She sat on the sofa and pulled a big cushion onto her lap to keep her knees warm, and tucked Archie up underneath it with his head sticking out of the top, and tipped the handbag upside down beside her so everything fell out.

There were lots of things in it today. Bits of paper with writing on, and some bottom wipes, and a sheet of gold star stickers, which she pulled off, one by one, from their backing paper and stuck to her top. She opened the zip on Mummy's purse but there were only a few coins in it today. The big shiny silver ones, and some round penny ones, with the queen's face on. No money notes. And no lollies. But she did find a box of little round white sweeties. Each one was wrapped up in some silver stuff and some had already gone. She pushed and pulled with her fingers and dug her nails in until she finally managed to push one out. It looked like a Smartie, but she'd never seen a white one before. She liked the orange ones best, or the red.

Sometimes she got her colours a bit mixed up, but she was getting better at it. And white was easy. White, like her teeth. Like polar bears. Like snow.

She popped one into her mouth and moved it around her tongue. It didn't taste like a Smartie. It didn't taste of anything. She sucked at it for a while but she didn't like it very much, so she spat it out, all soggy and powdery down her chin. She definitely liked the orange ones better, but there weren't any.

It was a shame there were no lollies. There was a lipstick at the bottom of the bag though, a bit messy without its lid. She ran it over her mouth, feeling it miss a bit as it slid onto her cheeks at either side. She tried to paint her nails with it, but it didn't look very nice, or feel very nice, so she wiped it all off again, rubbing her hands together and wiping them on her dress, making her knife cut sore again. Maybe she could use the lipstick to make the sweeties red? They might look better, and taste better then, like real Smarties. She tried to force another one out from its shiny stuff but her fingers were too slimy and slippery and she couldn't do it.

Lily left the contents of Mummy's bag where they were. There was nothing in there that she wanted to play with, and no lollies to eat, and even the end of the lipstick was broken now where she'd pressed it too hard against her nails. She picked up the mote and tried the buttons that usually made the kiddie programmes come on but there weren't any. She rearranged Archie again, so he could see, and then tried some different buttons.

There wasn't anything very good on at all. She'd seen a man in a white coat shouting some very bad words in a kitchen, and an old man lie down on the ground in the woods and shoot another man with a big gun until the blood sprayed right up out of his head, and a naked lady licking her lips and moving her bare bottom up and down in the air, before she gave up and went back to bed.

*

Agnes sat in her armchair in her newly washed dressing gown, with a cup of cocoa going cold beside her. It was way past her usual bedtime, and the central heating had gone off so the flat felt chilly, but she was still waiting for Smudge to come back. He never stayed out this long.

She had called and called, at the back and the front of the building, but nothing. Now it was a bit late to call him, to make too much noise in the hallway or out in the street. She didn't want to disturb the other residents or have anyone come down to complain. Her old trick of rattling a fork on a tuna tin hadn't worked either. But then, this was London, and London was heavy with noise. Who would notice, or care, if she made just a little bit more of it?

Maybe Smudge was out of earshot. Even just a few houses away, up a tree or chasing mice in someone's garden, he probably wouldn't hear her above the traffic. Or, if he did, he might well prefer to carry on doing whatever it was he was doing. Cats were very much their own masters, not at the beck and call of any human, whether or not that human held the keys to the food supply, otherwise known as the can opener.

She knew she shouldn't worry so much. He was well able to look after himself after all these years, and it wasn't as if it was snowing or blowing a gale or anything like that. But she loved him. Dear old Smudge, with his woolly fur and his deep growl of a purr, was all she had left to love, or that's how it felt most of the time. The thought of losing him was too unimaginable to bear.

*

'Twice in one day!' Patsy climbed back into the bed and curled herself against Michael's warm back, wrapping one leg over his and whispering into his ear. 'You insatiable devil, you!'

'Couldn't resist you, sweetheart. Now let's get to sleep. I'm shattered.'

'I'm not surprised.'

'You don't think she heard anything, do you?'

'Your mother? Well, the bed was banging a bit. But I expect she's asleep. It's late.'

'Hope so. It does feel a bit – well, strange – having sex here, with her just behind the wall. Disrespectful, you know.'

'Michael, you're not a naughty teenager. You're a grown man. It's allowed.'

'I suppose so.'

'Michael?'

'What now? Come on, it's time to sleep.'

'Did you ever . . . you know, do it here, in this bed, with Ruby?'

'Oh, God, Pats. Let's not do this now, okay? It's too bloody late, and there's nothing to say. I don't want to talk about the past. I'm not with Ruby any more. I'm with you.'

'I know, I know.' She snuggled closer and took a tiny nibble at his ear.

'Ouch!'

'Sorry. But, did you?'

Michael heaved himself up onto an elbow and turned to look at her in the almost darkness of his old heavily curtained childhood room. 'Probably. I don't know. Ruby was . . . well, different. She was kind of innocent. Young. Straight out of a children's home, and not used to dealing with things in the real world. With life. And I was with her for the wrong reasons. I didn't really love her, Pats. Is that what you want to hear? I didn't love her. But you already know that, don't you? We didn't have passionate sex, the kind that rammed the headboard into the wall. We didn't exactly make love either, not with meaning, the way you and I do. It was just going through the motions. Now please, stop all this nonsense and let's go to sleep.'

But Michael couldn't sleep. Half an hour later he was still lying there, staring at the ceiling, his mind whirring with memories he'd rather not have to encounter. It was something about being back here, in this house. It brought things back. All that playing at happy families. He knew now that it had all been one big stupid mistake. Except for Lily, of course, the one good thing to come out of it all. Lily was why he'd stayed for as long as he had, got caught up in those ridiculous wedding plans. It had felt like the next step. What people did. What he should do.

He pushed the covers back, trying not to disturb Patsy, trying to free himself of that awful claustrophobic feeling that was closing in on him again as he remembered all the wedding magazines and bits of satin lying about at the flat, and Ruby's childish excitement as she tried to choose between pink roses and white, and his mother gabbling about her outfit and her

120

hat, and his own growing certainty that he just couldn't do it. But he didn't need to be married to love Lily, did he? And he did love her. So much. Leaving her behind had been hard, and he couldn't help feeling that, however bad things were, he shouldn't have. Leaving Ruby may have been best for him, and in the long run maybe even best for Ruby too, but for Lily? He closed his eyes and tried to picture her tiny face. How was she doing without him? Was she missing him too? Ruby wasn't very experienced in the ways of the world, wasn't used to managing by herself, and he'd left her to do exactly that. Of all the mistakes he'd made, was that the biggest? No wonder he couldn't sleep.

But there were two sides to Ruby. He knew that now. Ruby was a lamb. A wide-eyed innocent, reliant for too long on other people, with way too much trust in her. But she could be a predator too, out to catch her prey. Was that too harsh? No, she had come after him. Set her sights on him, watched him from a distance, and from close-up too. And without setting off any warning bells. Just Ruby. Quiet, invisible Ruby. There was a determination there, a sense of purpose, that, when he finally worked it out, had come as a massive shock.

The day she had moved in to the house, his mother's latest protégé, quiet like she wouldn't say boo to a goose, he'd had a feeling he'd seen her somewhere before, but he couldn't remember where. She didn't say. Not then. Just settled into their home, quietly, like a mouse you hardly notice, until it creeps about at night in search of cheese.

But Ruby wasn't a mouse. She was a bloody tiger. With claws on her that sank into him, dug deep, refused to let him go. She'd shown him that all right, on the night he'd finally left. He'd tried to explain how he felt, to break it to her gently, but Ruby didn't do gently. Not any more. Everything had to be a bloody drama. Tears didn't cover it. Oh, no, it was never just tears with Ruby. It was full-on screaming, pleading, begging, down on her knees and clinging to his jacket so hard she tore the sleeve.

'But we were meant to be together,' she'd said. 'You can't go, can't leave us. We love you. We've always loved you . . .'

It was that 'always' that had unnerved him. Always, like before he'd even known who she was.

'But I don't love you, Rube,' he'd said, trying to stay calm. 'I'm sorry, really sorry, but you know that, really you do. We've just been making the best of things, and that isn't enough any more. Not for me. Not since I met Pats . . .'

'No, Mike. No. She's poison, that woman. Not right for you. How could you let her do this? Steal you away from me? From Lily? How could you let her do this to us?'

'I didn't *let* her do anything, Ruby. It's me. I'm doing this. My decision. I'm sorry. I am, but I'm not going to change my mind. But I'm not leaving Lily. Believe me, I would never leave Lily. I'll come back and see her, as often as I can. I'll keep paying the rent on this place, at least until the lease runs out. And I'll send money. Give me your bank account details and I'll make a transfer, every payday. Or I'll send cheques. Whatever. I'll make sure you're okay. That Lily's okay. And when things have calmed down a bit, we'll talk properly. Decide what to do longer term.'

But she'd wanted none of it. Not his money, nor his apologies. No short-term solutions or long-term plans. Just him. The one thing he could no longer give.

He rolled over and lay an arm over Patsy. She was breathing

quietly beside him, and he caught a faint whiff of her perfume, felt her pulse beating rhythmically against his hand. Patsy made it all worthwhile. Every terrible moment of breaking away from Ruby, of breaking her poor fragile heart, had been worth it. Except . . .

Lily. He had to do something about Lily. However much Ruby resisted, whatever Ruby said, however much she might fight to keep Lily to herself, the last living breathing part of him she had left, he knew that he had rights too. Lily needed him in her life. And he needed her.

CHAPTER ELEVEN

Ruby

Lily. It's like she's at the end of a long, long tunnel. We're under the water, and it's so dark, and there's just a tiny speck of light behind her, so I can hardly see her, but I'm trying to get to her, swimming hard against the tide. Every time I get closer, along comes a big wave, and then an even bigger one, pushing me back. Slap. Slap. Slap.

Her eyes are closed. I don't think she's scared. But I am.

And now we're at a funeral. Or I'm remembering one. And it feels the same. Scary, cold. 'There's nothing to be scared of,' he says, squeezing my hand. Mike. But I've never been to a funeral before, and this is his dad. How can he stand it? The dreary music, the black clothes, the sobs and snuffles into soggy hankies, the coffin with all those flowers on top. Carnations. Roses. Lilies

I smell them coming in through the door before I even see the coffin. The flowers, their scent all cloying and overpowering, like an air-freshener. Flowers that are bright and pretty, but can't hide what's lurking underneath. A box. Dark and claustrophobic, with a body enclosed inside it. I wonder what it's like to be inside that box? The lid closed. Nailed down. No air. No way out. I can feel it. The panic, wanting to scream, trying to scratch my way out.

But then I remember he's dead. He won't be doing that. He won't know anything about it. He's been snuffed out, like a candle. I think I should probably be crying like everyone else, but I'm not. I just want to escape, to get out of here, away from this tunnel, this box with lilies on top. Lilies. My Lily. I just need to get back to Lily.

I look at Geraldine, all white and still, and it's as if she's far away, somewhere else, nothing to do with me at all. Not really here. Her eyes are watering down her face, and I can see through the water – right through her – like she's a ghost. Then she starts to get smaller and smaller, further and further away, and the noise inside the chapel goes fuzzy and there's a humming and a ringing in my head, and I know without any doubt that I'm going to faint. That I am somewhere else now. Out of reach. Out of touch. And that I can't touch her either. Lily.

CHAPTER TWELVE

When Laura went into Lily's room on Monday morning, there was a man already there, sitting on the edge of the bed, with his back turned towards her. She hoped, for one fleeting moment, that someone had come to claim her mystery girl at last. A father, brother, boyfriend, husband. But, as soon as he turned round, she knew she was wrong.

He was tall and slim, no more than about thirty, if that, and dressed all in black except for the bright white dog collar at his throat.

'Oh. Hello, Vicar. I mean Father . . . ' She stumbled over her words, not quite sure how to address him. Was he C of E or a Catholic priest? How were you meant to tell the difference? Not that she'd have known what to call him even if she could.

He smiled and stood up, coming forward to greet her. 'Hi. Please, no formalities. Paul Thomas. But just call me Paul. I'm the new hospital chaplain.' He held out his hand, which was surprisingly warm, and gave hers a short but friendly shake. 'You must be Nurse Carter. Sorry, you couldn't be anyone else.

The ward staff have told me so much about you, but I don't know your first name. Or I've forgotten it. I do quite a lot of that!'

'It's Laura.'

'Ah, yes!' He gave her a big wide smile. 'And here bright and early too. An early riser like me? But no uniform today, I see.'

'It's a case of habit, I'm afraid. My shift in A & E usually starts at eight. But I'm off today. I just wanted to pop in and see how she's doing. Can't seem to stay away. Have they told you anything? Any change? Oh, God, you're not here because . . .' She lowered her voice to barely a whisper. 'Because she's about to die? You're not giving her the last rites or something?' Laura looked at the girl in the bed, still pale and peaceful, still breathing through the machine.

'No, no. Nothing like that. Don't upset yourself. She's doing fine. They tell me she came in wearing a cross, that's all, so I thought I'd look in, see what I might do to help. If she's a believer, she just might find some comfort in that. We were just saying a little prayer. Or I was, I suppose. I don't think she even knows I'm here. The poor girl remains nameless and friendless, I'm sorry to say. Except for you, of course. I hear you've been doing a grand job, taking her under your wing.'

'Someone had to.'

'No, they didn't. But you chose to, and I think that was a wonderful thing to do. She does look very alone, doesn't she?' He moved back to the bed and laid his hand over the small still one as it lay inert on top of the crisp white sheet. 'They say she's no better, no worse. Not much change at all. I suppose it's hard to be sure what's going on while she's unconscious. But, with a little luck, and a prayer or two, let's hope she'll be able to breathe for herself soon, eh? It's only a matter of time, I'm sure, until she's back with us, and then our little mystery will be solved.'

'Thank you. It's good to hear a bit of positivity.'

They stood silently for a while, both gazing down at the seemingly lifeless figure on the bed, but there was nothing awkward about it. For once, Laura didn't feel that urge to say something, anything, the need to be noticed and approved of, that usually came over her in the presence of a good-looking man, turning her mind to mush and her cheeks bright red. None of that, even though this Paul certainly was good-looking. Deep brown eyes, short cropped hair, slightly uneven but very white teeth, and spotlessly clean fingernails. Why on earth had she noticed those? It showed that he took care of himself, though. But he was a vicar, for goodness sake! Was it allowed to have those sort of thoughts about a vicar?

'Would you like to say a prayer with me? Just a few words before I go?'

Laura hesitated. 'I don't know. I'm not very religious really. I haven't been inside a church since Sunday school, except to go to a wedding. It's not . . .'

'That's fine. It doesn't matter at all. It's what's in here that counts.' He lifted his hand from the girl's and placed it, palm flat, against his chest, where his heart was. 'Just think good thoughts, Laura, healing thoughts. I'll see you again tomorrow perhaps?'

'Maybe, maybe not. I have to try to fit visits into my breaks, so I'm not sure when . . .'

'Well, whenever then. I'm sure our paths will cross again. It was good to meet you.'

And then he was gone, closing the door quietly, and leaving a vague feeling of hope and a pungent whiff of musky aftershave behind him.

*

Agnes woke up in her chair, her neck stiff from the way she'd been sitting. It took her a moment to work out where she was and to remember why she had not been to bed. Smudge! Oh, dear Lord, he'd probably been out there waiting on the steps all night and she'd fallen asleep and left him there.

Quickly she heaved herself up, feeling more than a little crumpled, checked her dressing gown buttons were done up to make sure she was decent, and headed out through the hall to the front door. He wasn't there.

The disappointment hit her like a brick, heavy on her chest, closely followed by a growing fear. Something had happened to him, she was certain of it. But, what to do? She must get herself dressed and go and look for him. Properly look. Knock on doors, ask people to check their sheds and garages. And the road. It was a busy one. The first thing she must do was check the road, look for him – or his body – in the gutters. She felt the tears come the moment the thought of him being dead entered her head. No, he couldn't be dead. Not Smudge. He was going to die peacefully in his sleep, when he was very old, and she would be with him at the end, holding his paw. She'd never been able to think of his death in any other way. Unless she went first, of course, and then William would have taken her place and made sure the cat's last days were good ones. It wasn't meant to be like this. On his own, lost, hurt, in pain.

Agnes dressed in the first clothes that came to hand, pushed all thoughts of breakfast aside and slipped her coat and boots on. Her imagination was running ahead of her, at super-fast speed, running riot. Should she ring William? She'd seen so little of him lately, but he could help her. She knew he would, if asked. He'd know what to do, who to call, how to make posters on his computer and, if there was a body, there'd be a burial to think about. She didn't even own a spade any more, and there was no garden to speak of. In the old cottage, Smudge would have been buried under the apple tree, and she could have placed some kind of marker with his name on it, and sat there every day with a cup of tea and talked to him. But not here. Not in London. It was too loud, too soulless, not a place where anyone, or anything, would want to die.

Hurriedly, she picked up her keys, and a small blanket just in case, and went out into the street to search for him.

*

William opened his eyes. The phone was ringing, over and over again. Whoever it was clearly had no idea of the time. He wasn't even up yet. Not that he bothered getting up early these days. He tried to burrow down under the duvet and ignore it but the insistent ringing didn't let up. They weren't going to hang up, whoever they were.

'Mother?' He'd known her voice straight away, when all she'd said was his name. He sat up, clutching the phone in one hand and reaching for his glasses with the other so he could see the clock. It was nine fifteen. Had he really slept so long?

'Whatever's wrong? No, no, speak slowly. I can't understand a word you're saying. What's the matter? Mother, are you crying? What? When? And you couldn't find him? Yes, yes, I'll be there. I'm coming, okay? And don't worry. We'll track him down. At least he's not been run over, or you'd have seen him. I'm sure he won't have gone far. Just sit tight and give me half an hour.'

If the damn car will start, he suddenly remembered, and grudgingly hauled himself out of bed and into the bathroom for a pee.

*

When Patsy opened her eyes it was to the gentle sound of Michael's deep-sleep breathing and the monotonous cooing of a pigeon outside the window. It made a change from the seagulls. She slipped out of bed and into the hall, enjoying the feel of warm carpet on her toes. The cold tiled floors back in Portugal were nice, especially in the heat of the day, but you couldn't beat a thick fluffy carpet between your toes when getting out of bed. It was good to be back in England, she realised. In spite of the weather and the traffic, she had missed it. Once things were sorted out here, she could hopefully get up to visit her own parents and her little brother in Cumbria. A few relaxing days at the lakes, with a good book to read, a huge hug from her dad and a plentiful dose of her mum's home cooking inside her, was just what she needed.

Geraldine's bedroom door was ajar and there was no obvious sign of her inside. Patsy pushed it open and padded carefully across to the window that overlooked the small front garden and the driveway to the road, making sure not to disturb anything that would alert Geraldine to her having entered her private domain.

Geraldine's car was no longer there. She'd gone. Off to the shop, presumably. Hopefully this meant they could have some time to themselves today, maybe take a walk on the beach or look at the shops down the famous lanes she'd heard so much about. They were supposed to be on holiday, after all, and it was Monday morning. A Monday morning, when they didn't have to get up, dress smartly and go into the office. No meetings, no deadlines, no pressure. Hers was a hectic job and it was good to find some space away from it for once. She'd hardly thought about the office at all in the last couple of days and was determined to keep it that way, to avoid opening emails, reading texts, taking phone calls, anything at all that might link her back to work. All the planning, seeking out new clients, matching them up with the right properties, making the figures add up. Oh, she loved it all right, thrived on it, but everyone needs a break from time to time, and this was meant to be it. Although, sooner rather than later, the prospect of confronting Ruby was going to rear its head. She wasn't looking forward to that at all, and she felt sure Michael wasn't either.

For now, it was good to be free to wander about the house alone, without having to put her clothes on or ask politely for every little thing. Was there any orange juice in the fridge? Any wholemeal bread? Was there enough hot water for her to please have a shower? Would anyone mind if she watched the news, or did it clash with one of Geraldine's soaps? Geraldine had not asked her to treat the place as home, or to help herself to whatever she fancied, and the constant feeling of being an unwelcome visitor in someone else's house was starting to drag her down.

She found some juice and poured it into a glass, emptying and discarding the carton with no feeling of guilt at all, and settled on a stool in the kitchen. What exactly had she done to alienate the woman so badly? And then her thoughts turned back to Ruby. Was that what it was all about? Michael and Ruby, the girl he had broken up with to be with her? Was Geraldine still fond of Ruby, still angry that her son had walked out, still hoping for some kind of last-minute reconciliation? According to Michael it had never been that serious, despite the fact that they'd lived together and had a child. Not true love, he'd said. Not passionate. Something he'd just fallen into. A mistake.

Yet, there had been a wedding planned, a dress chosen, a date fixed, before it had all gone wrong. It didn't really add up. Perhaps she should have asked more questions, got him to open up to her a lot more and a lot sooner, but men – and Michael more than most – didn't seem to like talking about the emotional stuff, the things that matter. It's in the past, let's leave it there, that's what he would say. What he *had* said, whenever she had pushed. Even then, whatever he had told her had usually had to be teased out of him in tiny reluctant doses, a bit like pulling teeth.

She had met Ruby a couple of times. The girl was pleasant enough, but quite plain and unpretentious, younger than she'd expected, and very eager to please. She remembered how she'd bustled about at the flat, fetching biscuits and plumping cushions and popping her head around the door every five minutes to see if they were okay or to ask what they were doing, and then withdrawing again when she realised it was all work stuff she didn't really understand.

Michael had told her Ruby had been brought up in care, and he later realised had been looking, perhaps too desperately, for someone of her own to love, and that he had turned out to be it. He'd told Patsy that he'd found it all quite suffocating at times, oppressive, once the feeling of being flattered by her attentions had worn off. Her utter refusal to listen to reason, coupled with her childish belief that love was something straight out of a fairy tale and could never be broken, had been hard for him to handle. He didn't want to be Prince Charming. He was just a man, with his fair share of faults. And when the end had come, she had not taken it well. Things had been said, screamed, thrown . . .

Poor kid. Poor, sad, damaged little girl.

Patsy closed her eyes, trying to imagine that final scene, the last goodbye she had only heard about in short snatches that didn't always quite join up. Now they were going to have to walk back into that world. The pent-up emotions, the anger, the volatility of a girl who had not yet found it in her heart to forgive, or even begin to forget. They must visit Ruby again, in that same flat, and try to work things out about Lily. It couldn't go on, this animosity, this refusal to let him have anything to do with his daughter, even to provide for her financially. She had refused to give him her bank details. Even though he had apparently been the one to open the account for her, back when he was working there at the bank, he couldn't be expected to remember the number. Or even the occasion. And, the last time he'd gone online and checked his bank statement, he'd seen that she wasn't even cashing his cheques. She was just being stubborn. That money was for Lily, and nobody, surely, wanted Lily to do without, to suffer, because of the way her parents were with each other. *Without* each other.

Patsy wondered, not for the first time, if she should feel guilty. She had taken away another woman's boyfriend after all, and a little girl's daddy, and it was inevitable that there would be bad feelings. All that blame and anger, directed at Michael but really meant for her. The other woman. The *wicked* other woman. Some kind of fall out was bound to result, for everyone concerned, and it was obvious now that that included Geraldine. A grandmother kept away from her only grandchild. Geraldine might come across as a difficult and bitter woman, but Ruby keeping her away from Lily, that really didn't seem right. It probably went some way towards explaining the way she was. A woman on her own, her son gone, her grandchild miles away . . .

These things were never easy, were they? But Patsy loved Michael, really loved him, and she was sure he felt the same. Relationships failed, didn't they? Every day. Mistakes got made, sad things happened, couples fell apart, but no one in this day and age was expected to just grin and bear it forever. Divorce was commonplace, accepted. And Michael and Ruby hadn't even been married.

But maybe she was just trying to justify herself, make herself feel better about what she had done. What *they* had done. If she had been the one he'd abandoned, how would she have reacted? How would she have felt? It wasn't surprising that Ruby had taken things so badly and decided to make things difficult.

If this had been a work problem she would have taken charge, negotiated, done a deal, made concessions if necessary, to get what she wanted. It was one of her main strengths, what she was good at, but this was different. This wasn't business, this was real life, Michael's life, and although she was a major part of it now, what to do next was his decision to make, not hers. But there was so much emotion involved, and that brought her back again to the knowledge that Michael was just not good at talking about the emotional stuff. That had been all too clear last night with his 'go to sleep' stance as soon as Ruby's name, and those intimate questions about their life together, had come up.

'Morning.'

She looked up as Michael's head appeared around the kitchen door, his hair all messed up from sleep, little dots of stubble all over his chin, the rest of him naked but for a towel, far too small, that was just about wrapped around his waist and gaped open at the side. Oh, he was gorgeous. She'd pull that towel away and press him up against Geraldine's fridge door right now if she had her way, even though the collection of tastefully arranged fridge magnets might just find themselves stuck somewhere they were not meant to go. But he had his serious face on, and it was pretty clear he wasn't in the mood for any more passion at the moment.

'I didn't hear you get up,' he said, looking around for his mother and realising she wasn't there. 'I'm just going to have a quick shower and a shave, and then I'll ring Ruby again. I've tried twice already, but it's engaged. God knows who she's talking to. And no luck with her mobile either. As usual. I just hope it's not one of her stalling tactics. She can't put this off any longer. We should drive up there today, see Lily and get her down here for a few days. She'll love a little holiday at Granny's, and a chance to play on the beach. If Ruby's even packed her stuff yet, that is. I told her what I wanted to do when I wrote, laid everything out as clearly and as fairly as I could, but I don't suppose she'll make things easy. Sorry, Pats, here I am rambling on. You didn't have any other plans for today, did you?'

Patsy sighed inwardly. 'No, no plans. Nothing that can't wait.'

'Good. We'll take it slowly then, give Ruby another call, leave mid-morning, whether she answers or not, and maybe get a spot of lunch on the way. It looks like quite a nice day, for a change. Rain's stopped.'

'Yes, okay. Fine. But, Michael . . . driving there could be a problem. Your mum's gone to work, and she's taken the car.'

'Right. I hadn't thought about that. Train then. Or I might give Mum a call and see if she wants to shut up shop and come with us. I know she'll see Lily when we bring her back later, but she might enjoy coming with us, and some time away from work will do her good. She seems a bit stressed, don't you think? Not quite her usual chirpy self.'

Chirpy? Patsy couldn't imagine Geraldine ever being chirpy. If she had to use any birdlike adjective, she'd probably have gone for beaky, or crowing, or even vulturine, if there was such a word.

'It'll give you two a chance to chat in the car too, get to know each other a bit better.'

'Oh. Right. You don't think it might look a bit like we've turned up mob-handed? Three of us? We don't want to antagonise Ruby, do we? And, in her eyes, I must be public enemy number one.'

'Hmmm. Maybe. Although you're not, of course. What do you suggest?'

'Leave me here. I don't mind, really. Or drop me off somewhere in London. Oxford Street. Westfield. I don't know. Somewhere I can just wander the shops for a while. I really think it would be better if it was just you today. And your mum too, of course, if she fancies going. We can hook up again later, after you're done. Have dinner together somewhere. McDonalds, if you like. That's what toddlers usually like to eat, isn't it?'

'You could be right, I suppose.' He came across the room and took her hand in his, bending to kiss it. 'I may love you to bits but you're still a stranger as far as Lily's concerned. It might be a good idea for you two to meet properly on neutral territory, well away from Ruby and her catty remarks. And a Happy Meal could just help to break the ice. Depending on what toy is on offer, of course! Give me a few minutes to get cleaned up and I'll call Mum, see what she thinks.'

Oh, I know exactly what she'll think, and what she'll say, Patsy thought as she found herself alone again, sunlight pouring in through the window and making patterns of light on the glistening worktop in front of her. She won't want me to be there, any more than I do. She'll shut the shop or ask that assistant of hers to take over for the day, and she'll agree that I should go off somewhere by myself, and she'll be at Michael's side, car keys in hand, like a shot.

For once, she and Geraldine would be in complete agreement. This was about family, and for now at least Patsy did not feel a part of it at all.

CHAPTER THIRTEEN

Lily woke up to the feel of a warm body pressed against hers, the softness of hair against her cheek. She was in Mummy's big bed. It felt warm and safe in Mummy's bed. The body next to her stirred and stretched, and Lily opened her eyes. An arm unfurled and gently touched her face. But it wasn't Mummy. It was a cat, the lovely big furry cat that lived downstairs.

'Hello, Catty.' Lily stroked his fur, and the cat rolled over onto his back and purred loudly in her ear. She wasn't frightened of cats. Not like dogs. Dogs could bite you and growl at you, and that's why Mummy never let her touch them in the park, just in case one wasn't friendly. Cats don't do those things. Or she hoped they didn't.

'This isn't your house, Catty. Are you lost?' It felt good to have someone to talk to again. It felt like she'd been a very long time on her own. Months, or maybe years. 'I think my mummy's lost too. But we can look after each other now, can't we?'

She sat up in the big bed and reached out instinctively for Archie. She couldn't see him at first. Then she spotted him, lying on the floor, where he must have fallen during the night. But the cat was lying across her lap now, paws outstretched, wanting her to tickle his tummy, and she couldn't reach over the side without disturbing him, so she left Archie where he was. Archie didn't move. He never did. Not by himself. He didn't say anything either. Archie was pretend; just a toy. The cat was real. Warm and noisy, and comfortingly real. And, although she was feeling hungry again now, and she really, really, really needed a drink, she stayed exactly where she was, with the cat, all cuddled up together, his loud purring filling the room, the crumpled picture of Daddy beside her on the pillow, and started to feel just a little bit less alone.

*

The journey had been easy. The car, with its battery back in place, had started first time, the traffic had been light and William had been able to park right outside the house, but he realised now he was here that he'd completely forgotten to stop off for the freesias. Not that she seemed in the mood to care much about flowers. Agnes was frantically pacing the carpet, back and forth, back and forth, enough to wear a hole in it, all thoughts of arthritic knees forgotten, looking distractedly right through him towards the street outside the window and asking him absolutely nothing, about himself, or the drive, or the weather. Not even a 'How are you?' It wasn't like her at all.

She was wearing an odd mishmash of things. A brown tweedy skirt with part of the hem coming undone, a pink blouse, a green cardigan with the buttons done up wrong. She'd dropped her coat and some sort of blanket thing on the back of her armchair but still had her ankle boots on, and a beige headscarf with pictures of horses all over it on her head, tied too loosely and slipping off to one side, revealing a tangle of grey, uncombed hair.

'Right, Mother.' He put his hands gently on her shoulders and tried to guide her to the chair, untying the knot at her throat and removing the flapping scarf that looked so out of place indoors. She was obviously agitated, and nothing short of reuniting her with her missing cat as soon as humanly possible was going to make her happy. 'Sit down, won't you? Tell me all about it. When did you last see him?'

'Last night, sometime in the evening.' Stubbornly, she remained standing and started pacing again. 'After nine, I think. He wanted to go out, so I let him.'

'Did he seem okay? Not sick, not off his food, or limping, or anything to indicate something was wrong?'

'William, you're sounding like someone off one of those detective programmes. Barnaby, or Morse. There's no need to interrogate me, you know. I'm not a suspect. If anything, I feel more like a victim. You'll be getting a notebook out next! But, no, everything seemed perfectly normal. Nothing wrong with him at all. He often goes out for a last stroll before bed, but he always comes straight back.'

'Sorry. Look, sit down, take the weight off your feet, please. You're making me feel all on edge. Let me get you some tea. Lots of sugar. Good for the shock.'

'That's all very well, I'm sure, but sugar is not what I need right now. He's old, he's been gone all night, and I need to be out there looking for him. I need to feel I'm doing something useful, not just sitting around like a spare part and, believe me, William, tea is not the answer.'

His mother might not want to sit, but he certainly did. He sank into a chair, feeling quite exhausted just from watching her, the tension in the room almost palpable. 'Right! Down to business, then. Have you asked the neighbours yet? The other residents here in the house?'

'No. I haven't seen them. I rarely do. And why would they know anything? I let Smudge out onto the pavement, through the front door. And it's a dangerous place out there, what with all the traffic . . .'

'Yes, but he's a wise old cat, and you've already looked out there, so we're going to assume he has not come to a sticky end squashed under the wheels of a bus, okay?' He saw her wince and realised he may have been a tad too insensitive, graphic even. 'So, the house neighbours first. Any one of them could have seen him, passed him on their way in or out, maybe even opened the front door and let him back into the building. Then we'll try some of the other houses down the street.'

'I suppose so.'

'But first, you're having tea. We both are. I insist. I bet you've not even had any breakfast, have you?'

He went through to the kitchen and filled the kettle, leaning against the table as he waited for it to boil. The room was small and cluttered, with too many plants on the windowsill and not enough room in the cupboards. He pulled out the jar of teabags and chose two cups from the many lined up in rows.

There was a thin grey cobweb trailing across the ceiling and dangling down from the corner above the cupboard. He reached up and grabbed the end of it and watched it disintegrate into a mini dust cloud. The place could do with a spring clean. Could you call it spring cleaning when it was autumn? He forgot sometimes that she was old, that reaching ceilings and keeping everything going by herself was probably getting a bit too much for her. Should he find her a cleaning lady, or a home help of some sort? The place could do with a lick of paint too. He could offer to take care of that for her, now that he had more time on his hands. The once lemon-coloured walls were showing signs of fading into a nondescript shade of murky cream, and there was a funny shaped brown stain on the ceiling that he did not remember seeing before.

'Mother?' he called to her as he poured the boiling water into the cups. 'How long has that stain been up there?' He pulled a kitchen chair over and stood on it, not 100 per cent sure it would take his weight, and pressed a finger against the mark. 'It's wet! I think you have water coming through here. What's up above you?'

'What are you talking about? What stain?' Agnes stood in the archway that separated her small hall from the kitchen and followed his gaze. 'Oh, well now, where did that come from? I'm sure I have no idea.'

'It's soaking wet up here. There has to be something leaking from upstairs.'

'I think the flats are all arranged the same way, so it must be from their kitchen. The young couple, with the little girl. Oh Lord, that's all I need right now.' Slowly she sank into the chair that William had just stepped off, and let out an enormous sigh. 'Please, William, forget the stain. Forget the tea. I just want to get on and find Smudge. Everything else can wait, surely?'

'We were going to start with the neighbours anyway, so let's go there first, to the flat above you, shall we? We can ask about the cat and the leak at the same time. See what they have to say for themselves. Kill two birds with one stone, so to speak. Come on, then. What are you waiting for? No time like the present. Coat back on, Mother, and don't forget your key.'

*

The post dropped onto the mat with a loud thud just as Geraldine's car pulled back onto the drive. Patsy could see her, and hear her, through the big glass panel in the front door, making some remark about the weather to the postman and him mumbling a reply as they passed each other briefly on the path. As Patsy bent to pick up the bundle of letters, Geraldine's key turned in the lock and the door swung open, almost having her fingers off.

'Sorry. Didn't see you there,' Geraldine said, which seemed unlikely considering the size of the glass. She was wearing a pair of jeans, just a little too tight around the bottom but immaculately tailored, with an ironed crease down the front, and a loose silver-coloured blouse that swung around her hips as she breezed past, taking the letters from Patsy's hand and carrying them into the kitchen, pulling the rubber band off them as she went.

'Mum.' Michael greeted her, pouring water from the kettle onto a waiting teabag in Geraldine's favourite cup. 'I'm so glad you're coming too. I could do with the moral support, and I know how much Lily will love seeing you. Let's have a quick cuppa and we'll be off, shall we? Traffic should be good this time of the morning. I'll drive if you like. I assume I'm still on the insurance policy? Oh, and Patsy won't be coming this time. I thought . . . well, *we* thought, that it might not go down too well with Ruby, so we'll drop her off somewhere on the way and meet up again later, okay?'

'Michael, do let me catch my breath for a moment. I'm only just in the door and you've not let me get a word in yet.'

'Sorry. I'm just excited, that's all. I haven't seen Lily for so long, and I can't wait.'

'I know, I know, but let me just open the post and drink my tea first, all right?' She put her handbag down on the table and took a seat next to it. 'And get me a biscuit, would you, dear? I haven't had a moment to myself since I opened up the shop this morning.' She fanned at herself with one of the envelopes, flicking a cool gust of air across her face. 'Oh, I do hope Kerry will manage by herself.'

'She'll be fine. You shouldn't worry so much. What's the worst that can happen? She's only got to sit and serve. It's not as if you're letting her loose on the accounts or sending her to the wholesalers . . .'

Geraldine didn't look convinced, but she nodded slowly, blew on her tea and sunk her teeth into a garibaldi as she flicked through her mail. 'Bills, bills and more bills,' she muttered, sending a tiny spray of crumbs out as she spoke, casting each letter aside, unopened, as soon as she'd identified its sender. 'Oh, and there's one for you here.' She turned it over and back again, looked at the childish handwriting on the front and the crooked strip of sellotape that held it closed at the back, then handed it across the table to her son. 'Posted on Saturday. It has the look of your Ruby about it, if I'm not very much mistaken.'

Patsy flinched at the use of that phrase 'your Ruby'. A slip of the tongue, or another sign of Geraldine's usual thoughtless brand of insensitivity? She couldn't help but wonder if Geraldine did it deliberately, acting as if Patsy didn't exist, just to stir things a bit and wind her up. She stood back, in the doorway, not feeling a part of their little family tableau, and watched as Michael took the envelope and stared at it. The little muscle in the side of his face had started to twitch the way it did when he was anxious, or angry. It wasn't always easy to tell the two apart with Michael. Either way, he went remarkably quiet.

'Well, aren't you going to open it?' Geraldine sipped loudly at her tea, dunked her biscuit in it until it all but fell apart, and waited.

Patsy watched Michael's chest rise and fall as he took in a deep breath and slowly let it out again, then he slipped his thumb under the end of the tape and prised the thing open, drawing out the single sheet of paper and reading through it, rapidly, silently, in his head.

'Right!' He slammed his fist down on the table, dropping the letter and making the teaspoon jump in his mother's saucer. 'It looks like war has been declared. If that's how she wants to play it, so be it. Two can play at that game. Come on, Mum, get that tea down you, and we'll be off.'

'But I haven't even changed yet.'

'You're fine as you are. It's not a bloody fashion parade. Come on, hurry up. The nerve of the girl! No, I'm not having this. Ruby making all the decisions. What makes her think she can call the shots? Lily's my daughter just as much as hers, and I'm going to see her today no matter what Ruby says. Sorry, Pats, but we don't have time to mess about. Would you mind if we leave you here today? I'm not in the mood for detouring to some shopping precinct. There are places here in Brighton if you want to buy stuff, or you could just have a quiet day on the beach? You don't mind, do you? Here, take my key so you can get back in. I'll call you later, let you know how things go. That all right with you?'

Patsy nodded. 'Okay. I suppose. If that's what you want.' To be honest, she didn't feel she was really being given much of a choice. 'But, Michael, what did Ruby actually say? Is she refusing to let you see Lily, or what?'

'Letter's there on the table,' he said, his voice edged with impatience. He pointed at it, angrily, not even looking Patsy in the eye. 'Read it for yourself. Bitch!'

Then he was gone, his mother scurrying after him, the front door banging fit to break, without so much as a kiss on the cheek by way of goodbye, leaving her not 100 per cent sure whether it was Ruby or herself he was calling names.

*

The knocking at the door made Lily jump. She wanted it to be the iron man back again. This time she would talk to him, and tell him her Mummy was lost. Sometimes only grown-ups knew what to do.

Knock! Knock! The cat's ears had pricked right up at the sudden sound, and his claws flicked out, scraping down Lily's bare arm as he jumped down off the bed, yowling, his tail almost knocking over the lamp on the cupboard beside it. It didn't matter about the scratch. He hadn't meant to do it. All she wanted to do was follow him, hold on to him, make him stay, so she wouldn't be on her own again, but he moved so quickly, running out of the bedroom and towards the door.

By the time she had climbed down to the floor and gone after him, all she could see was the tip of his furry tail disappearing as he shot out through the cat flap, leaving it clattering behind him.

In the hallway outside the flat, she could hear voices. A lady and a man, talking. It wasn't the iron man this time. It was someone else. Voices she didn't know. She heard the lady talking to the cat. 'Smudge, there you are!' the lady squealed, and Lily could tell she was all happy and excited, even though it sounded like she was crying too.

'See, I told you,' the man said. 'I knew he wouldn't have gone far. Ah, look, the poor old thing looks as pleased to see you as you are to see him. He's rubbing all round your legs! Probably hungry by now, and trying to say he knows who's got the tuna!'

Lily flattened herself on the floor and poked her hand out very carefully through the flap, the plastic rubbing hard against her sore arm. She wanted the cat to come back, but she also wanted someone to help her now, someone nice who would come inside and get her some food and a drink, and tell her where Mummy was.

'Now we just need to sort out this damned leak. Bloody great box left here on the step too, I see. Looks like some kind of parcel delivery. That doesn't bode well for someone being at home, does it? Smudge! Smudge! Get off there. Oh, God, Mother, he's only gone and peed on it!'

And then the knocking came again, heavier and louder this time. It was very close by, making the door shake in its frame, and Lily pulled her hand back inside, quickly.

'Naughty boy, Smudge. Oh, William, what was that?' It was the lady talking. 'Look. That flap down there. It just moved, I swear it did. Surely there's not another cat living here? I've never seen it, if there is.'

'Well, that could explain things. Maybe our old Smudgey has a girlfriend!' the man said, laughing. 'Not quite as old and past it as we thought he was, even if he can't control his bladder. No wonder he stayed out all night!'

Lily didn't know what to do. They were just behind the door, but she didn't know who they were. She could shout, or cry, or push her hand out through the flap again. She could get the kiddie step and stand on it and open the door, even though Mummy had told her she must never, never do that. Whatever she did, she knew she didn't want the people to go, like the iron man had when he'd just left the things outside and walked away.

'I'm sure I can hear something inside,' the man said. 'Listen. It doesn't sound like a cat to me.'

'Then, if it's a person, why aren't they coming to the door? Oh, I do hope everything's all right. You don't think someone's hurt, do you? That could be why Smudge went in. He's very tuned into human emotions, you know. I've noticed that before. He always knows when I'm feeling a bit down, or under the weather. Comes and cuddles up to me, he does.'

'Someone hurt? It's possible. Or hiding, more like! Not wanting to face us and own up to the water damage. I'll give it one more try.'

He knocked again. 'Hello! Anyone home?'

'That was definitely a sound just behind the door. Someone's in there all right! Oh, William, do something. Should we call an ambulance, or the police or something?'

'Stop panicking, Mother. You really do watch too many TV dramas, don't you? It'll be nothing. Look, I'll have a peep in through the cat flap, all right? If there's a body in the hall, I'm bound to spot it!'

'Stop mocking me, William, and just do it!'

Lily saw the flap move. She lay on the floor and watched, half terrified, half relieved, as big man-sized fingers pushed through and stayed there, holding it open, and an eye appeared, looking straight into hers.

'There is someone.' The man was talking to the lady outside again, but his voice was much quieter now. 'But it's not a body, Mother. It's a child.'

PART TWO

CHAPTER FOURTEEN

Ruby

Where does reality end and dreams begin? Who knows? I'm not sure which one I'm in anyway, but I'm not following him. Really, honestly, I'm not. It's lunchtime, and the sun's out. So are all the holidaymakers. And me.

The beach is crowded, and so is the pier, and all the seats are occupied. I remember the heat, the noise, the press of people. People eating their sandwiches and their chips, and licking ice creams, and the seagulls hovering. I watch him come out of the bank, loosen his tie, wipe his hand across his forehead and look up into the sun. He smiles. He's not wearing his jacket and I can see the sweat pool on his shirt, spreading under his armpit. Damp, dirty, real. There's a newspaper tucked under his arm, rolled up, clutched against his side. He pulls a pair of sunglasses from his pocket. Big, dark, aviator style. When he puts them on he disappears inside them. Anonymous, faceless, not Michael Payne any more. But I know who he is.

Mrs Castle says I'm too trusting, that I want to be everyone's friend but that it's not always possible to be. She's always telling me about boundaries, telling me to protect myself, to be careful.

Careful of what? He's not dangerous. He's nice. And he does like me. I know he does. He smiles when I go into the bank with the money. He doesn't pull away when my fingers touch his as I pass the coins through under the glass. I don't think he knows that I'm waiting for him to notice me. But I am, and he will.

I walk a little way behind him, tracing his footsteps, squinting into the light, dodging in and out of the crowds. He walks slowly, enjoying the day. I walk slowly too. Breathe slowly. Think slowly. He goes into one of the sandwich places, dipping into his pocket for change, and joins the queue. I wait, looking in shop windows, until he comes out again clutching a carrier bag, the newspaper still there under his arm. I know he's looking for somewhere to sit down, but there's nowhere. I walk behind him again, watching my own feet moving, making noisy footsteps on the pavement. In the end, he just plants himself on a wall, down by the sea, stretches his legs out, takes a triangular packet of sandwiches out of the carrier bag, and a bottle of water. I find a place on the same wall, further along, stretch my feet out in front, try not to trip anybody up. The wall feels hard, cold against my legs, despite the warmth of the day. He spreads his paper out and reads as he eats. I don't think he sees me, doesn't look up at all. I wish he would.

An older woman comes out of one of the shops across the road, clutching a bottle of water, waving, calling his name. I watch her cross, see him stand up and hug her, not too tightly, and without passion. She's too old to be a threat, anyway. Maybe his mother, a neighbour or an aunt? They talk for a while. Not long. She looks at her watch and goes away again. I wish he would hug me like that, but tighter, and for longer.

I wish he would sit easily beside me, and let the crowds go by and ignore them, and talk to me and listen to the sea.

I don't know what it is I can hear now, but it's there all the time, just like the sea. It rushes in and retreats, over and over again, making its whooshing sounds. It never seems to stop. It's there, even when I'm asleep. Am I asleep now? I don't really know. I'm not sure where I am at all. But the sea keeps moving in and out. I hear it above, behind, inside everything else. Continuous. Calming. Careful. And I feel warm, protected, safe.

She told me I was good for him. The woman by the sea. Geraldine. She said I was like a breath of fresh air. Fresh, sea air.

She was there with me later. When Lily was born, when there was nothing but pain. Air. Gas and air. Breathe it in, Ruby. Breathe. Deep, deep breaths.

She held my hand, let me squeeze it as I wriggled and screamed, stayed with me when they decided to cut. I try to move my hand now, to reach for her fingers. Or his. She's not here, and neither is he. But Lily is, and she's not a baby any more. She's bigger now. Walking, talking. She's reaching out her hand to me. If I could just stretch that little bit further, touch her fingers through the glass . . . But I can't. I look away, towards the sea. Michael finishes eating and throws his crumbs to the birds. And when I look for Lily again, she's gone.

CHAPTER FIFTEEN

William pushed his hand further through the flap and touched the smaller one on the other side of the door. It was hot and damp, and it didn't pull away.

'Where's my mummy?' The voice was tiny and high. It was a little girl, her blonde hair matted into rat's tails, lying on the floor, her eyes wide and pleading. As she gripped his fingers, hard, he heard her start to cry. Great sobs seemed to shake through her. He could feel her hand tremble as it gripped on to him for dear life.

'It's okay. Don't worry. Is Mummy not in there with you?'

The child shook her head. 'No,' she gulped.

'Well, I'm going to find her for you, little one. Everything's going to be all right, I promise. Now, can you tell me your name?'

She opened her mouth, but no words came out, just a huge sob.

'It's okay. You don't have to tell me if you don't want to. My name's William. All right? William. And I'm not going to hurt you. I'm here to help you. Now, tell me, where did Mummy go? Do you know?'

She shook her head, just enough to register a no.

'Can you open the door for me? Can you reach?'

The child didn't answer.

'Did Mummy tell you not to open the door?' Still nothing. He lifted his head for a moment, just by an inch or two, and coughed, trying to clear his mouth of dust.

'Oh, William, what shall we do? Do you think she's really on her own in there?' Agnes put the wriggling cat down in the hallway and lifted her hands to her face, covering her eyes for a moment, then running her fingers up over her forehead and through her hair. 'I mean, you hear about these things, read them in the papers, about children being abandoned, left alone. Mothers going to work, or out for the evening, or even on holiday, and leaving their children locked in alone. But, here? Here, right under our noses? How could she do a thing like this? And where's the father?'

'Let's not jump to conclusions, Mother. Anything could have happened. First things first.' He turned his attention back to the little girl, still clinging to his hand. His shoulder was pressed hard into the floor and his neck was stiffening up. He couldn't stay down here much longer.

'Okay, can you stand up now and see if you can open the door for me? I won't go away, I promise. And I will find out what's happened to your mummy, but we have to get the door open first, don't we? We have to get you out of there.' He eased his fingers out of her grasp and watched her slide back, away from him. He could see that her feet were bare, and so were her legs, small and pale under a shiny blue dress that was badly crumpled and undone at the back. 'Good girl. Tiptoes now.

Find something to stand on if you have to. That's it. Good girl. Now try to turn the catch for me.'

William raised his head from the dirty floor and slowly stood up. There was dust in his hair and in the back of his throat. As he tried again to cough it free, he could hear her moving something around behind the door.

'That's it. Just twist it and pull. Can you do that?' He could feel his mother beside him, gripping his arm, and the cat, still weaving his way between their legs, rubbing, purring, hoping to be fed.

Then the lock clicked and the door opened, inwards, just by a crack at first, and her fingers appeared, wrapped around the door, tugging at the edge, and there she was, tears streaming in lines down her dirty face. A toddler, half naked, her legs smeared with excrement, her eyes red and sore from crying, her arms held up, covered in streaks of blood, just begging to be saved. Agnes let out a gasp and rushed forward, scooping the girl up, the tiny arms latching immediately and oh so tightly around her neck.

'Oh, my God. William, just look at her. The poor little mite. Come on, I'm going to get her downstairs quickly and clean her up. I bet she's had nothing to eat or drink either. However long must she have been in there by herself?'

'God knows.' William pushed the door fully open and hovered on the threshold. The phone was making that howling noise they made when they'd been left off the hook. He picked up the receiver and dropped it back in its cradle. Sounds coming from the lounge told him that the TV was on. Or maybe a radio. 'Hello?' he called. 'Anyone at home?'

'Oh, don't be ridiculous,' Agnes said. 'If anyone was in there,

I think they'd have made themselves known by now, don't you? Unless . . . Well, you'd better take a quick look, just in case someone's . . . ' She stopped, not wanting to say the unthinkable in front of the child who was now snuggled in close to her, her little chubby legs tightened around her waist, her sobs smothered in Agnes's woolly chest as she bent to kiss the top of her head. 'And see if you can find something for her to wear while you're in there. The poor thing's so cold, and she's half bare, with her dress all undone, and no socks or tights or anything. Then I think we'd best call the police, right away, don't you? There's something very wrong here, William. Very wrong indeed.'

*

Laura usually went to see her mum and dad on her days off, but she was tired, more so than usual after working several long days in a row, and she just wanted to take things easy, stay in with a packet of biscuits and a pile of magazines and whatever the TV had to offer.

Gina, her flatmate, was working today, so she had the place to herself. Gina had left early for her shift, trying to creep about but not quite managing it. When she'd dropped a cereal bowl on the kitchen floor, the sound of smashing china, not to mention the barely suppressed swearing, had reverberated through the bedroom wall, and Laura's plan for a lie-in had been scuppered before it even started. It was hard to relax knowing there were still little sharp pieces of broken china scattered about the corners of the kitchen floor, and a heap of last night's mucky dishes teetering in the sink. So, she'd got up and taken the bus to the hospital to see Lily. Stupid behaviour on her day off, but the girl had got to her.

Now, back at the flat, she was watching a doctor on the TV talking about flu jabs to protect the elderly. As if she didn't get enough medical stuff at work, now she had to listen to it at home as well. It reminded her that winter would soon be setting in. Another Christmas on the way, another round of snow and ice and transport delays, woolly hats and scarves and furry boots, and cramming onto the bus at the crack of dawn when it was still dark, let alone all the patients coming in who'd slipped over on the ice or couldn't stop coughing. She would have to get a flu jab herself to keep all those germs at bay. How depressing!

What she needed was something to cheer her up, a bit of fun, something – or someone – to bring some sparkle into her life. She was only twenty-four. She shouldn't be sitting about with nothing but the housework to look forward to, letting life pass her by. Laura smiled to herself. Fantasy time. She closed her eyes. A boyfriend, that was what she needed. Tall, dark, Johnny Depp-style handsome. Someone to go for a walk in the park with, kicking at the piles of crispy leaves and feeding the ducks, would be nice, or to stroll round a museum with, or just go for pizza. But a fantasy was all it was at the moment. Likely candidates had been a tad thin on the ground lately. It was a nice day out there too, for October. There was a peep of sun between those clouds. Ideal dating weather, if ever she saw it.

It had been all of eight months since she'd split up with Kevin. Not that he'd ever been the love of her life, or that she even missed him all that much, but she did miss the idea of him. Someone she could call 'my boyfriend', who would walk into parties by her side, not necessarily even holding her hand but at least sharing a bottle of beer they'd bought together at the offie on the way, and who could make up the numbers when she was asked for a meal somewhere and stop her being the odd one out stuck at the end of the table and calling for a taxi for one to get her home. It made her look less sad and desperate, sound less alone somehow, when there was someone in her life to take on the boyfriend title and hang onto it past the first couple of tentative dates. And who wasn't so keen to get straight into her pants that he forgot to ask what she liked to drink or what kind of films she preferred or, worse still, forgot her name.

Of course, there was always the vicar guy she'd met this morning. Paul. He had seemed really nice. A genuine sort of a person, but then a vicar would be, wouldn't he? She'd felt very comfortable around him, less flustered. And despite the tiredness and the TV and the mess waiting to be sorted out in the kitchen, she found that he kept popping back up into her thoughts. His hair, his eyes, that slightly crooked smile. He was certainly her type, in the looks department at least. But boyfriend material? A vicar? She laughed. Probably not.

*

Agnes was wiping the little girl's arms and legs with a soapy flannel when William let the police in. She hadn't been sure if she should try to make her sick, in case she'd swallowed any of the headache pills he'd found lying about, but she seemed okay. Scared, tired, hungry, dirty . . . But not ill. She wasn't sure whether to take her knickers off either. They were clearly on back to front. Or whether she should undress her completely and pop her into a warm bath. The girl could certainly do with it, but Agnes had seen too many crime shows on the telly. She didn't know what the child had suffered. Who might have done what to her, before they'd left. The police might need evidence, want to take photos, do DNA tests. She didn't want to put herself in a vulnerable position, be accused of something unseemly. From what she could gather, it was a risky business these days, touching a child, no matter how well intentioned. But she couldn't leave her smeared in faeces, or bleeding. It wouldn't seem right.

There were two of them. A young male copper who hardly looked old enough to be out of school uniform, and a woman, mid-thirties probably, clearly the senior of the two.

'She was covered in filth. Maybe I shouldn't have, but I couldn't just do nothing,' Agnes said, defensively, but the woman smiled at her and signalled for her to carry on.

'Right. Mrs Munro, isn't it? Just tell us what happened. You found her by herself, is that right? In a neighbouring property?'

'Well, technically it was my son, William, who actually found her.'

The officer turned to William, hovering in the doorway of the bathroom. 'Sir?'

'Well, there was water coming in through the ceiling. In the kitchen. Obviously from the flat above. And my mother's cat had gone missing.' At this point, Smudge decided to appear, working his fluffy body in slinky slalom patterns around the policeman's uniformed legs. 'Well, we found him, as you can see. But what I'm trying to say is—'

'Oh, for heaven's sake, William!' Agnes was losing patience and was only too happy to take over. 'We went upstairs and knocked. Nobody answered the door, but Smudge, my cat here, came out through their cat flap, and we were sure we could hear someone still inside, behind the door. To cut a long story short, it was this little thing. All by herself. And just look at her. Covered in her own mess, and half starved to death. She guzzled a whole glass of milk no sooner I'd put it in her hand, not to mention the jam sandwich. All children love jam, don't they? Strawberry —'

'So there was no sign of a parent there with her?' the female officer interrupted. 'No responsible adult at all?'

'Nobody. William went in and checked, in case there was anyone unconscious in there, or a body or anything. Which, thank God, there wasn't. And to turn off the tap and empty the sink, to stop the leak getting worse. The phone was off the hook too. But all that only took a few minutes, and since then, well, we've both been here with her and she hasn't said a word. Nothing. Won't even tell us her name, will you, darling?' Agnes dabbed the child's legs dry with a towel and carried her through to the living room, one arm under her bottom, as she cradled her head with the other. 'But my son did have a quick look round for anything that could be useful. There was a handbag, but it was all tipped up, like the little girl had been in there, you know, rummaging about the way kids do. And a purse, but nothing much in that. Nothing with names or numbers. And there were these.' Agnes reached for the packet of pills from the table where she'd put them so she wouldn't forget. 'We thought they might be important. You know, just in case she . . .'

'Right. We'll have to call Children's Services.' The police-woman smiled at Agnes. 'At the council,' she explained. 'Part of the Social Services department. We'll see what they have to say, and they'll probably sort out somewhere safe for this little one to go until we can find out who should be with her, and, more importantly, why they're not.' She turned to her colleague. 'Ambulance first, I think. These are only aspirin, and there are one, two . . . Six missing from the packet altogether. Nothing to say she took them all, or any of them, but I don't know how bad these might be for a child this age to take. We'd better get it checked out. Just as a precaution. Better safe than sorry. Then we'll have to go for Powers of Protection. That'll give us seventy-two hours anyway, a chance for the parents to show their faces before any big decisions have to be made. But let's make those calls first, okay?'

The younger one nodded. It was pretty clear this was all new to him, but he had his notebook out already and went out into the hall to make the necessary calls.

Agnes slumped into her armchair, taking the sleepy child with her. 'They'll take her away, will they?' She watched the girl curl into the folds of her lap. 'After the hospital check, I mean. Off somewhere to be looked after, by strangers?'

'A foster carer, probably. Only very temporarily, maybe just for tonight, until we can track down her mum and dad, find out what's happened. That's our priority now. Do you know them? Know who they are? Anything about them that might help?'

'No. They kept to themselves. As do I, I suppose. We did have a little talk a while ago, the mother and me, but, I'm sorry, this sounds terrible, but I can't even remember her name. She's young though, very young. Hardly more than a kid herself. And, as for him, I haven't seen hide nor hair of him for ages.'

'Never mind. Let's take a look in the flat then, shall we?'

'Don't you need a search warrant? To break in and hunt about?' Agnes was remembering all those crime shows again. Drug searches, and stolen goods, and escaped prisoners on the run.

'Not if it's open, and there's a risk to a child involved. We're not going to do any damage, don't worry. Just try to find out what's happened here, and look for some ID. Could you lead the way, please, Mr Munro? You did leave the door open for us, didn't you?'

Agnes could see William close his eyes and take a big gulp of air. He hadn't! The damn fool boy had closed it behind him. Now they'd have to force their way in, break the door down. She knew about these things. She'd seen it once, on an episode of Morse.

*

Patsy was enjoying being by herself. Much as she loved Michael, staying in his old childhood home, and sharing it with his mother, was becoming a strain. There was a strong breeze coming off the sea, lifting her hair and flapping it back behind her ears, and she was glad she'd decided not to wear a skirt or it would surely have been a battle to keep it where it was supposed to be, somewhere south of her knicker line.

She'd just strolled past Geraldine's shop. It was easy enough to spot, with its *Bits & Bobs* sign in dire need of a lick of paint, and its cluttered window display. The whole place looked dated, in need of a makeover, but it was Geraldine's business, and not her place to say. There was a young girl working behind the counter. The famously inept Kerry, no doubt. From where she was standing, Patsy thought the girl looked competent enough, ringing up some tacky souvenir on the till, dropping it into a paper bag, handing out change. It wasn't as if the place was heaving with customers either. Patsy doubted that it ever was.

Kerry waited until the customer left and then sat down on a stool behind the counter and nibbled at her nails. With her thin straight hair pulled back into an untidy ponytail and her maroon nylon overall looking like something from an old corner grocery shop from the sixties, the poor thing could do with a makeover of her own.

Patsy walked on. It was best to keep her opinions to herself, keep her nose out of Geraldine's life. The sea was up ahead, glistening in the sunshine, the aroma of fresh coffee wafted out from an array of cafes, and the prospect of bigger and better shopping brought a smile to Patsy's face, offering a much more inviting way of spending the day than wondering about Geraldine and her sorry little gift shop.

She hadn't spent any time alone for weeks. Months, even. Since she'd persuaded Michael to follow her to the Portugal office, there had seemed little point in him looking for a flat of his own. They had become a couple quickly. Too quickly, some were no doubt saying, and there was a definite case for keeping work and pleasure apart, as she well knew, having seen others in the office rush too quickly into instant coupledom after some drunken kiss at a party and then come a cropper even quicker, then have to find a way to carry on working together afterwards.

But Michael moving in with her had seemed the right thing to do. She had no regrets. She loved him, loved being with him, and the line between work and pleasure had, for her, always been a thin one. Her life and all its strands had come together in a way she could never have imagined since she'd met Michael. They lived together, worked together, played together, and their sex life was still new and exciting, still in the exploring stage.

If it wasn't for his mother, his ex-lover and his child, then everything would be as near perfect as it could possibly be. But, she told herself, settling down at a pavement table and ordering a frothy cappuccino and a bun, most people come with baggage of one sort or another, don't they? He was twenty-eight. No man of that age, barring some kind of monk, would have a completely clean slate. Past relationships would be echoing through their lives in one way or another, no matter who she hooked up with, and she wouldn't swap him. Not in a million years.

'Mind if I sit here?'

Patsy looked up and was surprised to see it was the girl from the shop, Kerry. She'd taken off the overall and let her hair fall down over her shoulders, so she looked like a different person altogether, like someone suddenly unshackled and relishing her freedom.

'No, feel free.'

The girl had no idea who she was. Why should she? They'd never met.

'Lovely day,' Patsy said, feeling mischievous, wondering if

in starting up a conversation she might be able to find out a little more about her mother-in-law to be, maybe even dig up a bit of juicy dirt.

'Is it?' The girl shrugged. Her loose cardigan hung off her shoulders as if it was three sizes too big, and her skin was pale and spotty, although she'd tried to cover it with an inexpertly applied layer of make-up that didn't suit her.

'Well, weather-wise it's pretty good, considering the time of year.' Patsy crossed her legs, slipping out of one of her high heels and letting her foot dangle, relishing the cool air where a blister had started to form. She should have packed some more suitable shoes. 'But not so lovely for you, by the look of things. Having a bad day?'

Kerry yawned. 'Oh, don't mind me,' she said, beckoning to a passing waitress and ordering a king-size burger, chips and a Coke. 'Work's just getting to me a bit. I'm in a shop, just up the road there, and I'd been due to finish early today, but the boss had to dash off somewhere without any notice at all, and she just expects me to stay on late and hold the fort. I had a date lined up, see, and I've had to text and put him off. A new guy I've only just met. Here on holiday and going home tomorrow, so that's that chance blown. So, I've closed up and snuck out for an early lunch. Stuff holding the fort, that's what I say. There were other things I'd been hoping to hold tonight!' She blushed and let out a little scream of embarrassment. 'Oh, that must have sounded awful. Hands! I only meant hands!'

Patsy laughed. 'Oh, dear. It's tough when work pushes the old love life aside, isn't it? But she's that sort of a boss, is she? A hard taskmaster?'

'Oh, she's all right really. Just me moaning. I don't have much in the way of qualifications – well, none to be honest – and she was the only one around here to give me a job and to help me find a place to stay as well. I know I should be more grateful. She's got a soft spot for people like me, I think. The waifs and strays, she calls us. You know, kids having a bit of trouble at home, chucked out of school, that sort of thing. She's not a bad old bird once you get past the outside layer. I'll miss her if the shop closes.'

'Oh, dear,' Patsy said again. 'Is that likely?'

'Dunno. I know she's been looking at the books a fair bit lately, and we're lucky to get more than a couple of hundred quid through the till most days, so it's on the cards, I reckon.'

They sat in silence after that, until Kerry's food arrived and she proceeded to smother it in ketchup until it looked like some kind of bloodbath from a horror film.

So, Geraldine was hiding a heart of gold, was she? Well, Patsy had yet to see it. It could explain why she still seemed so attached to Ruby, so loyal to her, despite the fact that Michael had decided to leave her behind. Perhaps Ruby had been one of Geraldine's waifs and strays? Someone she took pity on and tried to help. Michael had told her that Ruby had come to live with them but had never fully explained why. It would certainly fit.

Patsy glanced over at the crusty ridge of ketchup congealing around the edges of Kerry's plate and trying to do much the same around the edges of her mouth. She nodded a brief goodbye and went inside to pay her bill.

*

Gina picked another tiny fragment of broken china out from the rubber sole of her shoe with her fingernail and plonked the shoe back on her foot. That was the last one, as far as she could tell, but her nail was chipped now and catching on the threads in her tights, and her last emery board was so old and flat it was about as much use as rubbing her nail along a sucked lolly stick.

It had been one of those mornings. A bit of a niggly headache from too much wine and nowhere near enough sleep the night before, the accident with the bowl in the kitchen and nowhere near enough time to stop and clear it up properly, and now this.

She had seen plenty of sick children in A & E before, many of them dripping with blood or screaming in pain, but this was something else. The first time she'd come across anything quite like it. An abandonment case. A child who looked no more than two or three, not only found alone, but who'd been that way for some time, apparently. Nobody knew just how long, but from the state of her when she'd been found, they'd said it must have been days rather than hours. Now she was quiet, half asleep but still clinging tightly to the old lady in the funny clothes who'd come in with her, trailing an ambulance crew and a couple of police officers, one male, one female. They always seemed to bring a policewoman in when there was a child involved.

Nobody seemed to know the child's name or her date of birth, or where her parents were. Everyone was trying to help, but she could see they were mostly just getting in the way, crowding the tiny cubicle as the ambulance crew completed their handover, a student nurse dug out a teddy to make the little one feel more at ease, and the doctor did her best to calm things down and just do her job. An open pill packet was produced and the doctor peered at it. Gina heard her count. Six missing from the foil. Aspirin. Not good, but nothing too terrible, so long as the poor kid hadn't taken more than one or two. They'd do tests, take bloods, to make sure, if they had to, but the most likely option, from looking at her, was that she hadn't taken any at all. You couldn't be too careful when it came to drugs. Drugs and children didn't make for a good mix at all, but nobody would want to put this little one through any more trauma if it wasn't absolutely essential. The doctor would probably take a 'wait and watch' approach for now.

They all seemed to be talking at once over there, enough to disturb the patients in the other cubicles. It was bad enough at the best of times, with nothing but a collection of animal print curtains and plastic chairs separating them, and their young occupants in pain or scared already. Or in many cases, both. The little girl who was the centre of everyone's attention wasn't in pain but she was undoubtedly scared. She looked bewildered, her thumb stuck deep in her mouth, her eyelids beginning to droop, with no interest in the second-hand teddy at all, but still she clung on to the old lady with a vice-like grip that said she'd never let her go.

'No name for her yet, I'm afraid.' Gina pulled her attention back, startled by the sudden appearance of the policeman now leaning on the desk, just as she was wiggling her foot around to try out the comfort of the shoe and about to go over and do something about the noise. 'We have an address, obviously, and your reception staff are checking that on the computer. We have officers in the flat now too, checking things over, so it won't take long to get some kind of formal ID.'

He was young, not much more than Gina's own age, and looked almost as white and terrified as the child. In fact, he looked pretty much as he probably felt, like a spare part, out of his depth, talking too much, trying to find something useful to say that she didn't already know.

'Is she hurt, do you think?' He was clearly upset. Like one of those new young coppers who'd just seen their first dead body. She'd come across one or two of those over the years, and held the bowl as they'd spewed up the contents of their stomachs. 'Has anyone . . . ' He went on, almost in a whisper. 'Well, you know, has anything bad happened to her? Apart from just being on her own, I mean, and the pills?'

'Abuse, you mean? Sexual? No, there's no indication of that. Not that is obvious, anyway. She's hungry and a bit dehydrated, and she has quite a few superficial scratches and cuts. She's very quiet, but her pulse and BP were fine in the ambulance. Someone will try to talk to her soon, about what happened to her, I'm sure, when Social Services get here. Yes, she's drowsy, so she may have swallowed some of the pills, but there are no real signs. She doesn't seem to have a tummy ache and she's not been sick. Besides, they won't have tasted very nice, so I think probably not. It could simply be that she's tired, and who can blame her?'

She looked across again, saw yet another woman approaching the bed, and gave out a deep sigh. 'Oh, for God's sake, the poor child must be overwhelmed by all this. All these people, and now Social Services have turned up, right on cue! Your uniforms and radios probably aren't helping either. Can't you shut them up while you're in here? It's all just going to scare her, and every other child in here, for that matter. Why can't they all just back off and let us deal with this for now? She's perfectly safe here. She's not a criminal, about to run off. It's not as if we've got a suspect here to interrogate, is it?'

She stood up and strode the few feet towards the cubicle, the clackety noise of her shoe on the hard floor indicating the presence of yet more undiscovered chips of china. The officer followed at her heels, not saying another word. At least she'd put him in his place, but something still needed to be done to stop this whole thing becoming some kind of circus. It would be the press and the TV cameras next, if word got out.

'The doctor will need to get a proper look at her now, and I don't think it's helping having so many people here, do you?' She raised her voice, holding out an arm to try to ease everyone back. 'Could we perhaps all step back for now so I can close the curtain and give her a bit of privacy?' She could feel the reluctance in the air, even as they started to move. 'But perhaps you'd like to stay?' Gina turned to the elderly lady with the little girl, wrapped up in a blanket, still stuck tightly to her chest, and lowered her voice. The woman who'd just arrived from Social Services nodded her reluctant approval and went straight to the policewoman in search of facts.

'She does seem to have become very attached to you, doesn't she?' Gina smiled, helping to ease the old woman down into a chair, noticing how anxious, how drained she looked, how her cardigan buttons were done up wrong, and then, clucking a series of soothing 'there, theres' into the child's ear, she very gently started to prise the little arms away from the wrinkled neck. 'Quite literally, in fact!'

'We've got the address she was found at on the records.' It was Diane from the reception desk, peeking her head through the gap where the curtains met. With her head there amongst all the rabbits and squirrels and hedgehogs on the material to each side of her she looked like Mr McGregor turning up in the vegetable patch, and Gina had to suppress a giggle. 'Someone called Ruby Baxter. She lived there around three years ago, anyway. She gave birth here at the hospital, to a girl. Caesarian section. But we can't be sure this is definitely her. People move a lot, and this one hasn't been back for any kind of treatment since. Nor the child, which is unusual. Most will have some hospital involvement by the time they're three, if it's only a fever or a thumb stuck in a door or something.'

'I'm sure you're right. Looks likely it's them though, doesn't it? The child's age, if nothing else . . . ' She turned to the old lady. Agnes, she'd said her name was. 'Ruby Baxter. Does that name mean anything to you? You're the neighbour, right?'

'We met once or twice. I hardly knew her. Couldn't remember her name when they asked me. But, yes, Ruby, that does sound familiar. I do think that's what she was called.'

Gina reached over to the bed and patted the little girl's hand. 'Ruby. Is that your mummy's name?'

The child stared back and grabbed on tightly to Agnes's hand, but said nothing.

'Right, I won't push her. Not if she doesn't want to talk. But I bet this is little baby Baxter, and a fair bit bigger than when she was last here.' Gina looked back at Diane, her face still hovering in the gap between the curtains. 'Thanks, Diane. Oh, before you go, who was listed as next of kin?'

'Someone called Michael Payne. Fiancé, it looks like. Want me to give him a call?'

'Can't do any harm, can it? Let's hope there's a mobile number. If the only number we have is for the flat she came from, we already know he's not there.'

The doctor finished her examination and the child was soon almost asleep, her fingers loosening on Agnes's and finally letting go as her arm dropped limply down onto the bed. They'd taken the Disney dress off her and found her some pyjamas to wear, and the student nurse had been delegated to stay by her side to keep a close eye on her, when one of the police radios crackled into life.

The policeman came over to the desk again. Some of the colour had flooded back into his face now it looked like the little girl was likely to be okay, and she noticed how freckly he was, right across his nose and cheeks. 'Officers have been into the flat now, nurse. Mum is confirmed as Ruby Baxter. Age twenty-two. They found documents at the premises. No driving licence or passport, so no official photo ID, but there were family photos that should help us to find her, or recognise her, at least. No sign of the fiancé. No evidence he lives there either. No shaving stuff, or anything like that, so it's unlikely he does. And she's still a Baxter, so it doesn't look like she married him in the end, does it?'

'Well, I can see you'll make a great detective one day, Constable. Real little Sherlock, aren't you?' She smiled at him. 'Only teasing. But at least we're getting somewhere. And the child? Got a name for her?'

'Yes. It's Lily. There was her birth certificate, red book,

vaccination records, stuff like that, all kept together in a drawer by the bed. And more photos, of the two of them together.'

'Thanks. I'll let the doctor know.'

Lily? Gina closed her eyes, tapping a pen idly against the desk in front of her. Lily? She definitely knew that name from somewhere. It took her a moment to reach back into her memory banks and drag it out. Lily. Wasn't that the name of the girl Laura had been jabbering on about, and visiting as well? God knows why. She'd been run over on Saturday. Two days ago. And now she was lying upstairs in Intensive Care. Wasn't that her name? Lily? She was sure Laura had said she was young, no more than early twenties. A real mystery girl, with some sort of religious cross round her neck, and a caesarean scar. Could that be her? Ruby Baxter, the mum? It certainly seemed to fit. But why would she have called herself Lily if her real name was Ruby? Unless she was calling out for her daughter, of course. Yes, that must have been it. It had to be her. It was just too much of a coincidence, wasn't it? If she was the missing mum, hit by a car and pretty much out of it since, it would certainly go some way towards explaining why the child was alone.

'I think you'd better get hold of one of those photos, Officer. It could help you ID the mum a lot sooner than you'd expected. Your missing Ruby Baxter could just be here, right under our noses all along.'

*

'Why on earth haven't you got a satnav, Mother?' Michael muttered. He was getting tired of relying on street signs and some badly-folded ancient map that Geraldine kept in the glove compartment, but she had nodded off to sleep beside him and was no help at all. After all this time, he should know the way like the back of his hand, of course, but when he'd taken a side street to avoid a huge queue of traffic up ahead he'd somehow lost his bearings and God knew where they were now.

He thought he could hear his mobile ringing somewhere, muffled, a long way away. He must have left it in his coat in the boot. Oh, well. It would only be Patsy asking if they were there yet. Or Ruby, finally answering the messages he'd left on her mobile this morning. Sod her, they were nearly there now. She could wait and say whatever it was to his face.

He thought back to her letter. It was so typical of Ruby. She had to make everything so hard, declare some indefensible war, and do it in a way that gave him no chance to fight back or argue his case. She couldn't just pick up the phone and talk like normal people. Not until she really had to, like now, no doubt desperately trying to stop him from turning up at her door. Some kind of last minute excuse, pretending Lily was sick or they had to go out somewhere vitally important.

It seemed that Ruby just couldn't accept that things change, that relationships sometimes don't work out, and that seeing Lily, finding a way to share her, make sure she had what she needed, was something separate from all of that. It was so like her to just put up the barricades and dig her heels in. Threatening him with legal action was so petty and childish. Not that she'd have any grounds. He'd left them, yes, he had, no denying that. But he'd tried to do the right thing, tried to call, sent presents, money . . .

Why did she have to be so difficult? He wasn't trying to take his daughter away, just to have proper access, the chance to be a part of her life again. Any court in the land would say that it was best for Lily to stay in touch with both of her parents, surely? And Ruby, of all people, should understand that. She'd never known her own dad, and only had sporadic contact with her waste-of-space mother as she grew up. Even that had stopped by the time she was ten, and God knows what had happened to the woman after that. Drunk herself to death, probably, from what he'd heard about her. That old biddy, Mrs Castle, was more of a mother to Ruby than her own flesh and blood, still sending cards and calling from time to time long after Ruby had left the children's home and the woman herself had officially retired. Didn't Ruby want a more normal life for her own daughter? With two parents who loved her, even if they chose to do it from separate homes?

He pulled the car into Ruby's road. There was nowhere to park, as usual. The building just about had room for two spaces on its short gravel drive, though both were occupied by cars he didn't recognise, but then it had been a while since he'd lived here. He looked up at the windows. One of Ruby's was open a crack, the curtain billowing about, so she must be at home. The rest were closed, dark, telling him nothing. They could all be new people here by now, for all he knew. Not that he'd ever got to know any of the old lot properly when he was here. Too much time at work, too much time taken up with the baby, too little time for much of anything else. A motley collection of vans and old bangers filled up the few legitimate reserved residents' spaces in the road, and even the pay-by-meter parking slots further along were all full.

Swearing under his breath, Michael drove along the road, turned the corner towards the little scrappy bit of grass they laughingly called a park, and found a space near the gate. This was where they'd brought Lily in her buggy on sunny days, and sat and watched the bigger kids messing about on the climbing frame. He wondered if Ruby still did that, if they might even be here now, with Lily whooshing down the slide, or on the swings, pushing her little legs backwards and forwards to make herself go higher. She could probably do that now. She would have changed so much since he'd last seen her. They do, don't they? Change in weeks, at her age. He wondered what she was like now, how many teeth she had now, whether she could write her name, how long her hair had grown ... Oh, he'd missed too much. He wondered, briefly, if he would even recognise her, but that was absurd, of course he would. He was her daddy, still her daddy, always her daddy. And things were going to change from now on, no matter what Ruby had to say about it.

After several attempts he managed to ease the car into the tight space, albeit at a strange angle and with the wheels a few more inches from the kerb than he would have liked. 'This will just have to do,' he said, swinging his door open and almost knocking a passing cyclist off his bike. He peered into the park but everything looked still and quiet, the small playground empty. She wasn't there. He walked slowly along to the meter. How long would they need? If things went well, and Lily was packed and ready to go, they could be out again in minutes. Then again, if Ruby wasn't playing ball, the wrangling could take a while, especially as he'd prefer not to do it in front of Lily. Thank heavens for his mother. Maybe she could act as some sort of calming influence, or take Lily to the swings while things were sorted out. Would an hour be enough? Two? He tipped all the coins from his pocket out into his hand and fed them in. What the hell? It was only money. Some things were more important.

'Come on, Mum,' he said, walking back to collect her, helping her with the door as she stretched and opened her eyes. 'It's time to go and find that daughter of mine. And more than likely dodge the odd flying rolling pin, if Ruby's up to her old tricks again.'

'That bad, eh?'

'Mum, you didn't read the letter. It's going to be that bad, believe me.' He was already striding on ahead of her, glad he'd hung onto his keys when he'd moved out. If Ruby played silly beggars now, at least they could let themselves in. He could hear his mother's heels clattering along the pavement behind him, trying to keep up. 'Come on, let's get on with it, shall we? If my Lily's in there, I'm damned sure I'm going to see her no matter what Ruby might say.'

*

It was quiet after his mother had gone with the ambulance, the police car hot on its heels. William supposed he would have to go after her sooner or later, to give her a lift back home from the hospital, but for now he'd make a start on doing something about the stain on the kitchen ceiling. It had always helped him, in times of stress, to have something practical to do. Using his hands somehow removed the need to use his brain, or to engage his feelings. Maybe all men were like that? Looking for ways to push their emotions aside and just be the providers, the fixers, the hunter-gatherers they were originally designed to be.

He'd been an idiot shutting that door, he knew that, but you don't always stop to think, do you? Having had a quick look around for possible bodies, sorting out the sink and the phone, and having a rummage through the contents of the upturned bag, there'd seemed little else he could do, other than get back downstairs to his mother and wait for the police to arrive. He wasn't good with children. Well, he'd never had any of his own, had he? And although his heart went out to that little scrap of a thing, he wouldn't have been a lot of use in cleaning her up or knowing what to do with her if he'd found her by himself.

He hadn't even looked around the flat for something clean for her to wear, as his mother had suggested. He didn't like the idea of opening drawers and cupboards. It felt too intrusive, in someone else's home. He'd just wanted to get out of there fast. Thank God for his mother and it wasn't often he'd had cause to say that. She'd done her share of nagging, putting her two-pennyworth in, letting her opinions and her long-suppressed feelings be known, especially during the divorce, but underneath it all she was still the rock his whole life had been built upon, and that's just what she was being now. Solid and dependable and surprisingly loving, to a child she didn't even know, when all he would have done alone was crumple.

It wasn't long until more police arrived. There were four separate bells outside, and they'd rung on his mother's. He'd gone to the front door and let them in, had a few words in the hall, but he didn't follow them up the stairs. Not his place, and he didn't want to come across as some rubbernecker, hanging around the scene of the crime, being more curious than was either necessary or seemly. He wasn't sure how they did it but they were soon inside the flat. He could hear their boots stamping about upstairs, the thump-thump noises reverberating through the ceiling. So, it was true what they said about the police and their clod-hopping size nines!

He stood on a chair and prodded at the stain again. It was still soaking wet, a muddy-looking brown ring at its edges, spread out now like the open petals of a flower, so it occupied the whole of the corner and was making its way in a trickle down one of the walls. At least there wouldn't be any more water adding to it now he'd cut it off at its source. He just had to let it dry out before he decided what to do. With luck, it would need nothing more than a coat of paint. He'd have to do the whole ceiling while he was at it, but it was a small enough room. Worst case would be to have to replaster some of it first.

William climbed back down and put the kettle on. Would his mother have any alcohol in? The thought of plain tea just didn't work. He definitely needed something a bit stronger today, after all the trauma of the last hour or so. He rooted about in a few likely places but the best he could find was a drop of cheap sherry, the kind she put into trifles, and then hardly enough left in the bottle to cover the bottom of a cup. Not quite the brandy he might have wished for. Not tempted by the thought of mixing them together, he downed the sherry first, straight from the bottle, shuddered, then made himself the strongest tea he could and stirred in four spoons of sugar. Strong, sweet tea. It's what they always had in films, for the shock. It was so strong, it came as a surprise that the spoon didn't stand up by itself in the cup!

What else did she keep in these cupboards? Where were all the important papers? The insurance? Did it cover this sort of thing? Leaky ceilings, thoughtless neighbours, careless acts committed by children too young to know better? He'd better ask her for the policy details and check, although there was usually an excess that basically meant you ended up paying most of it anyway, or all of it if you didn't want to lose the no-claims. Bastards! They had you over a barrel whichever way you looked at it really, didn't they? A bit like solicitors. Robbers, the lot of them.

Of course, they might be able to claim against the other people's policy. He didn't think they owned the flat though, the young couple. When Agnes had bought hers, they'd found out that two of the others in the house were still in the hands of its original owner and were let out. He was fairly sure the flat above was one of them and, from the odd occasion he'd spotted them, he didn't think they looked old enough to own it. Or to have a mortgage, anyway. Oh, why did everything have to be so complicated? He'd just get hold of a tin of cheap emulsion, bring the stepladder over, and do the job himself. Just get on with it. It wasn't worth the hassle of fighting anyone else over money. Susan had taught him that.

There was more noise now, out in the hall. He had thought the police had gone by now. It had all been quiet up there for the last ten minutes or so. He guessed that they'd found what they needed, but now there were footsteps again. Back for more already? Should he go out there, offer them tea, ask them if there was any news? He was the one who'd found her, after all. But, when he opened the door, it wasn't the police coming down the stairs, it was two other people entirely, about to go up.

CHAPTER SIXTEEN

Ruby

She is sitting in Mrs Castle's sitting room, drinking tea. Same woman, different place. She's Michael's woman, the one he was talking to by the sea. His mother? I don't know. But why is she here, where I live? Is she following me now, the way I followed him? The stalker stalked. A shiver runs through me.

They both smile at me as I walk in, don't ask me to leave. Mrs Castle introduces me, as if I count. Maybe I do. And the woman takes my hand, only for a moment, before I fade back into the wallpaper. Her hand is warm, pale, weak. Like Mrs Castle's tea. And she is called Payne. Like Michael. So I'm right, it is his mother. Turns out they're friends, her and Mrs C., in the same club or something, raising money for the same good causes. I suspect I am regarded as one of them. The good causes that is, not the members of the club. I am someone in need of care, someone to be saved. And all the others just like me. A cause, but not necessarily good. If she knew what I am thinking, about her son . . .

'Victoria sponge, Geraldine?' Mrs Castle makes them herself. Cakes, scones, biscuits. Sells them sometimes at fairs and stuff. I

189

like to help her, but I'm not very good at it. The cooking. They never come out looking quite straight somehow. All a bit out of shape. But I'm not bad at the selling. She says I have the gift of the gab. Over-friendly. Push, push, push. Never giving up. Dog with a bone, she calls me. There are times when that's a good thing.

The woman takes a slice and opens her mouth around it, and I see the jam ooze out from between the layers, like a trickle of thick, gooey blood. Her hand reaching up and wiping it not quite clean. I look away, because I can't look at her any longer. Her mouth, still red and wet. The mouth that has kissed his cheek. The hand that has held his hand.

She sips her tea. Bone china teapot tea.

Not the old slot machine tea. Polystyrene cups, not enough milk, or too much, and sugar in sachets, if we're lucky. In hospital corridors and doctors' waiting rooms, she waits with me, tuts at the delays, flicks through tatty magazines, looks at her watch, holds my hand. Not Michael's, but mine. Waits for the baby that was supposed to link us together, always. My baby, and Michael's. And hers. The beginnings of us, the four of us, as a family. A real family, at last.

But where are they now? All of them? Any of them? Why am I on my own again?

CHAPTER SEVENTEEN

Laura gasped into the phone. It was one of those moments, when what you are hearing is so startling that it takes your breath away.

'So, her name isn't Lily at all?'

'No, I already told you. Oh, do keep up.' Gina was beginning to sound annoyed with her, which was a bit much coming from someone who'd smashed up half the kitchen and left her to clear up the mess. 'Lily is her daughter's name. The little girl I have right here in A & E. The one you've been sitting with and talking to these past couple of days is called Ruby. Ruby Baxter, age twenty-two, and at the moment looking pretty much like the bad guy.'

'But she didn't get hit by a car on purpose, did she?'

'Of course not. But she shouldn't have left the kid on her own either, should she? And now we've got Social Services sniffing around, which isn't surprising. Anyway, I thought you'd want to know, or about as much as I do, anyway. Got to go. On my break, and I'm already late back. See you later. My turn to cook.'

Laura put the phone down. So Lily was really Ruby. For a minute or two she felt a bit daft, all that time she'd sat by the bed calling the poor girl by the wrong name. Not that she'd got much response, so she probably hadn't even heard her. Still, it was good to know she'd been identified at last, that there was a real name to put to the face and hopefully, soon, a real family on its way to claim her.

It was mid-afternoon and Laura was still slopping about doing nothing. She hadn't planned on going out again, but now, suddenly, she knew she had to. Not that the hospital would normally be her first choice of destination on her day off – twice – but she had to do it. To go and talk to Ruby again, and to tell her they had found her daughter and that the little girl was okay. God, how that must have been playing on her mind, knowing the child was all alone, and her needing to get back to her. If her mind was working at all.

Laura heated a quick bowl of soup out of a tin and gobbled it down so quickly she burned the roof of her mouth and had to swig down a glass of cold water to ease the pain. You'd think nurses would be used to dealing with pain. But not when it was their own. She swore that even the smallest things hurt her more than they did anybody else. Her dad always called her a wimp, but he smiled when he said it. 'Who'd have thought you'd ever become a nurse?' he'd joke. 'Even the sight of an Elastoplast used to bring you out in a sweat when you were little!' But he was proud of her, she had no doubt about that.

She let her tongue worry at the blister forming rapidly inside her mouth, until the flap of loose skin came away and she spat it out, feeling the raw patch it left underneath. She dragged a brush through her unruly hair and tied it up, wishing she'd had time to wash it and straighten it properly, then pulled on a nice dress and some boots, and slicked a mascara wand over her lashes. She might as well try to look half decent. You never knew who you might meet. Her mind flicked back, quite spontaneously, to the young chaplain, Paul. He'd want to know, wouldn't he? Perhaps she should find him and tell him about Lily. No, about Ruby. She must try to get used to calling her that.

If she was quick she should just catch the bus that was due by at any minute. She grabbed her bag, slammed the door behind her and started to run, her heart pounding in her chest. Because she knew now who Ruby was, or because she was running, or because of the strong possibility that she was about to see Paul again? She didn't know which, and she didn't care. Boom, boom, boom, her heart echoed the rhythm of her feet as her boots pounded along the pavement, and she had the distinct feeling, a warm and hopeful and breathless feeling, that everything, for Ruby and for herself, was at last about to change.

⁂

As soon as the man on the stairs had explained what was going on, Geraldine and Michael had run back to the car – no mean feat in the shoes she was wearing – and driven at high speed to the nearest hospital. It had been some jumbled story about cats and floods and packets of pills. None of it made any real sense. All they knew for sure was that Lily had been found by herself and had been taken away in an ambulance.

'Is this the right place?' Geraldine stopped to get her breath and looked around the waiting room full of teenagers with crutches, old people with pale grey faces, and various heads leaning resignedly over sick bowls. There was a drinks machine and one packed with chocolate and crisps, discarded cups scattered everywhere, an untidy pile of dog-eared magazines, a payphone surrounded by cards advertising taxis, and a queue at the desk. 'Is there where they would have brought her?'

'I don't know, Mother. But this is A & E, so I guess it has to be.'

'But, Michael, these people are all adults, and they're sick. Surely Lily's not sick? I don't understand. And where's Ruby? Why wasn't she at home?'

He was rummaging in the pockets of the coat slung carelessly over his arm, putting the car keys away, trying to find his phone. There was a notice on the wall showing a drawing of a mobile phone with a big red X through it. Typical! 'I don't know Mother.' God, how was he supposed to know? Anything at all? This was all as alien to him as it was to her. He shook his head and put the phone away, feeling the anger rising involuntarily and aware that, if he wasn't careful he'd be directing it at her. 'Oh, for God's sake, get a move on.' They stood together in the slow-moving queue, listening to the man in front rattle off his details before being asked to sit and wait, Michael's foot tapping impatiently. It was cold in the waiting room, the doors continually opening and closing again, silently, whenever anyone approached, like the jaws of a shark capturing its unsuspecting prey and swallowing it whole. It seemed that far more people came in than ever went back out. Where did they all go? Shunted away into side rooms and cubicles and wards, names called, files and papers changing hands, anxious relatives following in the slipstream, whispering into mobile phones they weren't supposed to use, sipping terrible tea. Michael slipped his coat on to keep warm, jiggling noisily at the bunch of keys in his pocket, impatient for his turn.

At last!

'My daughter. Lily. I've been told she's here? What's happened to her? Is she all right?'

'Full name? Address?'

Michael reeled off the details and waited as the woman checked her computer screen. 'Ah, yes. I believe one of my colleagues has been trying to contact you. If you could just wait for a moment please, sir. I'll get someone to come out and talk to you.'

Geraldine clutched at her son's arm. 'It will be okay, Michael. Nothing bad will have happened to her. It's just a precaution, bringing her here. You heard what that man at the flat said.'

'Yes, Mother, I heard. And I didn't like what I heard. Hungry, dirty, scared. And tablets. Tablets! What was Ruby thinking? Why on earth did she leave her all by herself? There's police and Social Services and God knows who else involved now, so don't tell me it's okay, because it clearly isn't.'

'Mr Payne?' A young nurse was approaching, holding out her hand. 'I'm Staff Nurse Gina Willis. I've been looking after your daughter. Don't worry. She's fine. Really. Now, if you'd like to follow me?'

The nurse led them along a once-white corridor that smelled of something overly clean and distinctly clinical, and through a door marked 'Paediatric Accident and Emergency' with a picture of a giant teddy etched into the glass. She ran her hands under a tub of gel attached to the wall and gestured for them to do the same.

It was a large square room, with a wide, paper-strewn desk

sweeping along one wall, and a collection of cubicles lined up around the other three. Each cubicle was bounded by a colourful curtain, covered in assorted animal prints. From behind one or two came the sound of tears and the occasional whine. Quite a few were empty. Michael could guess where Lily was right away. A young policeman was loitering outside the cubicle in the corner, and a middle-aged woman with a huge handbag and a notebook in her hand stood up from a chair and was making a beeline for them across the room. She didn't look like a doctor, that was for sure.

'Mr Payne?'

'Yes. Michael. And this is my mother, Geraldine Payne . . . '

'Mrs Freeman, but please, call me Barbara.' She nodded at each of them in turn, shifted her belongings over, clumsily, from one hand to the other, and finally held the free hand out to shake. 'Children's Services.'

'Yes, right. But can I see my little girl now, please? Whatever it is you have to say, can it at least wait until I've seen that she's all right?'

'Of course.'

The nurse, Gina, moved ahead of them and pulled the curtain aside. Lily was on the bed, curled up in a tight little ball, fast asleep, dressed in oversized pyjamas, a teddy encircled in her arms. An old lady was dozing in an armchair at her side, her cardigan askew, her shoes off and tucked under the bed.

'Lily!' Geraldine gasped and sped forward, her shoes squeaking on the shiny floor.

'Leave her, Mum!' Michael grabbed at her arm and pulled her back. 'Let her sleep.'

'Oh, but Michael . . . It's so long since I've seen her. The little sweetheart! Look how she's grown. She must have been so frightened, all on her own. I just want to pick her up and cuddle her. Don't you?'

'You will. We both will. But, for now, let her sleep. Who knows what she's gone through?' He moved toward the narrow bed, slowly, stepping carefully so as not to bump into the woman in the chair, and stroked his daughter's head, very gently, as if she were made of glass.

'Mr Payne . . . ' Barbara whatshername stepped forward again. 'As you must appreciate, this is a difficult situation. The police have informed us that the child . . . ' She referred briefly to the papers in her hand. '. . . Lily was found alone, and every indication is that she had been alone for some time.'

'Some time? How long is some time?'

'Look, can we just step outside the cubicle please? We don't want to disturb your daughter. And Mrs Munro here, well, you might not want her to hear anything confidential.' They were back outside the curtain now, but not far enough away to stop Mrs Munro hearing every word, if she wanted to. Who exactly was Mrs Munro anyway? There was something familiar about her, but he wasn't sure why.

'There are a few things we need to talk about, Mr Payne, in the absence of the girl's mother, and before we can go any further. You are Lily's father, I assume? And you do have parental responsibility?'

'Yes, I'm her father. Of course I am. Parental responsibility? What does that mean? That I look after her? Pay maintenance for her? We don't live together any more, her mother and me, if that's what you mean. But she is my little girl, and I have always done my best for her.' His voice came out in a choke. 'She's mine, and I love her.'

'I'm sure. So, just a few questions. You are not, were not, married to Lily's mother?'

'No.'

'But your name is on the birth certificate? You were acknowledged as the father?'

'Absolutely.'

'I believe the police did find the birth certificate among certain papers retrieved from the premises, so it shouldn't take us long to confirm. Do you have any ID, Mr Payne?'

Michael felt around in his pockets. 'Not on me. Well, just a credit card, but I don't suppose that counts, does it?'

'Passport? Driving licence?'

'Who carries their passport about with them? I came up here from Brighton today, not bloody France!'

Geraldine winced. 'Michael. There's no need—'

'No, I know. Sorry. I think I might have my driving licence in the glove compartment of the car. I tend to shove it in there with all the insurance stuff when I'm driving in England, sharing Mum's car, just in case I get stopped. It's outside, in the car park. I'll go out and look if I must. That's if the car hasn't been towed away by now, because the exorbitant car parking ticket we paid for has run out already. Three pounds for an hour? What's that all about? Robbing the sick and vulnerable. What if I turned up dying of a heart attack and I didn't have the right change? Neither of us had? It's a bloody disgrace.'

'Michael.' Geraldine was giving him one of her glares. 'Not

now. I know you're feeling wound up, but do try to stay calm. This is all very stressful, for all of us, but shouting and swearing isn't going to help anyone. Money is not our top priority right now. And anyway, it's hardly Mrs Freeman's fault, is it?'

'Mr Payne, I can understand that this is all very upsetting for you.' Barbara Freeman lay a tentative hand on his arm. 'I'm just trying to make things easier. If we are satisfied that you are Lily's father, that you have parental responsibility, that you are able to take proper care of her and she knows you and appears happy to go with you, then we should be able to release her into your care. As soon as the hospital say she's fit to go, of course. If not, then a suitable foster carer will be found for her, at least for tonight, and until the mother, Miss, er . . . '

'Baxter. Ruby Baxter.

'Until Miss Baxter is awake and able to help us establish—'

'Hang on a minute. You said, until she's awake? You mean you know where she is?'

'Well, yes. I'm sorry, Mr Payne. I had assumed that someone would have told you.'

'Told me what?'

'That she's here, in the hospital.'

'What? Then why on earth isn't she here with Lily now? And what the hell was she playing at, leaving her alone in the first place? Wait until I get my hands on her, the stupid bloody girl!'

'Mr Payne . . . ' It was the nurse again, her hand on his shoulder, easing him towards a chair, her voice calm and soothing. 'Listen to me. Ruby hasn't been able to tell anyone anything. We only made the connection between her and Lily this afternoon. Ruby is in intensive care. She was hit by a car two days ago, around lunchtime on Saturday, and she's been unconscious ever since. We had no idea who she was until today. She's broken a leg and a couple of ribs, but more worryingly, her head took quite a knock.'

'Two days?' Michael interrupted. 'You mean Lily has been on her own, in that flat, for two days and nights?'

'It looks that way, yes.'

Michael ran his hands through his hair and stared at the floor. He couldn't quite take it all in. 'And Ruby? How is she now?'

'The staff up on the intensive care unit will be able to tell you more than I can. All I know is that she suffered a severe injury to her head – to her brain – and that she's been very poorly indeed. She's not out of the woods yet, I'm afraid. Not by a long way. She's had an operation to relieve some of the pressure, but I'm sorry, Mr Payne, she is being heavily sedated for now. And that means she hasn't woken up yet.'

Geraldine leaned against his shoulder, her hands shaking. 'Oh, Michael,' was all she was able to say, before her legs gave way and the nurse hurriedly pulled up another chair.

*

Patsy was starting to wonder what was going on. No news is good news, so they say, but today no news felt very much like something had gone horribly wrong. She'd avoided going back to the house. It smacked of Geraldine, from its chintzy furniture with the carefully placed cushions to its stark, uncluttered worktops and lemon-scented loo, and it wasn't somewhere she could feel at ease. Not yet.

While the weather stayed reasonably warm it was just nicer to stay outside. There was always something calming about being by the sea, even when it was blowing a gale or packed with holidaymakers, which, thankfully, it was not. It reminded her of Portugal, her other life. Would they get back there as planned? With everything sorted out, regular access to Lily, the chance to develop as a little, occasional, family of their own, without all the hassle? Or was Ruby going to put a spanner in the works again?

She'd already been round the shops twice, bought herself a pair of shoes, two tops, a lipstick, two more cups of coffee and an ice cream. She'd sat on a bench and watched the dogs straining against their leads along the prom, eager to get down onto the beach, the passing of distant boats out on the horizon, the funfair rides whirring away high in the sky at the end of the pier, a child's abandoned red balloon bobbing unsteadily in the shallows. Lily was scared of balloons. She remembered Michael telling her that. One thing to avoid if they ever did make it to some sort of birthday party for Lily. Or to McDonalds.

How much longer could she just idly wander about or sit here doing nothing but worry? Were they still going to have that burger later, or should she show willing and get some food shopping in, go back and make a start on something for dinner? If Lily wasn't with them, for whatever reason, then she for one would not be opting for a cheeseburger and chips out of choice. Michael wouldn't be in the mood for food at all.

She looked at her watch again. The sun had lowered itself in the sky and there was no longer any need to squint to read the tiny diamond-encrusted dial. Five thirty-three. They'd been gone hours. They must have arrived in London ages ago, and should be halfway back by now at least, if all had gone to plan. But there had been no call, no text, nothing. Her gut feeling, especially having read Ruby's vitriolic letter, was that things had very likely not gone to plan at all.

In her head, she started to play out little scenarios, hastily put-together stories of what might be happening. The best involved nothing more than a bit of heavy traffic and Michael's phone battery being dead, but in the worst versions Ruby was refusing to let them take Lily at all, refusing to even let them in, barricading the door, threatening to cut her wrists or something. From everything she'd heard, she wouldn't put it past her. A silly immature girl, a drama queen, a head case . . . Pick any one and you wouldn't be far wrong, according to Michael. But then, he was hardly unbiased, was he?

She wanted to believe the best of Ruby, to give her the benefit of the doubt, to believe that she would do what was right for Lily, as any mother would, or should. But Patsy was not a mother, and who could say what thoughts and feelings took over when you're trying to protect your child, and yourself, from being hurt? When you honestly think you've been badly done by? If she was Ruby, would she want to hand over her child, willingly, into the arms of the enemy? Probably not.

Patsy shook her head. She should stop all this. Recriminations didn't help anyone, and she had never set out to cause pain. She had simply fallen in love, and with a man who loved her back. What's done is done. Stop now. Stop worrying, and wait. All would become clear soon enough, when they got back.

She gathered up her bags and checked where she'd put the key, fingering it in her pocket, dreading what was to come. It was time to go home. No, that didn't feel right at all. Not home. Just time to go back. Somehow she couldn't imagine a time when she would ever be able to call Geraldine's house home.

*

The nurse took him as far as the door. 'She already has two visitors. If you could just wait a few moments while I go in first and find out if they're ready to leave. We don't like to crowd the room.'

Michael stared at the closed door. Through its small glass window he could make out a high bed, wires, and lots of machinery. There was a man with his back to the door, and a woman sitting in a hard chair to the right. He couldn't see their faces, had no idea who they were. For now, he couldn't quite bring himself to look at the bed or the lifeless shape inside it that must be Ruby. He wished he'd brought his mother with him, but he'd left her with Lily, in case she woke up. A familiar face, in an unfamiliar place. She would need that, poor kid. No, his mother was certainly better at this kind of thing. But he'd felt it was something he should do alone, at least to start with, while he found out what was what.

'Who are they? The visitors?'

'We've not known who she is, you see, your Ruby. One of our nurses, Laura, has befriended her. That's her in the chair. She's been calling in every now and then to sit with Ruby. Felt sorry for her, I think, having no one of her own to worry about her. And the other one's Paul . . . He's our hospital chaplain.'

'A priest? Why is there a priest?' Michael felt a sharp stab of fear, a sudden realisation that things here could be very serious indeed. This wasn't just Ruby being difficult, Ruby causing her usual problems. This was Ruby in danger. Unconscious, swathed in bandages and looking so small, buried so deep beneath all the unfamiliar machinery that, when he peered through the glass, he could hardly see her at all. They could lose her, couldn't they? Right now, today . . . Lily could lose her. He clasped his sweaty hand over his mouth, and hoped to God he wasn't about to throw up. 'Ruby's not . . . She's not going to die, is she?'

'We very much hope Ruby is not going to die, Mr Payne.' The nurse placed a cool hand on his wrist. 'It's just routine, honestly. A courtesy visit, if you like. Ruby was wearing a cross round her neck, you see. We thought he might be a help, a comfort to her. You know, if she is a Christian . . .'

'I'm not sure that she is really.'

'Well, as I say, if you could just hold on a tick.' She leaned on the door and slid inside the small room. The noise of the machines grew louder, then receded again as she closed the door behind her, leaving him alone and shaking outside.

They came out almost straight away. The woman he'd seen in the chair was more of a girl, about his own age, probably younger, pretty, with her hair swept up into some kind of loose untidy pony tail. The man was tall, thin, a few years older. He wore black, except for the dog collar, and was holding out his hand. 'Mr Payne? It's so good to see you. Paul Thomas. We were beginning to think poor Lily . . . I'm sorry, poor Ruby here was never going to be claimed!'

'Well, I'm not exactly claiming her. Just come to see how she is and what I can do. We're not together any more, you see, Ruby and me. But she doesn't really have anyone else. Just me, and my mother. And Lily, of course.'

'Your daughter?'

'Yes. Do you know about Lily? You called Ruby Lily just then . . . ?'

'A case of mistaken identity, I'm afraid. The last word she said before she blacked out, apparently. Everyone just assumed she was trying to tell them her own name.'

'But she was asking for Lily?'

'Looks like it. This is Laura, by the way. Staff Nurse Carter.' The girl smiled up at him.

'No uniform?'

'It's actually my day off. But I came in specially when I heard she'd finally been ID'd. I was working in A & E, you see, when she was brought in on Saturday. She was in a bad way, and on her own. I've been sort of keeping an eye on her since then, in case there was nobody else, and today . . . Well, I just wanted to be here when our mystery girl finally found her family.'

'That's very kind of you.'

'Not at all. I'm really glad you've come, and I'm sure she will be too. Nice to wake up to a face you recognise, not some stranger like me!' That was exactly what he'd just been thinking about Lily waking up and his mother being there beside her, the need for a familiar face. The girl must have been reading his mind. 'You can go in now, if you'd like to?' she went on, nodding towards the door.

Michael hesitated. She was right, of course. Ruby would need someone with her when she woke up, just like Lily did. But not *him*. He was the last person Ruby would want to see, wasn't he? And, if he was honest about it, he was scared. The enormity of what was happening in that room was too much for him. He didn't want it, couldn't face it. He shouldn't have to . . .

The uniformed nurse was just coming out of the room, her latest checks completed. She held the door open and nodded encouragement, but the prospect of what he might find in there was far too daunting.

'Do you want to be alone with her, or would you like me to go in with you?' Laura Carter seemed to sense his unease, and Michael nodded. He had never felt so grateful to a complete stranger in his life.

'Yes, please. If you wouldn't mind. I know it's your day off, and I don't want to keep you. For a minute or two, maybe? I'm just so new to all this. Never really had much to do with hospitals, except when Lily was born, and that was different, wasn't it? Nobody was actually ill or anything. Even when my dad died, we never had to . . . Well, he died without any warning, so there was none of this to contend with.' It was all just so completely out of the blue, so overwhelming. He'd come up here today expecting trouble, but just an argument, a slanging match, the usual Ruby-style battle. Not this. Never this. 'I'm sorry, but I'm a total coward. Don't even like the sight of a drop of blood when I cut myself shaving, and they let me leave the room when Ruby had the caesarean, so this . . . '

'It's okay. No need to explain. Come on.' She took hold of his elbow, nodded a goodbye to the priest and gently guided Michael into the room. 'She's just asleep, that's all. Try to ignore the machines. They're only there to give her some support. She's still Ruby. She won't bite!'

'You clearly don't know Ruby!' For the first time all day, Michael smiled.

'A feisty one, is she?'

'You could say that.' He edged towards the bed and forced himself to look at her. Her face was deathly pale, her eyes closed, and there was a tube in her mouth, a bandage around her head. Her hands lay on top of the covers, utterly still, and almost as white as the sheet. He'd never seen her look so young, so small, so vulnerable.

'Not today though.'

Despite every effort to be strong, his feet faltered, stopping a foot or two from the bed, and he felt his hands tremble where he'd put them, squeezed into tight fists deep inside his pockets. He closed his eyes for a moment, fighting the urge to run, and felt an unexpected tear break loose and start to roll down his cheek. 'Oh, my God, no. Not today.'

*

'Hello.' Geraldine eyed up the strange old lady who had been dozing in the chair by the bed and had just opened her eyes. 'We haven't met, have we? I'm Geraldine Payne, little Lily's gran. We went to the flat, you see, my son and I – to Ruby's flat – expecting to see Lily, and then all this . . . Look, it was very kind of you to come here with her. We do appreciate all that you've done.'

The woman sat upright and ran a hand over her crumpled clothes, presumably in an attempt at straightening them and making herself look more presentable. 'Not at all, not at all. I'm sure anyone would have done the same. The poor child was so scared, in that flat all by herself. She was hungry and none too clean, but most of all she just seemed to want a cuddle. Someone to pick her up and hug her. I was more than happy to be that person.'

'Thank you.'

'It must have been very lonely for her. Hard to imagine, really. Being all alone like that, having no human contact for so long. No one to look after her.' She sighed as if she knew only too well how that felt. 'She's too young to understand, isn't she?'

Geraldine closed her eyes. 'Oh, it doesn't bear thinking about, does it? Anything could have happened to her.'

'Well, luckily it didn't. Nothing too terrible anyway.' The woman leaned forward and held out her hand. 'I'm Mrs Munro, by the way, as I expect they've told you. But do call me Agnes, please. You must have met my son earlier, at the flats?'

'Ah, yes.' Geraldine nodded. As she took Agnes's hand and held it in her own, she noticed how thin it was, wrinkled in long deep furrows from wrist to fingertips, and, despite the overbearing clammy warmth in the ward, remarkably cold. The woman must easily be in her eighties, by the look of her.

They sat in silence for a while, each watching the sleeping child in the bed beside them.

'The social worker woman? Has she gone?'

'No, worse luck. Just popped out for a coffee, so she said, but I'll bet she's phoning her office while she's out of earshot. They'll be plotting now, deciding what to do. Which reminds me, I need to make a call myself. To my assistant. At the shop I run. Would you mind just keeping an eye on Lily for a moment?'

'Of course not.'

Geraldine stepped out into the corridor and called Kerry from the payphone, telling her what had happened and issuing a few half-hearted instructions. For the first time in ages, it didn't seem to matter much what was happening at the shop. She had bigger things to worry her now.

When she went back, Agnes was starting to gather her few things together. She picked up a carrier bag and passed it to Geraldine. 'The dress she was wearing. They took it off to examine her. It didn't really fit anyway,' she said. 'But I expect you'll want to take it home.'

Geraldine peeped inside. It was the Disney princess dress she'd bought for Lily's second birthday, almost a year ago. She could still remember her running about in it, spilling great dollops of creamy birthday cake down the front, refusing to take it off even at bedtime. Fancy her still having it after all this time. No wonder it didn't fit.

Agnes made an unsuccessful attempt at standing up, gripping the sides of the chair to give herself some leverage. 'Oh, my damn knees. The trials of old age. But I shouldn't still be here, I know. Time I got out of your way. It's been a traumatic day. Well, for all of us, obviously. And tiring. I'm sorry I nodded off there for a while, but now I must call my son and see if he can come and collect me. Have they said if she's all right now? Health-wise, I mean. And if she can go home?'

'They've bathed and dressed her cuts and scratches. I think they're just waiting now, to make sure there are no ill effects from the tablets she may have swallowed. But, as for home, I don't know. There's nobody there to look after her at home, is there? I'm not sure these Social Services people are going to let us just drive her away to Brighton. That's where I live, you see. We were expecting to take Lily down there for a few days today, for a little holiday.'

'But they're surely not going to stop you? You're her family. It's not as if you did anything wrong. She's going to need you more than ever right now.'

'I have no idea. I hope not. I'm not even sure what rights we have, if any. Nobody's saying much at all. I suppose they're still hoping to talk to Ruby. Find out what happened. Why she left her alone. There are bound to be investigations, consequences . . . Oh, dear. It's all such a mess.'

'How is young Ruby? They told me she's here.' Agnes was perched on the edge of her chair, somewhere halfway between sitting and standing, and looked as if she was wedged there, for the time being at least.

'Had some kind of road accident and is still out cold, so they say. It sounds bad. Very bad. I dread to think what could have happened to her. Or still might. Michael's gone up to see her, then I suppose we'll know more.' Geraldine let out a huge sigh and shook her head. 'Oh, Ruby. You silly, silly girl. How on earth did you let this happen?'

'I'm sure it was in no way deliberate. I don't really know your daughter-in-law, but . . . '

'Oh, she's not my daughter-in-law. Not technically anyway. They never actually married.' Geraldine sighed again. 'Never will now.'

'Sorry, I didn't realise. Young couples these days . . . Well, anyway, I didn't know her well, as I say, but from what I saw, she did always seem to be very close to little Lily.'

'Yes, she was.'

'She must have had her reasons for going out like that, and leaving Lily behind.'

'I'm sure she must. I just can't think what on earth they were.'

'But there is one good thing, you know.'

Geraldine couldn't for the life of her imagine what that might be. 'Really?'

'Just think what might have happened if she'd taken the little one out with her. That car might have hit the pair of them, and then what?'

Geraldine clutched her hand to her mouth. 'Oh, I hadn't thought, but you're right. That would have been awful. Lily's so small. And if she'd been in one of those little buggy things she wouldn't have stood a chance, would she? It could have been tipped up, crushed, smashed to smithereens. Oh, Agnes . . . I know I've said it before, but it really doesn't bear thinking about.'

Their conversation was cut short then by a muffled sound from the bed. Lily was waking up, stretching her legs out and opening her eyes, fixing them first on Agnes, straight in front of her, and then slowly turning to Geraldine. 'Granny?' she said, her voice very small and sleepy, tinged with curiosity. 'Am I going to go to your house now?'

'I hope so, darling.' Geraldine moved forward, throwing her arms around Lily and planting a big red lipsticky kiss on her cheek. 'Oh, Lily, it's so good to see you. Granny has missed you so much!'

'Yuck,' said Lily, quickly wiping the kiss away with the back of her hand as she sat herself up and pushed Geraldine's arms away. 'Mummy didn't come home. Are we going to find her now?'

'Yes, I think we are. Soon. Very soon. Your daddy's gone to look for her now.'

'Daddy?' Lily swung her legs over the edge and climbed off the bed. 'I saw Daddy. He was under the pillow.'

Geraldine had no idea what she meant. 'Did you? Well, he's not under the pillow now. He's right here, in the hospital, with us.'

'Can I see Daddy now? Can I?' Lily tottered the few paces it took to reach Agnes and held her arms up to be cuddled again. Curling into the old lady's lap, she stuck her thumb, dressing and all, into the corner of her mouth and gazed at Geraldine, still sitting on the bed. 'Granny . . .'

'Yes, Lily?' Geraldine fought back the instant wave of jealousy that was sweeping over her, seeing her granddaughter with this stranger, her small arms locked around her, her face squashed lovingly against that funny little green cardigan as they both perched rather precariously on the edge of the chair.

'Where's Archie?'

Geraldine had no inkling who Archie was. A friend? A pet? Some new boyfriend Ruby was seeing? She felt a lump rise into her throat. Oh, how little she knew about her granddaughter now. It had only been a few months but things changed so quickly. She should have made more effort, should never have left it so long.

'I don't know, darling. We'll ask Daddy when he comes back, shall we? He'll know where Archie is, I'm sure.'

Agnes looked at her and smiled, almost apologetically. Don't worry, the smile said. You're her granny. It's you she loves, not me. She's still confused, still uncertain about what's happening. 'Well, I think I should be going. Let you sort things out now, as a family.' She tried again to stand, tried to hand Lily over to her grandmother, but the little one clung like a limpet.

'No. Stay.' Geraldine smiled back. No use blaming the woman. If Lily felt secure with her, then so be it. She had as good as rescued her, after all. 'A few minutes more, anyway. Here, give me the number and I'll call your son for you. We could wait for Michael to come back and use his mobile. I've left mine in the car. Or use the payphone outside, if you'd rather do it now?'

'Yes, all right. It's very kind of you. He'll be wondering what's happening, I'm sure. William. His name's William. Munro. Well, obviously it's Munro! But you must let me give you the money for the call.'

'No, no, it's only a few pennies. Now, you stay right there with Lily for a minute or two, at least until Michael comes back. I know he'll want to thank you.' She stood and stretched, ruffling Lily's hair while she waited. 'So, do you have the number, Agnes?'

'Oh, yes, of course. Just give me a moment to think. I have

it written down on a pad by the phone at home. I don't call it enough to know it off by heart, you see. It will come to me in a minute. Oh, but he might still be at my flat, of course. That's one number I do know!'

That's sad, Geraldine thought, taking both scribbled-down numbers and heading for the phone. Not being sure of her own son's number. Another case of life, and time, and distance, coming between an ageing mother and her grown-up son . . . She knew that scenario only too well. Could she reel off Michael's number without the aid of her address book? Probably not. They might have something more in common than met the eye, she and this old lady. But, of course, she was just being fanciful. She knew nothing about Agnes's life. She might have a husband, and ten children, and hordes of grandchildren who visited every day, for all she knew.

But somehow, watching the way she clung to Lily, and Lily clung right back, she knew she was right. Agnes was not just alone, but lonely, and the two weren't always quite the same thing.

*

It was two hours later, with the Munro woman long gone and his mother hardly able to keep her eyes open, that Barbara Freeman finally gave Michael the good news. 'You can take Lily home this evening, Mr Payne,' she said, smiling, but the smile didn't quite reach her eyes and he still wasn't sure he could trust her. 'Doctor seems happy with her, and says there's no reason to keep her overnight. I think she's had enough separation for a while. It's her family she needs now. Obviously we can't stop you taking her wherever you like. You are her father, after all. But . . . '

'But you'd rather we didn't swan off back to Brighton?'

'We will be calling a case conference, getting together to talk about Lily, within the next week or so, to decide a plan of action. It's routine in cases like this. Of course we all want what's best for her, and your input into that process will be very important. It would be useful to everyone if you stayed in the area.'

'She's not at any risk, you know. Not when she's with me.'

'I'm sure that's true, but decisions are going to have to be made, to determine what risk there might be if and when she is returned to her mother's care. I'm sure you can understand our concerns. So, can I ask, where do you expect to be staying?'

'At Ruby's flat, I suppose. *Our* flat. I've still got a set of keys. Still have my name on the lease. So, my mother and I can squeeze in there for a day or two, and then Lily can at least have some normality, sleep in her own bed . . . '

'That's good. How are you taking her home? You have a car here? And a properly fitted car seat, I assume?'

'Car seat?'

'For Lily. You do realise that, by law, she can only travel in a regulation seat?'

'Well, no, I hadn't thought . . . '

'But you were going to take her to Brighton today?'

'In the back seat. On my mother's lap. I don't know. I hadn't really thought about that. I suppose I should have, shouldn't I?'

She looked at him sternly, then wavered a bit and forced a smile. 'I have one with me. A car seat.'

'You do?'

'I could drive Lily home for you if you like. I would like to take a look at her living arrangements anyway. Kill two birds with one stone, save coming back and bothering you tomorrow.'

'Well, yes. All right. You could follow me maybe? Or I'll come with you and Lily, and Mum can drive our car home. I don't feel I should leave her alone again. With a stranger, I mean. No offence. But I'll have to come back here to the hospital, won't I? Tomorrow. To see how Ruby is, maybe let Lily see her. How will I . . .?'

'You'll have to acquire a seat, I'm afraid. Or come on the bus.'

He looked the woman right in the eyes, expecting some kind of defiance, and saw nothing there but compassion and a hint of tiredness. She meant well. Just doing her job.

'Right,' he said, in the calmest voice he could muster. 'Let's get her discharged and out of here then, shall we?'

It was only halfway out to the car park, their three pairs of feet scrunching in unison across the ground in the encroaching gloom of another cold wet evening, that he realised. The woman had a car seat in her car. Why? Had she come here expecting to take Lily away with her? To fill in her forms, tick her little boxes, and drive her off somewhere, still alone and scared, to be with strangers? He slowed to let his mother catch up, holding Lily against his chest, pulling his coat closed around her, as he watched the woman open up the back door of her car and beckon him forward. Thank God they'd got here when they did. A day later and his daughter might have been taken away from him.

They were almost at the front door of the flat, the two cars parked one behind the other, when he remembered Patsy. He hadn't called her. In fact, he hadn't given her a single thought since the moment they'd walked into this awful mess all those hours ago.

CHAPTER EIGHTEEN

Ruby

My mother has black hair. I think it's black. Although she's right here in the room with me, I can't see her very clearly. She keeps turning her back, walking away from me and then, just when I think she's gone, she comes back again, another day, with some dirty second-hand doll in her arms, or a bunch of over-ripe bananas.

Her name is Dorothy. I know that because Mrs Castle calls her that as she pours the tea, but I just call her Mummy. She smells of cheap soap, or maybe it's talcum powder, and too many peppermints – and booze. I don't know if I knew that then, but I know it now. I think it's gin. Sweet, almost like perfume; on her breath, her clothes, her skin. The soapy smell wafts alongside it but doesn't disguise it.

Mummy wears flat shoes with soft bendy soles. They are not always very clean, but they are always very quiet. I think that's why I don't hear her leave sometimes. I feel the silence, look round from playing with the doll, and she's gone. The tea is still warm in the cup, and she's hardly sipped it. I run to the window and climb onto a chair and I can see she's already out of the

Vivien Brown

gate, the top of her head showing over the tall hedge, bobbing up and down as she walks away, tipping back to face the sun as she swigs something from a bottle. I feel Mrs Castle's arm behind me, steadying the chair, making sure I don't fall. She does a lot of that. Steadying. She's very good at it.

'Shall we go and make some cakes, Ruby?' she says. 'Pink or white icing? You choose.' In the kitchen, I pound the spoon around in the bowl, crushing the sugar into the marg, crash the eggs against the side, and try to get rid of the smell of her. But it's there on the doll. When I pick her up, it's in her dress, in her matted, nylon, second-hand hair.

I start to cry, right into the bowl, tiny trickly raindrops landing on a bed of flour, and I mix them in quickly so they disappear and I can pretend everything's going to be all right, and wonder whether the cakes will taste of my tears.

CHAPTER NINETEEN

'Where are we all going to sleep?' Geraldine sank into Ruby's sofa, kicked off her shoes and pushed away a mound of scattered toys with her toes. She glugged down what was left of her milkless tea, made a space on the cluttered coffee table and deposited the empty mug.

'Take Ruby's bed. I don't mind. I can't say I really fancy sleeping in it again, to be honest with you. I'm happy enough on the sofa. Not sure I'll be able to sleep much anyway.'

'And we need to eat, Michael. I took a peek in the fridge freezer and there's virtually nothing. In fact, the door wasn't properly closed, so whatever there was is probably ruined anyway. Is there anything nearby? A late-night grocery shop? A takeaway place? We need the basics. Milk, bread, juice for Lily, something for breakfast . . .'

'Don't you think we should get Lily to bed first?'

'Well, she must be hungrier than the lot of us, poor soul. The odd biscuit and a bag of crisps at the hospital, and whatever the old lady downstairs gave her, isn't going to do the trick, is it? She needs fattening up. A treat, to take her mind off what's been happening.' She looked across at Lily, sitting silently on the carpet, surrounded by the big chunky pieces of a giant floor puzzle Michael had found in a cupboard, but not showing much interest in trying to fit them together. 'You were talking about McDonalds earlier, weren't you?'

'It's very late.'

'In the circumstances, I hardly think we need to clock-watch, Michael. Can't you just pop out in the car and fetch something back? Something with chips, milkshake, one of those boxes with a toy. It will cheer her up. I don't know about you, but my stomach feels like my throat's been cut. Please. Anything . . . '

'But I can't leave Lily. After the time she's had, she needs me.'

'She'll be fine with me. Now that social services woman has finally gone we need to try to get things back to normal. Lily can have a bit of granny time. Maybe she can help me to clean up a bit. There's an awful smell in her room, and a nasty stain on the carpet and I'll have to change the beds. I couldn't help noticing they are both a bit crumpled, and Lily's is decidedly damp. Where did Ruby keep the spare sheets?'

'Don't say it like she's in the past tense, Mother. Airing cupboard, I suppose. And I need to call Patsy. She must be wondering where in the world we are. I need to explain what's been going on, though I hardly know where to start, and I'll have to tell her we won't be back tonight.'

'Or for quite a few nights, I should imagine. Whatever are we going to wear? I didn't set out with the intention of not going back. I've got nothing with me. No toothbrush, no nightclothes, no spare underwear . . . '

'Least of our problems.'

'Even so, we do have to be practical.'

'Try something of Ruby's.'

'Michael, you may not have noticed but we are about forty years and a good three dress sizes apart.'

'The Munro woman then. Agnes. Go downstairs and ask her. She may have something, a spare nightie or a dressing gown to see you through tonight at least. Maybe she can let you borrow a pair of knickers too. I can just see you in pink flannelette, or some of those old-fashioned knee-length thermals!' He laughed, circling his arms out wide around his hips in a poor imitation of how she might look in an old lady's underwear. 'Oh, don't look so shocked. I'm kidding. I'm sure we can find a shop in the morning. For now, just keep the ones you're wearing on. Nobody, as far as I know, has ever died of wearing their pants two days in a row. Or go commando if you have to.'

He picked up his keys and wallet, tucked his phone into his pocket, kissed Lily on the top of the head and went off out in search of food. He'd be a while, Geraldine was sure. He'd be on the phone to that Patricia as soon as he was out of earshot, so there was plenty of time to have a good nose about.

She started with the big cardboard box that had been waiting outside the door, more curious than Michael obviously was to find out what was inside. It was clothes, mostly men's shirts, and a pile of hangers. She couldn't think why they were there, and when she lifted one or two out they smelled a bit strange. Musty. She carried the box in and dropped it down in the corner of the kitchen, folded down the ironing board, brushed up a pile of biscuit crumbs into the dustpan and ran a mop around the floor. Gradually, the place started to look tidier, and smell fresher.

In Lily's room, the small window at the top was slightly open, bringing in a chilly breeze and, despite the whiff of old nappies that pervaded the air, she quickly banged it shut and eased the curtains across. She found a spray bottle of carpet cleaner under the sink and hastily sprayed and scrubbed at the carpet until the worst of it had been sorted, trying not to breathe in as she worked.

The bed needed stripping, and she was pleased to find, as she pulled the sheets off, that there was a plastic covering underneath so at least the mattress had survived without staining. She found clean sheets and pillow cases piled up in the airing cupboard, and swiftly and efficiently restored the bed and the room to some kind of order, aware all the while of Lily standing behind her in the doorway, her thumb locked firmly in her mouth, watching every move she made.

'Come on, Lily. Would you like to help Granny to make Mummy's bed nice and clean now?'

'Is Mummy coming home?'

'Soon. Not tonight though. Remember what Daddy told you, on the way home in the car? Mummy's a little bit poorly, and she needs to have a good long sleep to help her get better.' She knelt down beside Lily and kissed her on the forehead. 'So, tonight Granny will be sleeping here, in Mummy's bed. We can have our breakfast together in the morning and then we can go to the shops. Would you like that? Just you and me.'

Lily nodded, grabbing hold of Geraldine's free hand as she carried yet more sheets through to the other bedroom.

'Archie!' Lily let go of her hand and ran excitedly into the room, bending down to scoop up a toy from the floor. 'You naughty bear, where have you been?'

So, this was the mysterious Archie! For the first time since they'd brought her home, Lily was smiling. She sat on the carpet telling Archie everything she could remember about her trip in an ambulance and her hospital stay, much of it completely made-up.

Geraldine smiled. She just wanted to sit down on the floor with her and hug her but she knew she must be starting to smell unpleasant by now. The mingled scents of bleach, dust, damp bedding and poo had worked their way into her hands and hair. She opened the wardrobe, hoping that, if she stripped off and jumped into the bath later, there might be something she could wear afterwards. Maybe a loose robe or something but, as she'd suspected, Ruby's few clothes were all clearly way too small. As she ran her hands through them she noticed that they only filled half the wardrobe. The rest of the space was packed with shirts. Men's shirts, all neatly pressed and on covered hangers. Odd. If Ruby had found herself a new man, surely there would be other stuff. Evidence, dotted about the place. An extra toothbrush, a can of shaving gel, some trousers . . . Geraldine closed the door. Curious though she was, it wasn't her business any more, what Ruby did, or who she saw.

She began working on the double bed, pulling off sheets and easing the quilt from its crumpled cover. As she tossed the pillows out of the way and onto the floor, she saw what looked like a small piece of shiny card. It was wedged between the top of the mattress and the headboard, but it was only when she picked it up and turned it over that she realised what it was, and what it meant. A lump came up into Geraldine's throat and she fought back an unexpected tear. It was an old picture of Michael.

Despite everything, it would appear that Ruby might still have feelings for her son after all.

*

Laura fought her way to the crowded bar and came back with three halves of lager and a handful of crisp packets. 'Oh my God, what a day!' she said, thumping down onto the long cushioned bench seat in the window.

'You weren't even at work, were you? I thought it was your day off?' Fiona broke her way into a bag of cheese and onion, closely inspecting her pink-painted thumbnail, holding it under one of the frilly wall lamps in search of enough light, as if she feared it might have got irrevocably chipped in the process.

'It was. But, Fi, you won't believe what happened . . . '

'That girl's kid only went and turned up,' Gina butted in, never one to stand on ceremony and eager to get the story told so she could get on with the serious business of getting drunk. 'Seems Laura's mystery girl had gone out and left her daughter by herself before inconveniently walking under a passing car.'

'Gina! Don't be so heartless. She can hardly have meant to get run over?'

'I suppose not. But what a lot of fuss. The police and Children's Services barging in, and the old lady who found her, then the little girl's dad and grandmother rolling up as well. Give me a kid with a plain old broken wrist or a burst appendix any day! Patch them up and send them on their way.'

'So . . .' Fiona was trying to catch up but was struggling to take it all in. 'They know who she is now then? Your Lily?'

'Yes, only she's not called Lily at all. The child is.'

'I'm confused now.'

'When aren't you?' Gina retorted, somewhat cruelly. 'Now, let's stop all this work talk and get back to what we usually talk about on a night out.'

'Men!' all three of them chorused together, dissolving into uncontrollable laughter that sent Fiona into a choking fit when a chunk of crisp went down the wrong way.

'Talking of which . . .' Gina's eyes were trailing a small group of men who'd just come in, slipping their jackets off as they moved across towards the bar. One of them already had his wallet out and was asking the others what they wanted to drink.

'Hmmm, four of them, and only three of us.' Fiona, always the most forward, had stopped laughing and was considering the possibilities. 'Awkward. But at least it gives us some element of choice. I'll take the blond one. I've had enough of tall dark strangers lately. I fancy a change.'

Laura cringed. She didn't know where to put herself. They'd obviously heard what Fiona had said, or they'd realised there were three pairs of curious female eyes staring in their direction. Either way, they were staring right back now, amused smiles on their faces, and she just wanted to hide herself away, under the table, behind a pot plant, anywhere. Fiona and her big mouth! She could feel her face burning red as the one with the wallet looked straight at her and she immediately saw who it was. Even without the dog collar, he was instantly recognisable, unmistakeable. It was Paul Thomas. Out of her league, quite possibly the man of her dreams, untouchable because he was a priest, Paul Thomas. He smiled, held up a hand to his mouth and wiggled it up and down in a clumsy sort of 'can I get one for you?' gesture and, when she shook her head, he turned away, busying himself with a twenty-pound note, then juggling pint glasses and change.

She had just enough time to compose herself before he was elbowing his way through the busy pub and bringing his friends over to join them at their table. Introductions were made all round, and Fiona quickly squashed herself along to make room for Ian, the blond one she'd clearly already earmarked for herself, to sit down next to her while the others went in search of extra chairs.

'Well, Laura,' Paul said, once he'd placed his chair right in front of her. 'How about our Ruby then? Good to know she's found her family. Or should I say, that her family have found her? Thanks for letting me know, by the way. Now all we have to pray for is that she'll wake up.'

'Oh, she will.'

'How can you be so sure?'

'She has a daughter to live for, doesn't she?'

'Is it really as simple as that?'

'I think so. Little Lily's just as likely to bring her back as any one of your prayers. Love can be a powerful thing. The maternal kind especially.'

'Touché!' He laughed. 'Not really a believer yourself, then?'

'In God? I'm not sure. In love, absolutely.'

As soon as she'd said it, she wished she hadn't. But then they got caught up in other conversations around the table, about football and the weather and who was watching that police drama thing with the old Doctor Who in it, and more drinks were bought and there was talk of them all going for a curry together, and even though both kept popping in and out of Laura's thoughts, neither Ruby nor love were mentioned again for the rest of the evening.

*

Patsy had only picked at her dinner. She had made a quick lasagne just in case, and left enough for Michael and his mother on plates still being kept warm in the oven, but it would be overheated and ruined by now. She scraped the leftovers from her own plate into the bin and turned the oven off.

Something must have gone badly wrong or they would all have been back hours ago. Briefly she imagined them all chatting, laughing, eating without her, Geraldine peering suspiciously at her burger and asking how much fat was in it, Michael wolfing down his fries in big handfuls, like he always did, and adding extra salt. But, no. If that was where they were, he would have called. Something was wrong.

She dug her mobile out from her bag and checked again for messages. Nothing. She had tried calling a couple of times but it just went straight to voicemail. Either out of signal or, more likely, switched off. He obviously didn't want to be disturbed. In a way, she was glad to be apart from it all. Michael and Ruby's arguments weren't her arguments. She would have just been a bystander, an unwanted hanger-on, if she'd gone with them, maybe even a catalyst, adding to the already volatile atmosphere and making it all ten times worse. Still, it would be good to at least have been kept in the loop. A few minutes to send a quick text couldn't be that hard to find, surely?

She was just starting to wonder if perhaps she should give up on any of them making an appearance, wash up, watch some TV and get herself ready for an early night, when the phone finally rang. The sudden burst of *You make me feel like dancing* broke into the silence and made her jump. It had seemed a good choice for a ringtone when she'd bought herself a new phone a few weeks back, a bit of fun that represented how Michael made her feel, but now it just sounded inappropriate and flippant. She would change it later.

'Michael? Where are you? What's going on?' She tried hard to keep her voice light, not to come across as the nagging partner keen to check on his every move, but she wasn't sure she'd succeeded.

'Everything's fine. Well, not fine exactly, but it's being sorted. Oh, God, Pats, it's a long story . . . I don't know where to even start but I'm afraid we won't be back any time soon. Ruby's been in some kind of accident. She's in the hospital. And so was Lily for a time, but she's out now, and back at the flat.'

'No! That's terrible. What happened? Is she all right? Lily, I mean. Well, Ruby too, obviously. But, oh, you know what I mean.' She was rambling. She must stop that. Stop, Patsy. Let him talk. Just listen.

'Ruby was hit by a car. Pretty badly. She'd left Lily at home by herself. God knows why.' He went quiet for a moment, long enough to make Patsy peer at the screen to make sure they hadn't been cut off, and then he was back. 'Look, Pats, we're going to have to stop here, for tonight at least. I need to go back to the hospital in the morning, let Lily see her mum if that's allowed, and the Social Services people are involved now, so I've more or less promised not to leave the area. Will you be all right there by yourself? Or do you want to come up? It's a bit crowded here. I'm stopping over at Ruby's, by the way. And Mum too, of course.'

Patsy took a deep breath. 'No, Michael. I don't think me coming there would help anyone at all, would it?'

'It would be great to see you, though. I could do with the support. And a hug. Someone to make everything seem more normal, you know . . .'

'Normal? Nothing about this sounds very normal to me. No, I'm fine here. Honestly. You're better off without me getting in the way. You must be short of bed space as it is, and you won't catch me bunking in with your mother! In fact, if you're not coming back for a while, I might just catch a train up to see my family. We were going to go up there soon anyway, weren't we? It's been ages since I've seen them. It'll give you some time to sort things out. I promise I'll be back, as soon as Ruby's okay, as soon as you need me.'

She realised he'd gone silent again. 'Michael? Are you still there? Did you hear what I said?'

'Oh, Patsy, sweetheart.' She could hear the sigh that escaped in the pause between his words. 'What if Ruby isn't okay? What then?'

'Is that a possibility? Is it that bad?'

'Yes, I think it is, but I couldn't take it all in. It all came as such a shock, all the medical stuff, the jargon they use, and I'm not good with illness. Never have been. You know that.'

'Neither am I.' Patsy remembered being sick on the plane. The taste, the smell, that awful gagging feeling. Just the thought of it almost brought her lasagne rushing back up into her throat. 'But tomorrow will feel different, won't it? Get a good night's sleep and you'll be better at asking the right questions. And anyway . . .'

'Yes?'

'You've got Geraldine with you. She can be pretty formidable, I bet. She'll soon suss out what's what. You just concentrate on Lily. How is she anyway?'

'Beautiful. And big. I can hardly believe how much she's grown. And she's not hurt. Just a few bumps and scratches. In fact, she's remarkably okay, considering what she's been through.'

'That's all that matters then. Lily. Healthy, and spending time with her daddy.'

'I suppose so. Look, Pats. I have to go. None of us has eaten, and I don't want to leave Lily for too long. Even with Mum. I'll call you in the morning, all right? Let me know if you head off up to your parents. Don't be gone too long. I miss you already.'

They made their usual kissing noises down the phone and Patsy waited for him to say 'I love you' before they hung up. She hated being the first to do it, knowing he was still there, still connected. The three words were like a signal they had always used to show that the call was over. A bit like 'Roger, over and out', but with more feeling. But when she looked at the phone, it was back to its blue sky wallpaper screen, and he was gone, the magic words unsaid.

Right. Onto the internet, and check the train times. She couldn't sit here, twiddling her thumbs in someone else's house, waiting for a man to say he loved her when his thoughts were so clearly elsewhere. Time to spend some time with her own family. She was looking forward to that, with or without Michael.

It was only later, when she'd ripped off the nylon sheets and replaced them with pretty cotton ones she'd found in the drawer under the bed, and was tucked up with a magazine and a cup of tea, her route worked out, her train tickets bought and her case repacked, that she suddenly remembered something Michael had said. Social Services? How did they come into the picture? Didn't they only get involved when there had been neglect or abuse? No wonder Michael had sounded so stressed. Whatever it was Ruby had done, if that lot were sticking their oar in, then things must be serious. You read about these things all the time. Perhaps they would take Lily away, put her into care or something, or perhaps they would hand her over to Michael permanently. Might they do that?

Oh, my God! Patsy let her tea go cold beside her, the magazine stuck open on the same page across her lap. Things could be about to change beyond all recognition. She could be a stepmother a lot sooner than she'd expected. And a full-time one, at that. What would happen then, to her career, her home, her relationship with Michael? What would happen to her life?

*

'I think we should ask if there's anything we can do to help.' Agnes was at the table, still in her dressing gown, eating porridge, when William came in, dripping rain and leaving a trail of muddy footprints across her kitchen floor.

'Haven't we got enough to worry about trying to fix your ceiling?' William pulled off his wet coat and the slightly damp jacket he'd been wearing underneath, and dumped a carrier bag of paintbrushes and old turps bottles on the worktop, alongside an almost full giant-sized tin of emulsion he'd found at the back of his garage. Susan had abandoned it as 'not quite right' after just a few brush strokes when she'd wanted to decorate the hall at home, and it was close enough in colour to the paint his mother already had up there. All these shades of white looked pretty much the same to his untrained eye anyway, once you got past the fancy creamed buttermilk and fluffy cloud names. If it didn't match, which, let's face it, it probably wouldn't, then he was happy enough to paint the whole room if necessary, ceiling and walls all the same colour. He had nothing much else to do.

He hadn't slept well. Despite his assertion that it was none of their business, and that simply being the ones to find the child and rescue her did not give them automatic rights to be included in whatever happened next, he had found it hard to put the little girl out of his mind.

'But I'd like to do something for them. Offer them breakfast at least. You can be sure that fridge up there is not packed with bacon and eggs, and they probably haven't even got their own toiletries with them. Imagine not being able to brush your teeth properly.'

He wondered when exactly his mother had last had any teeth of her own to brush. As far as he knew she kept hers in a glass at night, fizzing away in some kind of tablet stuff. But that was being unkind. He knew she meant well.

'I suppose so,' he said, half-heartedly, hoping she might let the whole thing drop, but there was no chance of that, it seemed.

'William, they may not even have milk.'

'Is that really the disaster you're making it out to be? Will the world as we know it come to an end without milk? Anyway, you said he went out last night, in the car. The shops are less than a quarter of a mile away. I'm sure he would have picked up the basics at least.'

'Even so . . . They must have plenty to worry about without having to trudge round the supermarket. And that poor girl in hospital still.'

William sighed. He'd have to go along with it. 'Right. What is it you want me to do?'

'Just go up there, will you? Knock and ask.'

'Ask what, exactly?'

'Well, just be neighbourly. Invite them down here. For a cup of tea, or a bite to eat or something. I'd like to know how little Lily is, and perhaps see her. So, just find out if we can . . . Oh, I don't know. Use your imagination. Meanwhile, I am going to get myself washed and dressed.'

William stared after her as she hobbled out of the room. He heard her bedroom door close, and moved through to the living room where he sat for a while in the old armchair, trying to summon up the energy, the will, the courage, to venture upstairs. Whatever could he say that didn't sound like an intrusion? Like they were a couple of curious old bystanders nosing into others' misfortunes?

He looked at his watch. It was only twenty past nine and, for all he knew, they might still be asleep. Yesterday had been a traumatic day for everyone, and a tiring one, not to mention the stress and the worry that poor family must be feeling. But he knew from bitter experience that when his mother got an idea into her head she could be extremely persistent and frighteningly unwavering, and consequently virtually impossible to ignore. The many outpourings of vitriol that had followed in the wake of his separation from Susan were testimony to that.

He felt Smudge move with a sudden furry flick against his leg. The old cat appeared by his side, asking for food. He must have been hiding underneath the table.

He plonked some cat food in a bowl and replaced the water in another, then took a deep breath and stepped out of the flat into the cluttered hallway. The child's buggy was still there, pushed against the far wall, although the other one had gone. The woman up on the second floor must have taken her baby out somewhere. There were a couple of flyers on the mat inside the front door, pizza ads by the look of them. He didn't bother picking them up. It was still too early for the proper post.

One of the young men from the flat at the top came down, nodding as he stopped to tie up a shoe lace on the bottom step. He was dressed for a cycle ride, in black lycra leggings, already wearing his helmet and carrying a bottle of water. He wondered what they did, this one, who he thought was maybe called Jason, and his skinny flatmate. For work, that is. They certainly seemed to keep odd hours, but if they liked to keep themselves to themselves, it was no business of his.

All he was doing, of course, standing here gazing into space and pondering other people's lives, was putting off going to the flat upstairs. He wasn't quite sure why he felt so awkward about it. They seemed nice enough people, not likely to bite his head off just for being friendly.

He squeezed past the lad in lycra and took the stairs two at a time, the most exercise he'd had for weeks, and the surefire way of making sure he just gone on with it and didn't have the chance to change his mind. He tapped very gently on the door. If they were still sleeping it off, he didn't want to be the one to wake them, but it only took a few seconds until there were sounds of movement from inside.

It was the woman who opened the door. She was still in the jeans and blouse she'd been wearing yesterday, but her hair was freshly washed and still quite damp, and she was wearing more make-up than she had before. In a way, she reminded him of Susan, well turned out and made-up this early in the morning, even when she probably had nowhere special to go.

'Oh! It's Mr Munro, isn't it? What can we do for you?' The smile lit up her face, accentuating the little lines around her eyes.

'William, please . . . And it's more the other way round actually. My mother was wondering, well, we both were – if there was anything we could do for you. You know, to help. It can't be easy for you, landing here unprepared. Breakfast perhaps, if you haven't already eaten?'

'That's very kind of you, but we couldn't put you to all that trouble. Look, come in for a minute, won't you? My son is just getting Lily dressed. Can I get you a tea or something? I would like to say thank you for yesterday. For finding Lily . . .'

William waved her thanks away with an embarrassed flick

of the hand and a shake of his head, and stepped over the threshold into the flat. It looked different now, tidier, everything back where it was supposed to be. It was hard to imagine that just yesterday that little girl had been trapped here all by herself.

'Tea would be lovely. Thanks.'

He followed her into the living room. There were a few toys on the floor but the handbag and its scattered contents had gone from the sofa. The smell had gone too, a slither of fresh air wafting in through a partially open window. He didn't like to sit, not without being asked to, so while she went off to the kitchen to boil a kettle he stayed standing, looking out of the window at the street below. Life going by, in a flurry of dripping umbrellas and splashing puddles and mushy leaves. It was exactly the same scene he had glimpsed from his mother's window just moments before, but the view was subtly different from up here. Different angle, more bird's eye, more panoramic.

There was a big white van pulling up outside, the driver obviously looking for somewhere to park. A large man with a bald head jumped down and started to make his way up the small driveway, feet scrunching through the gravel, and up the steps to the door. He didn't ring any of the bells on the wall, just walked straight in so someone must have left the front door open. Probably the cyclist, still fiddling about in the hall. The bald man was carrying a large cardboard box, not unlike the one they'd found outside the door when they were trying to get to Lily.

Before he could think any more about it, the woman came back in. Geraldine, that was her name. He'd been trying to remember it ever since she'd let him in. 'Sorry. No milk,' she said, apologetically. 'Michael only thought to buy a pint last night and it's gone already. Would you like it black? Or a coffee instead?'

'It's okay. Don't bother. Really. I wasn't thirsty anyway. And I meant what I said about breakfast. Come down to us, all of you. I can promise you milk aplenty, and my mother does a mean fry-up, if you fancy it. By the way, there's a van outside. *Iron Maiden,* it says on the side. The driver's just let himself in. Anything to do with you?'

She shook her head. 'They're a rock group, aren't they? *Iron Maiden?* What would they be doing coming to see me?' She giggled, flicking her hair back, and William couldn't help noticing her eyes. How blue they were, and how they sparkled as she laughed

He laughed back. 'Heard about your legendary head banging, perhaps? Come to offer you a job as their roadie? Answering your fan letter?'

'I don't think so.'

'Oh, you're wrong. It is you they're after!' William turned his head towards the hall where the sound of a sudden thumping on the door had made them both jump. Geraldine went to answer it.

'Morning, love.' The bald man was on the step, as broad as he was tall, filling the doorway. He spoke with a very loud and very strong London accent. 'Where's young Ruby then? I called for the stuff the other day and she weren't here then neither. It won't do, you know. I ain't got all day to keep coming back 'ere willy-nilly.'

'Stuff?' William could hear Geraldine put on a new voice, much posher than the one she'd been using just seconds before.

Susan used to do that too, usually when she was talking to washing machine repair men, window cleaners, people like that. It was a defence mechanism, he knew, a way of sounding authoritative, to stop them taking advantage, adding on ludicrous call-out charges or trying their luck with a bit of flirting over a cup of tea. William wandered out into the hall and stood behind Geraldine. Safety in numbers, in case of trouble. He wasn't sure he liked the man's tone.

'Yeah, the ironing, love. I've brought her another lot, but she's behind. Not handed over the previous yet. There isn't a problem, is there? Boss won't be too pleased if it's not done.'

He dumped the box he was carrying at her feet and peered into the flat. 'Ready, is it?'

'I'm sorry.' Geraldine was flustered, William could tell. 'I'm afraid I have absolutely no idea what you're talking about.'

'Then let's start again, shall we? Ruby does the ironing, I pick it up, I bring her the next lot, she does it, I pick it up, she gets paid. Get it now?'

'The box, Geraldine . . .' William stepped forward and placed a calming hand on her arm. 'There was a box outside when we were here yesterday. Where is it now? Did you bring it inside?'

'This, do you mean?' She disappeared into the kitchen for a moment and came back, dragging the box along the carpet.

The man bent and opened it. 'Not done, is it?'

'Well, no. It would seem not. But we didn't know anything about it, did we?' She turned to William for support. 'Only, Ruby . . . she's in hospital at the moment. We don't actually know how long for. So, I'm afraid the ironing is the last of our worries right now.'

'Sorry 'bout that, but he won't like it. She could lose her job over this.' He stood and scratched his head, the light from the bulb behind him shining in great glary patches across the top of it where the raindrops hadn't quite dried. 'I suppose I'd best take it all back then. And the lot from the day before. Where's that then, eh? Don't know what he's going to say about any of this. She could at least have let us know, Ruby, I mean. About not being able to do it. She's usually pretty reliable. Have to get someone else now.'

'No!' William stopped him, just as he was about to walk away, balancing the two boxes now, new and old, in his burly tattooed arms. 'It's all right. Leave them. We wouldn't want Ruby to get into trouble or to lose her job. Or her pay. You say there's some more somewhere? We'll find it and it'll be done. All of it. Later today. Five o'clock suit you?'

'Well, it'll have to, I suppose. Five though? No later. No messing me about. I'll come back at five, right?'

'Right.'

William took the boxes from him, fumbled them back to the floor and closed the door.

Geraldine was looking at him as if he'd gone mad. 'Ironing?' she said. 'Two boxes of ironing? How are we going to get that lot done in time?'

'My mother.' William grinned. 'She said she wanted to do something to help. And, as it was her cat that weed on the box . . . Oh, don't ask! Well, I think she just may have to wash some of it first!'

*

'Lovely eggs, Agnes.' Geraldine wiped her mouth with a paper serviette and put her cutlery down. 'So big too! Where do you get them? They're not supermarket, are they?'

'Thank you, dear. No, there's a little man comes round. Brings them to the door, every Friday. Farm eggs, they are. Free range. I don't like to think of those poor hens all cooped up in boxes, not being able to see the light of day or peck about in the grass, do you?'

Michael watched Lily dip her soldier into the runny yolk of her third egg. She was eating like a small horse this morning and, despite constant questions about her mummy, had definitely got much of her spark back.

'This is so kind of you,' Geraldine went on. 'Feeding us up like this.'

'Not at all. It's so good to have someone to cook for. I spend too much time on my own these days, and you don't always bother to make proper meals, do you, when there's no one to share them with?'

Geraldine shook her head, as if she understood only too well. And so, Michael couldn't help noticing, did William.

'I have to do something about getting a car seat later on today, for Lily.' Michael frowned and shook his head. 'Got to stick to the law of the land, and keep that Freeman woman happy.'

'It's not just rules for the sake of rules,' Geraldine said. 'It's to keep Lily safe, Michael. On the roads. And, after what's happened to her mother, you must surely see how important that is.'

'Yes, of course. It's just more hassle though, isn't it? Still, we can't have anything else happen to Lily, can we?' He ruffled his daughter's hair and closed his eyes for a moment. 'It might take time, so it will have to wait for now. I think we'd better get over to the hospital first, to see what's happening with Ruby. And I'm hoping they might let Lily in to see her, if the tubes and stuff aren't too intimidating for her. Depends what they say. So . . . does the bus that stops on the corner take us there? The number . . . oh, I don't remember. I always had a car to get about when I lived here. I'm not very up on public transport.' Michael drained his cup and started to lift Lily and Archie from their shared chair.

'Oh, yes, dear, it does.' Agnes smiled at him. 'There's just the one route that comes along here, so you can't go getting on the wrong bus! And it stops right outside the outpatients' entrance, so you'll only have to walk through to the lifts. I go there for my arthritis, you know, every six months or so. They say I may need a new knee. Well, two if I'm lucky, but they only ever do the one op at a time. There's a waiting list, of course. Still, it only takes twenty minutes or so. The journey, not the operation! Yes, about twenty minutes, door to door, though you can never tell, what with the traffic.'

'What about you, Mum? Coming with us?'

Geraldine looked at her watch. 'Well, to be honest, I think I'd be better employed here, getting some supplies in. If you leave me the car. There's still washing to do. Sheets and things and I really should help you with all that ironing too, Agnes.'

'Nonsense. I'm a dab hand with the steam iron, so long as I can sit down while I'm doing it. As I was saying, the old knees aren't what they were. But William could help you out today, I'm sure, couldn't you, William? If you wanted to go into town, or to the supermarket. Show you where things are. Maybe even help you to get that car seat sorted out while your son and granddaughter are out. There's a Mothercare, I think, in that big new shopping centre. He's very handy when it comes to lifting and carrying, aren't you William? I don't suppose these car seat things are light.'

Geraldine was about to protest but William was already on his feet. 'At your service, madam,' he said, bowing like a chauffeur and pulling his car keys out from his pocket. 'And I am happy to take my car. It's bigger than yours. More room for packages.'

CHAPTER TWENTY

Ruby

He's here. When Mrs Payne offered me the job in her shop, I knew it was only as a favour to Mrs Castle. She probably didn't really want me. Well, who does? Not even my own mother, wherever she is these days. Or my dad, wherever, and whoever, he is.

I hadn't expected her to give me a room too. Mrs Payne, that is. Or keep saying 'Call me Geri', because I can't. Not yet. I'm eighteen but I know I can't stay here any longer. Children's homes are for children, and I'm not a child any more. She has a nice house, with a spare room, and we do get on. It's so kind of her, though it doesn't stop me from being scared. Or from calling her Mrs Payne, still.

And now he's here, helping her to load my things into the car. Her son, Michael. I don't know if he recognises me, from the bank, our hands hovering over the coin bags this last year and a half, my heart banging loud enough to set the alarms off, my eyes burning into his back as I follow him along the street. If he does, he doesn't say so.

I don't have much. Not a lot to call my own. Clothes, a

couple of pairs of sturdy shoes, my shampoo and stuff, and the doll, the latest one. I don't know why I've kept her. I'm not a child.

There's nothing worth anything, really. Pretty much like me. The basics, enough to get by, but nothing out of the ordinary. Most of it is in carrier bags, all my worldly goods, and it doesn't even fill the boot of the car. I feel a bit small, unimportant, not even owning a proper suitcase. I bet Mrs Payne has a whole matching set.

My room is the smallest in the house, just like I am, but I can shut the door and be alone, and nobody comes in without knocking. Which is nice. Private. I like that. Through one wall I can hear the bathroom, the running of taps, the flushing of the loo, a gurgling from the pipes in the night. I have even heard a fart or two sometimes, loud ones, which isn't as funny as it sounds. And once, only once, I heard her crying, but I didn't say anything. Not then, not ever. Through the other wall I should be able to hear Michael. I know he's in there, sleeping just inches away, with only a layer of bricks and plaster to separate us, but I never do.

It's an odd feeling, being independent, cut adrift, on the verge of my own adult life. I wonder if everyone feels this way at my age, or is it just me? And the people like me? The care home kids, with nowhere of their own to go, nowhere to belong.

Michael wears boxers. Blue, white, grey. I've seen them on the line. Size fifteen shirts and black socks that all look the same and sit in rolled-up pairs on the worktop when his mother sorts the laundry. I never see pyjamas. I think about that a lot, when we are one each side of the wall. Michael, without pyjamas.

I never normally hear him, but now I do. He sounds a long way away, further than the other side of the wall. I don't know what he's saying, or doing, or thinking, but I know he's here.

CHAPTER TWENTY-ONE

He couldn't stay in the room any longer It just felt wrong. Too warm, too oppressive, much too scary. Lily, gripping his hand so hard, was suddenly all clammed up with nothing to say, her eyes as wide as saucers. He shouldn't have brought her in. Yet she wanted to see her mummy, and needed to.

God knows what she made of all this. Ruby lying there, so still. No hugs, no chatter, no smile. This was not the mummy Lily knew.

They said they were cautiously optimistic, whatever that meant. The swelling, bleeding or whatever it was, had stopped, gone down. He didn't understand it all, but the treatment was working. Time to reduce her medication, take her off the machinery, let her breathe for herself. Very soon now. Time to try to bring her back, out of her sleep, to wait for her to open her eyes. And then . . .

It was the not knowing that was so bad. Not knowing when, or if. Not knowing if there might be any damage, anything lasting, that would change her. They'd warned him it was possible. The loss of some of her normal functions, for a while, for longer, forever. He didn't really understand what that meant.

That she might not be able to walk, talk, think, maybe even wee, for herself? He didn't want to consider those things at all, even if they were just worst-case scenarios, but they'd said they were things he should be aware of, just in case. Things they could discuss, if and when . . .

Then there was the not knowing what Social Services might decide to do. Because it wasn't over yet, far from it, whatever might happen to Ruby. There would be more questions, judgements, decisions, and most of them taken right out of his hands, he'd bet.

One thing he did know was that nothing would ever be quite the same again. For Ruby. For Lily. For himself. Whatever happened here today, or tomorrow, or the day after, things – so many things – were about to change.

He took Lily out into the corridor, closed his eyes, allowed himself to breathe properly at last. He gulped in a big deep breath of hospital air, let Lily ride the lift up and down a few times and press the buttons while he let his thoughts seep in, bought her a chocolate bar in the shop. He wanted to get back on that bus and hotfoot it out of this awful place. Go as far away as possible. Pretend it wasn't happening. Run. But something – Lily – made him stay.

They went for a walk outside, in the grounds, killing time for a while. Pretending everything was normal. Scrunched through some leaves, splashed their fingers in the cold water of the fountain, sat for a while on the slightly damp wall where some of the nurses were eating or chatting in between the bouts of rain.

'Daddy?' Lily said, kicking her little legs, her shoes bouncing off the wall, her forehead crumpled into a frown. 'Are you going to go away again?'

'Only for work, sweetheart. And not just yet.' He put an arm around her and pulled her closer, snuggling her into his jacket and lowering his chin to rest on her hair. 'But I will come back and see you lots and lots.'

'And will Mummy go away again? When she's better? Cos I don't want to be on my own. I didn't like it.'

'No one is ever going to leave you on your own, ever again. I promise you.'

'Daddy?' She lifted her chin and stared at him for what seemed like a long time, as if she was trying to tell whether what he said was true. 'Can I have an ice cream?'

Michael laughed. How quickly a child's mind could flit from one thing to another. From something so worrying to something so simple. 'You most certainly can. Let's see what they have in the shop, shall we?'

They went in, hand in hand, and Lily made her choice, and then, with a strawberry ice lolly dripping slowly down her arm, she happily sat out on the wall again and together they counted all the red cars coming in and out of the car park, then the blue ones, and then the yellow. Not so many of those. And it was a good feeling, talking, playing, just spending time with his daughter. He had missed her so much.

After half an hour or so they went back inside, not because he wanted to but because Lily said she needed to go to the toilet. She was jiggling about, pulling a face, her small hand clutching at her clothes below the tummy line, as if she was trying hard to hold it in. He wasn't sure how men were meant to manage things like that on their own, not when the child was a girl. Maybe he should have put a nappy on her. Was she properly trained yet? He didn't know. He hadn't thought.

But he had to do something quickly now, or there would be a puddle he would have even less of a clue about dealing with, so he took her into the Gents, just inside the main doors. He ushered her straight into a cubicle, covering her eyes with his hand, so she wouldn't have to see the line of men with their zips open lined up at the urinals. So she wouldn't catch sight of anything she shouldn't and start asking questions he preferred not to answer.

She was his little girl, and it was his job to protect her. From all the bad things in the world, and from having to confront them even a moment sooner than she really had to. He hadn't done a very good job of it so far, but things would be different now. When Ruby woke up, they would talk. Properly talk, not stand their own separate ground, ignore each other, shout, sulk. They would talk and work things out, so Lily would be safe and happy and nothing like this could ever be allowed to happen again.

He did the best he could wiping Lily dry with a wad of loo paper and pulling up her knickers, but skipped the hand washing bit. Despite their backs being turned, there were too many men with naked dripping penises on show for his liking, or for hers. There would be gel in the dispenser by the door to the ward. They could use that. Because he knew he had to go back up there, to be near to Ruby, to wait, and hope, and see this thing through to the end, whatever that end might be.

Much as it all scared the life out of him, and much as he knew how much Ruby despised him, and that he would probably be the last person she'd want to see, there should be someone there for her, when the moment came. *If* it came. Oh, God, he so hoped that it would. And if she did wake up – no, he must be positive. *When* she woke up, he knew that it shouldn't be some nurse she had never met standing there, or some do-good vicar she had no faith in. No. He owed it to her and to Lily. He knew it had to be him.

*

'So, tell me about your husband. What was his name?'

'Kenneth. Well, Ken, really. Everyone called him Ken.'

William bit into his iced bun. It was very slightly stale, but, despite eating one of his mother's big breakfasts, he was hungry enough again not to complain. He watched Geraldine take a slow sip of her coffee and replace the cup very carefully in its saucer. She looked tired and pale, like the last day or so were finally catching up with her.

'You told my mother you were widowed. Sorry, I was washing up, and I couldn't help overhearing. That kitchen is pretty small! But it must be hard for you. Having to cope alone, I mean. Especially when there's a family crisis like this. I hope you don't mind me asking, but when did your husband die? Just tell me to shut up if I'm being too nosey.'

She didn't reply, just turned her head and gazed out at the traffic going by several floors below. The window had been left open just an inch or two, presumably to let some of the heat out, or the cool air in, but it wasn't really working. The glass was steamy, with little trickles of moisture running down onto the sill. William undid the top button of his shirt and loosened his collar. He gazed around at the other customers, some of them in dressing gowns and slippers, and at Geraldine in her jeans, and knew he was overdressed. The sweat was starting to drip down the back of his neck and his head was throbbing, but he turned his attention back to her. She looked like she was miles away, in a world of her own, her eyes still fixed on something beyond the glass.

'Sorry,' he said, stirring his coffee again and watching the milky patterns swirl around its frothy surface. 'If you don't want to talk about it, that's fine.'

'No, no, I don't mind.' She turned back towards him and forced a smile. 'Actually, I rarely do get the chance to talk about it. Or him, what with Michael being away, and there's nobody else really. I don't have sisters or brothers. There's just Kerry, who helps me in the shop, but it wouldn't be fair of me. She's young. She wouldn't want the burden of it. Wouldn't understand.' She clenched her left hand several times, squeezing until her knuckles whitened, as if trying to release the tension. Then her fingers stretched open and finally came to rest against the plastic table top, and he saw the dull glint of her wedding ring under the lights as she started turning it round and round, slowly and absent-mindedly, with her thumb. He couldn't help noticing how loosely it fitted.

William thought about reaching across the table and taking her hand in his, but it probably wasn't appropriate. He wasn't all that good at this kind of thing, and, much as she looked as if she needed a friend right now, the last thing he wanted was for his actions to be misconstrued.

He was about to say something, anything, just to try to make her feel more at ease when, in a sudden thud of swooping grey, a pigeon plopped itself onto the thick grey concrete ledge outside, flapping its wings hard against the glass. Geraldine jumped back in surprise, her hand flying up and knocking the sugar bowl across to the opposite side of the table, and they both laughed nervously as the pigeon took off into the sky again and disappeared. But it seemed to break the ice and, as soon as she'd composed herself and gathered up all the scattered sugar sachets, she took a deep breath and started to talk.

'Ken. He's been gone just over two and a half years now,' she said, her voice small amongst the hubbub of the place as a steady trickle of customers queued at the counter, rattled coins and clattered cutlery, some chatting loudly into mobile phones, trying to be heard above the din. 'Two years and six months and – let me see – five days, to be precise,' she went on, seemingly oblivious of everything around her, 'It was very sudden. A heart attack. We were down by the beach, early in the evening. It had been a nice day. An April day, without the showers. We'd had a stroll along the pier and we were sitting on a bench, resting our legs, watching the waves. Talking, you know how you do, about inconsequential things. About the seagulls diving down for people's scraps, a bit like our pigeon friend here, and the way some mothers just let their children run about screaming, and the terrible price of the ice creams we'd just had, and how we were sure they cost more the nearer to the pier you bought them ...'

William nodded, trying to remember similar conversations he might have had with Susan, but failing to conjure up even one.

'One minute he was fine. A bit quiet, maybe, but I just put that down to the sea air and him being tired after our walk. And then, he just keeled over. None of that clutching at his chest stuff you see in films. No cry of agony or attempt to utter a few last words. Nothing like that at all. He just toppled over right next to me, and died there on the spot.'

'That must have been a terrible shock for you. Frightening.'

'It's hard to remember now, exactly how I felt. I don't think I even knew at the time. Numb, I suppose. But, yes, it was frightening. It was all so unreal too, like being in a bad dream. I kept thinking it couldn't really be happening and I would wake up soon and he'd still be sitting there next to me, not stretched out on the concrete with all these people gathered around us, watching. Oh, the ambulance came quickly, I've no complaints there, and everyone tried, they really did, but he was already gone. Just like that.' She lifted her hand and clicked her fingers. 'Like snuffing out a candle. The light had gone from him, in an instant. I think it sort of went from me that day too, if you know what I mean. I haven't felt properly alive since.' She took another mouthful of coffee and leaned back in her chair. 'Just going through the motions . . .'

'I'm sorry.'

'Not your fault.'

'Oh, I know. But it's what we all say, isn't it? When there are no words that fit. And I am sorry. You know what I mean. For your loss.'

'Thank you.'

Another pigeon landed on the ledge outside the window, or maybe it was the same one returning for another try. They both sat in silence for a while, watching it pecking about at some specks around its feet. William was about to break a piece from his bun and toss it out through the gap, but he was too late. Someone at the next table stood up and banged on the glass, shooing the bird away.

'You'd think they'd do something about them, wouldn't you?' Geraldine said. 'It's not very hygienic, it being a hospital and all.'

'They're not doing any harm though, are they? And they have to eat somewhere, just like the rest of us. I'm not sure I would have chosen this particular restaurant myself, given the choice.'

She laughed. 'Beggars can't be choosers, I suppose. The coffee's not bad though, and at least the floor's clean.'

William chuckled and changed the subject. 'Your Lily. She's a tough little thing, isn't she? Seems to have come through her ordeal remarkably well. How old is she, exactly? Not even three yet?'

Geraldine sighed. 'It's her birthday next weekend. I expect her mother has something planned. You know, a little party, an outing or something. Or maybe I should say *had* something planned.'

'She'll be fine, you know. Lily.'

'I hope so. It's just that . . .'

He waited, but she didn't go on.

'Look, Geraldine, I can see this has been a terrible shock, but they say she's all right, don't they? Little Lily. Nothing a few days rest, a decent meal or two, and plenty of cuddles can't put right. Whatever happens now, whether she gets to have her party or not, there will be other parties to come. Lots of them. That little one looks like a fighter to me. Gets some of that from her grandma, I shouldn't wonder.'

'And Ruby? What about Ruby?'

He shook his head. 'Well, nobody can tell yet, can they? When she might wake up.'

'Or *if*.'

'Don't say that. They seem hopeful, don't they? Maybe when your Michael comes down from the ward, there will be some news, eh?'

'Lily needs her mummy. Whatever her faults . . .' Geraldine lowered her head into her hands, her elbows pushing hard against the table. 'I should have seen this coming, you know. Ruby not coping. A crisis waiting to happen. I should have done something. Done more . . .'

He reached over and tentatively placed his hand on her shoulder, trying to reassure her, pleased that she didn't push him away. 'Do you want to talk about it? They say it helps.'

'No.' She lifted her head. 'Thank you, but no. It's something I'll have to try to put right myself. If I get the chance. We just play the waiting game now, I suppose, don't we? What is it they say? All things come to those who wait. Patience. It's a virtue, apparently.'

He nodded. 'She'll be okay. I'm sure she will. Whatever's happened between you can be put right.'

'I hope so. I do love her. Well, both of them really. Lily, obviously, but Ruby too. She's like the daughter I never . . . Well, perhaps the daughter I *should* have had. Yes, she's young, and

258

headstrong sometimes. Stubborn. But it's not her fault, the way she is. She didn't have the best of starts in life. I always felt a sort of responsibility towards her, when she came to work for me, when I took her in, but it was more than that, in the end.'

'I didn't realise she worked for you.'

'Used to. Not any more. Lived with us too, for a while, when she first came out of care. I offered her a room, as a favour to a friend more than anything, but I liked having her around. A bit of female company, for a change.'

'Is that how she met your son?'

'I'm afraid so. Met him properly anyway, although she'd seen him before, she told me, in the bank where he worked back then. She moved in, and then she got herself pregnant, not long after. Well, no, that's not actually possible, is it? *He* got her pregnant, my stupid son, thinking through his trousers, never his head. Then, with Lily still so small, they were off to London, without a backward glance. No thought for me. New job, new start. It all happened so quickly. Always was weak, my Michael. Oh, he's a charmer, all right. Never had any trouble attracting female company, and he was always going to do well in his career. He just has a way about him, you know? Everybody likes him. But he can be so easily led. Just look at how quickly this latest floozy got her hooks into him. Whisked him away to sunny climes, as soon as looked at him. So, it probably is all my fault, isn't it? All of this mess. For bringing them together in the first place, under the same roof. Michael and Ruby, that is. I had no idea what floodgates I was opening.

'Even so, I should have stuck by her after Michael left her. But she didn't want me there. Wanted to do it all by herself, to prove she could, I guess. I tried. Phoned, suggested she come down to visit or that I go to her, but it was a long way to drive just to risk having the door slammed in my face. I think it all reminded her too much of her past. Her mother was an alcoholic, you see. Couldn't look after her. Or wouldn't. She said Michael was just like her mother. Not the drinking, but the rest of it – giving her a life, some hope, and then abandoning her, snatching it all away. Said she didn't think she'd ever be able to trust anyone again. And that included me, apparently. I thought she just needed time, to calm down, adjust. She wouldn't be the first wronged woman, would she? Or the first one having to manage without a man? And at least hers was still alive. Not like my Ken . . . But it wasn't about me, was it? Not about my misery. I really should have tried harder . . . '

'Don't be so tough on yourself. I'm sure, whatever happened, none of it was your fault.'

'But if she'd had me there, for some sort of back-up, babysitting or whatever, she wouldn't have gone out and left Lily on her own, would she? God knows what was going on in her head. Was Lily acting up, and she just needed a break? Time to herself? Did she just step out for some air? Was she shopping, meeting a man? Not that any of those are valid excuses. Maybe we'll never know . . . '

They sat in silence for a while, Geraldine opening the new packet of pink pills she'd bought earlier, pushing two out of their foil and slipping them into her mouth. She picked up her coffee mug and drained it, swallowing hard, then sat back and closed her eyes. 'Damn migraine,' she muttered. 'I always get them in times of stress. Far too often these days, in fact. And I shouldn't be drinking so much coffee. It's a trigger, you know . . . '

William watched her, concerned, but at least he was discreet enough not to ask any more questions.

'I wish I knew what was happening,' she said after a while. 'Surely there should be some news soon? What's taking Michael so long to report back? I texted him a good hour ago. He knows we're here, waiting, new car seat at the ready. All he has to do is pop down and let us know how things are. Then we can go back to the flat and work out what to do next, about Lily, and about getting her, and ourselves, back home to Brighton. I can't leave Kerry in charge for much longer. I really should call her again.'

'I'm sure everything will be fine. Best not to worry. It can't change anything.' William moved his spoon around in his coffee and tried to change the subject. 'Phew, why's it so hot in here?' He half stood, shrugged out of his jacket and turned to hang it on the back of his chair. 'It's enough to make you feel ill.'

'You'd be in the right place if you were!' She snapped out of her thoughts and turned her attention back towards him. She'd looked like she'd almost forgotten he was there for a moment or two. 'Every other customer seems to be a nurse or a doctor.'

'You're right. And with most of the others in their pyjamas, I suppose they can't risk it getting too chilly, can they?'

She laughed, and he could feel the mood lighten.

'So, William, you haven't said what you do.'

'Do?'

'For a living, I mean. You must have a good boss, letting you take time off at short notice like this.'

'Oh, no. No boss to worry about. I don't really do anything. Not any more.'

She looked at him quizzically.

'I was made redundant, you see. Almost two years ago now, from an accountancy firm. Yes, I know. Boring! I've yet to meet anyone who gets excited by the word *accountancy*, but it was a job, something I did for more than thirty years, and I wasn't bad at it.'

'So why did they let you go?'

'The firm were losing business hand over fist, and my area was the first to suffer. Helping the self-employed do their tax returns, that's what I specialised in. Builders, shops just starting up, small businesses generally. I even had a cattery on the books. Out in the country, lots of moggies spending their holidays in snug little cages, fed twice a day and with the radio on all the time for company. I enjoyed the site visits to that one, and it was better than some of the hotels I've stayed at in my time, believe me!'

Geraldine smiled, curling her fingers around her empty mug as if to keep herself warm.

'But it's so easy nowadays for people to tackle their own tax. It's all online. And, once I'd helped them through year one and they had a good idea of what's involved and what expenses they could claim, they'd ditch the accountant and have a go at it themselves in year two. Another client down the drain, and me not far behind. Writers, quite a lot of them, too, thanks to my dear departed wife . . . '

'Your wife's dead? And there's me going on about my Ken. Oh, I'm so sorry.'

'No, no. Not dead. Just gone. Departed. We got divorced, earlier this year, and I can't say I'm sorry.'

Geraldine nodded. 'Not a happy union then?'

'Not towards the end. We were leading fairly separate lives by then, and we parted on a two-year separation. We'd not been properly together for a while, but it hadn't really been quite *that* long. Still, I didn't mind lying. No point in contesting it, trying to force someone to stay when they've so clearly had enough. I think she just stopped needing me. Too much going on in her life that I was never a part of. She worked for a publishing company, you see. Susan. Still does, in fact. Finds a lot of new talent. Nurtures them, as she likes to call it, and she did put a fair bit of work my way, usually when their first royalty cheques started arriving. So she wasn't all bad.'

'Publishing! That's the sort of career I would have liked, I think. I used to love reading. Novels, autobiographies. Always had my nose in a book when I was younger, or lugging carrier bags full of them to and from the library, before . . . Well, before life got in the way. Did she deal with anyone famous? Your ex?'

'To be honest, I used to tune out whenever she got started. Book talk can get pretty tedious. Boring. A bit like accountancy talk, I suppose.'

'You weren't boring me. Far from it.'

'Good! No, I could tell you a few names, actually. The authors I took on, tax-wise, I mean. But I'm not sure I should. The writers I've met do tend to be a bit precious. They're creative types, not necessarily good dealing with money, especially if they get a bestseller on their hands and there's more of it flowing in than they're used to. Big spenders too, some of them. I don't suppose they'd want me telling the world their business, or that they're broke!'

'Ah, but you're not telling the world, you're only telling me!'

'That's true. Let's get another coffee and perhaps I can be persuaded to spill a few secrets.'

Geraldine stood up and reached for her purse. 'Done!'

'Put your money away. This is my treat.' He winked at her as he got to his feet and guided her gently back into her seat. He hoped that Michael might take a little longer yet. There was no hurry to get back, move the car seat from his car to theirs, help Geraldine to carry in her new clothes or the groceries, and certainly no hurry to get back to his mother's ceiling and the steamy heat of all that ironing. Nowhere else he needed to be, or wanted to be. Ridiculous though it sounded, sitting either side of a plastic table with this almost stranger, surrounded by old men in crumpled pyjamas, with the car parking fees racking up outside and a young woman's life hanging in the balance somewhere up there on the sixth floor, he hadn't felt this relaxed, or this comfortable in a woman's company, in ages.

*

Patsy gazed out of the train window at the trees and fields rushing by, a landscape dotted with sheep and little clusters of brick houses, and cut through by the occasional road. This was the real England. Proper countrified England, with all its emptiness, sweeping greenness and tranquillity. Portugal may be hot and sunny, and it was pretty damn good at blue, but it had no idea how to do a truly lush and typically English green.

She had left the rain behind, hovering like a soggy grey sheet over the sea, and felt her spirits start to lift as she came into a dusty and damp London, humming with noise and throbbing with life. Resisting the temptation to shop, she had bumped her small case onto the tube to Euston and just managed to catch the train in time. A pale sun hung in the sky now, peeking out between drifting patches of cloud as she settled into her seat and let the train take her home. The further north she travelled the brighter the weather, and her own mood, seemed to become.

The seat beside her was empty, and the woman in front was already asleep. Slipping out of her shoes, Patsy tucked her feet up under her, ran her fingers over the thin gold chain that circled her ankle, briefly catching one of its tiny links on her engagement ring, and rubbed at the broken blister still sore on her heel. She was heading for her childhood home, for her old bedroom which she knew would still look exactly the way she'd left it, her dressing gown still hanging on the back of the door, her over-sized Christmas-present slippers poking out from under the bed, her walking boots and waterproof coat cleaned and waiting in the hall ready for the next time she took them tramping over the hills. She could be a different person there, shake off the super-efficient, super-poised woman she was at work, and just be herself again. Closing her eyes, she could almost smell the wide expanses of well-trodden grass, the cool clean blue-white air that lay over the lakes, hunks of her mother's homemade bread cooling on the range, and the unmistakeable whiff of damp dog.

She didn't realise she'd nodded off to sleep until the train shuddered to a noisy halt, late in the afternoon, and there was her brother Matt jumping up and down on the platform outside and banging excitedly on the window.

*

The room was so much quieter now. No hissing, no whirring from the machines. Just Ruby, looking as if she was asleep. Looking alive. Not quite so still any more. The tube gone from her mouth. A hint of colour in her cheeks. Just the bandaging around her head to show that she was not merely a girl asleep in her bed and dreaming. That she was sick, and there was still some way to go.

The first step was over. She had started to breathe by herself. She hadn't died. These were good things. Miraculous things. Now they had let him into the room, Lily hovering beside him, half hiding behind his legs.

But Michael knew the biggest hurdle was yet to come. What had been happening all this time, in that head of hers? What was going on in her brain? Was it healing? Was it going to survive? Intact and undamaged? Would Ruby be able to do all the things a young girl of twenty-two should be able to do?

He felt himself gulp, swallow hard, as if he was the one struggling for air. Would she still be the same Ruby, when this was all over? The same simple, trusting, but maddeningly hot-headed, girl he had known? She had to be. Oh, God, please, please, she had to be. For all their sakes, but especially for Lily's.

He closed his eyes, felt Lily's tiny sweaty hand wriggle in his, and quickly opened them again.

As he watched from the back of the room, saw the doctor

leaning over Ruby, the nurses moving about efficiently, charts being filled in, he could have sworn he saw her move. Saw her fingers start to twitch. Just a flicker, but enough. Enough to bring an air of hope to the room.

Lily had seen it too. 'Is Mummy waking up now?' she said, her hand slipping out of his as she took a tentative step nearer to the bed.

He looked across at the nearest nurse. Raised his eyebrows in a silent question. Saw her smile and nod.

'Yes, sweetheart,' he said, hardly daring to believe it was true. 'I think she is.'

CHAPTER TWENTY-TWO

Ruby

When Michael came into my room, I was in bed. It was a very cold morning in January, frost on the grass, the windows misty, but under the covers I was as warm as toast. Geri always keeps the heating off at night and it takes time to kick back in. I think Ken likes it that way. Saves money, I suppose. I've noticed that he always keeps his socks on though. Big thick woolly ones, even with his pyjamas. Warm feet, warm heart. Isn't that what Mrs Castle used to say? Or was it hands? I wonder if it works the other way too. Cold feet, cold heart . . .

He does seem a bit of a cold fish, her Ken. With his cold fish feet, his cold fish toes and his cold fish fingers. I giggle to myself about that. But he is. Cold, I mean, whatever the weather. I don't ever see them hold hands or kiss. Not in front of me, anyway. Not the way I thought couples were meant to do. Maybe that's just because they're old, and the fire has gone out. But what do I know about couples? Where I come from, everyone is pretty much on their own.

I was wearing very little that morning. Just a thin nightshirt that barely reached to my knees. White, it was, with flowers on the front. Nothing else. He'd brought me tea. He didn't usually. I think she'd gone out to work early, and who knows where Ken was? I don't think he was in the house. Even if he was, he'd never been inside my room, and wasn't likely to start now.

I don't really remember how it happened. Not clearly. Just that it did. And how much I wanted it to. Kicking off the covers, raising my knees, reaching for the mug and feeling it shake, heavy and hot, in my hand. My nipples reacting to the sudden rush of cold air and standing up like buttons behind the cloth of the shirt. And Michael noticing, and pretending not to. My hair all messy and tousled from sleep, the soapy fresh tang of his skin, him holding out both hands to steady mine, to guide the mug to the safety of the bedside table, my bare knee knocking his arm, the nearness of his face to mine. Oh, the nearness. Neither of us moved away. He still held my hands, held my gaze, lowered himself onto the edge of the bed – said something. What was it? Something about the time or the weather or what was I going to do today? It was my day off from the shop. I remember that. No plans. No hurry.

His hands reaching across the counter at the bank. How many times had I dreamed of them? Warm, strong hands, sliding the money under the glass, pulling back, away from me. And now, here they were, not pulling back. I leaned forward. No glass partitions, no watching eyes, no hurry. I leaned forward, and I kissed them. Without thinking, without saying anything, without shame. Pulled his hands up slowly to my lips and kissed them. I felt the thin cloth move as I moved, felt the cold air ripple up my exposed skin, felt his hands slide away from under mine and slide up beneath the shirt and find me.

I loved it, and I loved him. More in that moment than ever before, or since.

Mike came into my room. Stood by the bed, watched me, touched me, entered me. Only once, but once was enough. And then there was Lily. Tiny inside me, then growing, growing, like a little miracle. She brought us together, Mike and me. Lily, the glue that bound us together. And when she was born, she was like all my dolls, all those other Lilys and Betsys, merged into one and brought to life. But better. More beautiful. More perfect. Half his, half mine. More mine than anything had ever been before. From the day she came I loved her. More than anything, or anyone. And love can't be divided, or shared. She is mine, and Mike's. Not *hers*. Never hers. I can't let her have her, take her . . .

Lily.

'Is Mummy waking up now?'

I hear her voice, and I know she's here. In the room with me.

It's cold, and I am wearing very little under the covers. Just a thin piece of cloth. Where is Geri? She must have gone to work, left me here to sleep in. Michael has brought me tea. I have brought him nothing but trouble. I try to raise my knees, but they don't move. *Won't* move. I can feel my fingers. Just. And then they start to tremble. A flicker of a feeling. But I know that if I can just reach out, I will be able to touch her. Lily. My Lily. All that matters to me in all the world. Just Lily.

'Is Mummy waking up now?' I hear it again, like an echo. Round and round, far away, swirling in circles inside my head. I feel my eyelids move, struggling to open. I want to see her. Need to see her.

There is a long silence. I can feel hands touching me, eyes

watching me, everything and everyone stopping and waiting. For me.

'Yes, sweetheart. I think she is.'

And then I do.

PART THREE

CHAPTER TWENTY-THREE

Laura was sure the woman had tried to commit suicide. It didn't matter what story she told, about taking too many pills by accident, about not meaning for it to happen. Anyone could see it had been real, and how close she had come to succeeding. A cry for help, or maybe even a genuine attempt to end it all, to escape from something she flatly refused to talk about.

It seemed such a terrible thing to say, in the face of the woman's obvious anguish, but Laura was almost glad she had this patient to worry about now. Someone whose troubles were big and deep and heavy enough to have brought her here. Someone whose plight reminded her why she had wanted to be a nurse in the first place. To help, to heal, to make a difference. And now . . . Well, administering an antidote, talking to her, walking her up and down, giving her a shoulder to lean on, it all helped to take her mind off Ruby and the wait for news.

'Julie, I can't do that,' she said again, trying to guide the woman back to her bed. 'You shouldn't leave the ward. Not yet. You're not ready.'

'But it wouldn't take long. Ten minutes. I have to talk to God.' The woman clutched at Laura's wrist, pulling her towards the door. 'Please. You have a chapel here. I know you do. You don't have to come with me. Just turn your back, let me slip out. I can find it, follow the signs. You can say you knew nothing about it. Just for a little while. Please. I need to talk to God. It's important.'

'Julie . . .'

'You don't understand, nurse, just how important it is. What I've done, it needs to be . . . forgiven.'

The chapel. Laura knew where it was, had passed its doors often enough, but she'd never been inside. Had never felt the need, nor understood its power. Yet, for this woman, it was clearly desperately important, that urgent need to unburden. And whatever it was that troubled her, it had been bad enough for her to try to take her own life, no matter how strongly she denied it.

'But there may not be anyone there. You know, a priest . . .'

'Oh, that doesn't matter. I don't have to see a priest. What I have to say is between God and me. I just hope He'll listen . . .'

They had passed the bed again, on their slow circuit of the ward, and were nearing the exit door. Julie limped a little, her toes red and sore from being more or less dragged from her home by her distraught husband, the bruises already big and blue on her arms from where he'd gripped her and shaken her and then tried to carry her in his haste to get her here. Now all she wanted to do was leave.

'Please. It's not as if you can hold me here, is it? Against my will, I mean. I could walk out any time I like.'

'Technically, yes, you could. But I don't think you'd get very far. For a start, you don't have any shoes with you. And, besides, you're far too weak to leave. Julie, you swallowed a lot of pills.

You're lucky your husband found you and we were able to help you so quickly. You've not long been properly awake, and you can hardly stand unaided. So, why not wait? Until the doctor says you can go. The chapel will still be there later, won't it?'

'No. I'm sorry . . . ' Julie stopped for a moment and bent forward, almost double, holding her hands across her stomach, taking a slow breath in and out again before moving on. 'But I have to. And before my husband comes back. He'll only be gone a few minutes, and I don't want him to know. Or to stop me.' Then, with an almighty effort, she straightened up, pulled herself free of Laura's restraining hands and headed for the door.

There was nothing Laura could do but follow. The woman was too ill to go alone.

Maybe we really will be so quick that nobody will know we've gone, she thought. Except it wasn't right. It was against the rules. She was meant to say if she left the ward, and especially if she took a patient with her. But if she ran back inside now, Julie would be gone, wandering the corridors, staggering about by herself. She couldn't let her do that.

The lift came quickly and, before she could change her mind, they were both inside.

The chapel was down in the bowels of the place. It had pale wooden double doors with stained glass panels, and a sign outside that invited them to come in, day or night. Julie held tightly to Laura's arm with one hand and eased one of the doors open with the other. Inside there was just the sound of their feet, squeaking on the wooden floor, to break the almost eerie silence. Julie stopped a few paces in and crossed herself. Head, heart, side to side. Mumbling a prayer under her breath.

'You're a Roman Catholic?'

'Oh, I've tried not to be, believe me. Tried to leave it all behind, but I can't. It's in me, always has been, all my life. There's no escape.' She lowered herself into the nearest seat and bowed her head.

Laura looked around. There was a narrow band of red carpet along the central aisle, little kneeling stools covered in tapestry pictures, a simple cross above the small altar at the front. There were flowers too, in vivid pinks and oranges and reds. So colourful, so cheerful. But the woman beside her looked like she had a grey doom cloud hanging over her head, weighing her down.

'Shall I leave you alone for a minute or two?' She felt a bit uncomfortable, as if she was intruding on someone else's most private thoughts. Like a stranger at a funeral, hovering outside the grief.

'Yes, please. I'll be fine here. What I have to say won't take long.'

'Well, only a few minutes, mind. I'll be just outside and when I come back for you I want you back up to that ward super quick. No arguments. Okay?' Laura touched her shoulder and tiptoed away.

It was almost as quiet out in the corridor as it was inside the chapel. She glanced at her watch. Five minutes. That was all she would give her. While she waited she would grab the nearest phone and call A & E, to tell them where they'd gone and when they'd be back.

'Laura?'

The voice behind her seemed to come out of nowhere and made her jump. She turned and there was Paul, dressed in his usual black, sandwich in hand, coming around the corner from the lifts.

'Well, we don't often see you around these parts.'

'Never, actually. My first time inside! But it's very nice, isn't it? Your chapel. Very peaceful and bright.'

'What did you expect?' He laughed. 'A cold damp cave? We do like to be warm and welcoming. A place for people to rest and relax, have a little think or a little cry. They come for all sorts of reasons. Yes, to pray if they want to, but it's not compulsory!'

'That's why I'm here, actually. A patient of mine. She's in there now, having her own little moment, talking to God.'

'Would she like to talk to me, do you think? Could I be of any help?'

'I don't know. She's a Catholic, and you're . . .'

'And I'm not! No, that's true, but it doesn't usually matter, not really. A listening ear, a kind word. We're all of us capable of that. We do worship the same God, after all.'

'Even so, I get the impression she probably just wants to be on her own in there. For a while, anyway.'

'How long have we got then?'

'How long?'

'Until you have to go in? I'm assuming you're lurking out here until she's finished, not just on the off-chance of bumping into me?'

Laura giggled. 'Five minutes. Ten, at a push.'

'Right then.' He peered at the triangular packet in his hand. 'Cheese and pickle on brown. Fancy half?'

'I'm meant to be on duty.'

'Aren't you allowed a bite of a sandwich while you're on duty? Come on, I'm on duty too, and we all have to eat. Follow me.' He turned around and pointed to a smaller door marked 'Staff only' that she hadn't even noticed. 'My own little hidey hole. My place of escape when the going gets tough.'

'And does it? Get tough?'

'Sometimes. No more than in your job though, I'm sure.' They went in and he closed the door behind them, pointing her towards a threadbare armchair. It was low and wide, its big squashy cushion swallowing her up like a sponge. Once she'd sat down, he pulled out a small wooden chair from under a cluttered desk for himself.

Laura spotted the phone and remembered. 'I just need to call the ward. May I?'

'Be my guest.' He lifted the receiver and handed it to her. While she explained what was going on to the nurse who answered, he busied himself ripping at the corner of the sandwich wrapping with his teeth.

'I got this from that friend of yours,' he muttered, when she'd handed him back the phone. 'You know, one of the girls you were with, in the pub. I didn't know she worked here in the shop. Shows how much I notice.'

'Fiona?'

'Yes, that's the one. I think my mate Ian was quite smitten with her actually.'

'Really?'

'He took her number, you know. I'm pretty sure he's going to ask her out.'

'Oh!'

'Is that a good thing? He wouldn't be treading on any toes? She's not already spoken for? Not married or anything?'

'Oh, no. Not married . . . Or anything!'

He opened a drawer and rummaged about inside, finally producing a paper plate that looked like it had seen better days. From her armchair she couldn't see it clearly, but she was fairly certain it had *Happy Birthday* written in the centre.

'And you?'

'What about me?'

'Married? Or anything?'

Laura laughed. 'Definitely not.'

'So, I was wondering . . . ' He kept his head down, taking his time to separate the sandwich into its triangular halves and place her share carefully on the plate. 'If you might consider maybe going out with me one evening? On a . . . well, on a date.'

He looked up then, his eyes capturing hers, holding her gaze as he passed the plate. A date? She hadn't seen that coming. Hadn't expected it at all.

'But . . . ' she mumbled, balancing the plate on her knees. 'You're a vicar.'

Now it was Paul's turn to laugh. 'It's allowed, you know. As I think you may have mentioned just a moment ago, I'm not a Catholic. Same God, different rules.'

'Oh,' was all she could say, seeing a red flush rise up in his face and knowing she probably had one to match.

'Oh? Just Oh? Look, I'm sorry. I didn't mean to embarrass you. Or to be too forward. If you're not interested, just say. I'm not usually in the habit . . . '

'No, no. It's not that. You just took me by surprise, that's all, but it was a nice Oh. Honestly. A very nice Oh.'

'A nice enough Oh for you to say yes? To a date? Friday night. Rock concert. Heavy metal. Just a little local gig. I've got two tickets.'

'And you want someone to come along and fill the second seat?'

'No, I want *you to* come along and fill the second seat. Subtle difference. Not that there will be a lot of seats. Standing up mainly, I'm afraid. We need room for all the head banging, you see!' He laughed. 'The band are mates of mine, actually. They're quite good. Loud . . . but good!'

'Heavy metal? You really are full of surprises, aren't you? And I suppose you'll be telling me next that the band are all vicars too!'

He smiled. 'How did you guess? Yes, they are. Well, two of them, anyway. So, you'll come? You're not on duty or anything?'

'Not on duty, no. And, yes. Yes, I will come. Heavy metal vicars is something I really do have to see!'

'Oh, and did I mention the motorbike? Are you all right with travelling on that? I've got a spare crash helmet but you'd have to bring your own leathers.'

'Leathers? But I haven't . . . '

'I'm joking!' He laughed so hard his half of the sandwich nearly fell off its plate. 'Oh, I'm sorry, but you are such an easy target! I do have a car as well. Can't roll up to visit the sick and dying looking like a Hell's Angel, can I? I can see I'm going to have to show you just what we vicars are really like, when we get our dog collars off.'

'You take it off? Wear normal clothes?'

'Of course I do. I don't want everyone to know what job I do when I'm out having a good time. I bet you don't go out clubbing in your nurse's uniform, do you? Now, come on, eat up, or your patient will have given up on you and done a runner.'

'I don't think so. In fact, I'm probably going to have trouble dragging her away. She's . . . Well, asking for forgiveness, apparently. For something. I don't know what. Maybe you . . . '

'Well, I don't do confession as such but, as I said, I can be a good listener. Let me go in first. If I'm not out in five, come in and get me. Or her! My lunch can wait.'

He stood up, hesitated for a few seconds, then bent down and kissed her. It was only a tiny peck on the cheek, just to the left of her nose, the kind of friendly gentle kiss that passes between friends, but when she lifted her fingers to her skin she was sure she could still feel it there, all warm and comforting, long after he'd gone.

*

'Mum!' He was coming towards her across the café, little Lily tugging at his hand.

Geraldine stood up, her heart pounding. Were those tears in his eyes? In Lily's? She couldn't be sure, not from this distance. But something had happened. There was no doubt about that. She could feel William get up too, his hip knocking the edge of the table, the crockery rattling as he moved. But she couldn't look at William now, didn't want to see that look of pity that would sweep across his face if . . .

'She's awake, Mum. Ruby's awake.'

She felt her knees buckle, her shoulders fall. 'Oh, thank God. Thank God.'

His arms were around her now, holding her up. 'It's early days, and there are lots of tests and things to be done, but it's looking promising. And she knows who we are, Mum. I'm sure she does. She hasn't said anything yet, she's still very drowsy, but her eyes . . . When she saw Lily . . . '

Geraldine breathed in the warm male smell of him. It had been a long while since he'd hugged her so tightly or for so long. Since anyone had hugged her. 'Oh, Michael, that's wonderful. I was scared. So scared, that Lily was going to . . .' She lowered her voice, suddenly aware that Lily was standing there, hearing every word. 'That she might lose her mummy, or that I was going to lose . . . '

'No, that's not going to happen, Mum.' He patted her awkwardly on the back, then pulled away a little. 'She's going to live,' he said, very quietly. 'As for anything else, any sort of disability or mental . . . Well, you know what I mean. The next few days will tell, and whatever happens we'll deal with it, won't we? Look, we'll talk later, okay? Away from Lily, I mean . . .'

'Would you like me to go now?' William was hovering, clearly not sure of his place. 'So you can go back up and see her together? I can always come back later, to drive you all home.'

'No, no.' Michael held out his hand and shook William's. 'You've been great today, driving Mum about, and keeping her company in here and we wouldn't want to put you to any more trouble.'

He turned back to his mother. 'What Ruby needs now is time, some peace and quiet, and plenty of rest. She opened her eyes but she's not what you'd really call properly awake. Not really with it. She's still got a lot of recovering to do, and I don't think we should crowd her. They say they'll know more tomorrow. So, how about we all go home now?'

'Are you sure? Shouldn't one of us be here? You know, in case . . . '

'Don't think about any in cases, Mum. Let them do their jobs, eh? They can look after her better than we can. Come on, let's make a move. Then we won't have to take up any more of Mr Munro's time. We can pop the car seat thing into our car as soon as we get back, and then Lily and I'll be all set to come back here whenever we need to. You too, if you want to. But it won't be tonight.' He looked at his watch. 'God, it's only half past three but I'm knackered already. It's bloody shattering, all this hospital lark.'

Geraldine gave him a withering look. 'Michael. No swearing. Not in front of Lily. Walls have ears, you know.'

'Do they, Daddy?' Lily said, looking up puzzled. 'Can they hear what we're saying? Did they hear you say bloody?'

'Right, let's go then, shall we?' William spoke into the short awkward silence, and slipped his jacket back on. 'If that's what you want. I just hope we've been out long enough for my mother to have finished all that ironing!'

'That's a point. Maybe we should give her a bit longer.' Michael laughed. 'We don't want to get caught having to do any of that ourselves, do we?'

*

Patsy sat in the garden, huddled inside one of her dad's baggy jumpers, and listened to the birds. It was amazing how different they sounded when there were no cars or planes or conversations going on. Like a dream world she'd almost forgotten existed.

'Here, love.' Her dad came across the grass bearing a tray and placed it precariously on the little wooden table beside her. It was a bit of a rickety old thing, cobbled together from the remains of an old wardrobe, but he'd made it himself, so there was never any question of throwing it away or replacing it with one of those fancy plastic jobs. 'I've brought you some lemonade. Homemade, with plenty of sugar. I know how much you used to like it when you were small, especially when you had something on your mind. This stuff's seen you through many an exam, and the odd bit of boyfriend trouble, if I remember rightly.' He lowered himself into the second chair, each positioned perfectly to catch the dying rays of the evening sun without missing out on the view.

'I don't have boyfriend trouble, if that's what you're inferring.'

'Of course not, love. Not my place to infer. Or to interfere. But if there is anything . . . '

She took the glass of lemonade and sipped at it. Yes, it was good, just how she remembered it. Fresh and fruity, with just a tang of sourness, despite the copious amounts of sugar. The effect on her teeth didn't bear thinking about.

'So . . . Tell me about this Michael of yours. I know we met him once before, but only briefly. And now, well, now you're going to marry the fella, and I for one would like to know a bit more about him. I'm sure your mother—'

'Yes, I know, Dad. Mum has her doubts. She's worried. She's made that perfectly clear. Thinks we should have waited longer, that I haven't known him more than five minutes, that I should have brought him here for vetting or whatever. But I'm twenty-seven, Dad. We're not teenage runaways. I . . . *We* do know what we're doing.'

'Where is he, then? The two of you would be up here for a few days, that's what you said on the phone. Some time next week, we'd thought. I half expected some sort of formal chat, if you know what I mean. You know, him asking me for your hand.'

'Just my hand? How about my head and my body, and my arms and legs?'

'Well, the rest of you too, obviously.' He brushed her attempt at humour aside. 'But then you turn up on your own, several days ahead of schedule, only giving us a few hours' notice and half a story. What are we supposed to think? No sign of your fiancé. No explanation. Your mother hasn't even got the beds ready yet.'

'Beds? We can share just the one, Dad. We do live together in Portugal.'

'I know all that, but old-fashioned, that's us. We did things properly in our day. Engaged for two years, your mother and I, and it was single beds for us, I can tell you. Your grandfather would have had a fit if I'd waltzed in expecting hanky-panky under his roof before the wedding day! There's your brother to consider, too. Don't forget he's only fifteen. What sort of message or ideas would it be giving him, at his age?'

'Times change, Dad. Stop sounding so old.'

'I am old. Or I'm starting to feel it anyway. It's not as if we see you often these days. So, if we're not meeting your young man this time, then when? Only, we would like to get to know him properly. You know, as a future son-in-law. Find out what makes him tick and all that . . . '

Patsy sighed. 'He's got family problems, Dad. He would have come if he could. Still might, if he can get away.'

'Ah, yes. Family. That ex of his, I suppose. And the child. What's her name again?'

'She's called Lily and she'll always be a part of his life, and of mine now too. You can't wish her away.'

'I didn't mean . . . '

'Oh, never mind. The lemonade's lovely, and thanks for caring, but nothing you say is going to change anything now. I have this . . . ' She held up her finger and flashed her diamond at him. 'And that means I'm going to marry him. Not Andrew Piper, or Johnny Smith, or any of the other local lads you've had lined up for me over the years. Oh, don't pretend you don't know what I'm talking about. I'm a big girl now, and you have to let me make my own choices. Okay?'

'Okay. Point taken. And I won't pry any more. But if he comes up here to join you, you'll have to tell your mother about the beds situation. It'll be more than my life's worth!' He chuckled, taking the empty glass from her hand. 'Now come on inside for your dinner. It's starting to get chilly out here. Your Mum's made a chicken something or other and roast potatoes. I bet you don't get those in Portugal. Not made with real goose fat, anyway. Matt's just finishing off his homework, then I've promised he can have you to himself all evening. Monopoly, TV, computer games, whatever he likes. Us oldies will get out of your way. We're due at the Pipers for bridge tonight. I hope that's okay, that you didn't have other plans? That lad has really missed you, Patsy, love. '

'I've missed him too. And it is great to be back home, Dad, really. Just don't worry about me, all right? Or Michael. Things will work out fine, just you wait and see.'

Would they? She certainly hoped so. Patsy took a deep breath, put on her best smile and followed her dad back towards the house, the overpowering smell of too much garlic wafting out from the open kitchen door and across the grass to meet them. Her mum never used to cook with garlic. She was strictly a plain meat and three veg kind of a woman, and always had been. It was probably her idea of what Portuguese food was like, giving Patsy what they both believed she wanted, trying hard – too hard – to make her feel at home. But it didn't matter what they ate. It was the being here, back with her parents, old-fashioned and traditional though they were, and the air and the view – and her lanky, loopy, nutter of a brother – that made this place home. And in that moment she knew that, one bed or two, Michael or no Michael, she didn't really want to be anywhere else.

*

Lily had a bad dream. Mummy was all wrapped up in lots of white sheets, like a mummy from a scary grown-up film, making funny breathing noises and she was staring at her and not saying anything, and then, when Lily tried to jump on the bed and get a cuddle, Daddy pulled her back and wouldn't let her. And Granny said Lily couldn't come to her house ever again because she'd wet the bed and made too many marks on the carpet and left the tap running. And then she lost Archie and couldn't find him anywhere, not even under the bed. Then she woke up crying, and Granny came and carried her into Mummy's bed and cuddled her up tight, and kept the light on, but Mummy wasn't there, and neither was Archie. And the bed didn't smell of Mummy any more, like she was never coming back, and the photo of Daddy was gone, and everything was different and dark and scary and sad.

CHAPTER TWENTY-FOUR

Ruby

I feel weird. Like I'm waking up from a bad dream. I'm only half here, the rest of me still somewhere else, buried in a hazy place I want to tear myself away from but can't. Like when they buried me in the sand that time at the beach, on a day trip, just my head sticking up into the sunlight, with my cap on back to front, my arms and legs pinned down, bogged under by the sheer soggy weight of all that sand. But I wasn't scared. I laughed, because I knew they would get me out, digging with their plastic spades, and their eager hands. Mrs Castle in her deckchair, watching and listening, a battered straw hat on her head, a *Woman's Weekly* in her lap. Sand flicking into my eyes, into my ears.

There was no sand when I opened my eyes. Just noises, echoes bouncing off walls, and faces peering in at me. Not the children on the beach. Strange faces, ones I didn't recognise at all, in a circle, all around me, like a halo. But, she was here too. My eyes drawn to her. Lily. Why was she here, on the beach? Wide-eyed, and small, and white. Behind all the others, like a tiny dot. And my mother. I think I saw my mother, her head bobbing up down through a window, before she disappeared again, like she always does.

It's warm, and they've gone, and I've been asleep again. Something hurts. My head. My leg. This isn't right. Still healing, someone said, holding my hand. Or was it my wrist? They come and go all the time. Touching, looking, talking. To each other, to me, about me. But I'm still only half here, only half listening.

It's funny that all I really want is to fall back into sleep. They say I've been doing that for a while. Sleeping. They say they were waiting for me to come back. Now I am back, now I am here, but I just want to sleep again. Deep, peaceful sleep. To make it all go away. All the thoughts, and memories, and truths and half-truths and lies, that wash over me while I lie here under this bare white ceiling, with nothing else to think about, nothing else to do.

The next time I hear them, I try harder. Much harder. I reach for the hand, without knowing whose it is. I peel my eyes open and drag my gaze away from the stark whiteness of the ceiling, and struggle just that little bit harder to stay awake. I open my dry lips and try to say her name. Nothing comes.

'Hello, Ruby,' a voice says, close to my face. 'Welcome back. Don't try to talk just yet. Just squeeze my fingers. Do you know where you are?'

Of course I know where I am. Do they think I'm stupid? I move my hand, just enough for the voice to feel it. Yes, I'm trying to tell her. Yes, I know where I am. I'm on the little bus thing, going home from the park, my head nodding against the glass, the sun streaming in, the noise of the younger ones buzzing around me as they squeal and scream and giggle, the rhythm of the wheels on the road thudding and clicking in time with my breathing, only half awake.

But I can feel that the wheels have stopped turning, and that the sun has gone, and so has the glass with my mother behind it, and the screams around me sound different. Are different. One of them might even be mine.

What have I done? Where is she? It feels like I'm watching a film. The replay of a film, in slow, slow, motion, with my fingers frozen over the buttons, unable to move. Even the bits of the story where I run are in slow motion. And I want to scream out loud, that Lily isn't here, that I know I shouldn't leave her, should never leave her, but I do, I have. And I can't rewind it, can't make it stop, can't change it.

I'm at the door and watching her. She's sleeping like an angel. And there's rain. I do remember the rain. But what happens next? I can't see it, can't stop it. Just the flying, the flailing, the falling . . .

In slow, slow motion, the faces come back. Huddled around me again, and this time I can't lift my head at all. Or my arms. And I'm suddenly frightened. Stuck in the sand, cold, wet, alone, with no plastic spades to save me.

I'm watching the film play again and again, but it isn't over. I know it isn't over. It's stuck in freeze-frame. Me in the sand. Lily at home. Lily alone. And I don't know the ending yet. I need to know the ending.

What happens to me? What happens to Lily? After I leave her.

CHAPTER TWENTY-FIVE

'Oh, well.' Geraldine was scribbling something on a scrap of paper. 'Another day, another dollar.'

Michael looked up from the computer screen, 'You're not talking about work, surely?'

'Oh, I don't know. I want to be here for you and Lily, and to see Ruby. But the shop can't run itself, can it? I've been making a note of a few things that I need Kerry to do, but in reality I think it might be time for me to get back down to Brighton and take over the helm myself. Some time today, maybe?'

'And what does Kerry say?'

'She says she can manage. That everything's okay.'

'Then it probably is.'

'Do you think I should stay here then? I could tell her to close up for a few days, I suppose. The poor kid must be run ragged by herself, no matter what she says. But there's still the banking to be done, and the suppliers . . . '

'Mum, do what you think is best. But, if you ask me . . . '

'Yes?'

'That shop is looking more and more like an albatross around your neck.' Was that even a real saying? He sometimes felt he was turning into his old gran who used to talk in clichés and riddles that, when he was little, hardly meant anything at all. 'Close it for a while. Take a break. Put yourself first. Give Kerry a break too. What's the worst that can happen? You lose a few quid in takings, and have to pay her to do nothing for a week or so. It's not as if you're broke, is it?'

Geraldine sat back down. 'You could be right. And you'll need the car, won't you? To get to the hospital.'

'We managed all right on the bus. We can again, if we have to.'

'No. You're right. I have to stop letting the shop rule my life. I'll call Kerry.'

'Good.'

'What are you up to there? On that computer? Where did it come from? I thought you said Ruby didn't have one.'

'Your friend William brought it over. Kind of him, wasn't it?'

'My friend?'

'Well, you spent time with him yesterday. You looked like you were getting on well enough. Anyway, he's downstairs at his mother's now, painting her ceiling. It's just a cheap laptop, but he said I could borrow it. He also got me one of these dongle things on his way over, so I could get onto the internet.'

'Why?'

'Just things I wanted to look at.'

'Work? You're as bad as me, Michael. Leave all that emailing stuff for a while. You're supposed to be on annual leave, aren't you? After all, as you said to me ... ' She tried to imitate his voice, but didn't quite get it right. 'What's the worst that can happen?'

He laughed. 'Just give me half an hour, Mum. Why don't

you call Kerry, then take Lily for a walk to the park, or pop down and have a cuppa with Agnes? Then we can all go to the hospital together, okay?'

She took her time. He could hear her on the phone in the hall, then banging about pouring Lily a drink and rummaging around for a packet of biscuits. She would never dream of turning up for tea, unexpectedly or otherwise, without an offering of some kind in her hand. But, eventually, she was gone.

Alone at last. He grabbed his mobile, and Patsy picked up hers on the second ring. 'Patsy? Oh, it's so good to hear your voice. I've missed you! No, there's no news yet, I'm afraid. Well, not since yesterday. I still have no idea how long I'm going to be here, but I have been looking up some stuff on the net, and I really don't like what I'm reading. Yes, about head injuries . . . There's all sorts of things that can go wrong. Waking up is no guarantee of anything. She's likely to be confused, disorientated, agitated, angry, have personality changes, memory loss . . . You name it and it could happen. She might even have some kind of lasting brain damage. No, I know, the internet is a dangerous thing, tell me about it. But I can't just shy away from this stuff any more.'

He took a pause and waited for her to speak. Waited for some kind of reassurance, some declaration of undying love and support.

'Michael, I don't know what to say.' Her voice sounded dull, clipped. 'Or what you expect me to say. But a "How are you?" might have been nice.'

*

Fiona bit into her sandwich and wiped at the trickle of mayonnaise that had somehow squirted out and found its way to her chin. The weather was colder today, and sitting outside was not an appealing option, so they'd found a corner of the canteen – or *cafeteria* as the hospital preferred to call it – as far away from the patients as possible. A persistent pigeon hovered on the tiny window ledge outside, hoping for scraps.

Gina toyed with her teaspoon, clinking it rhythmically against the side of her cup, and yawned into her other hand, while Laura rubbed the skin of her apple so vigorously against her uniform sleeve that she was in danger of breaking through to the flesh.

'Want to talk about it?' Gina said, clearly recognising the signs.

'Nothing to say really. Just a few things on my mind. You know, the usual. A patient who came damn close to topping herself, but refused to say why. The light at the end of the tunnel for poor Ruby at last and . . . Oh, yes. The chaplain asked me out.'

'What?' Both the other girls were suddenly sitting up straight and bouncing in their seats.

'When did this happen?' Fiona spluttered, bits of crumb launching themselves across the table. 'How? Where?'

'You'll be asking me *why* next! It was yesterday, actually. In the little cupboard he laughingly calls his office. Just after he kissed me. Or was it just before? It's all a bit of a blur, to tell you the truth.'

'Kissed you? You dark horse! You didn't say a word about it last night when you came home.' Gina grabbed Laura's arm, sending the apple flying. 'You did say yes, didn't you? Oh, please, tell me you said yes.'

'I said yes.'

'Well, thank God for that! Or maybe that's what he said? Your chaplain. In one of his little chats with the almighty!'

'He's not *my* chaplain. And, honestly, he does not talk about God all the time. Or *to* God either, for that matter. He's surprisingly normal, underneath the obvious.'

'Oh, yes? Went that far, did you?'

'Gina, stop it. I meant that he likes ordinary things, just like other blokes. Beer, for instance, and music, and motorbikes.'

'And sex?' Fiona chipped in.

'I really wouldn't know.'

'Oh, come on. We need facts. Juicy facts. You can be so boring sometimes! Just make sure we're the first to know when you find out.'

'So speaks the dating expert! At least mine will turn up.'

'Hurtful, Laura. Not nice!' Fiona feigned indignation.

'Now, now, girls. What are friends for, after all, if not to share in each other's downs just as much as the ups?' said Gina, ever the peacemaker. 'And if you can't fix it, then laugh about it, that's what I say.'

So they did.

*

William put his paintbrush down on a sheet of newspaper. It was surprisingly hard work, painting a ceiling, even a small one, what with all that stretching up above his head, and it didn't take much to give him an excuse to stop.

'You know, I'll miss Geraldine when she's gone.' Agnes had just seen Geraldine out and had come wandering into the kitchen again, supposedly to make more tea, but he was sure she only did it to keep an eye on what he was doing. As if he was a little boy again and she had to make sure he didn't splash his poster paints on the floor or get mucky fingerprints on the door handles.

'She's been a bit of company for you, that's for sure.' He ran his hands under the tap, went and found the biscuit tin, which the two women had left lying open in the other room, and sat down with it at the table. There was still paint under his nails but he didn't suppose it would do much harm if he swallowed the odd drop. It hardly seemed worth a thorough scrub when he'd be back up the stepladder in a few minutes getting covered in another lot.

'So have you, these last few days. Been company, that is. It's nice having you around, Son. I haven't seen so much of you in a long time.' She turned her back and busied herself with the kettle. 'But, no, it's more than that, with Geraldine. She's a nice woman. A very nice woman. Not just a passing stranger, but someone I think I could get to call a friend. And, at my age, with one funeral following another, I don't have too many of those left any more.'

'Shame she lives in Brighton then. I don't suppose we'll see much of her once this business is all over.'

'Oh, I don't know about that, William. I can't imagine her being parted from her little granddaughter for long, not now they've been reunited. They're off to the hospital together now, in fact. She and that son of hers, taking Lily to see her mother. It all makes me feel quite . . . Well, sad, in a way.'

'What does?' He dipped his hand into the tin, rummaged beneath what was left of Geraldine's digestives and found a broken custard cream at the bottom. They always had been his favourites. No good for keeping himself in trim, probably, with all that gooey creamy stuff sandwiched in the middle, but the broken ones didn't really count, did they?

'Everything being so quiet again, once she's gone. I'm not looking forward to that. It's sad how easily relationships seem to break down these days. I mean, up until the last two days, she hadn't seen that little one in ages. Then there's the father, going off like that, for months on end, with some other woman, and now waltzing back in as if he's never been gone. Why can't families just stay together any more? Your father and I would never have dreamed of running off anywhere, leaving you – leaving each other . . .'

'Is this relationships rant of yours another dig about me and Susan? I did try to make it work. You know I did.'

'No, no. I can't pretend to be sorry about that. Only . . . Well, I am sorry that you didn't find the right woman early enough, when you were younger, settle down and be happy, have children.'

'Too late for all that now, Mum.'

'For children, maybe. But not the settling down part. You can find love at any age, you know.'

'Really? Love, eh? Are you trying to tell me you're having a fling yourself? Who is it? The milkman?' He laughed, choking temporarily on his biscuit so she had to lean across and pat him on the back.

'That will teach you to mock. Not that we even have a milk-man these days, haven't seen one in all the time I've lived here. But you could do a lot worse, you know. Than to take up with someone like Geraldine, I mean. Nice-looking woman, easy to talk to, has her own business. You'd even get a ready-made grandchild!'

'Mother, honestly! Are you matchmaking?'

'You won't do anything about it yourself, so someone has to.' She poured the hot water into mugs, swirled the teabags around for way too long, and added a hefty helping of full-fat milk. 'You need looking after, and I'm too old and this flat is too small for me to be able to do it any more. I don't even have the room to do a proper family Christmas dinner. That lovely old table I had. It could seat ten, at a push.'

'Ah, I see. The house move again. You've never quite forgiven me for that, have you? Nobody actually twisted your arm, you know, and when were there ever ten of us? You'd have had to invite half the street to fill that table, and this one's fine for just the two of us. It's even coped with five this week. At a push, admittedly. Then there was all the waxing and polishing that old table always seemed to need.'

'I wasn't forced into moving, that's true, but I was certainly persuaded, and rushed, and against my better judgement. Oh, yes, I accept the old place was getting too much for me to manage, but I think, with hindsight, you – okay *we* – didn't take enough time to consider the other options, and this flat, it just isn't right for me, not really. I don't feel at home here. I don't feel settled as if it's my "forever home", as they say on the property programmes. Okay, I know it's near the shops and the buses, and you're not too far away if I need you, but I'm just not a city girl at heart.'

'Girl?' He smiled, raising his eyebrows at her.

'Yes, go on, rub it in, why don't you? I'm no spring chicken any more, but that's even more reason why the years I have left should be good ones, spent where I want to be and where I feel at home.'

'Which is where, exactly?'

'I haven't quite decided. But I do know it's not here. And, yes, it might be nice to have more than just the two of us around the table. To be able to entertain sometimes. Geraldine and her little family have shown me that. I like having company. I miss it. I even enjoyed doing that heap of ironing. I haven't had anybody but myself to iron for in a long while. I'm lonely here, William, and I want to do something about it. Don't interrupt.' She put up her hand to stop him. 'So, while I've still got the value of this place and money in the bank, and a mind of my own that's still, thankfully, in working order, it's not too late to change things, is it?'

'Well, I suppose not. Just let me know when you've decided, won't you?'

'Oh, I certainly will, William. You can be sure of that. Loud and clear. From now on, I fully intend to speak my mind.'

As if there was ever a time when you didn't, William thought, but he knew better than to say it out loud. Still, she had a point about Geraldine. She was a nice woman, and it was about time he found himself one of those.

*

'She's doing really well.' It was the young nurse again, Laura, the one who had befriended Ruby while she'd been asleep, if that was even possible. She was just leaving the ward, squirting the gel onto her hands, as they arrived.

'What does that mean, exactly?' Geraldine was looking anxiously along the gleaming white corridor, as if every step she took along it, every step nearer to Ruby's room, was going to bring her closer to something she just didn't want to confront. 'Is she properly awake? Will she know us? Is this all going to be too much for Lily to cope with?'

Laura placed her newly scrubbed hand on Geraldine's arm. 'It's okay,' she said. 'I've just been getting to know her properly myself. She's groggy, still a bit sleepy, but I got a smile out of her! Just give her time to recover. Everything's looking very promising. There's nothing to be scared of, really. No nasty machinery now, no wires or blood or anything.' She bent down towards Lily and patted her head. 'And you'll be fine, won't you, little one? You're going to see Mummy again, and that will make Mummy so happy.'

Michael thanked her, watched her open the door and walk away. 'Ready, Mum?'

Geraldine nodded, held tightly on to Lily's hand and, after they'd checked in with Cora at the desk, followed her son into Ruby's room.

Her eyes were closed but she wasn't asleep. There was a shaft of light filtering in through a gap in the half-closed blinds, shining right across the bedclothes in a straight line, like a laser beam. From somewhere outside a bird was calling loudly and they could hear the rustle of the trees below the window, moving in the wind.

Ruby tried to lift her head off the pillow as they came towards her, opening her eyes and making a strange croaky sound that was somewhere between a laugh and a cough as soon as she saw her daughter.

'Mummy!' There was no stopping Lily. She tugged her hand away from Geraldine's and launched herself onto the bed, flinging her arms out in front of her, her little legs flaying out behind, as she landed in a star shape, her face instantly buried in Ruby's neck.

'Lily.' Ruby winced. Her voice was small and weak, but she managed to lift her arms, despite the cracked ribs, and wrap them around her daughter, the small warm body pressed against her, their faces so close it was as if they were breathing each other in.

'You didn't come home, Mummy. Archie and me, we were on our own. And we didn't have anything to eat.' Lily was choking back tears and clinging to Ruby like she would never let her go.

'I know. I know. And I am so sorry.' Ruby was stroking her daughter's hair and hugging her close. 'Mummy loves you so much, and she is never going to leave you again.'

'Ruby . . . ' Geraldine approached very slowly, not sure of the response she was going to get.

'Geraldine?' Ruby looked up, gazing into her face, puzzled for a moment.

'Hello, Ruby love. I've been so worried about you.'

'Have you?' Ruby's voice was muffled, coming from behind Lily's hair.

Geraldine couldn't be sure if Ruby was crying. She was struggling, and mostly failing, to hold her own tears back, no matter how hard she was trying to be strong for Lily's sake. It was just so awful, seeing Ruby like this, all damaged and alone.

'Mind Mummy's head now, Lily. And her poorly leg.' Michael laid his hand on the back of Lily's head and stroked it. 'Ruby, how did this happen? What were you thinking, leaving our daughter like that?'

'Leaving our daughter? No, *you* did that. Not me. Remember?' She closed her eyes again. She looked exhausted. 'If you hadn't done that . . . '

'You're saying it's my fault? Good God, it was you who did this to her, not me! You can't just go out and leave a two-year-old to fend for herself. Something terrible could have happened to her. It damn nearly did.'

'Michael.' Geraldine's voice was steely. 'This is not the time, nor the place. Now, if you can't be in this room without starting another row, then I think you should wait outside, don't you? Ruby is not ready for this. And Lily certainly isn't. They say only two visitors at a time anyway, so I suggest you go and take a walk to clear your head. Lily – and Ruby – will be fine with me for a while. Bring us back a coffee, why don't you, and something cold for Lily. Twenty minutes, okay?'

He made a fuss, but he went anyway. Probably glad of the excuse, Geraldine thought, waiting until the door had closed silently behind him. He wasn't good with hospitals, and being with Ruby always brought out the worst in him. Too much alike, those two, that was the trouble, both rushing into things without thinking them through properly first.

'Geri . . . ' Ruby hadn't called her that in a long time. 'Thank you.'

'What for? Kicking my angry son out of the room? He will calm down, you know.'

'Is he right though? Did I do it? What he says?' She lay back down, worn out, her grip loosening around Lily's shoulders. 'I can't think. It's just a muddle, a big mess. And all I can remember is the rain. It was only for a few minutes. Not long. I don't like her to get wet. Lily. My Lily. She's still so little. So little . . .' Then Ruby drifted back into sleep.

*

Barbara Freeman rang early in the afternoon. She was having some kind of strategy meeting with the police to talk about what had happened and whether any legal action was likely to be taken for neglect. Michael cringed when she used that word. It all sounded so terrible, that between them, he and Ruby had failed their daughter and were about to be branded as bad parents, or worse.

'There will then be a full meeting – a case conference, we call it – within the next week or so, so we can determine if Lily needs to become the subject of a child protection plan. That will include ourselves, the police, probably someone from Lily's nursery . . . We will need to study Ruby's own social services records, including the children's home where I understand she spent a good part of her childhood, in care. We do need to get the full picture, you see.'

'You're talking about putting Lily's name on some kind of at-risk register? Like kids from violent homes? With drunken fathers who beat them up, and drug addicts for mothers?'

'Not necessarily, but yes, that's essentially what a plan does. But it happens for all sorts of reasons. Nobody is suggesting that you or Ruby are violent, or fall into those categories at all, or that Ruby's own childhood history necessarily has any bearing, but we do have to do whatever is needed to make sure Lily is safe, that she's not left alone again, not put in unnecessary danger or left in a position of vulnerability . . . '

'I see.'

'It's looking unlikely that Ruby herself will be well enough to attend, but I would appreciate it if you could be there, Mr Payne. Your mother too, if you believe she is going to continue to play a significant part in your daughter's life. Don't worry. It's not as frightening as it may sound, but it is a serious matter. Some kind of close supervision is almost certainly going to be required, if Lily is to stay with Ruby, so we can keep an eye on things for a while. I'm sure you'll want to have your say, and to be party to any decisions that are made about Lily's future.' She promised to come back with a date and a time as soon as things had been arranged, then rang off.

Michael collapsed into a chair. Lily's future? Much as he may have had his moments with Ruby, bad moments, he had never envisaged a time when Lily's future might not be spent with Ruby. Was she really a bad mother, the kind to neglect her child – to go out and knowingly leave her alone? You only had to have seen her and Lily together earlier on, clinging to each other on that hospital bed, to know that she loved her. So, why? What could possibly have gone so horribly wrong, in the few months since he had left?

He had tried to help where he could, but this was no longer

just about him visiting or sending money. If there was some doubt about Ruby's competence or her ability to care for Lily properly, then he had to step up to the plate now and do more – whatever it took – to keep those two together. Because, however he felt about Ruby, he could never be party to anything that took Lily away from her.

*

'I don't know if you have any plans.' William shuffled from one foot to the other on the doorstep. 'But I have an hour or two to kill now. Waiting for paint to dry, basically. Oh, dear, that sounds like some old cliché, doesn't it? What people do when they're bored! Sit and watch paint dry. Which I'm not, by the way! Bored, I mean. But I just wondered . . . Well, if you might fancy a run out somewhere in the car?'

Geraldine watched him fiddling with his collar, tiny specks of paint still freckling the backs of his hands. The poor man looked flustered. She couldn't think why.

'It's not a bad sort of a day, weather-wise, and I imagine there can't be an awful lot for you to do, you know, to keep you occupied, when you're away from home like this. Not brought your knitting or your library book with you, I bet. Perhaps a bit of a walk, tea and scones in a little teashop, or maybe visit an art gallery? Whatever you fancy, really. What do you say?'

'But what about Lily?'

'Oh, bring her with you if you like. I don't mind. You have the kiddy car seat now, after all.'

'Do you know, William, I think perhaps she would benefit

from spending a few hours with just her father. A bit of bonding time. I'm sure he would too, after the news he's just received. But I can tell you about that as we drive, can't I?'

'You'll come then?'

'Of course. Why not? I'd love to. Do I need my coat, do you think?'

'Not a bad idea. It's quite a nice day, but you never know when the rain might decide to come back.'

'Pop inside for a mo then, while I find it. Can't have you hanging about on the landing. I'll just need to say goodbye to Michael and Lily, and tell them where I'm going. Where are we going, by the way? Only, you mentioned tea and, to be honest, I seem to have drunk nothing but tea – and the occasional coffee – since I got here. I'm swimming in the stuff. I don't suppose we could run to something a bit stronger, could we?'

'Pub?'

'Sounds good.'

'By the river? Watch the boats go by?'

'Sounds perfect.'

Within minutes she was sitting beside him in the car and they were weaving their way through the traffic. While he concentrated on getting past a bus that had stopped to disgorge a gaggle of noisy schoolchildren she studied his profile. He wasn't bad looking for a man of his age. What must he be? Fifty-six? Fifty-eight? Just a little younger than she was, she'd guess. His hair still had some colour to it, despite the greying around the ears, and he did have rather nice eyes. A dusky kind of brown, from what she could see behind his glasses, which were already starting to darken in the sunlight.

'You mentioned news?' he said, glancing across at her briefly before returning his attention to the road. 'Not bad news, I hope?'

'The woman we saw at the hospital. Children's Services. They're planning some kind of meeting to talk about Lily. Michael's worried they may try to take her away from Ruby, or watch her like a hawk from now on, at the very least.'

'They wouldn't give her to strangers though, surely? Not when she has a dad and a gran who could have her?'

'Who knows what they have in mind? I wouldn't want to take her away from her mummy, and neither would Michael. That wasn't what we came here for. To see her, re-establish some kind of regular contact, have her for a little holiday, that was all. We're waiting to find out when this meeting's likely to be, then perhaps we can still take her down to the sea for a few days. She'll enjoy that, I think, after what she's been through.'

'It must have been tough. How's she coping?'

'Surprisingly well. She's sleeping okay, by and large, as long as we leave the light on and she has that toy of hers to cuddle up to. Just one bad dream, but it soon passed. Remarkably resilient, aren't they? Kids.'

'I wouldn't know really. Not had a lot of experience with children myself.'

'Oh, you never had any? I'm sorry. I hope that didn't sound horribly insensitive.'

'Not at all. Just one of those things. A fact of life. Now, let's head for the bridge, shall we? I think we'll have better luck finding somewhere suitable on the other side. Have you eaten? I know it's a bit of a funny time for a meal, but I'm actually quite peckish. I seem to have got by today so far on Weetabix and custard creams.'

Vivien Brown

'Ha! Me too, but it was cornflakes, and a couple of digestive biscuits with your mum, in my case.'

'Excellent!' He put his foot down as the lights went green and they drove onto the bridge. Below them the river shimmered in the sun, its streaky grey surface moving and rocking with the remains of the tide, little boats chugging up and down purposefully, a bunch of gulls swarming and squawking overhead, reminding her of home.

'Oh, I do love London. I should come up more often.'

'Yes, you should.'

They drove on in silence for a while, the busy streets and tall buildings gradually giving way to more open space, more room to breathe. William opened both windows by a few inches, and a gentle breeze wafted across the insides of the car and out again, ruffling Geraldine's hair.

'It's very good of you, William, to look after us all like this,' she said, turning towards him, her hand touching his sleeve before quickly pulling back. 'The driving, the shopping, sorting out the computer for Michael. And now you're fixing the ceiling, so we don't have to worry about contacting the landlord or claiming on the insurance – your mother told me. I mean it, it's more than we could have expected. And if there's any expense involved in that, you must let me know.'

'Oh, I had the paint already lying around doing nothing and plenty of time on my hands too, so it's no trouble. Beats sitting around, knitting!'

They both laughed.

'For all you know, I might love knitting. If only I had the time.'

'And you don't?'

'Every spare minute gets used up running the shop, or worrying about it. Behind the counter, at the wholesalers, balancing the books. It's taken over my life, what with everything falling on my shoulders now, since my Ken died. We used to do it together, you see. It was easier then. A pleasure, even. Something we shared. I don't even know why I'm still doing it, on my own, and at my age.'

'Then why are you? Couldn't you retire early, start enjoying life, pass it all on to Michael?'

'Oh, I've suggested it, but he's not interested. Especially now he's working abroad, with this Patsy girl.'

'Sell up then?'

Geraldine leaned back in her seat and gently rolled her head around in small circles, stretching her tense neck muscles. 'It's a possibility, that's for sure. And one I've been thinking about lately. But I do have another plan. An idea I've been toying with. I'm just not sure if it could work . . . ' Her voice faded into a thoughtful silence and William didn't press her to explain.

'Ah, here we are. This place looks okay, don't you think? Tables out by the water. A nice bit of grass.' He pulled the car off the road and slid it into a corner space in the car park.

Before she could even unclip her seatbelt he was out and walking round to her side of the car, opening her door, offering his arm. 'Madam?' he said, bowing slightly and raising an imaginary hat. 'Shall we?' And, arm in arm – how exactly had that happened? – they strolled across the car park to the little terrace and selected a table looking out across the river, before William disappeared inside to find a menu and order the drinks.

'Oh,' Geraldine said, very quietly, to herself, as the realisation of her situation began to sink in. 'I think I just might be on a date.' Pulling her coat around her shoulders at the sudden shiver that ran through her, she wasn't at all sure how that made her feel.

CHAPTER TWENTY-SIX

Ruby

I saw Lily today. Properly saw her, not just a blurry vision, at the back of the room, that I wasn't sure was real. I touched her and held her, and let myself cry into her hair. Not that I could have stopped myself if I'd tried. But, after that, when they'd all gone, someone from the police came and asked me questions. About how I left her, and when, and why.

It is starting to come back. As my head clears and the fog lifts. Only snatches. It's as if it's all there, waiting to be remembered, but just out of reach. I didn't do it on purpose though. I never would. I know that. I hope they know it too.

All I want now is to get better and get out of here and be with her again. I told them how much I love her, but I'm not sure they really cared about that. They certainly didn't write it down.

They say they know who ran me down. Some young lad. Said he just panicked and drove off after he'd hit me, but his conscience got the better of him and he handed himself in within half an hour of it happening. They asked if I remembered anything about it, about being hit, but I don't. Not a thing. Look what he's done to me. It's all his fault. It must be. What happened to me. To Lily. He kept me away from her. Kept me here.

But it seems there were witnesses, and they say I just stepped out, head down, not looking, that the driver didn't stand a chance. The police say they are unlikely to press any charges for dangerous driving or anything like that. For driving off, maybe, leaving the scene, but not for hitting me. So, he gets off scot free while I . . .

Oh, God. It's not nice, talking to the police. Raking over rights and wrongs, feeling like a criminal, when it's me that's the victim. The nurses didn't let them stay long though, that's one good thing. Needs her rest, they said. I could feel my hands shaking, while I spoke to them, and again now, when I reach to my throat, to Lily's cross, like I always do when I'm nervous, but it's not there. I must ask someone about that. I hope it wasn't stolen – anything could have happened while I was gone. Anything.

CHAPTER TWENTY-SEVEN

William wandered from room to room. He had loved this old house once. Years ago, when he'd first moved in and its high ceilings and creamy walls rang with possibilities. He was going to buy big furniture, hold parties, take up gardening, make wine. But none of that had happened.

He had been used to a small bachelor flat before. The vastness of the space suddenly available to him came as a shock. There was much more hoovering to do, and some of it on stairs, which he never did get the hang of. Two loos and a much bigger kitchen to keep clean, cobwebs taunting him from high-up corners, bigger bills to pay.

Within months he was wondering if he had made a mistake. By the time he got home from work he couldn't face the housework. The place, like himself, began to take on a tired air and the parties dream just seemed to fade away. Dust settled on his few ornaments, so he packaged them away in boxes. Who needed souvenirs of holidays he could barely remember? Or ornate vases, when he didn't know one end of a flower from the other and on the odd occasion he had bought himself a bunch they'd died within days. Outside, there were the weeds and lawnmowing to contend with, cracks in the driveway, paint starting to peel from the window frames. He allowed himself to settle into a kind of cluttered, dusty, make-do existence. If no one saw it all or had to live amongst it but himself, then why should it matter?

Then, along had come Susan. And he knew then what the house, and he, had needed. A woman's touch. Now, as he looked at his home with a critical eye, he could see that, since she had gone, things had reverted to the way they'd been before she came. He was not good at domesticity. Like his mother, he was just ticking along, biding his time, living in a place that was too big for one, that had no real meaning for him now and knowing deep down that life could be better somewhere else but not knowing where that somewhere might be. At least his mother was determined to do something about it. All he felt was a numbing apathy that, if he wasn't careful, would see him slip slowly into a lonely cobwebby old age.

He had really enjoyed his afternoon out with Geraldine today. Oh, nothing had actually happened between them. They'd not fallen into each other's arms and declared undying passion. Nothing like that. A couple of drinks and a bite to eat by the river, watching the swans glide by, chatting about nondescript things. It had taken him out of himself. Did that make any sense? He wasn't sure, but it had been a new experience, being with a woman who wasn't out to belittle him, who wanted nothing from him, one who looked at him as if he was a man who might have something interesting to say.

When he'd dropped her back at the flats, he'd been tempted to ask her out again, to tell her what a difference she had made to his day, to reach out and kiss her on the cheek, but it had not felt right. He had no idea how she might feel. Or how he felt himself. She would be off back to the coast any day now so there was no real future in any of it. Which was a shame.

He hadn't gone in. Agnes asking questions was the last thing he needed, so he'd seen Geraldine as far as the door, got back in the car and just driven. He couldn't even remember now where he'd gone. Just around, with the windows down, letting the cool air start to clear his head, waiting for his thoughts to settle.

The house sighed around him. Agnes was right. Well, she usually was, of course. Sometimes you just had to take the bull by the horns and make things happen. Good things. Positive things. They sure as hell didn't happen all by themselves.

He wondered what the house might be worth these days. It was a good part of London. Desirable, as the estate agents would undoubtedly say as they rang up the pound signs in their heads. What exactly was keeping him here? Without Susan, without a job, he had no ties any more. Except his mother, and she wanted to get out too. Would it be so bad to contemplate moving somewhere new, maybe even doing it together? Property outside London was so much cheaper. If they were to pool their resources they could afford something big enough to allow them each their own space. Maybe a house with a separate granny annexe, or two houses in the same street. Enough to be able to keep an eye on her without living in each other's pockets. There'd be plenty of money over to pay a cleaner. He'd had enough of battling with that damn vacuum, with its tubes and attachments and clogged filters, and his mother wasn't up to it these days, her arthritic knees growing stiffer and creakier by the day, although she was still surprisingly nifty with an iron.

Would she want to do that? Buy somewhere together? He didn't have to say anything to her yet. Wouldn't want it to look like he was pushing her into anything, making decisions for her again, or making assumptions that she was getting past the living alone stage and might need a bit more support. No, one step at a time. It was just a vague idea at the moment. He'd check out the house prices on the internet first, see what he might get for this old place.

He almost ran up to the third bedroom, the one he laughingly called the study despite it being more of a junk room now, filled with stuff he hadn't looked at in months, and a tatty desk in the corner. But when he got there the desk had nothing on it but a couple of chewed pencils, and he remembered that he'd lent his laptop to Michael. He'd have to go round tomorrow to ask for it back. Then he might get to see Geraldine again, if she was in. It was the perfect excuse.

But he shouldn't need excuses. It was time to be proactive, to take charge of his life. If he was ever going to change things, he had a feeling it had to be now. And before Geraldine was gone.

*

Lily liked having Granny to stay. Granny made yummy dinners, and her hands smelled nice, and she let Lily stay up late. She always set a special place at the table for Archie, and gave him his own bowl and spoon. When she tucked her into bed she sang funny songs Lily hadn't heard before. Ones she said she used to sing to Daddy when he was as small as she was now. There was one about someone running around the town at night in his nightgown. That one made Lily laugh because it said 'willy' in it, and the boys at nursery had told her that was a rude word. And one about Granny's glasses, which was funny too, because Granny didn't wear any.

Lily hadn't been to nursery this week. Granny said she'd phoned them and told them why, and that she liked to have her at home, to make up for lost time. Lily didn't know what that meant. She hadn't learned how to tell the time yet. But, with Granny here, they could do things together, like making cakes and licking the spoon, watching cartoons and walking to the swings, and they could go and visit Mummy every day. Lily missed Mummy lots. She didn't like seeing her with her leg all covered up like that or with the bandage on her head.

Granny had bought her a doll and a doctor's kit, with bottles and bandages, a tube to put in your mouth and an ear thing to listen to people's hearts, so she could practise making Mummy better. She didn't like the doll much. It felt cold and hard. Not like Archie who was so soft and floppy and warm. She didn't like it but she didn't say so. Mummy had always said it was rude to say things like that if someone had tried especially hard to be nice. That it might hurt their feelings. Like when Steven at nursery had said he thought Akbar's funny red top made him look like a fat tomato and Akbar had cried. It wasn't nice to do that, to make people cry. Lily had cried a lot when Mummy wasn't at home, and she didn't like crying.

Lily used the bandages in the doctor's kit to wrap up Archie's head so it looked like Mummy's, except Archie's kept slipping down over one eye. When Archie's head got better, she told herself, then so would Mummy's, and they could both take their bandages off together.

Lily left the doll sitting on the floor in the corner. It had long dark hair and a plastic face and it kept looking at her with its big open eyes that didn't shut even if you laid it down. She gave it a name because Granny said she should. She called it Nancy, like the girl at nursery she was a bit scared of because she had one eye that looked the wrong way. She wondered if her doctor's kit had anything magic in it that could fix Nancy's poorly eye. Probably not, or a real doctor would have done it by now.

But all that mattered now was that Mummy would be coming home soon. She hoped it would be in time for her birthday and that there would be a bouncy castle, and a rabbit, just like she had asked for. And, while she waited, she took extra good care of Archie, and his head.

*

Michael couldn't sleep on Ruby's old sofa much longer. It was too soft and too lumpy, and it was starting to give him a permanent backache. And it was way too short. He had two choices. Either to lie on his side and bend his legs up, almost to his chest, to make them fit, or lie flat on his back and leave them dangling, unsupported, over the edge.

It was three in the morning and he couldn't sleep, but it wasn't because of his legs. It was because of his head. There was too much going on inside it. Too many what ifs? Too many scenarios playing themselves out behind his eyes, like watching a thriller series on TV, with all the highs and lows and the long waits between episodes, not knowing what is going to happen at the end of this one, or the next, or when the whole thing comes to an end, and finding it even harder to guess.

He knew that his loyalty now had to be to Lily. Harsh though it seemed, he had to make sure that Lily was safe and happy, and if the powers that be made any kind of decisions about her, he had to co-operate with them, and try to stay a major part of his daughter's life, no matter where that left Ruby. He felt very sorry about Ruby. It wasn't her fault he didn't love her. He had tried to make a go of things. He really had. But when his life had started to change, when new work opportunities had come up, he had felt he had to go with them, to move on, and Ruby had not kept up, not kept moving along with him. Moving to London had been bad enough, done with reluctance and a lot of tears, but she would never have wanted to go to Portugal. Even without Patsy in the equation, he knew they would have come to an end — a natural, inevitable end. There wasn't a strong enough bond to hold them together. No bond at all, except for Lily. But what sort of life would Lily have had if he had given up his ambitions, and her parents had stayed together without love, simply because they felt they must?

Ruby had been very young when they'd met, the two of them thrown together under the same roof. She was not very worldly-wise, not used to coping with things by herself, and she was needy. Growing up in that children's home, without parents of her own, had probably played a huge part in making her that way, so again, he knew it was not her fault. He should have known better though, been more strong-willed, more determined to say no.

Ruby had been his mother's latest pet project back then. She had a habit of helping young girls she thought were vulnerable, finding them jobs and homes, giving them a kick-start in life if she could. But neither he nor his mum had known that Ruby already had some schoolgirl crush on him, long before they'd properly met. Perhaps, if either of them had realised that, his mother would have done more to keep them apart. But it was wrong to blame her, or Ruby. He had been weak, seen a pretty girl more or less offering herself to him on a plate, and, as many young men would have done, found himself led by the mysterious inner workings of his groin instead of his brain, and taken advantage of the offer. And, oh boy, had he had to live with the consequences.

He thought back to those final weeks, the slow, seeping away of their life together, after she'd figured out he was getting close – too close – to Patsy. He should have had the courage to tell her himself, of course. Be honest, for a change, but it hadn't been hard for her to guess. She wasn't stupid. He couldn't remember ever seeing her so upset, so distressed. She'd storm out sometimes, slamming the door, and disappear for hours. Leaving him with Lily, and his guilt. Walking, she'd say, when she came back. Just walking, to clear her head. But he didn't think it ever did clear her head.

Was that what had happened now? Had she stormed off, walked off in a huff for some reason, leaving Lily behind? This time, he hadn't been there to hold the fort. Hadn't been there for Lily. Nobody was.

He owed her something. He knew he did. Some support, some understanding, some help in proving herself to the authorities. But he couldn't stay with her, couldn't even contemplate moving back in and trying to make a go of things, to get the Social Services people off their backs, because he didn't love her. He loved Patsy. With all his heart.

Turning over, rearranging his pillow and giving it a good thump in an attempt at making himself more comfortable, he thought he heard a noise behind him. He raised his head and squinted into the darkness. His mother was up, out of bed, padding through to the kitchen.

'Oh, sorry. I thought you'd be asleep.' Geraldine stopped in the doorway. 'I didn't wake you, did I?'

Michael hauled himself up to a sitting position and stretched. 'Nope. Couldn't sleep.' He kept his voice to a whisper, mindful of Lily asleep in the next room. 'How about you?'

'Same,' she whispered back. 'Too much going on. Too much to worry about. Do you fancy a cuppa? I was going to make myself one, to see if it helped.'

'Go on then. I might as well join you in the kitchen. This damn sofa will be the death of me.'

They pulled the kitchen door closed behind them before turning on the light. The last thing they would want now would be to wake Lily.

'I keep thinking about poor Ruby.' Geraldine sat down opposite him as she waited for the kettle to boil. 'I want to do something to help her. I still feel responsible for her.'

'You're not.'

'Maybe not, technically. But I grew very fond of her, you

know, when she was living at home with us. With you . . . To all intents and purposes, she's my daughter-in-law, or as good as, and she's the mother of my grandchild. I don't want to lose touch with her again.'

'Then don't. Just don't expect me to have her back. It's not the answer.'

'There really is no chance . . .? For Lily's sake?'

'Mother. I've just got engaged to Patsy and it's Patsy I want to marry, Patsy I am *going* to marry. Not Ruby.'

'But I'd been so looking forward to it, Michael. To the wedding, and to Lily's christening. We could have been a real little family, the four of us. Well, we already were, weren't we? For a time. I wanted that to go on, to be legal, official, permanent. The Paynes, together against the world. You know, all for one and one for all. I felt I needed that, after losing your father. Some stability again, some happiness, some hope for the future.' She paused, stood up and made the tea at the sink, stirring slowly, before fishing the soggy bags out of the cups and turning back towards him. 'I'd bought a hat, you know.'

'Mother! How many more times do we have to hear about that bloody hat? People can't go ahead with misguided unwanted weddings just because you have bought a hat. And, anyway, you can wear it to my wedding to Patsy, if it matters that much.'

'I don't think so, dear.'

'Why don't you like Patsy, Mum? Why can't you accept her for who she is and not condemn her as some sort of marriage wrecker? She's never done anything to deserve the way you treat her.'

'It's not that I don't like her. I hardly know her . . . '

'Then get to know her! Look, Mum, Patsy's here to stay. I love her. She will be my wife, part of the little family you say you want so badly. I'm sorry that family isn't quite the one you envisaged, but I can't do much about that. Go ahead. See Ruby, take responsibility for her if that's what you want, and keep her in your life. It will be good for Lily, and good for you. I'm happy about that. But try to find a little corner of your heart for Patsy too. It doesn't have to be one or the other. You could have both. Think about it, Mum. Please.'

'I have, as it happens. Believe me, I'm not usually prowling about in the middle of the night like this. I've been lying awake too, and thinking. About the future, and what's best for all of us. Remembering something I had always planned to do, before you running off like that changed everything. About the shop . . . '

'Mum, we've had this conversation before. I know you want out. I know it's all getting too much for you. Sell it if you like, but it's not for me. I'm no shopkeeper. I don't want it. Not now. Not ever.'

'Oh, don't worry. I know that only too well. And when I'm gone the house will come to you, just as it should. But the shop . . . Well, it's not you I've decided to give it to.'

'Really?' He raised an eyebrow and looked at her quizzically.

'No, Michael. I'm giving it to Ruby.'

CHAPTER TWENTY-EIGHT

Ruby

I got out of bed this morning. First time, with help. I didn't go anywhere, just tried to keep my balance with a woozy head and one leg in plaster, used the portable loo thing and sat in a chair while they sorted out the sheets. Then she came. The Social Services woman, Mrs Freeman. She didn't stay long. She asked me things, about my life and Lily's, how we spend our days. I did my best, tried to say what she wanted to hear, but I know it wasn't enough. She said she'd be back tomorrow, when I was stronger, when I'd had more time to rest, and to remember

I quite liked her. She only wants what's best for Lily, I can see that. To make sure Lily is safe and that I am coping with things. She wrote lots down. Talked about support networks, nodded a lot, told me not to worry. It made my head ache though. It does that most of the time anyway, but all the questions made it worse.

I'm getting better, I think, though I still feel very tired, and lifeless, and sad. I'm glad they've moved me out of that room, my little sterile prison cell, now that I'm awake and talking and moving, and not the gibbering wreck they'd feared I could be.

Yes, I can blink and hear and speak and count and write. I can just about manage the alphabet backwards, although I'm sure there are lots of people who haven't had a bang on the head who can't. And yes, I know my name (despite the fact that half the hospital thought it was Lily), what year it is (though what day it is took me a while to figure out), and who's Prime Minister (even if I wish they weren't). All written down in their forms and their files, evidence that I'm back and I'm whole and all I need to do now is heal.

So, I'm in an ordinary ward, with other people in it. Not on my own any more. Someone to talk to, a bit of activity going on, which beats that awful unnatural silence, I suppose. When you're used to a bouncy almost-three-year-old morning, noon and night, silence feels very strange. But I know I'm not right yet. I'm far from feeling like me – the real me. That could be a good thing, couldn't it? The real me did something stupid, something dangerous and unforgivable, didn't she? Changing, becoming someone else, if I can manage to do that, can only be a good thing.

I've tried to work out how long I've been here. They've told me it's Thursday, so that's what I said for the test, but I know it was Saturday when I went out of the flat, when I ended up in the road.

There was someone hovering over me in a yellow jacket, and I tried to tell him about Lily, and then I woke up. Here, in hospital. All in an instant. Somewhere in between, there have been days and nights that have slipped by unnoticed, when I've had things done to my head and my leg, when I've slept and dreamed and remembered things, and tried and failed to wake up, and been monitored and tested and talked to . . . Life has gone on without me in it.

It's a scary thought, being here but not here, alive but not properly functioning, not even breathing for myself. What if I had never woken up at all? What would have happened to Lily then? Separating a mother and her child is wrong. Look what happened to me, always waiting for my mother to come, and always disappointed, even when she did. Is that what they are going to try to do to me? To Lily? Is that why they're asking me all these questions? Trying to take her away from me?

I want Lily with me, growing up with me. I want her to have everything I never had. To find someone, get married. Give me grandchildren. It's hard to think that far ahead, to imagine Lily all grown up, and me old with wrinkles and grey hair and bad knees like the old lady downstairs.

I suppose I should just be happy to be alive at all. I look down at my leg, all encased in plaster, and my toes, with just a smattering of old red polish still clinging to the tips of my nails, and I know I'm a mess. A stupid single mother, struggling along with no family and no friends and not enough money, never asking for help, even when I need it, trying to do it all by myself, bubbling with rage and hurt and foolish pride. This is what they call a wake-up call. It's a turning point. It has to be. And I know it has to stop.

CHAPTER TWENTY-NINE

Patsy dipped her spoon into a creamy peach yoghurt that reminded her of the colour of Geraldine's sheets and listened to her mum and brother bickering. It was something about him leaving the top of the cereal packet open. Again. So trivial, so unimportant, yet so familiar. They all knew that the cereal wouldn't be around long enough to go stale, open packet or not. Not with an appetite like Matt's to contend with. But the bickering never meant anything. It was the background soundtrack to her life. Of all their lives. Mum and Dad having a go about something that bugged them, she and Matt fighting back in a half-hearted way, putting up a token resistance before doing what they'd been asked to do in the first place. Keeping the peace, because they all knew the peace was so important. Too many of their friends had suffered broken homes, their parents shouting, splitting up, divorcing. They were all grateful for the stability they had, and treasured it.

Sometimes it was as if she had never been away, was still that happy-go-lucky teenager she had been when she'd last lived here full time. But things were different now. She was in a relationship with just the sort of man her parents had always been so anxious to shield her from. She had to try to see him through their eyes. Leaving his partner, living apart from his child. Now he hadn't come up with her, was held back by problems created by those very people he was supposed to have left behind, what must they be thinking? She knew they were only looking out for her, but she had to make it her mission now to stick up for him, to present him as the husband they could believe she deserved.

'Now,' she said, when they'd finished eating. 'You put your feet up and read the paper, Mum. Get started on the crossword. Let me do the washing-up.'

'No need. We've got a dishwasher now.'

'Really? I thought Dad was your dishwasher. Far cheaper to run than an electric one too.'

'Very funny, love. No, your dad thought it was time we moved with the times. The Pipers have had one for years. Swear by it too.' She bent and slotted their bowls and spoons into the wire tray inside the machine and closed the door.

'Forget the Joneses. We're keeping up with the Pipers!' Matt laughed, just dodging out of the way in time and running out of the room to fetch his school bag as his mother swiped at him with a tea towel.

'What's the tea towel for, Mum? If the machine's going to take care of the dishes?'

'Old habits die hard, love. It just seems to jump into my hand whenever I go near the sink! There are only so many new tricks you can teach an old dog.'

Patsy followed her mum through to the living room and sank down onto the sofa beside her. 'What you said about new tricks . . .'

'Yes?' her mother reached for a pen and opened the paper at the crossword page.

'You will be okay with Michael, won't you? I do know he's not quite what you'd hoped for. For me to end up with, I mean. He's not a Piper, for a start! But I hope you can get used to him, to accept him, and us as a couple. Because he's lovely really, once you get to know him. Already having a child doesn't make him a bad person, or a bad prospect. I do know he's right for me. That he's the one. You know what I mean by that, don't you?'

'About being the one? Of course. I always knew your father was the one. From the first day I met him. Love at first sight it was, for me. But—'

'I do wish you wouldn't always have a but.'

'I worry about you, that's all. About you getting hurt.'

'I'm not going to get hurt, Mum.' But she crossed her fingers, in a stupidly superstitious way, where her mother couldn't see, just in case she was wrong. Just in case whatever was going on down in London was about to change everything and prove her wrong.

'Have you heard any more from him then? Your Michael?'

'Not today yet, no. I'll give him a call a bit later, before he sets off for the hospital.'

'You are telling me everything, aren't you? Not hiding anything from me? Because, whatever's going on, whether you think I might like it or not, I'd rather you tell me the truth.'

'I told you yesterday, Mum. About Ruby and what's happened to her. About Social Services. There's nothing else. As to what happens next, I really don't know yet. But when I know, you'll know. Okay?'

'Okay, love. You just seem a bit down, that's all. So . . . With your dad off to the golf course, and your brother about to leave for school, let's have a nice girlie morning, shall we? Just the two of us. We don't often get the chance nowadays. There must be other things we can talk about, apart from your love life! Or something you fancy doing while you're here? Maybe you'd like to go shopping later? There's a lovely blue top in Addison's window that you'd love. It'd suit you, I think. My treat. Shopping will get us out of the house and into the fresh air, at least. Can't beat fresh air for blowing the cobwebs away.' She put her crossword back down on the coffee table. Patsy could see she'd only got as far as filling in one answer.

'Right! Shops it is then. Maybe I can find something for Lily while we're at it. Presents are the way to a child's heart, aren't they? It's her birthday coming up soon, and I have to break the ice somehow.'

'You haven't met her yet?'

'Not properly. Once, a long time ago, when she was sleepy and ready for bed, before Michael and I . . . Well, anyway, this week was going to be the big "getting to know you" holiday, you know. Me becoming part of her life, but the plan sort of went awry at the last minute. A present will help though, won't it? Children like presents. What do three-year-olds want these days?'

'Well, let's see. When you were that age, it was dollies and all the paraphernalia that went with them. Little outfits, a doll's pram, feeding bottles that looked like they emptied by magic . . . Remember that little chubby doll you had? With the annoying cry whenever you sat her up and took the dummy out of her mouth! Annabel, you called her. I bet she's still here somewhere, up in the loft. Oh, those were the days, Patsy love. I sometimes wish we could go back, do it all again. Wouldn't that be grand? Still, I don't suppose children have changed all that much over the years, have they? You can't go far wrong with a doll.'

'That's what I'll do then. Get her a doll. That cries!'

'You won't be able to bribe her though. You do know that, don't you? She'll have to like you, for yourself, not just for the presents. Kids are no fools.'

'I'll try, Mum. But none of us can make people like us, can we? It's been hard enough with his mother . . .' Patsy picked up the paper from the table and gazed at the crossword for a moment, seeking something to distract her. 'Oh, I've got one! Seven down. The clue is: "Suffocate favourite back inside. She's wicked." Ten letters. So, if suffocate is smother, and the favourite is a pet, spelt backwards and dropped into the middle, then it has to be stepmother. And a wicked one, at that! Especially with all that smothering going on, I suppose. That's how we're always portrayed, isn't it? We stepmothers. Cinderella, Snow White, Hansel and Gretel – they all have this evil old bat who gets jealous and tries to ruin their lives. There's even that awful woman Colin Firth almost marries in *Nanny McPhee*. Wicked, the lot of them. And me about to join them. You know, Mum, I'm beginning to think I'm onto a loser here before I even start!'

*

Neither of them was working today, so Laura and Gina had treated themselves to a spa day. They had days like this from time to time, when they needed to get away from the wards and the stresses of London life, and unwind.

'It's tomorrow then? Your hot date.'

Laura could only just hear what her friend was saying over the loud bubbling sounds of the Jacuzzi. She sidled nearer, moving along the underwater ledge until their bikinied bottoms were almost touching, and leaned her head back against the edge. Rivulets of rapidly churning water ran up the side of her neck and burst over her face.

Laura was surprised it had taken Gina so long to get round to the subject of her love life. Probably because up until now she'd been too busy talking about her own. Or bemoaning its absence, more like. 'I wouldn't say hot, necessarily. Not as hot as this water, anyway. No, cosily warm will suit me, to start with. It's been a while, you know, since . . . Well, since Kevin and I split, and I'm in no rush to chuck myself in at the deep end again quite so quickly.'

'Loving the water references, Laura. You'll be not wanting to make waves next, or go up the creek without a paddle!'

'Ha, ha! Very funny, I'm sure.'

'So, how's your hit-and-run girl getting on? Ruby?'

'Fine, I think. I haven't been back, not now she's properly awake and got her family around her. Professional distance, and all that. I've got another one playing on my mind now. Attempted suicide. Wouldn't talk about why, either. I gave her the Samaritans leaflets, tried to get her to talk to someone from Psych, but she wouldn't have it. Seems God is the only one she'll talk to. And Paul, but I suppose that's almost the same thing! He spent quite a while with her down in the chapel, but of course he won't tell me a word of what went on. Now she's gone home, with everything unresolved, so who knows if she might try it again. I'm half expecting her back any minute. So, Ruby's the least of my worries. There are only so many patients you can get over-involved with at once. You know that.'

'Oh, I don't do it. Don't let myself. Bloody nightmare taking all that stuff home with you, especially if it's sick kids. Way too upsetting. Still, I think you might have caught yourself a good one there, Laura. In Paul, I mean. Professional, caring, able to keep a secret . . . '

'Not bad looking either.'

'That's true, from what I saw of him the other night anyway. Let's hope he measures up in other ways, eh?'

'Gina! Really! I can't think what you could possibly mean.'

'Well, I do seem to remember you telling me once – I think you must have been fairly drunk at the time – that your Kevin had a very large . . . ' There were others in the water with them now and she couldn't rely on the bubbles to drown her out, so she leaned over and whispered the end of the sentence in Laura's ear.

'I did not!'

'Oh, yes you did.'

'Are you denying it?'

'That I said it, or that he had a   ?'

'Don't bother. You've already given the game away. Even in this hot water I can tell a blush when I see one.'

'Gina, you are terrible. There's more to finding the right man than the size of his . . . '

'Cassock?' Gina asked, and they both fell about in fits of

giggles, the bubbles going straight into their open mouths and forcing them both to splutter and cough it out again, much to the disgust of the two elderly ladies in one-piece costumes and rubber swim hats who were already tutting loudly and edging away from them in the water.

*

Geraldine led the way, peering into each separate four-bedded room as they walked tentatively along the ward. When they found Ruby she was sitting in an armchair, only half-awake, her broken leg propped up on a stool, a newspaper open on the bed beside her.

Lily bounded forward, pushing curtains aside, chattering excitedly about some cartoon she'd been watching before they left home, and plonked herself very quickly and proprietorially on Ruby's lap, all the drama of the last few days seemingly forgotten as she helped herself to a banana from Geraldine's bag.

'It took us a while to find you,' Geraldine said, planting a kiss on Ruby's cheek. 'But it's lovely to see you out of that awful intensive care place and looking so much better.'

Geraldine handed over a pile of magazines and a selection of fruit, pulled over a plastic chair from a small stack by the door and settled herself in it at Ruby's side.

'You don't have to stay, Michael,' Ruby said, wrapping her arms around Lily to stop her slipping off her lap, she was squirming about so much. 'We both know we'll struggle to keep the pleasantries up for long. Go. I wanted to talk to your mum by herself anyway.'

He looked at Geraldine and she nodded. 'Not a bad idea, Son. Come back for us later, eh? Give us an hour or so. I wanted to talk to Ruby too. About that little matter we discussed last night. Go and call Patricia again . . . Sorry, I mean Patsy. I'm sure she must be wondering what's going on.'

Michael didn't take much persuading. 'I'll leave Lily here with you then. You will look after her, won't you?'

Geraldine gave him a withering look. 'I think that, between us, we are perfectly capable of doing that, Michael. Please don't try to teach your granny to suck eggs.'

They watched him walk away, his hands in his pockets, his shoes squeaking on the shiny floor. At the door he turned and waved goodbye to Lily, but Ruby had eased her off her lap and let her sit on the edge of the empty bed where she was now too engrossed in a colouring book his mother had produced from the depths of her bag to notice.

'So . . . '

'Look, Geri. It is still all right to call you Geri, isn't it?'

'Of course. Why ever not? You said you wanted to say something to me, on my own?'

'Yes, but I hardly know where to start. My head's still all over the place. I can't quite seem to be able to hold a thought in it for very long. Everything's still very muddled. I think it's having those days taken away from me, when I didn't know where I was, that's left me a bit, well, jet-lagged I'd have to call it. Like my mind hasn't managed to catch up with my body yet, or the other way round.'

'That's okay, love. You take your time. Getting over something like this is not going to happen overnight. You've still got a way to go, you know. Whatever it is, it can keep. I'm not going anywhere. Other than back to Brighton, that is. Which I will have to do soon. But, no rush.'

'No, no, what I have to say can't be put off, and it won't take long. It's just that . . . Well, I wanted to clear the air between us, to make sure things were right again.'

'No need.'

'Yes, there is. Every need. Geri, I don't know quite what went wrong, between you and me. It was Michael who left me, not the other way round. I didn't think I'd done anything wrong. But I was the one left to cope, as if I was being punished. And I didn't think that was fair. So I told you not to come and see me, and I'm so sorry about that now. It was stupid of me. I was feeling so mixed up and I know I was being my usual stubborn self, but I didn't want your pity, and the truth is that I might well have thrown you out if you had come. You'd have been like a reminder. Of him. You know, you even look like him sometimes. I couldn't bear it.'

'Oh, Ruby.'

'But, the more I think about it now, the more I can see why you had to take his side. There's nothing more important in all the world than our children, is there? Of course you had to stick by Michael, whatever he'd done. He's your son. Your only son. I can't imagine a time when I would ever turn my back on Lily. I'd support her, love her, stick up for her, no matter what she did, always. She could murder someone and I'd still be there telling the world she was innocent, sneaking a file into the prison inside a cake to help her escape! Michael is your flesh and blood, and I'm not. I do understand the difference.'

'Oh, Ruby . . . ' Geraldine said again. She glanced at Lily, making sure she was still busy with her crayons, not listening. 'That's not it. Not at all. It was never really about sides. Yes, I know it's Michael I should have been angry with and, believe me, I was. Still am, to be honest. But I felt kind of deflated. Let down. I don't think I'd ever felt so sorry for myself. Your wedding cancelled, and all the plans and dreams I had for you—for the pair of you – gone. Broken, in an instant.'

'But . . . '

'No, let me finish. There was the gift, you see. My wedding gift to the two of you. I'd had all the papers drawn up, everything was arranged. I'd made up my mind. I hadn't told you because I wanted it to be a surprise, but I was giving you the business, Ruby. Lock, stock and barrel.'

'The shop? You were giving us the shop?'

Geraldine nodded, taking Ruby's hand in hers.

Ruby looked shocked. 'Did Michael know?'

'Not then, no. But when I told him later, he said he'd never wanted it. Wouldn't have accepted it. Had a career of his own, plans of his own. He said it was my dream, and his father's, to run a shop, but it had never been his. I so wanted to pass it on, to see it go on and grow and thrive as a family business. It could have set you both up for life. You could have done what you wanted with it. Changed the name, changed the stock, hired your own staff, made your own mark. I had faith in you, both of you. I wouldn't have interfered.'

She sighed, pausing for a moment before going on. 'Then

suddenly he was leaving, and there was no wedding, no you, no Lily, and everything came tumbling down around my ears. No family future, no rosy retirement. I know you've struggled to cope, Ruby. I've seen that. Taking in ironing. Bills piled up in the kitchen – which I will be paying, by the way. I've struggled too. Oh, not for money. Just with life, or what's left of it, without Ken. Without you and Michael, and Lily. The shop's still mine, of course. I'm still there, wishing I wasn't, doing it all on my own.' She shrugged her shoulders. 'Huh! And not very well either.'

'Geri, I'm sorry. I wish it could have been different, but he cheated on me, slept with another woman, and then he ran away. Said he'd only stayed as long as he had out of duty. That he didn't love me. Never had.' Ruby turned away, looked out of the window, took a breath. 'Not in the way I loved him.'

'And do you still? Love him?'

'No!' Ruby answered almost too quickly, then closed her eyes and paused for a second or two, before composing herself and going on. 'No, Geri, I don't. It's over with. Done. Finished. What would be the point?'

'You won't be wanting this, then?' Geraldine reached into her bag, brought out the photo she'd found under the pillow, and handed it to Ruby.

'Where did you . . . ?'

'It was in your bed, Ruby. It speaks volumes, love.'

'No. That was just me being childish . . . Lonely. I don't know, I was probably just using it to help me remember when things were good between us. When the fantasy was still strong, when I thought he could do no wrong. Please don't think this means I still love him. I have to let all that go now. I mean, look at Patsy.

She's glamorous, clever, a real high-flyer. And there's me, in my baggy T-shirts and tatty trainers. She's who he wants now and I have to accept that. Move on.'

She held the photo up high, gazed into Michael's crumpled black-and-white face and, after a moment's hesitation, handed it back to Geraldine. 'Here! You keep it. I don't need it any more. Lily will be at school in another year or so, then I can change things, really change things, look for a part-time job, a proper job, and start to make something of myself. There will be life after Michael, you just wait and see.'

'That's my girl!'

'*Your* girl?'

'Oh, yes. If I'd had a daughter . . .' But she had, of course. Had a daughter, a long time ago, when she was only fourteen, and she'd given her up. The only thing she could have done, at the time. But she'd never given her up in her heart. She swallowed hard. It wasn't something to burden Ruby with. Or anyone. ' . . . Then I'd want her to be just like you.'

Geraldine saw the tears spring up in Ruby's eyes, and tried hard to stop herself from crying too. She'd held on to her secret for so long that suppressing it came as second nature to her, but it still hurt. Knowing all that she had missed.

'Do you mean that?'

'I wouldn't have said it if I didn't. My God, girl, you had me so worried. I thought you were going to die. But you didn't. So now, I'm going to look after you. Like I should have done all along.'

Like I promised myself I would, Geraldine thought. To make amends. To give you, and all those other girls, the chances in life I was never able to give to my own.

'Thank you.' Ruby was holding her hand now, totally oblivious to the storm of emotion she was struggling so hard to hold back. 'And I'm sorry about the shop. It was very, very generous of you, wanting us to have it. I used to love my time there, you know, when I was working for you. I just wish I could do something to help you now.'

'Well, maybe you can. And that's what I wanted to talk to you about. Because I've decided exactly what I'm going to do, about the shop, and about you and Lily too.'

CHAPTER THIRTY

Ruby

I can't believe it. Me, the owner of a shop! I'm already thinking of how I can change things, update the stock, make
it work. Walking before I can run, that's what Mrs Castle
would have said, and often did. When I tried to make bread,
after only ever doing fairy cakes before, and forgot all about
it for days, the dough left to rise and go smelly, in the airing
cupboard, among the towels. When I tried to get the bus back
from the shops because it had started to snow, and ended
up twenty miles away, in the wrong direction. When I fell in
love with a man I had never spoken to and who didn't even
know I existed.

No more running. Walk, Ruby, walk. It's time to slow down
now, to think before I do anything rash. Like running out in
the road, without looking.

Geri says we should keep Kerry on. She's a good kid, got her
problems but tries hard, reminds her of me at that age. I have
to listen to Geri, learn from her, take my time. It will be funny
being the boss though. Telling someone else what to do. I feel
sometimes as if I've spent my whole life doing what others tell

me to do, what others want. And suddenly I'm being treated like an adult, with a mind of my own, with some say over my own future, and it feels good. Just don't blow it, Ruby. Don't blow it. Like you always do . . .

CHAPTER THIRTY-ONE

Michael took the car out of the hospital car park before the parking fees started to hike up again, and drove back to the flat. If his mother was serious about taking Ruby back to Brighton with her, setting her up in the shop, then he needed to talk to the Freeman woman. This would make a difference, wouldn't it? To their meeting, and their decisions about Lily's future. Ruby wouldn't be on her own any more, struggling. She would have a job, an income, a home, and with a responsible woman – Lily's own grandmother – to support her. Surely they would see that this made everything all right? Michael would then be able to go back to Portugal, back to Patsy, knowing that Lily was happy, knowing she was safe.

The flat felt cold, empty, abandoned. There were toys on the floor, including that awful doll with the staring eyes his mother had bought, his bedding was still in a jumbled heap on the end of the sofa, and there were dishes piled up in the sink. He'd had to more or less force his mother away from her natural clean-up mode and out of the door to get to the hospital on time, assuring her that nobody was going to give a damn whether or not they'd done the washing-up.

He had never really liked this flat, or this road. It had served its purpose, given them a cheap base to start off their life in London, but it had always felt too small, too claustrophobic, too hemmed in and noisy after the open spaces and clean sea air of Brighton. It hadn't been fair to bring Ruby here and then leave her, he knew that now. It wasn't where she belonged. In fact, he was quite surprised she had stayed. Moving back to Brighton after they'd split up would have been the obvious thing to do, and cheaper. It would have made things easier for him when he visited too, if his mother and Ruby had been closer together, killing two birds with one stone as they say. Had she stayed in London in the hope he might come back? Or because doing nothing, not making decisions or changes, was easier than the alternative? Or was she just being bloody-minded, stubborn, cutting off her own nose to spite her face?

Still, she was going to do it now, wasn't she? Move back home, take on the shop, give Lily the sort of wonderful childhood he himself had had growing up by the sea. His mother hadn't done a bad job with him when he was a kid, so he knew he could trust her to do the same for Lily. If Ruby accepted the offer, of course – with Ruby, nothing could ever be taken for granted. Perhaps he should have stuck around at the hospital, waited to hear Ruby's answer. Knowing her, she just might say no.

He put away Barbara Freeman's number for now, just in case he was jumping the gun, and called Patsy instead.

*

Agnes stood at the back window and looked out over the yard. Was she the only one who had remembered it was little Lily's birthday on Sunday? They were all so busy trundling backwards and forwards to the hospital and worrying themselves sick about the child's long-term future – still to be determined by the Children's Services department – that they seemed to have forgotten her immediate future. The party she had hoped for and told her grandmother all about, with a bouncy castle and presents. It hardly seemed likely now that any of her little friends would be coming. She hadn't been to the nursery all week so no invitations would have been handed out. That yard outside could never accommodate a castle, whichever way you tried to squeeze it in.

William had a garden. Quite a big garden, though heaven knows how long the grass was by now, and how dense the weeds. It had been a long time since she'd visited, and her son was no gardener. Maybe they could give Lily some sort of party there. How much did it cost to hire one of these bouncy things for a day? Even without other children to share it, she knew Lily would enjoy it, and the poor soul had had precious little enjoyment these last few days. It could be her present to the child. Hers and William's.

William was upstairs now, talking to Michael. He'd said he'd called round to pick up his laptop, but she'd seen the disappointment in his eyes when he'd realised his timing was all wrong and Geraldine was not at home. She was going to have to give the pair of them a bit of a nudge if they were to get any closer together before Geraldine went back to Brighton. Agnes had been quite a good matchmaker in her day. Several of her friends had met and married their perfect partners with a little help from her, but that was many years ago, in the days of weekend dances and country walks and Saturday afternoon cinema. It was all online dating and nightclubs nowadays. Not really William's scene at all.

However, it was the party she should be concerning herself with now. Getting William busy on the computer looking for an inflatable castle, or something like it, would at least keep him here for a while, in time to see Geraldine come back, with any luck. Then she could invite her, and Michael and Lily, down for tea and suggest it to them all. After that, she decided, as far as romance goes, it was going to be up to William. She couldn't hold his hand and wipe his bum for him all his life.

*

'Mum, I've decided I'm going up to see Patsy. Well, not just to see her, but hopefully to bring her back with me. This was meant to be our holiday, and I've hardly seen her. I know I've needed to put Lily first, but it's not been very fair to Pats, and I miss her.'

He pulled the car into a parking space a few doors along from the flats and waited for her to object.

'That's fine.' Geraldine smiled at him, placing a hand on his arm. 'I understand, and I'm more than happy to look after Lily for a day or so. If you think that will be okay with the social people?'

'I'm her dad, and you're her gran. We can go where we like, do whatever normal families do, apparently. We don't have to report our every move. It's not us who's under investigation, is it? Not us who left a two-year-old by herself . . . '

'All right, Michael. Let's not start all that again. What's done is done. You will remember it's Lily's birthday on Sunday, won't you? I'm sure she'll want you here, especially if Ruby is still in hospital.'

'Of course. I'll be back. Or *we* will.'

'Good.'

Michael scratched his head. He hadn't given his own needs much thought in recent days, but he realised now that his hair probably needed a good wash – and the rest of him! Maybe he'd have a long soak in the bath before he set off, make sure he was all clean and scrubbed up for Patsy. He pulled the key out of the ignition and opened the car door, but didn't climb out. 'So . . . Ruby. You said *if* she's still in hospital? Do you think there's some chance she could be out for Sunday?'

'Just wishful thinking. Nobody's said.'

'What about the shop? Did you ask her?'

'I did.'

'And?'

'And . . . She said yes. She'll need some training, a lot of handholding to start with, and she's still got her injuries to contend with, but I think in the end it could be the making of her. Naturally, they'll give up the flat here and both come to stay with me, at least to start with. There's plenty of room. You are okay with that, I presume?'

'Mum, I think it's wonderful. I can go back to work knowing my daughter is in safe hands and that she's away from London. It's the ideal solution for them, and for you. What will you do with all that spare time when you've handed things over?'

'Start to have a life of my own again, I hope. It's been a while.'

'That's good. You'll be getting yourself a toyboy and learning to line dance next!' He laughed as they both got out of the car and walked back towards the flat.

'I may well do that, Michael. My options are well and truly open.'

'I'd better get on to the Freeman woman then. This is all going to make such a difference to their worries about Lily, I'm sure. Not the toy boy part, but the rest of it. The stability, the support, a real chance to prove herself. It's just what Ruby needs.'

'Do it then. Do it now. Remember to stress that it's what *Lily* needs. That's what counts. Oh, and if they've set a date for that meeting we're meant to go to, you make absolutely sure you're back for it.'

'Of course. You know, I wouldn't miss that. Lily's still my top priority. But, one other thing . . . '

'Go on.'

'Can I borrow the car? It's by far the quickest and easiest way for me to get to the lakes, especially if I go now, this afternoon – and the best way to get back again in a hurry.'

'But, what about us visiting Ruby? I do think Lily should still see her mummy every day, don't you?' She stopped and peered along the street. 'Where did you say that bus goes from again?'

'Forget buses. I'm sure there's a certain neighbour who'll be only too happy to drive you.'

'William? Oh, I can't keep imposing on the poor man.'

'I don't think he minds, Mum. In fact, I think he really likes to do it – I think he really likes *you*!'

'You do?' She turned away and started to climb the steps to the front door, but not before Michael had seen the look on her face. Embarrassment, yes, but pleasure too. He hadn't spotted it before, but there just could be something brewing between those two.

CHAPTER THIRTY-TWO

Ruby

I can feel myself getting better, stronger, all the time. They say it's my age that's helping me to recover so well and so quickly, beyond all expectations, fighting my way back like this. And my determination too. Sometimes being a stroppy cow can be a real advantage, apparently!

But recovery goes beyond the physical, doesn't it? It's more than my head wound healing, or my leg bones knitting themselves slowly together like a scarf. When the visitors have gone and it's quiet, just the old lady snoring in the bed across the way and the sound of the nurses chatting at the desk in the hall, I can't seem to shake away all the stuff that's in my head. It's like this stupid bandage is keeping it all in, not letting anything escape and, until I deal with it, I won't really have recovered at all.

Michael. It all comes down to Michael. I can't bring myself to think of him as Mike any more. That name came from a different time, a different place. And it was only ever me that used it. To his mother, and to just about everyone else, he has always been Michael. When he comes here, to the hospital, he hangs back, stands awkwardly behind his mother, not sure what

357

to do or say. He doesn't want any of this. He has a new life now, and I'm just a reminder of the old one.

He's been at the centre of things for too long. What I think and feel and do. It's hard now to believe just how much I used to fantasise about him, building him up in my mind as some kind of Mr Perfect. But he's far from perfect. I know that now. Perhaps, in another life, one not blighted by our own mistakes, we could have been friends. I think it's time to let him go. Forgive. Forget. Like I probably should have done with my mother all those years ago. Accepted she was part of the past and stopped hoping for more than she could give. But I was a kid then, and I'm not now.

I have to let Lily see Michael, because he is not like my mother. Never was. He loves her, and he won't let her down. She needs him in her life. She needs a mummy and a daddy. I, more than anyone, should know that.

A nurse has come over to the bed. The middle-aged one, with the big bosom and the little rolls of fat on her arms. 'Everything all right, lovey?' she says. 'Need anything for the pain?'

'No, thanks. Everything's fine.' As she walks away, her soft shoes padding across the ward, I tell myself that it is fine. It really is. Or, if it isn't now, it very soon will be.

Lily was so happy today. She drew me a beautiful picture with her crayons. Said it was her and me on the beach at Granny's house. It didn't matter that I had a huge head and a stick body and a few too many fingers. We were there together, side by side, with a big blue wavy sea behind us and a yellow spikey sun in the sky. I know it means this is what Lily wants. Us together, the two of us, living by the sea. Me with my big head and all.

Well, it feels that way at the moment, what with the bandages. Who wouldn't feel a bit big-headed, knowing they were going to be the owner of a shop!

I have my necklace back. Michael had taken it home for safe-keeping, and Geri brought it back in for me today. My fingers keep going to it, touching, twiddling. It's the cross I'd bought for Lily to wear at her christening, but that didn't happen, did it? No wedding, no christening. Everything altered, her cross slid onto a longer chain and kept here, with me, where it belongs, keeping Lily near. It makes me feel more like me again. It's like a talisman. It makes me feel lucky. I am lucky. To have people who care about me. Lucky to be alive.

Now all I have to do is make them see I'm not the terrible mother I'm sure they think I am. The police, Social Services, Michael . . . Because I'm not. I made a mistake, I know that – a big, bad mistake. I need to tell my story. Because I remember it now. All of it. The story of what happened that day. Why I left her.

I hope they will listen to me, believe me, understand. Forgive me. Everything I did was for her. Everything I do. Because I love her, and always will. Lily. My Lily.

CHAPTER THIRTY-THREE

It was dark when Michael arrived. He had never been to the house before, wasn't sure he'd be able to find it without street-lights or a satnav, but here he was.

The woman who answered the door was illuminated by the hall light behind her, standing out of the surrounding darkness like a picture in a frame. She was the spitting image of Patsy, only older. They'd met once before, fleetingly, in London, about a year ago, but she had looked different then, all dressed up for a trip to the theatre, and he and Patsy had not yet become a proper couple then, so they had shaken hands in passing but he had not paid the woman a lot of attention. Now, everything was different. She was his future mother-in-law, and she would be more wary. He needed to get off on the right foot this time.

She was wearing a loose blouse and a pair of what his mother would call slacks, with an apron over the top, slippers, and her hair tied back off her face. She looked sort of homely. She also looked surprised.

'Oh! It's Michael, isn't it?' Her hand flew to her mouth. 'Oh, dear, we weren't expecting you tonight. Just look at the state of me. Whatever must you think?'

'So sorry, Mrs Walker. I didn't mean to just barge in, and you look perfectly fine to me. More than fine! But . . . Well, I was really hoping to see Patsy. She is here?'

'Oh, yes, she's here. Of course she is. Come in, come in.' She opened the door wider and ushered him into the hall. 'You must call me Betty, now that we're almost related. Please.'

'Thank you, Betty.' He took her hand as if he was about to shake it but changed his mind at the last minute and pulled her towards him for a kiss on the cheek instead. He could see the blush rise in her face as she drew away, and a little girlish giggle escaped from her mouth.

'Oh,' she said, withdrawing her hand slowly from his, and steadying herself against the wall. 'Let me just call her for you. She's upstairs helping Matt with some maths problem he's stuck on. Come in and sit down.' She showed him through into a pleasant enough lounge and pointed him towards a pink chintz armchair. 'Let me get you a cup of tea or something while you're waiting. Have you eaten?'

'A quick chicken sandwich and a bag of crisps on the motorway. That'll do me for tonight. But, yes, tea would be nice. Milk, no sugar.'

She closed the door behind her but he could still hear her, hurrying up the stairs, the shuffle of her slippered feet somewhere up above him, then the pounding of heavier, faster feet running back down.

'Michael!' The door burst open again, flung back on its hinges, and Patsy was upon him, her arms wrapped vice-like around his neck, the smell of fresh shampoo and her sexy designer perfume mingling together to instantly arouse his senses. 'I am so glad to see you. Why didn't you say you were coming? I only spoke to you this afternoon and you didn't say a thing!'

'Surprised?' He was pushing himself against her, crushing her ribs between his encircling arms, breathing her in.

'More than surprised. Ecstatic!'

He pulled back and looked into her eyes. 'Is it okay if I stay? A day or two at the most. I'll have to get back for Lily by Sunday.'

'Of course you can stay. Oh, I have missed you so much.' She was kissing him now, raining little rapid kisses all over his face.

'Oh, do it properly, woman!' he joked and bent her over backwards, his lips full on hers, just as her mother came back in with a tray of tea.

'Ahem,' she coughed. 'Don't let me disturb you two lovebirds! I assume you'll be stopping, Michael, so I'll go and make up the small bed for you in the spare room.'

'Mum . . .'

'No, Pats.' He held out his hand and stopped Patsy before she could say any more. 'That's fine, Mrs Walker. Very kind of you. I appreciate it.' He felt in the carrier bag he'd brought in with him and pulled out the box of chocolates he'd hastily acquired in the motorway service station shop. 'These are for you. A little thank you for your hospitality, especially at such short notice.'

She put the tray down and took the box from him, beaming from ear to ear. 'Very kind of you. My favourites too. But, really, there was no need.'

'I beg to differ, Betty. And, tomorrow, perhaps you'd let me take you and your husband . . .'

'Frank. I'm sorry he's not here to meet you. Annual General Meeting at the wine club . . . '

'If you'd let me, and Patsy of course, take you and Frank out for a meal. Your son too, if he'd like to join us.' He'd spotted someone who could only be Patsy's teenaged brother hovering behind his mum in the doorway. 'It will save you having to cook. You shouldn't have to, what with me being an uninvited – well, unexpected – guest. I'm sure you can guide me to the best restaurants in this neck of the woods.'

'Oh.' She was pulling off her apron, as if she'd only just remembered it was there, and straightening her hair. 'That would be very nice. Very nice indeed. But I'm sure you young people would prefer to be by yourselves. Not lumbered with two old fogies like us.'

'Nonsense. Old? Betty, you don't look a day over thirty-five. You must have been a child bride. But I would quite like Patsy to myself for a little while now, if you don't mind. I thought maybe we could go out for a walk, and she could show me some of the lovely countryside I've heard so much about. What I'll see of it in the dark anyway!'

By the time they got back from their walk, hand in hand, and with little clumps of damp grass stuck to the back of their coats, there was no more talk of spare rooms or single beds. Mrs Walker had changed the sheets on Patsy's double and placed a vase of flowers on the bedside cabinet, and was happily reintroducing Michael to her husband, with a hazelnut cluster in her mouth and the menu for the best restaurant in town, retrieved from the back of the kitchen drawer and more than a little crumpled, in her hand.

*

Paul Thomas hadn't been to see Ruby since she woke up. It was very remiss of him and something he had fully intended to put right, but there had been so many other demands on his time and somehow it had been put off over and over again. Now, as he entered the ward, he felt almost guilty for his prolonged absence.

'Good morning. Ruby, isn't it?' He approached the bed with some trepidation.

'Yes. Do I know you?'

'Paul Thomas. You won't remember me, I know. The last time I saw you, you were asleep. Upstairs, in Intensive Care. The nurses had asked me to visit, so I did. A couple of times.'

'Oh. That was kind of you.'

'You were wearing a cross, they told me, when you were brought in, so it seemed appropriate. I can see you have it back on. Lovely. We were all very worried about you, you know. I hope you don't mind, but I have been praying for you too.'

She was looking at his clothes, her eyes drawn to his collar, and to his kind smile. How could she possibly mind? 'No, of course not. I just hope it did me some good!'

'It's hard sometimes, to know what's best. What a patient might want, when they can't speak for themselves.'

'It's all right. I am a kind of Christian, I suppose. Not that I go to church nowadays, but I did, when I was small. My mother was – *is* – a member of the Church of England. Lapsed, I shouldn't wonder, but I don't really know. It's a long time since

I've seen her. Still . . . I don't mind you praying for me. It's your job, after all.'

'It certainly is! And a very rewarding one at times. I must say, seeing you awake and so obviously on the mend counts as one of those times.'

'Would you like to sit down?'

He pulled up a chair, close to the bed, and sat on it. 'And how is your little girl?'

'You know about her?'

'Oh, yes. I won't forget Lily in a hurry. Or her name, anyway. It's what we all thought you were called for a while.'

'They've told me that. But Lily – the real Lily – is doing well, thank you. Spending time with her daddy, and her gran. I'm beginning to realise how important it is to have back-up, people who can take charge when we can't do things for ourselves. That's why I'm grateful to you too, for coming to see me, a total stranger, when I was sick. It's nice to know there are kind people about, people who care when there's nobody else. There was a nurse too, wasn't there?'

'Laura, yes.'

'She came to see me, but I was still very woozy then. I'd like to see her again, properly. Do you think . . .?'

'I'll ask her.' He could feel his face redden, hoped she wouldn't notice, or would blame it on the heat in the ward. 'When I next see her.'

'Thank you. And about Lily . . . '

'Yes?'

'I was thinking about having her christened. I was going to do it once before, but things happened. Things that got in the way. I don't want a big fuss, just a quiet ceremony, but I want to do it soon. Coming so close to losing her, or I suppose I should say her coming so close to losing me, has shown me not to put things off any more. To just get on and do them, while I can. We never really know about tomorrow, do we? If it's even going to come?'

'No, we don't. But we do have to have hope. And faith, that there is another place, another life, after this one.'

'I don't know about that. I came quite close to finding out though, I suppose, so I do hope you're right. Would you, then? Christen her for me?'

'You wouldn't rather it was in your own church? The cere-mony conducted by your own parish priest?'

'I don't have one.'

'It's been a while since I've conducted a christening.'

'But you know how?'

He laughed. 'Yes, I know how. I feel honoured to be asked, to tell you the truth. There's no duty more important than bringing the next generation to God. You would need godparents, of course.'

'I'm already thinking about that. But I will be moving out of London when I get out of here. To Brighton, where I grew up. Do you know it?'

'Ah, yes. Many a happy hour spent as a boy, among the pebbles, with my bucket and spade.'

'So, I'd like it done here, before I go. Next week, or the one after?'

'I tell you what I'll do, Ruby. I will come back later, with my diary, and with Nurse Laura if I can get hold of her.' He blushed again, at the thought of getting hold of Laura. 'And we'll see what we can sort out for you. How does that sound?'

Then he stood, shook hands, quickly made the sign of the cross, and walked away.

*

'So, what do you think?' William looked at his mother as she turned back from the sink and eased herself down into a chair at the kitchen table. He was hoping to pick up at least some sort of clue as to what was going on in her mind, but her face gave nothing away.

'Together?' She wiped her hands dry on a small towel she kept on a hook by the sink – he could see the fraying hole she'd forced through it to create a makeshift eye to hang it up by – and offered him a biscuit from the open tin. 'You think we should move together?'

'It makes sense, doesn't it? Me on hand when you need a lift somewhere, you to do my ironing . . . '

'Ah, now we're getting to the real reason!'

'That was a joke, Mother, and there are lots of reasons, all real ones, why this could work.'

'But where?'

'I don't know that yet. Obviously it would have to be somewhere we both felt happy with. Not too countrified. We are both of us getting older, and it would be sensible to stay near a largish town, if not actually in one, for all the amenities we might need. Hospital, supermarket, library, buses, trains and so forth. Not London, though. I've been here way too long. So I do want to get out now, once and for all.'

'Well, I can certainly agree with you there. I never wanted to come here in the first place. If it wasn't for Susan . . . '

'Let's not go there again, eh? Susan's gone. It's just us now. Let's do what *we* want, for a change.'

'But, sharing a home? It's a big step. What if you met someone? Wanted to get married again? What would happen to me then if your new wife wanted me out?'

'What if *you* met someone and wanted *me* out?' He laughed as she rolled her eyes and slapped him gently with the towel she was still holding in her hand. 'It won't be a problem, honestly. We'll find something with two front doors, a dividing wall, an annexe, I don't know. I'm not saying we have to live in each other's pockets. Just think about it, will you?'

'I already have. And it's a yes.'

'As easily as that? I expected you to put up a fight. Go all independent on me.'

'I may be many things, William, but I'm not daft. I still know a good deal when I see one, and I am not in the habit of looking gift horses in the mouth. So, let's get both places on the market, shall we? Get the ball rolling. At my age, I can't afford to wait around. But, before we do that, while you still have a garden to call your own, we have a party to organise.'

'Still intent on doing that, then?' He sat back, scratched his chin, and thought for a moment. 'Right, I can book the bouncy castle. That's the easy bit. But the lawn . . . '

'You'd best get home and mow it then, hadn't you? And don't

forget the food. We can't have a party, even a small one, without food.'

'I'm no good at any of that stuff. What do three-year-olds eat anyway?'

'William, use your initiative. There's someone not a million miles away from here who knows the answer to that, and she'll be only too happy to help you, I'm sure.'

'You mean Geraldine?'

'Of course I mean Geraldine. Who else?'

As William moved towards the door, all set to go upstairs and see if she might be at home, he could have sworn he saw his mother wink. Only out of the corner of his eye, so he might have been mistaken. Whether she'd winked or not, she had an unusually smug look on her face. It must be because she was getting out of this flat that she so clearly hated. He had always felt guilty about her being here, about Susan and her pushy ways. But that was behind them now, and they were both ready to move on. He was so glad he'd finally made her happy.

*

'Ruby? Hi. Remember me?' Laura approached the bed cautiously, Paul following a few paces behind her.

The girl looked up and smiled. It was good to see her smile. Good to see her awake and alert and some way near to being normal again.

'Of course I do, Nurse. Can you stay a while, come and sit down, talk to me?'

'I'd like that. And call me Laura, please. I feel like we're already friends.'

'I suppose we are, although you've known me a lot longer than I've known you. Still . . . friends . . . I like that, and I could do with one of those right now.'

'Well, Paul – the Reverend Thomas here – said you wanted to see me. So here I am.'

'Yes. Hello, vicar. Did you look at your diary? For the christening?'

'I did. And I have it here. It's fairly clear, as it happens. I've scribbled down a few possible dates, which I can leave with you. I'm sure you'll want to discuss it with the rest of the family and you'll need time to talk to the prospective godparents.'

She took the slip of paper from his hand. 'Can we meet again? In a day or two? Make some arrangements, when I've spoken to everyone?'

'Of course.'

'Well, you know where to find me,' she laughed. 'I'm not going anywhere for a while.'

'I'll leave you to it then. In the capable hands of Nurse Carter . . .'

Laura watched him as he laid his hand gently over Ruby's, gave her a reassuring nod, then turned to go. 'See you later,' he mouthed. 'Seven-thirty.'

'So, was there something special you wanted me here for? I'd be happy to talk you through anything you're not sure about? The operation, your days in the coma, what we talked about . . .'

'I don't think I did a lot of talking, did I?'

'No, but *I* did. I wondered if you heard any of it? If you

remember me being there, talking to you? They do say that some patients do hear everything. People talking to them, telling them what's happening in the world, making tapes, playing music . . . '

'No. Sorry. Not a word. But there is something else. Something I have remembered. From before . . . '

'Before the accident, you mean?'

'Yeah.'

'And you want to tell me about it?'

'If you don't mind. I thought about telling *him*. The vicar. But that would make it seem more like some kind of a confession, and it's not that. Confessions are for when you've done something bad, aren't they? For telling secrets that you want to keep secret, but still want to be forgiven for. And it's not like that.'

'Okay. What is it like?'

'It's the truth. That's all. Just the truth.'

'About . . .?'

'About Lily. About why she was alone. Why I wasn't there.'

'Are you sure you shouldn't be telling the police? Your family?'

'Oh, I will do. But sometimes I think they've all already made up their minds. You know, Ruby being stupid, thoughtless, selfish. Ruby not thinking before she acts. Ruby so childish, so wrapped up in herself . . . You won't judge me like that. You won't have those pictures in your head of what I'm like, what I've always been like. Because you don't know me. So, I think – I hope – that you'll listen, give me a fair hearing. Let me tell it like it was.'

'I don't have long, Ruby.' Laura looked at the watch on her chest. 'I'm due back in A & E soon. I'm only on a break.'

'This won't take long. I promise.'

'Then I promise too. Tell me, whatever it is, and I won't say a word. I won't interrupt you. I'll just listen. The way you did, lying in that bed day after day, when I talked to you. Okay?'

Ruby nodded, re-arranged herself in the chair until she was comfortable, closed her eyes, and told her story.

'I remember standing in the doorway of her room and watching Lily sleep. She's so cute when she's asleep, her hair in sweaty blonde curls around her ears, that little bear she loves so much pressed to her face, her eyelashes flickering as she dreams. It's hard sometimes to believe that we made her. That we made something so perfect.

'I knew I had to answer it, you see. The letter he'd sent. I'd screwed it up at first, chucked it in the bin, but knew that wouldn't solve anything. So I fished it back out, flattened it, read it again, every last word of it, and thought about what I wanted to say. And I had to do it then. Right then. I knew that. I couldn't put it off any longer, or stand there all day just looking at our daughter, much as I would have liked to.

'I went into the kitchen. I pushed the breakfast bowls aside, put the half-empty cereal box and what was left of the milk away, slid the latest bill across to join the others in the pile, and tipped the contents of my bag out onto the table to look for a pen. Tissues, wipes, purse, keys, a furry pink lipstick without its lid . . . All the usual tat. An "I've been brave" sticker the dentist had given me for Lily but it wouldn't stick on her mac, and an open pack of cheap supermarket aspirins . . . The ones they say she might have swallowed, I suppose.

'There was an old black biro, a bit smeared with the lipstick

– not that I ever wear the stuff nowadays. I yanked the top off the pen with my teeth and went and got the notepad I always keep by the phone. I looked at my wrist, expecting to see my watch, but it wasn't there. I must have forgotten to put it on. My head's like a sieve these days, even before I got the bang on the head. Too little sleep, too many thoughts battling away. I'd been up since Lily'd got me out of bed just before six, spent half the morning still in my pyjamas, done a massive pile of ironing. But I was finally dressed, and she'd crashed out for a nap. The clock on the kitchen wall said it was ten to twelve. I remember, because it meant I'd only got ten minutes until the post got collected from the box outside the post office. There's only one collection on a Saturday. Twelve o'clock on the dot. Just ten minutes left to do it, before I changed my mind.

'But I knew I wouldn't change my mind. The answer was no. That's all I had to tell him – Mike – in the clearest and firmest way I could. Just no. He'd left me, you see, for this other woman, gone off to live with her, and now he was demanding the right to just waltz back in and take her. Lily. I wasn't having it. Any of it.

'I was sucking at the end of the pen and wished I hadn't. All this pink gunge from the lipstick went between my teeth, and over my tongue. I swigged the dregs from my coffee mug, to get rid of it, then wished I hadn't done that either. Too strong, too cold. Just like Mike. Mike the Bike, I'd started to call him, since he pedalled off into the sunset and left me. Us, I mean. Left *us*. Just like that. How could he do that? To me? To Lily?

'Time was ticking. Just do it, Rube, I remember thinking. Tell the bastard he can't see her. That *she* can't see her. Because it was all about her really. Not him. He was her daddy. *Is* her daddy. But her . . . Poison Patsy, she was nothing. Why should I let her anywhere near my daughter? Share my Lily with a home-wrecker, with her high heels and designer suits, and her stupid false smile? Why now? Why, all of a sudden, did they expect to sail back in like some kind of white knight and his whore and whisk her away from me? Visits? Access? Holidays? What would it be next? Joint custody? Lily spending half her life in another home, another country? No, I couldn't let that happen.

'I could hear the rain bouncing off the window, trickling down the pipe from the broken guttering two floors up. Another miserable day, in a long line of other miserable days. I sat and twiddled with the chain around my neck – this chain – tying it in knots around my finger. I do that, when something's troubling me. That, or bite my nails, but they're already down about as low as they can go without drawing blood. Just look at them. Hardly up to *her* standards, are they? She probably gets them done at some posh salon. I wouldn't be surprised if the only thing she ever nibbles is bloody caviar.

'It's Lily's cross. Real silver. We bought it together, for her christening. The christening that never was, because we'd decided to wait, decided that getting married should come first. The right order. The right thing to do. That's almost funny now, isn't it? The thought that Mike was doing what was right.

'Anyway, I read through his letter again. I looked at the unfamiliar address at the top, the postmark, the fancy foreign stamp. I'd never checked it out on the map, but he was living somewhere in Portugal. All blue skies and golden beaches and glorious sunshine, I'll bet. And he calls it work! He never got a job like that when he was with me. A glorified bank clerk, that's all he was, until he tried to move up in the world and she got her claws into him.

'That just made me even more determined than before. I couldn't let him do it. Not come and take her off to Brighton, without me. I couldn't trust him. Not any more. Well, why should I, with his track record? He might have taken her abroad, right then, kept her there, never sent her back. You read about it all the time, don't you?

'I'd had the letter for days already, putting off answering it. But it had to be done, before he got back and started knocking at the door. It was actually quite easy once I got started. So the paper wasn't as posh as his, and the envelope was one of those brown ones that came with the usual junk mail in it, and I'd covered over the franked bit and tried to recycle it. Saves the environment. Saves the cash. God knows, there's little enough of that these days. The cheques he sends are all still on the shelf over the fireplace, uncashed. We don't want his money. He only sends it out of guilt anyway.

'He said, in his letter, that he'd be back in England for two weeks, that he wanted to see Lily, that I could contact him at his mum's – Geraldine – down in Brighton, but then he'd be here in London to collect her on Monday or Tuesday. That I should have her bag packed. The nerve! Said that he'd have her back with me for her birthday, and maybe we could all spend it together. All. He meant *her* when he said that. Not just him and Geraldine, but *her*. That Patsy.

'I rummaged about in my bag for a stamp, hoping I'd only have second class and he'd have to wait just that bit longer. But, no. First class it was. My last one, as well. At least neither of us would have to prolong the agony any longer than necessary. Best it was all made clear as soon as possible. Much as I would have liked to make him sweat, he needed to be told. *She* needed to be told. Soon.

'I wondered why he'd kept it so formal, writing instead of phoning. It was all so businesslike, as if he was ordering something from a catalogue or complaining about his bank charges – as if we're strangers – but I knew he was writing for a reason. Probably keeping copies of everything, for his solicitor, as some kind of evidence, in case I gave him trouble. Or more likely, he knew I'd hang up on him if he rang.

'I could have ignored the letter, just like his cheques and his parcels, left it in the pile with the bills, or ripped it to shreds. I would have liked to rip him to shreds, come to think of it. It's what he deserved. But, no. I had to think strong. *Be* strong. Protect myself, and Lily. There was nobody else to. It was time to sort this out once and for all. No contact, no access, no bloody Patricia fawning over my child, pretending she likes kids, wanting to play at mummies and daddies, when I knew she cared more about looking after her phoney fingernails than a toddler, and she'd run a mile at the sight of a dirty nappy.

'So, I did it. Poured it all out onto the paper. All the anger and frustration came rushing out like a flood. Stay away from her. From us. We're fine. We can manage. We're better without you, that's for sure. Fight, and I'll see you in court. I wasn't sure about that last bit, if he might see it as a threat, a challenge he had to stand up to. Not that I can afford lawyers. I can hardly afford the bills, or even to top up my mobile. That's lying dead somewhere, in a drawer in the bedroom, I think. Useless, cheap and nasty thing. Still, I've got the landline, at least until the next bill comes and I can't pay it. Who needs two phones anyway? It's not as if I've got anyone I need to call. Or want to call. Thank God for the benefits system and the power of the bloody steam iron, or we'd be starving by now.

'But I didn't want to see him and I didn't want Lily to see him either. Not if *she* was going to be there. I remember licking the flap of the envelope, but it wouldn't stick. Second-hand ones don't, so I bunged a strip of sticky tape across it. Peeled the stamp from its backing and slopped that on too, a bit wonky, but so what? Not quite the image I'd intended, but it's what's inside that matters. My stomach was churning. It is now, just thinking about it. Me saying that to him, just before he left. Those exact words. That it's what's inside that matters. That I wanted him to stay, forget her flashy clothes, her posh job and the bulging bank balance that goes with it, her painted-on face. She doesn't love you. I'd said that too, not knowing if it was true. She doesn't love you. Not like *we* do. I may not be glamorous, but it's what's on the inside that matters. Kindness, caring, what you feel for your family. It didn't make any difference though. Didn't stop him going . . .

'It was five to twelve when I'd finished. It had only taken me five minutes. But if I didn't get it posted it would sit around until Monday and he'd be pacing up and down at his mother's and getting angry, chasing me for an answer. So I grabbed my plastic mac and Lily's, and pushed my feet into the nearest pair of battered trainers. The rain was pounding at the windows. I can almost hear it now, it was so heavy, and it obviously wasn't going to stop. Not in time.

'I opened Lily's door and looked at her. She was still fast asleep, snuggled down deep, and she looked so angelic, like one of those cherubs you see on a Christmas card, all chubby like you just want to snuggle her up tight and cuddle her till she pops. There was a picture book that had dropped off the bed, one we'd got from the library, and it was lying open on the rug, and her tiny fingers were clutching at her bear, the tip of his ear all soggy in her mouth.

'The rain just kept hammering, harder and harder, at the glass, rattling the catch, like someone was banging nails, rat-rat-tat, at super-fast speed, and I knew it wasn't about to ease off any time soon. I was going to shut her window but it was only open a smidge. She was snuffling in her sleep and I thought the fresh air would do her good. She rolled over onto her side then, towards me, as if she sensed I was there, watching her. Lying there, all warm and soft. And safe. I thought she was safe.

'The post office is only around the corner. I had three minutes left – if I was lucky – to catch the post before it went, and there just wasn't time. Time to wake her, get her coat on, carry her down to her buggy in the hall, lug it down the stone steps outside. She'd struggle. She'd cry. She's always grizzly if she's woken up before she's ready.

'I looked down to the street below, onto the tops of people's wet heads and the curves of the umbrellas. It was absolutely pouring out there. She'd get drenched, catch a cold. Just having her with me would slow me down. I dropped her coat back down onto a chair and slipped into mine. I remember how I fumbled trying to do up the zip. I'd go by myself. It'd be quicker, easier. I wouldn't even need a bag, just the keys to get back in. Two minutes. That's all it would take. I'd let her sleep, and I'd be back so quickly she wouldn't even know I'd been gone.

'It was one of those snap decisions, you know? Best for her. Best for me. I mean, what could possibly happen to her, left there in her own bed, for just a few minutes? It never even occurred to me that the worst thing that could happen might happen, but to me, not her.

'So I did it. I pulled my hood up over my hair, and stuffed the letter into my pocket with the keys and then I ran, as fast as I could, out of the flat, down the stairs and into the street, pulling the front door closed behind me. Leaving her behind.'

Laura had been sitting quietly, just listening, as she'd promised, but now she couldn't help the sharp intake of her breath as Ruby stopped talking, reached for the beaker of water next to her bed and took a gulp. 'And that's when you got run over?'

'It must have been. I don't really remember that part. I just know it was chucking it down with rain. I could hear my trainers sloshing through the puddles, ankle deep, feel the rain splashing up the back of my legs and trickling down my face from my fringe where my hood didn't quite cover it. There were still people about though. Saturday shoppers. I bumped into someone, a big bloke carrying a bag that must have been a lot heavier than it looked because it gave me a real whack as it thumped against my hip, and it almost threw me off balance. Him too, I think. I heard him shout after me, but I didn't stop to listen. I knew I didn't have the time.

'The postman was already there. He had the front of the

box open, so I pulled it out, the letter, and took a last look at it. I think I even spat on it. Can you believe that? Like a final message for the two of them that I wasn't to be messed with. But he was closing up, the postman, and it was too late to post it through the slot, so I dropped it straight into the top of the open sack. He gave me one of those looks. A sort of *"you can't do that"* look. But I already had. And that was that. Done.

'I stopped for a few seconds to catch my breath, resting against the post box as the postman muttered something I couldn't hear, but rude probably. I just stood there and let the rain fall on me as he got into his van and drove off. My hair was soaked, my hands, legs, feet. Inside my trainers, my socks felt damp and squishy, and my toes were cold. I felt like one of those drowned rats Geraldine used to talk about every time a speck of rain fell on her perfectly arranged hair. Oh, so what? I thought. What the hell, I'm soaked already. Let it do its worst!

'The letter was on its way, and I was finally standing up to Mike – no, Michael – and sticking up for myself at last. This was good stuff. A real turning point for me and for Lily. I felt almost proud of myself, in a funny sort of way, but I was crying anyway. Don't know why, but I was. I do that sometimes, when Lily's not around to see. I do try to hide it from her, Laura. Honestly, I do. I may not always manage it, but I don't want her upset. It's our mess, mine and Mike's, not hers.

'Anyway, I started to run again, knowing I had to get back to her. My head must have been down, I think, to keep the rain from hitting my face, and I was watching my own feet, driving through the puddles, sloshing along, listening to their rhythm. My laces had come undone and the ends were brown with filth, flapping behind me, skipping and bouncing off the pavement. I thought maybe I should stop to tie them up, but I just wanted to get home. But then . . . Then I was in the road, lying on my back, and I had no idea how I'd got there. I must have stepped off the kerb. Right into the path of a car, the police say, but I don't remember that at all. It hurt though. A lot. I do remember that. Then there were people around me, swirling in and out of the blackness, and a weird buzzing sound everywhere, and someone was screaming, wailing, and I think someone spoke to me, lifted me up . . .

'The next thing I knew I was opening my eyes and looking at Lily, all small and fuzzy, as if she was very far away, and everything that had been so black was suddenly bright, bright white. And it wasn't Saturday any more.'

Laura squeezed her hand. 'You were here. In the hospital. Safe. You're okay now, Ruby. You're on the mend, and doing really well.'

'Am I? Doing well? I don't think I am, not with Social Services and the police digging away, trying to make up their minds about me, the girl who abandoned her baby. You don't think I'm a bad mother, do you? For leaving her? Because I didn't abandon her. I didn't. I wouldn't. It's not as though I was out clubbing or anything, if that's what they all think. I only meant to let her sleep, to keep her safe. I was coming right back.'

'I know you were.'

'But I shouldn't have done it, should I? Shouldn't have left her, even for a few minutes? I do know that now, and if I could go back and change things, I would never do it again. As if some stupid letter was worth what happened to Lily. I'd rather he saw her every day, took her away and looked after her himself, than let anything terrible like that ever happen to her again.'

'Then that's what you have to tell them, isn't it? What you've just told me. I think – though you don't have to listen to me – that you need to stop hating Michael now, stop fighting him, and start working together. For Lily.'

'I don't hate him. How could I hate him? It's *her*. Patsy. She's the one I had to keep away from my baby.'

'But you do know you won't be able to do that, don't you? Not if they're together, and staying that way? Not unless she poses some sort of threat, a danger to children, and she doesn't, does she? Look, I don't know her, but is she really that bad? Couldn't you give her a chance? For Lily. I think if you can do that, Ruby, you'll be halfway there.'

*

Patsy closed her eyes and felt the familiar lulling motion of the boat. Growing up here, and knowing the area so well, took nothing away from the excitement she still felt every time, when everyone was aboard, the wind was in her hair, and the boat set off across the deep and beautiful lake. Forget aeroplanes. Give her a boat any day!

It was good weather, for the time of year. The recent rain had passed and there was a hint of sun breaking through a widening gap in the clouds. It would be half term soon and then there would be more people about, more bustle. Today the boat was half empty, or half full, depending on how you looked at things, and many of their fellow passengers were wandering the deck, holding hands, chasing after wayward toddlers, pointing binoculars and cameras at the distant shoreline.

'It's nice here.' Michael's arm was around her shoulders and, although her eyes remained closed, she knew he was gazing out across the water, taking in the sheer beauty of the scenery, as all the tourists did.

'Just nice?' she said, sleepily.

'Fantastic, then. Peaceful. Breathtaking. All those things. You know I'm not that great with words. I'm more of an actions man. I can do a mean line in kissing though.'

She opened her eyes just as his lips landed gently and expertly on hers.

'Do your parents like me, do you think?' he said, pulling reluctantly away. 'Have I passed the test?'

'The chocolate helped! And the offer of the meal. You know how expensive that place is? The menu she showed you had cobwebs on it, it's so long since they've been able to justify the expense of treating themselves. Worth it if it brings her round though. Where Mum leads, Dad will surely follow. I don't think I've ever seen you turn on the charm quite that strongly! For a man who says he's not great with words . . . '

'I do know three words actually.'

'And what might they be?'

'I. Love. You.' He said it slowly, moving his finger over her face, landing it in a different position with each word. Right cheek, left cheek, the tip of her nose.

'The only ones you need, as far as I'm concerned. I love you too, Michael.'

'Good. We'll be okay then, won't we? Whatever happens next.'

'With Ruby?'

'Forget Ruby. I mean with you, Pats. You are going to come back with me, aren't you? Don't worry, we don't have to sleep at the flat. We can get a nice hotel room somewhere nearby for Saturday night.'

'Just nice?'

He laughed. 'Fantastic, peaceful . . . Oh, I can't remember what I said now, but all of those. With a huge bed and a TV and chocs on the pillow, and everything. We'll sleep there and then go straight to Lily's party. It'll only be a small one. None of us know many people to ask. Just so long as Lily gets her castle and her cake. Mum's sorting it all out, with her new best friends from downstairs. We'll take it slowly, carefully, I promise you. I'm not chucking you in feet first, Pats. Just come and meet Lily, be as pleasant as you can to Mum, not that she deserves it, and start to be a part of the family. The doll you showed me . . . I meant what I said last night. It's perfect. Mum bought her one in the week. Awful thing that gives everyone the evil eye. Honestly, you wouldn't want to wake up in the night and see that at the end of your bed! But yours has a nice face. Lily will love it. And she'll love you too. Just you wait and see . . . '

*

Laura was still not ready. She'd been late back from her break and had stayed on to make up the time, then missed her usual bus home. Now she was finding it difficult working out what to wear. Rock concerts tended to mean jeans and T-shirts and leather jackets, but it was only a small local venue – more of a pub's back room from what she could gather – so the usual rules might not apply, and she wanted to look her best. Trickiest of all, she'd never been out with a vicar before. Twin sets and pearls came horribly to mind, but she quickly pushed the image aside.

By the time his car drew up outside she was in her fifth outfit, the previous four scattered over the bed and spilling onto the floor. She imagined it would get quite hot at a rock concert, so she'd settled for a thin lacy jumper and a knee-length twirly skirt, fifties style, with her hair piled up and held with a scarlet clip. If she hadn't got it right now she never would.

'You look sensational,' Paul said as she opened the front door, whipping out a big bunch of white roses from behind his back. Real florist ones, not Tesco's.

He was in jeans, T-shirt, leather jacket, the very clothes she had dismissed for herself. But, on him, they looked exactly right. And no dog collar. He looked like any regular guy. Not a vicar at all.

'You don't look bad yourself, Paul, and thank you, these look lovely. Come in. Just give me a minute to find a vase, and we can be off.'

He hovered while she poured the water into the only vase she owned and started to trim the ends off the stems. It had been a long while since anyone had bought her flowers. The occasional grateful patient, which didn't really count, but it had never been Kevin's thing. Paul had avoided the obvious red roses cliché and opted for white. She liked that. She had a good feeling about this evening.

'You can sit down, if you want.'

'No, I'm all right. I'd rather stand here and watch you. There's something very soothing, very captivating, about watching a woman arranging flowers. The soft petals, the soft hands, easing each bloom into just the right position . . . '

'Paul!' She giggled. 'You must see it all the time, in church. All those little old ladies from the WI with their carnations and chrysanthemums, helping to decorate the altar.'

'Not quite the same, believe me.'

Laura didn't know what to say after that. He obviously liked her, and she liked him too – a lot. But she felt on dodgy ground. This was new territory, scary territory, but tonight she was determined to forget he was a vicar and just pretend he was an ordinary boyfriend, to act just as she would on any other first date. She would go with the flow, have fun, not worry about where it all might lead. Just enjoy the ride, as her friend Fiona would say. Far more important – most of the time – than the destination.

But tonight did have a destination. It was called The White Bear. When they arrived, pushing past the motorbikes lined up outside and making their way into a small crowded room with closed curtains, a bare wooden floor and a rather dusty air, the first person she saw was Fiona.

Paul went straight to the bar for drinks and Laura pushed her way through to grab her friend by the arm. A leather-clad arm, too! 'What are you doing here? Not come to spy on me and the rev, have you?'

'You should be so lucky. No, I do, surprisingly, have a date of my own tonight. A real-life proper one, not the internet kind. And with a very hunky bloke. You've met him, actually.'

'I have?'

'The other night, in the pub, when you only had eyes for one particular person, and therefore clearly missed the fact that I had managed to pull too!'

'Not . . . Er . . . What's his name? Ian? Paul told me his friend had asked for your number.'

'The very same! And, no, before you ask, he is not a vicar.' She swung her arm around, in a sweeping gesture that encompassed the crowd pressing in around them. 'Although half the room are, apparently. You'd never guess, would you? That all this rock and roll, motorbikes and beer stuff goes on behind closed doors down at the chapel. I've been here about half an hour already, and they are a very nice crowd. Not *that* many vicars, to be honest, I may have exaggerated a bit! But the ones that are vicars are all very normal. Do you know, I think I might just have struck lucky this time. With Ian. Third date already! We've been out three nights in a row – yes, I know, I should have told you – and I really, really like him. Beats internet hook-ups any day. And I don't think he's going to suddenly run out on me or leave me sitting like a wallflower paying my own bar bill either.'

'About time you nabbed yourself a good one. You certainly did keep it quiet. No hint. Not like you at all. And three nights in a row, as well. He must be keen. I'm pleased for you though, you dark horse you! Where is he?'

'Getting ready to play. He's the drummer.'

'Then come and stand with us to watch them play. Can't have you hanging about by yourself and getting into mischief.

Going out with a rocker. Whatever next? This must make you some sort of groupie!'

'No, I am certainly not going to play gooseberry to you two, not on your first date. And it's okay, Ian's already introduced me to plenty of people so I won't be on my own. You just enjoy the show, girl. And whatever comes after!' Then she was gone, back through the crowds, just as Paul returned with two halves and, linking his arm through hers, led her to a couple of stools with 'Reserved' signs on them, right up near the stage.

'I thought you said standing room only?'

'Perks of being mates with the band.'

'Can you get me a seat at the front in church too? Perks of being mates with the vicar?' she laughed.

'Any time, Laura. Any time. But we tend to call them pews, and I have to warn you they can be a bit hard on the bottom. Seriously, though, I'd really like you to come and see me at work.'

'Only if you come and watch me cleaning out a bedpan!'

'I think I might pass on that offer, thanks. But, you could come to little Lily's christening. Watch me do my bit.'

'I'd like that.'

'You know, if it wasn't for her, and Ruby, we might never have met. They don't usually have much call for my services down in A & E.'

'Not even for attempted suicides with a desperate urge to talk to God?'

'It's no good fishing, Laura. You know I am not going to tell you anything about Julie. Not that she told me anything scandalous. She just needed a shoulder to cry on. But, if she had, then it would have been in the strictest confidence.'

'Spoilsport!'

The guitarists were warming up now, their strumming wailing out through enormous speakers, one of them right next to her head, and Ian was settling into his seat, flexing his drumming muscles. Laura could see Fiona at the other side of the small makeshift stage, her eyes fixed on him as if he were a real rock god and this was Glastonbury or Wembley, not a backstreet pub charging a fiver to get in.

No, if it wasn't for what had happened to poor Ruby she wouldn't have met Paul, it was true. There's usually some good to come out of the bad, if you stayed open to the possibilities life throws at you. Clouds with silver linings and all that. Fiona wouldn't have met Ian either. Or not yet, anyway. Fate had a habit of bringing the right people together in the end though, if it was meant to be. She'd watched *Sliding Doors*, and cried at the end, plenty of times. As Paul squeezed her hand and smiled at her, sending a lovely warm safe glow right through her, she wondered if that was what was happening here. Something that was meant to be.

Then the band launched full steam ahead into their music, so loud that her hands flew up to cover her ears and she could feel the floor shake, and Paul was rocking on his stool, one arm slung loosely across her shoulders and, after that, it was impossible to hear herself think at all.

CHAPTER THIRTY-FOUR

Ruby

I've been thinking a lot, about what Laura said. Lying here, hour after hour, not always being able to sleep, it's all I can do. Think.

It's going to be odd not being with Lily on her birthday. It's not as if she's had many of them, and this one will probably be the first one she really remembers. I mean, I don't remember much from before I was three. You don't, do you? I hope that means that the time she was on her own in the flat without me will fade and blur and eventually disappear too. I'd hate her to have nightmares about it, to feel I let her down, that I did a bad thing, didn't care. I've had enough of that when I think of my own mother, and it still hurts, even after all this time.

Family is so important. Having people you can rely on, who stand by you, whatever you do. Lily has a lot of years ahead of her until she's grown up. She's going to need us. All of us. Me, Geri, Michael, maybe even Patsy. I shudder at the thought. It's not easy to change the way you think about something, or someone, but I know I have to try.

Geri says she's going round to William's house today, so she won't be in to see me until evening visiting. William, the man who found Lily, and rescued her. She says she may bring him in with her, as she doesn't have the car. Not right to keep leaving him out in the car park or hugging a coffee in the canteen. It's time I met him properly, not just a nod every now and then at the flats when he's been visiting his mother and we've passed in the hall. I'd like to get to know him, and to thank him.

She's helping him to sort out what food to get for this little party they're having tomorrow, using his kitchen to make a birthday cake, childproofing the living room! I've told her where to find a couple of phone numbers, scribbled on a pad at home, of mothers I've met at the nursery. Just a few other kids for Lily to play with will make it more like a proper party for her. Not just grown-ups sipping sherry and wearing gaudy paper hats. I should have told her not to get balloons though. Lily's always been scared of them, but maybe Geri will remember that. Somehow I think she will.

Michael's still not back from Poison Patsy's – no, I mustn't call her that, not any more – so Lily will be with Geri today, at William's. It'll be good for her to have a garden to play in. And she loves helping with the baking. Give her a spoon to lick and she's in Heaven.

It's going to be a good life for us, going home with Geri. Having a garden, making cakes, earning my own money, can all become an everyday part of life again. The fresh air, and the fresh start, we both need. If Social Services will let me. If they believe me. But they will, I know they will, because I have Geri now, there to stick up for me, love me, care about me. Like the daughter she never had.

Bandages off tomorrow. Won't be long now.

CHAPTER THIRTY-FIVE

'What will you do about the business side of things, when you hand over the shop?' William took the coffee mug Geraldine offered him and eased his aching back into an armchair. This lawn mowing lark was a bit more strenuous than he had expected. 'I'm sure Ruby will relish being behind the counter, but I don't suppose she's going to be much of a whizz with the accounts, is she?'

'She's bright. She'll learn. Teaching her should keep me busy and involved for a while longer, I shouldn't wonder.'

'Only, I was thinking . . . I know you don't enjoy it, any of it, any more, and you obviously want out. I do have rather a lot of time on my hands since the redundancy, and it is my speciality. Small businesses . . . '

'William, are you offering to help? It's very good of you, but we really don't have the funds to pay you.'

'Who said anything about money?'

'I couldn't possibly let you do that.'

'Why not?'

'Well, we're in Brighton and you're in London, for a start.'

'Not for much longer.'

'What do you mean?'

'We've decided we're moving out, my mother and I. We've had enough of London, had enough of doing what other people want us to do. Well, what my ex-wife wanted us to do, to be precise.'

'Really? This all sounds very sudden. Where will you go?'

'Not at all sure yet. But I was thinking a bit of sea air might do us both good. Perhaps we'll pop down for a holiday, pay you all a visit, while we wait for the estate agents to do their job. You never know, if we like what we see, we might even move down permanently.'

'To Brighton?'

'Yes, to Brighton. Why not? I love a good seaside town, and they don't come any better, do they? But, one step at a time. Do you know, I haven't had a proper holiday in years. Time to treat myself, have a little fun. Brighton could be just the place.'

'With your mother in tow? Oh, I'm sorry, that sounded horribly rude. I didn't mean . . . '

'I know what you meant. She'll be fine. A bit of bracing sea air, a good dinner inside her and a TV in her room, and she'll be in bed asleep by half past nine every night. So, if you're interested in going for the odd drink, or maybe a meal, while we're there, just let me know. As for the accounts, I'd enjoy the challenge. A good set of accounts books to get my teeth into again. I might even start up again, go self-employed, look for new clients, generate a bit of income. Just part-time, you know, in between having a bit of a life of my own again. Maybe find an amateur dramatics group to join too, once I'm settled somewhere. I used to enjoy that sort of thing, although I never did find the courage to audition for a proper part!'

'Sounds fun. And, yes, a night out would be lovely. If you're down our way, I mean.' She looked down, as if inspecting a stain on the carpet, not quite willing to look at his face. 'I haven't really been out socially since my Ken died. But I'd like to. With you, I mean. It's time I got out and about again. All work and no play makes Jill a dull . . . Oh, whatever it is they say. But the accounts . . . I'm not sure "a good set" is quite the right way to describe mine. That's the trouble.'

'Well, we'll see what we can do about that, shall we? And about getting you out and about again too. Now, haven't you got icing a cake to get back to? Lily will have made a terrible mess of my kitchen if you don't go and supervise her soon!'

He watched her walk back to the kitchen, heard Lily squeal excitedly at something she said, took a long sip from his mug, and closed his eyes. Where had all that come from? About going to Brighton? When he'd come in from the garden and sat down, he'd had no idea he was going to suggest a holiday, let alone the possibility of moving down there for good. But now he came to think of it, it really wasn't a bad idea. Brighton fitted the bill. It made sense. It was a good-sized town, with a beach, nice shops, countryside all around. His mother would love it. He would love it. And it was where Geraldine lived, which really was the proverbial icing on the cake. With candles on!

*

Patsy rolled over in the hotel bed and reached for her knickers, which seemed to have disappeared under a mound of quilt somewhere down by her feet.

'Was it naughty of us not to tell your mother we're back? Expecting her to have Lily for another night?'

'What would you prefer? To have Lily here all night, in the bed between us? We could drive round and get her if you like. Not the ideal introduction to her future stepmum though. No, Mum loves having her. She wouldn't have minded, even if we had told her.'

'Then why didn't we?'

'Because, my beautiful fiancée, I wanted you all to myself for one more night. Without my mother knowing every move I make, or your family listening to every sound from the other side of the bedroom door. Just us. You and me. Going to bed in the middle of the afternoon, making as much noise as we like, not having to explain ourselves to anyone or fit in with other people's rules, and pretending we don't have a care in the world. Which, for tonight at least, we don't. Now, get your arse out of this bed and put your glad rags on. We are going out to find ourselves a bottle of champagne and the biggest steak this town has to offer.'

'I don't know how you can, after that huge meal last night.'

'I'll have you know that a young virile man such as myself can always find room for a juicy steak! It's what keeps our blood levels up . . . And other bits of our anatomy! Last night's dinner was about getting to know your parents, hoping they'll accept me. It wasn't really about enjoying the food, was it? Although I did, of course. At those prices, I was bloody well determined to. Do you think they did? Accept me?'

'You asked me much the same thing on the boat. Yes, I think so. You're not the big bad wolf any more, that's for sure. Whether you've quite progressed to Prince Charming we'll have to wait and see.'

'Well, come on then, Cinderella. You can't go to the ball as you are. Losing a glass slipper's one thing, turning up having lost your underwear is another matter entirely, although it could make for an interesting under-the-table game in the restaurant!'

'You are very naughty, Michael Payne. But I love you.'

'In that case, don't bother putting them on. Leave them exactly where they are. Because I love you too. And I'm going to show you just how much. Give us a kiss, Mrs Payne-to-be. The steak can wait.'

*

By Sunday morning, the garden was looking, if not exactly perfect, then at least neat and tidy. The grass was cut, the worst of the weeds hacked down, and William had even discovered a rather nice rose bush he'd completely forgotten was there. Not only set for a party, but all ready for the estate agents too, to take their photos and start showing off the assets of his home to the buying public.

He'd finally met Ruby last night. A nice girl. And so young to be carrying so much trouble on her shoulders. She'd rather tentatively asked him to be a godfather at Lily's christening, which had thrown him completely. He'd saved Lily's life, she'd said, and she wanted Lily always to know that, and to know him. The more he thought about the idea, the more he liked it. He had grown fond of the little girl, and being the one who had found her still gave him a weird feeling of pride that he thought might never leave him. He felt connected to her, unlikely ever to forget her, so, why not? It would give him the perfect excuse to stay connected, no matter how loosely, with Geraldine too.

The bouncy castle was ready at the bottom of the garden, in front of the tumbledown shed, its long power cables winding their way along the edge of the flower border, its constant blowing sounds surprisingly calming, and, despite a few threatening clouds, the sun was just about out and looking like it might decide to stay.

His mother was parked in a garden chair, the upright kind because of her knees, with a cup of tea and a bun, and Michael had just arrived with his fiancée in tow, Geraldine doing her best to be nice to her. The bells from a local church were ringing out somewhere behind the trees. Lily had been put upstairs in the hope she might take a nap and save her energy for the afternoon, but she kept creeping back down again, much to everyone's amusement. The other children were not due for another couple of hours at least, but a plastic-covered table of mini-food, much of it sweet and pink and covered in layers of cling film, already awaited them in the dining room.

So, this was what family life felt like. The generations all brought together, on assorted mismatched chairs, in a garden that smelt of newly-mown grass and last-minute baking. Too many people buzzing about, trying to help, getting in each other's way. The expectation of visitors, and conversation and fun. He knew he had missed out on so much, but it wasn't too late, was it? Surely, this, today, proved that it was never too late.

'How was your trip up to the lakes, Michael?' Geraldine sat beside her son, her foot playing idly with a long blade of grass the mower had missed, and sipping at a cup of tea.

'Fine. It's a lovely place, Mum, and Patsy's parents couldn't have been more welcoming.'

William saw the look that passed over her face. Even if her son had not done it deliberately, his words were certainly hitting home. Poor Geraldine. He knew how much she wanted to mend rifts, put things right. She only had one son, and she couldn't afford to alienate him.

'I'd like to meet them one day,' she said, smiling directly at Patsy. 'Well, I will, won't I? At your wedding. Have you thought about setting a date yet?'

'Er . . . No. Maybe next spring.'

'Oh, that will be nice. You will let me know if there's anything I can do to help, won't you? Make the wedding cake, perhaps? Or help you with the flowers.'

'Thanks. That's very kind of you.'

'And Lily will be a bridesmaid, I assume? I can't wait to see her in a pretty little dress. Pink, I think, don't you? Every little girl's favourite colour. Now let me fetch you another cup of tea. You both look so tired. It must be the long drive down this morning. Heavens, you must have set off at the crack of dawn!'

As she walked away, back through the open door of the kitchen, a look passed between Patsy and Michael that William couldn't quite fathom. A cross between incredulity and the stifling of a giggle. Whatever it was, he was sure things were changing for the better. He could almost hear the distant crack as a layer of ice softened around the edges and started, very slowly, to thaw.

*

Lily loved her castle. It was blue and yellow and springy as a kangaroo, and she didn't want to stop bouncing on it. Ever.

All the grown-ups were sitting in chairs. None of them wanted to join in. But Sarah and Josh were still bouncing with her, with their socks and shoes lined up next to hers on the grass. Up and down, up and down, bumping into each other, and knocking each other over, giggling so much that Sarah did a little wee and made a wet patch in the middle of the bouncy bit, so they were trying to keep to the edges now until it was dry. She wished they had a castle like this at nursery, or that she could keep this one, and take it home.

The old lady had opened up a big cardboard box that the man grumbled about a lot because she'd made him go and find it from some dark place in the garage, and now she was pouring tea from a big pot in the shape of a castle, just like the bouncy one but much smaller. The old lady looked very happy today, more than she usually was. Maybe it was because she liked parties. Maybe she would like to have a go at bouncing. Lily could hold her hand if she was scared, because grown-ups sometimes were.

She wished Mummy was here. Mummy always sat on the swings with her and climbed up the slide and raced her down, but only if nobody was looking, because grown-ups weren't allowed. She knew that Mummy would have bounced, if she was here, and if her leg wasn't broken.

Mummy told her, when they had gone to see her before bedtime last night, that the doctors were going to take the bandage off her head today and that underneath they hoped it would be all better, although they had had to cut off some of her hair which might look funny for a little while. Lily was going to take Archie's bandage off later and see if he was better too.

She'd put a bandage on her new dolly's leg too, and it was going to stay there until Mummy's leg was all mended. That would make Mummy feel better, knowing she wasn't the only one with a poorly leg waiting to mend. People had been writing their names on the white thing on Mummy's leg, and Lily had drawn a tree.

Lily liked her new dolly. It was soft and it had long hair made out of string, and big painted-on eyes and freckles. She had decided it was going to be called Molly. Molly the Dolly. She liked that.

Granny was waving her shoes at her now and telling her it was time to come off the castle and have a rest, to have a drink and eat some more food. Lily tried to stop bouncing but it was hard when the others were still doing It, making the floor move underneath her, and she kept falling over on her way to the front. But she managed to scramble off, the other children right behind her, and they all staggered over to where the grown-ups were, their legs still wobbly, giggling as they went.

'Time for your birthday cake, Lily!' Daddy said, carrying it out on a big tray. It was a square cake, the one she had helped

Granny to mix up in the bowl, with pink icing and her name written in a shaky line across it where she'd insisted on helping to hold the icing bag, and three tall swirly candles burning on the top. 'Come on, Lily. Blow, and make a wish.'

She wished, as hard as a wish can be, that Mummy would be coming home soon. And then, she didn't know if it was because of the sandwiches she had eaten much too fast so she could start bouncing, or the having to blow so hard or, as Granny said afterwards, because she was over-excited, but Lily knew all of a sudden that she was going to be sick. Nothing could stop it as it came rushing up her throat in a nasty big gloopy blob that tasted of old orange squash and boiled eggs, and spilled out down the front of her dress and onto the grass.

Lily looked around, helplessly, still coughing, her chest still heaving in big gasps like there might be more to come. Sarah and Josh just moved further away and waited for their helping of cake. Kids were always being sick. It was nothing new to them. Daddy was still balancing the cake tray and didn't want to let it go, and the old lady was stuck in her chair, moaning about her knees again, and the man just stood there like he'd never seen anyone be sick before, and Lily saw her granny jump up and rush off to get something from the house. A bowl, a cloth, a glass of water?

The pretty lady, the one who had given her Molly, sat very still with a shocked look on her face, as if she might be sick herself at any moment. But then, when nobody else did anything, she saw the lady take a big gulp like she was swallowing something that wasn't there, and then she stood up and came rushing towards her across the grass, opening her arms to her and hugging her in tight.

Lily wiped her sicky mouth on the lady's top, and the lady didn't seem to mind. She just cuddled her up, until Lily stopped coughing, and then she was all better again.

*

Agnes had the big box open on William's dining table now all the food had been tidied away and there was space again. Slowly and lovingly she unravelled the tissue paper from around each of her treasured teapots and held them, one by one, up to the light. She had really missed these wonderful old friends and to actually use one today, filling it with real tea leaves, waiting for them to brew, then pouring tea for everyone from its big deep spout, through a strainer into china cups, had felt just as it should. Magical.

If there was one thing she looked forward to, if and when she moved, much more than just about anything else, it was having her collection out again, properly displayed in a glass-fronted cabinet. Taken out and used, each in its turn. Oh, she knew getting them out now was pointless. They'd only have to be packed away again, but even so . . .

She sat down in one of William's old dark wooden chairs and listened. There was no traffic, no aircraft, no screaming baby two floors up. Just the peace and quiet of an ordinary suburban family house, in an ordinary road, one with more rooms than were needed, more memories than either of them wanted to relive. But it was what she wanted. An ordinary life, in a nice house somewhere, with her son close by, no noise, and her teapots lined up behind her, like her own personal army, reminding her of what mattered, of all that she loved and cherished.

William had said something about taking a holiday together. She wasn't sure about that. She couldn't leave Smudge in some cattery. He was too old, like her, too set in his ways. He'd hate it. No, she'd let William take his little holiday, by himself. There was unfinished business there, between him and Geraldine, she could tell. The future beckoned. Brighter than she'd ever hoped it could be.

Now, she'd ask William to drive her home. Smudge had been on his own for far too long today, and he'd be wanting his tuna. She left the pots where they were, on the table. Tall ones, round ones, tiny ones. All colours, all shapes, all ages. A bit like people, all thrown together in a motley collection, like we were today in William's garden, she thought. But somehow belonging together, just the same.

*

The children had gone home, Lily was fast asleep on the sofa, his mother was fondling her pots, and Michael and Patsy were still outside, making the most of the dying sun and planning their return to Portugal, and whether she should go on ahead and Michael extend his leave until the case conference thing was all settled. And William was on his own. Probably only for a few minutes. If he was going to do it, it had to be now.

William knew she would be in the kitchen, putting the last of the food away in the fridge, wiping surfaces, wrapping up cake. The bouncy castle company would be here soon, dismantling and carrying it away. He hoped it was gone before Lily woke up. He was sure she would find it upsetting seeing her dream toy being snatched away from her. Except, even though she didn't know it yet, there would be something even better waiting for her when she got down to Brighton. Geraldine had decided to get her that rabbit she wanted. A late present, but the one thing she wanted more than any other. And he already knew Lily well enough to know that she would give it some ridiculous name and feed it lots of carrots, and love it to bits.

Love. Love had been on his mind for a few days now. Or something that could so easily turn to love anyway. Was it too soon? Was it real? Did she feel anything like he did? Just a tiny spark, ready to ignite like the candles on Lily's cake? If not, he could wait, take it slowly, let it grow. But he had to know, and it had to be now.

William was not usually an impulsive person. Confidence was not high on his list of attributes. After Susan, he wasn't sure he really had any attributes. Not the sort to attract a woman like Geraldine, anyway. Nevertheless, something urged him on, polishing his glasses, combing his hair in front of the bathroom mirror, walking down the stairs, through the hall, into the kitchen, where she stood at the sink with her back to him, softly singing some song he didn't recognize but instantly adored.

She must have heard him come in because she turned, wiping her hands down her skirt, gave him an embarrassed smile and stopped singing. 'Oh,' she said. 'William.' Just that. But it was enough.

Taking her face, and every ounce of courage he could muster, in his hands, he gazed into her beautiful happy eyes for one long glorious anticipatory moment, and kissed her.

CHAPTER THIRTY-SIX

Ruby

Lily has brought me some birthday cake with pink icing on.
She saved me the piece with L for Lily on it, but if she hadn't
told me I wouldn't have known, it's so squashed. There's a small
round hole too, where one of the candles was and I have to pick
off a tiny blob of candle wax before I can eat the cake.

I don't have the bandage on my head any more. I think Lily is
happy about that. She keeps looking at my hair, where it's been
shaved back, but I'm starting to look more like her Mummy
again, and not the other sort of mummy, the Egyptian kind.
Together, and very ceremoniously, we peel the bandage from
Archie's head and check for imaginary, invisible scars, and Lily
pronounces that Archie is better too.

Michael doesn't stand back, the way he usually does. He's
sitting on the edge of the bed, stroking Lily's hair every now
and then. At one point, and just for a second, he reaches up as
if he's going to stroke mine, but he doesn't.

He tells me he's sorry, but it's not about the hair. He's sorry
about the way he's treated me, the way he walked away. Like

a coward, he says, covering his eyes with his hands. To think I used to dream about those hands.

He says he wishes things could have been different. Not us staying together, that would never have worked, but breaking up more gently, handling it better. I suppose it's as good as an apology. More than I had hoped for, or expected. I can see he means it, and that's something. It feels like we've turned a corner, and we're setting out on a different road now. Both going in the same direction.

We don't say much, because of Lily being here.

Lily doesn't listen to us anyway. She is too full of her party. It's all she can talk about. She tells me about her castle, and her presents, and that she is going to get a rabbit. I look at Michael, to see if it's true, and he says his mum can't keep secrets. Never could. So, yes, it is, as soon as they get back to Brighton. I'm pleased, because a rabbit is the one thing I had promised her, and shouldn't have, without knowing how or when I could ever make it happen.

I ask him where Geraldine is tonight but he's mysterious about it, tells me she has things to do, and that it's his turn anyway. He makes me feel that visiting me is a duty, one he'd rather get out of but knows he can't. I can't blame him for that. He's always been wary of hospitals, and what we had together is long gone. We'd been living like brother and sister for long enough, clinging to the wreckage, without passion, doing it for Lily, even before Patsy came along. I just hadn't wanted to face it. But now I can, and I do. And I want to make peace.

Lily shows me her new doll, with its funny freckled face and its bandaged leg, and she says the pretty lady gave it to her, the one who cleaned her up when she was sick, and who helped her sprinkle hundreds and thousands on her ice cream. I know that she means Patsy, although she calls her Pasty, which makes me laugh. Michael too. Lily laughs with us, even though she doesn't know why.

I never thought I would ever say this, but I'm going to ask Patsy to be a godmother at the christening. A big step, but she will be a part of Lily's life now, whether I like it or not, so it seems the right thing to do. And Lily likes her. I have to think about that. What Lily likes. What Lily needs. It's not all about me now. It's only about her.

I tell Michael, and he's pleased. He's not one for confrontation, really. He wants everyone to get along together, likes to take the path of least resistance. 'I've already asked William Munro, and I'm going to ask Mrs Castle too,' I tell him, and he says they're both a bit old for it, might not live to see Lily grow up, but he doesn't put up a fight.

I know that Geri still sees Mrs Castle, that they've stayed friends and I should make more effort to visit her, because Michael's right, she's getting older, and these things shouldn't be put off until later. In case later really is too late. She did a great job of steering me through my childhood, did Mrs Castle, and I know I can trust her to do the same for Lily. If life doesn't turn out the way I hope it does, she'll need people to rely on. William, who saved her, Mrs Castle who saved me, and Patsy, who much as I hate to admit it, seems to have saved Michael.

When Lily hears the word 'castle' she starts bouncing on the bed as if she's still on that bouncy one she keeps chattering about, and the doll falls onto the floor, temporarily forgotten, its big blue painted-on eyes staring up at the ceiling.

'Your mother will be able to wear her hat at last,' I say to Michael. 'At the christening.'

'I suppose she will. I never did see it. Did you?'

'Never. She's guarded it like the Crown Jewels. But I bet it's blue. Blue's her colour somehow.'

'And I bet it has feathers on it,' he says.

'Big floppy ostrich feathers, that tickle her nose and wave around in the wind.'

Just the thought of the hat and the feathers is enough to get me laughing again, laughing until my sides hurt, cracked ribs and all, and Michael laughs with me, for the first time in ages.

And, at last, I know with absolute certainty that everything is going to be all right.

ACKNOWLEDGEMENTS

First of all, thanks must go to my editor, Kate Bradley, who has shown such belief in this book, and in me. We met at a Romantic Novelists conference and somehow just 'clicked'. Working on this book together has been a pleasure and I know it is a better story because of her.

Thanks also to Vicky Vincent and Jane Robson, whose knowledge of Children and Family law and the workings of the Social Services system helped guide me through Lily's trauma and what came next. I have tried to show the process from the point of view of a worried family rather than that of a clued-up social work professional, and I hope I got it right in the end.

To Laura Hampshire, for sharing her inside knowledge of the social and working life of a busy hospital nurse, and for talking me through the initial assessment and treatment of A & E patients. If there are medical blunders in the book they are entirely mine, not hers.

To Louise Timothy and Lisamarie Lamb, who both had three-year-old daughters at the time I was writing this book and who gave me so much useful information about what a child of that age can and cannot do safely and successfully for

Vivien Brown

herself, especially if left to her own devices. It was amazing how much their responses differed, which just goes to show that age is not a clear definer of emotional or developmental milestones and that no two children are ever the same.

To the SWWJ, the RNA and Phrase Writers, three wonderfully supportive organisations for writers, whose members and meetings have been invaluable, informative and fun. They have kept me on the right path, provided encouragement, friendship and feedback, and helped me to see the much-needed light at the end of the long and lonely tunnel. And to my husband Paul, who always allows me the time, space and abundance of chocolate I need to write, whenever and wherever the compulsion strikes.

And last, but by no means least, thanks to all at Barra Hall Children's Centre, Hillingdon Library Service and the wonderful Bookstart programme, for giving me the happiest and most rewarding twelve years of my working life – until I became an author, of course! By spending time with so many children of pre-school age, and introducing them to the magic of books, I know I have helped to create the readers of the future. Without them we authors, and the books we write, have no hope of a future at all.